I Spy

CLAIRE KENDAL

HarperCollins*Publishers*

HarperCollins*Publishers* Ltd
1 London Bridge Street,
London SE1 9GF

www.harpercollins.co.uk

First published by HarperCollins*Publishers* 2019
1

A catalogue record for this book is
available from the British Library

ISBN: 978-0-00-825683-8 (PB b-format)

This novel is entirely a work of fiction.
The names, characters and incidents portrayed in it are
the work of the author's imagination. Any resemblance to
actual persons, living or dead, events or localities is
entirely coincidental.

Typeset in Lomba and Raleway by
Palimpsest Book Production Ltd, Falkirk, Stirlingshire

Printed and bound in the UK by
CPI Group (UK) Ltd, Croydon CR0 4YY

For my brother Robert

'You have almost completed your painting,' said I, approaching to observe it more closely, and surveying it with a greater degree of admiration and delight than I cared to express. 'A few more touches in the foreground will finish it I should think.—But why have you called it Fernley Manor, Cumberland, instead of Wildfell Hall, —shire?' I asked, alluding to the name she had traced in small characters at the bottom of the canvass.

But immediately I was sensible of having committed an act of impertinence in so doing; for she coloured and hesitated; but after a moment's pause, with a kind of desperate frankness, she replied,—

'Because I have friends—acquaintances at least—in the world, from whom I desire my present abode to be concealed; and as they might see the picture, and might possibly recognize the style in spite of the false initials I have put in the corner, I take the precaution to give a false name to the place also, in order to put them on a wrong scent, if they should attempt to trace me out by it.'

Anne Brontë,
The Tenant of Wildfell Hall,
Chapter V, 'The Studio'

Contents

Prologue An Interview   1

Now A Discovery   13

Then Black Star Sapphire   19

Now The Girl with the Two-Coloured Eye   30

Then Human Asset   39

Now The Two Tunnels   53

Then The Plague Pit   58

Now The Backwards House   67

Then The Forgotten Things   72

Now The Woman in the Room   83

Then A Quarrel   91

Now The Excursion   104

Then Provocations   112

Now Further Warnings   122

Then Eavesdropping   132

Now Persistence   141

Then Concealment   153

Now The Robin   163

Then Startling Intelligence   167

Now The Visit   188

Then A Meeting   206

Now An Assault   218

Then April Fool   235

Now An Ambush   248

Then The Handkerchief Tree   258

Now The Doors With No Knobs   269

Then A Misadventure   276

Now A Misdemeanour   284

Then The Studio   299

Now Further Intelligence   306

Then The Spin Out   314

Now Illegal Entry   319

Then The Memory Box   339

Now The Choice   348

Then The Drowning Place   363

Now Thorpe Hall   374

Now The Miniature   385

Now The Present   400

Acknowledgements   414

For those affected by the issues in this novel   416

Prologue *An Interview*

London, April 2013

The clear glass table meant that I had to work extra hard to stop my knee from jerking up and down. It was not a time to show nervousness. Maxine was on one side of the table. I was on the other.

'You are twenty-one, Holly. Correct?' She started simply, but her use of my first name was a warning. She had only ever called me by my surname.

'Correct.'

'Do you have many friends?'

'A few good ones.'

She nodded. I had never seen her nod before. Nodding is a gesture that suggests interest, and that wasn't something she normally allowed herself to show.

'It's good to be selective.' She smiled. I hadn't seen her do that before either.

'I'm glad you think so.'

'And your grandmother raised you?'

'Yes.'

'That's sad about your parents. What a thing to happen.'

'It was a long time ago.'

'You were two?'

She'd got it wrong on purpose. I was certain of it. 'Three.' Was I right to correct her? Should I have let it go? What was the best response? I needed to quit second-guessing what she wanted to hear and just say what was true.

'It was a car crash?' Maxine didn't have any notes. She didn't need any notes. She was in command of my 'facts' without having to write them down.

'Yes.' It was crucial to keep it brief.

'I apologise for the personal nature of some of the questions I have to ask you.' Had she really used the word 'apologise'? Maxine?

The lights in the room were unnaturally bright. The wall behind me was extremely white. But the wall behind Maxine, which I was facing, was a mirror of glass. It was a safe bet that it was one-way glass, and my performance was being assessed from the other side of it, in a darkened room. I imagined Maxine's boss, Martin, behind the glass, enjoying the peep show but appearing bored.

'You've known the Hargrave family for how long?'

'Since I was four. Most of my life.' I felt my lips trembling. My body was not under my control. I was losing it. Why did this woman scare me so much?

'Tell me about them.' Maxine settled in her chair, ready to be entertained.

'Peggy is the mother, James is the father. They have a daughter.'

There was that smile again. The indulgent kind you give to a difficult child. 'And the daughter has a name, I presume?'

'Sorry. Yes. Milly.' Maxine knew this already, despite the

pretence. I'd given permission for them to interview friends and family. I'd had to, though there weren't many. Peggy, James, and Milly. My list of three, because my grandmother hardly knew what day of the week she was living any more.

'You and Milly are very close, aren't you? Best friends, as they say.'

'I'd never tell her' – I flapped around for the right phrase – 'anything I shouldn't.'

'Of course you wouldn't. Milly's family moved next door when you were four?'

'Yes.' Elaboration was not my friend.

I reminded myself that these were the easy questions. The seemingly innocuous warm-up questions to lull me into the false sense of security that would get me to mess up and reveal every vulnerability I'd ever had. My stomach knotted, and I tried not to let myself panic about what might be coming.

'And you moved in when?'

'I was born in that house. My grandmother moved in to look after me when my parents died. Milly's family bought the house next door just before the two of us started school – she and I are the same age.'

'Your grandmother was quite old when she became your guardian, wasn't she?'

'Yes.'

Maxine smiled again, and I shivered so hard it must have been visible on the other side of the one-way glass. 'That can't have been much fun for a small child.'

I tried to think of what to say to this, but I took too long, so Maxine went on. 'You are close to Milly's mother? Peggy, you said?'

'Yes.'

'Peggy must have seen you as a poor little neglected orphan.' Maxine was a combination of effortful glamour and mess. Her hair was bottle-blonde but lank. Pieces of different lengths hung in front of her face, as if she'd hacked at them herself.

'I think she probably did, yes.'

'Tell me more, Holly.' That jagged curtain of hair was one of Maxine's tactics for hiding, though I managed a glimpse of hooded eyes that were grey that day but could easily be changed with contact lenses.

'I think Peggy wanted – she still wants – to protect me. To mother me, even.' I was saying too much when I needed to be spare in my answers. Part of what Maxine was testing was that I could be reserved, even under pressure.

'And Peggy's husband is around – James Hargrave. What is he like?' Maxine pushed her hair behind her ears. Not a Maxine gesture. Her mascara and eyeliner were heavy. She had gone for her usual indigo. No ordinary black for her. The foundation was caked on. Maxine was a woman of many faces.

'He runs the town pharmacy.'

'And?'

'James is very kind, but he doesn't say much.'

I didn't explain that it was as if Peggy had such a lot to say there was nothing left for James – and they both seemed to like it that way.

'Very kind? That's mild. You aren't damning by faint praise?'

'There is a lot to be said for real kindness.' As soon as the words were out, I wanted to take them back – she was going to think I was judging her, that I was rebuking her.

'I agree,' she said, but this didn't make me relax. 'And your grandmother is fond of the Hargrave family? As fond as you clearly are?'

'My grandmother hates pretty much everybody.'

Maxine laughed, something I hadn't seen her do even once during the residential phase of the recruitment process, which she was leading. Along with the other aspiring intelligence officers, I watched Maxine as if she were a superstar.

'But she worships James,' I said.

'You are admirably loyal, Holly, aren't you? Am I correct in thinking that you gave up your place at Exeter University to look after your grandmother? You were going to read Modern Languages?'

'I couldn't leave my grandmother alone. I'd been trying to delay putting her in a nursing home, so I enrolled on a BA in English at Falmouth instead of the Exeter course – I can commute to Falmouth pretty easily from our house. I'm due to graduate this summer.'

'You're predicted a first.'

'Yes. And I took every evening course they offered in French, Spanish, and German, to try to compensate for not being able to do Modern Languages. I'm fluent in all three – I studied them in school too.'

'You got As for all three at A level, and an A in English Literature. Correct?'

'Yes. And I can get by in Italian. I've been working towards a career in the Security Service for as long as I can remember.'

I had been obsessed with spies since I was a very little girl. My grandmother told me that my father used to play 'I Spy' with me, using the game to show me the world. I liked to imagine him in his blue-grey RAF uniform, pointing into the night, where he would soon be flying.

I Spy with my little eye, something far up in the sky . . .

. . . Moon.

When I was five, I tiptoed into the sitting room and hid behind my grandmother's brown-velvet wingback chair to peek at a film she was watching. I sat, cross-legged, on her scratchy brown carpet, so perfectly still and quiet she never knew I was there. To this day I don't know what the film was called. Only that it was about a spy who pretended to his family he was a boring businessman. Then, a bad spy injected him with truth serum, and this made him confess to his wife about his double life as an intelligence officer.

With the reasoning of a five-year-old, I decided to make my own truth serum and administer it to my grandmother, using the best available laboratory facilities. While she was cooking dinner, I sneaked into her bedroom and scooped out tiny spoonfuls of the lotions and scents on her dressing table, then stirred them into the moisturising cream she rubbed onto her face each night. My fantasy was that the serum would force my grandmother into revealing the secrets I was certain she was keeping about my parents.

When I was ready to begin the interrogation, I noticed that she had a bright-red and extremely bumpy rash on her cheeks. She never imagined the cause, and I crept back into her room to steal the cream away and dispose of it at the bottom of the kitchen rubbish so she would never use it again. I was frightened that I'd mortally injured her, but she seemed to recover quickly.

On my eighth birthday, *Harriet the Spy* appeared in my Christmas stocking, and Harriet became my absolute hero.

She carried her spy notebook everywhere, so I did too, writing little observations about everything I saw. I made things up as well. It was only later that I learned that spies were supposed to keep to what was true, and were trained to be cautious about what they put on paper – two principles I wasn't very good at heeding.

'I can see that you have been commendably strategic and goal-driven in wanting to join us.' Maxine gave me another of those intimate nods. 'But in this line of work, how far would you push it? You're *very* attractive.' Despite the appeasing gestures, Maxine shifted the subject with the suddenness of a window exploding in a storm. 'You know that.'

I blinked at this new Maxine. She was being kind but firm, friendly but still clearly the one with the power.

She pushed at me again. 'Where does the line come, Holly?'

I realised I was biting the side of my lower lip, a sign of the anxiety I wanted to hide. 'Emotional. Emotional involvement. That's the line I wouldn't cross.'

Maxine was in full-friend mode, pretending that the two of us were just ordinary women exchanging confidences. 'So as long as it isn't emotional . . .' her voice was gentle, understanding '. . . physical involvement is okay – to – a – point.' She tapped the table's bevelled edge with her index finger, picking it up and setting it down again a few centimetres further along with her last three words, as if counting.

'Are you asking – if I would sleep with someone for the role?' I imagined Martin on the other side of the one-way glass, controlling any impulse to sit up straighter or open his mouth wide. He wouldn't react at all.

'Now that you mention it.'

I thought I was saying the right thing, but I pictured Martin, no longer able to disguise his interest, sticking his feet out and crossing them at the ankles, leaning back in his chair and shaking his head. Because he could see that I was a fish being reeled in. 'No, No I wouldn't.'

'Are you sure?' Maxine said this as if she were trying to help me, trying to tell me I had given the wrong answer and should flip it.

'That would be like prostituting myself for the country. So no.' My shoe was tapping wildly against the white-tiled floor. I froze, and the absence of noise from it was too noticeable.

'Even if it was the only way to save your life and the lives of hundreds of others?'

I was flailing, trying to guess what she wanted to hear rather than saying what I thought. Which was the worst thing I could do. 'If it was for the role. I would be happy to – to go as far as I needed to for the role.'

Maxine's usual un-reactiveness was gone. She tilted her head, a questioning gesture of moral disgust, as if in disbelief that she'd heard me right. 'What if you had a boyfriend?'

'I would go – ahead – and tell him afterwards.' I was bobbing my head up and down, trying to signal that I meant what I said, that I *was* trustworthy.

Maxine's girlfriend pretence had vanished. 'So you'd cheat to get information.'

I had wanted the job with MI5 more than I ever wanted anything, and I had got so far and so close after multiple tests of my situational judgement and core skills. But it was rushing away from me faster than water down a drain.

Maxine shook her head. She said the most important thing she ever said to me. The thing I would replay all the time.

'You know, a physical relationship is not acceptable. You are making *yourself* vulnerable. It's all about using this.' She almost smiled. She placed a hand on each side of her head without actually touching it. 'Rather than that' – she lowered her hands from her breasts to her hips, again without touching herself – 'to get what you need.'

There was nothing left for me to do. I knew the implications of what I had said, and that there was no recovering from it.

'I think,' said Maxine, 'that this brings your interview to an end.'

When I was very little, my grandmother often chose my bedtime stories from Hilaire Belloc's *Cautionary Tales for Children*. Her favourite had a huge mouthful of a title. *'MATILDA Who told Lies, and was Burned to Death.'* This was probably because my grandmother hated my mother, and my mother's name was Matilda. It didn't occur to my grandmother that having a heroine who was my mother's namesake would only make me love her more.

Plus, my grandmother could never convince me that Matilda was really dead. 'It was a trick,' I would say. 'Matilda hid in a fireproof cellar but the story forgot to tell us.' I didn't confess to my grandmother that I often dreamed my parents were still alive, and it had all been a mistake. I never believed in the words 'The End' when my grandmother finished and snapped the book closed. I was convinced the characters continued on somewhere, and I would try to imagine the next phase of their lives for myself.

All in all, the effect of my grandmother's cautionary tales was not what she intended. They just gave me ideas about

the interesting things I could do, and alerted me to potential disasters so I could try to figure out how to avoid them,
though I didn't always succeed.

My grandmother was forever muttering about listeners at
keyholes being vexed, and eavesdroppers never hearing
good of themselves. 'That is what you must reflect upon,
Holly,' she would say.

The best response to this, like most of the things my
grandmother said, was the word, 'Yes', usually accompanied
by a solemn nod. But in truth, the only thing I reflected upon
was how to avoid detection.

Soon after they moved into the house next door, Peggy
discovered me lying like a tiger along a high branch of my
grandmother's apple tree. It was the end of summer, and I
was watching Peggy play with Milly on the other side of the
fence that ran between our houses, while James manned
the barbeque.

Peggy thought that this incident was an aberration. She
saw me as a sweet little girl whose loneliness and longing
for family had put her in danger, though it was Peggy's own
startled screech at seeing me in the tree that almost made
me fall out of it. But my spying was no aberration. I simply
made sure Peggy never caught me at it again.

Peggy was in the habit of leaving the laundry room
window open so she could dangle out the hose that vented
the hot air from her tumble dryer. The laundry room was
Peggy's favourite place for private conversations. I could
peek from my father's dusty first-floor study and see right
into that laundry room.

I loved my father's study, where I often hunted for clues

about my parents, though I only ever found one thing. A photograph of them on their wedding day, hidden in his copy of *A Tale of Two Cities*. I liked to sit and read in my father's old armchair, which was covered in green leather. I'd dragged it near the window. From there, I could monitor what was happening at Peggy's. If her washing machine and tumble dryer were off, then listening in was no challenge. In fact, I regarded such a circumstance as an invitation.

And that is how I came to hear Peggy and Milly talking together when I was back home in St Ives, two months after my disastrous final MI5 interview. As soon as I saw that the laundry room light was on and Peggy and Milly had gone in, I ran downstairs, slipped into the garden, squeezed through the rip in the fence Milly and I always used as a not-very-secret passage, and flattened myself against a tangle of Peggy's honeysuckle.

'She's so deflated,' Peggy was saying, 'since she's come home. I think she's embarrassed about the reason – she can't bear to look your father in the eye.'

I'd had to say something about why MI5 didn't give me the job, because Peggy and James and Milly knew I'd got to the final stage of the recruitment process. There was no disguising the outcome.

'She was brave to tell us, Mum,' Milly said. 'And fucking stupid.'

'You don't need to use that language, Milly.'

But Milly was right. I had been stupid to reveal the truth about the way I'd messed up. What had possessed me to give them the details? Perhaps I did it because it was the most un-spy-like action I could take, a kind of embracing of my failure. It was an act of self-sabotage I decided never to repeat.

'Sorry.' Milly didn't sound at all sorry. 'People say all sorts of shit.'

'Honestly, Milly,' Peggy said.

'She wanted us to see her real self,' said Milly. 'To see her at her worst and still love her. She knows she's not going to save the world by fucking someone.'

I imagined Peggy rolling her eyes in weariness at Milly's continued swearing. 'She'd never have actually done it,' Peggy said. 'Those recruiters were fools to believe she would.'

The scent of honeysuckle was choking me, mixed with the nearby roses I had been trying not to stab myself with. Somehow, though, a thorn caught my finger and my eyes welled up as I sucked away the blood and hoped that Peggy was right.

Now A Discovery

Five and a half years later

Bath, Tuesday, 25 December 2018

I know the day is going to be bad as soon as I see the kingfisher. He is so perfect, captured beneath the surface of the ice. He stops me in my run as if I have slammed into an invisible wall. Just like him.

I peer over the railings of the small bridge at the frozen water below, for a closer look. He must have been fishing, when the water thickened and trapped him. The vivid blue of his tail, and the dots on the top of his head, are clear beneath the thin layer above him. He is beautifully preserved in his ice cube. There is no sign he fought it, with those wings cupping his body so peacefully, his beak closed and pointed straight ahead.

I cannot bear to look any more, and if I don't get going I will be late for my visit to my grandmother at the nursing home. So I tear my eyes away and resume my run, trying to tell myself it isn't a bad omen, but knowing deep down that it must be.

· · ·

My grandmother has refused to get out of bed today, so Katarina takes me upstairs to her room. The door is open a crack, but not wide enough for me to see in. The sharp scent of lemon disinfectant makes the inside of my nose prickle.

'Who's that!' my grandmother says.

I push the door wide open. 'It's me, Grandma.'

'Who are you? I don't know you.' My grandmother rattles the safety rails of her bed like an angry child. 'You're not Princess Anne.'

'No. Sorry. It's just me. Just Holly.' It isn't possible for my grandmother to call me anything else. I moved her from the nursing home in St Ives to this one in Bath twenty months ago, and I told Katarina and the others who look after her here that Holly has always been my grandmother's nickname for me, but that my actual name is Helen.

'Go away. Go get Princess Anne.'

'After I've spent a little time with you.' I bend to kiss my grandmother's cheek. She is wearing the lilac night-dress and matching bed jacket that I asked Katarina to put under the tree for her. Katarina has arranged the pillows so that my grandmother is sitting up.

I move a slippery vinyl chair closer to the bed. I lift one of her hands. The skin is loose, and so thin it tears when she bruises. The surface is a jungle of liver spots and protruding green veins. Her fingers are bent as the gnarled branches of a weathered tree. 'Happy Christmas, Grandma.'

'Is it Christmas?'

'Yes.'

'Is that why you're wearing that ridiculous red hat?'

'Yes. Katarina gave it to me. There's going to be a lovely party downstairs. Will you let me help you dress? We can go together.'

'I had a feeling something was happening today.' She grimaces.

'It's also my birthday, Grandma.'

'How old are you then?'

'Twenty-seven.'

'Have you seen my Christmas present?'

'You're wearing it. It's a pretty colour on you.'

She examines her sleeve as if it were covered in bird poo. 'Not this.' She stresses *this* to make her disgust clear. 'My new photograph.'

The frame sits on her bedside table, beside a plastic jug of water with a matching tumbler in an unfortunate shade of urine-yellow. Almost immediately, my grandmother blocks it from my view, lurching her upper body to the side to try to grab at the photograph with her arthritic fingers. There is a crash, and a cry. 'Blast! Oh, oh oh!' She is screaming in frustration.

'It's okay. It's okay.' I am out of my chair and rushing to the other side of the bed. Water has sloshed everywhere. The jug has bounced onto the linoleum floor.

'Don't be upset.' I am already in her efficient wet room with its accessible shower and toilet and sink, grabbing a vinegar-smelling towel. I retrieve the frame from beneath the bed where it landed, and wrap it in the towel.

'Is Princess Anne all right?' my grandmother says.

I can feel my face creasing in puzzlement as I sweep

the towel over the floor with a foot. I study the image inside the frame. 'Oh my God.'

'Don't talk that way. You're a heathen – you cannot be my granddaughter.'

'But it really is Princess Anne.'

'Of course it is. Kindly answer my question, please.' My grandmother makes the words kindly and please sound like insults. 'I asked if Princess Anne is all right.'

'Yes.'

'I didn't hear you.'

Her ears are still as sharp as the wolf's, but I repeat the word. 'Yes.'

'No cracks?'

'Not even a hairline fracture.' I cannot tear my eyes from the picture, which has been cut from an article that appeared in a local newspaper last September. *Three whole months ago.* All that time, I was living my poor imitation of a normal life, not knowing this was out there.

Princess Anne's skirt and jacket are sewn from maroon and navy tartan. My grandmother is wearing her favourite dress. A background of dried earth, sprinkled with flowers the shade of wet mud. This is an adventurous pattern and pallet for my grandmother. Her white wisps of hair look lit from within.

My grandmother is standing, a wooden walking stick shaped like a candy cane in each hand, and care workers on both sides, ready to catch her if she crumbles. I think of my grandmother as tall, but she is stooped and tiny in front of Princess Anne, and looking up at her with a slant eye. My grandmother is not trying to please. My grandmother is never trying to please. Princess Anne bends towards her. The princess's back is straight and perfect and in line with her neck and head. Only the hinge of her waist moves. The impression is that she is paying homage to my grandmother, rather than the reverse, as you would expect. This is exactly how my grandmother thinks things should be.

My grandmother says, 'Will Princess Anne be coming to see me again soon, Holly?' Despite my shock, and my fear, a small part of me registers that at least my grandmother has remembered my name. 'As soon as she gets a chance, Grandma.'

I am not much of a royal follower. But staring at the photograph, I recall Princess Anne's visit, and the excitement it occasioned in the residents and staff at the care home. I was working that day, and happy to miss it.

Katarina hurries in, wearing a red Santa hat with a white pom-pom that matches the one she put on my head when I arrived. She has on a tinsel bracelet and necklace, too. 'Everything okay?'

'Just a water spill. All dry now.' I hold out the photograph. 'How thoughtful,' I say to Katarina. 'Is this from you?'

She nods. 'I think Mrs Lawrence likes it.'

'She does. That was so kind of you.' I am trying to seem pleased when I am anything but. But the damage is done. However I seem, it will make no difference now.

There is a tagline beneath the photograph. *The Princess Royal talks to Oaks resident Beatrice Lawrence, 93.*

It is the sight of my grandmother's name in print that makes my breath catch in a blend of fear and nausea.

All the things I have done. All the measures I have taken. Except for this photograph. This is what I missed. What I didn't foresee. A tiny thing that might make all the difference. The chance is small, but I know better than anybody that I must prepare for the possibility that this will lead him straight to me.

Then Black Star Sapphire

Two years and eight months earlier

Cornwall, April 2016

The three years since I failed to join MI5 passed slowly, with little to show for them. I spent the time taking care of my grandmother, moving her into a nursing home, and working behind the counter of the town pharmacy that Milly's father owned.

Everything changed when Milly helped me to get a new job as a ward clerk in the hospital where she worked as a nurse. On my first day, when there was a telephone call for Dr Zachary Hunter, I knew exactly where to find him. The click-clack of his shoes let me track him like the crocodile in *Peter Pan*.

I hovered in the doorway of a side room, watching Dr Hunter examine a patient whose eyes were closed. The woman's arm fell from the bed and dangled as he manoeuvred her.

'Dr Hunter?' Those were the first words I ever said to him. 'GP on the phone.'

I felt professional. I felt as if I were starring in a television drama set in a hospital. I felt proud that I was being so helpful. I was extra-diligent. I paid attention to absolutely everything and everyone. Already, I was on top of it all.

Dr Hunter's back was towards me. Otherwise, I might have seen that he was rolling his eyes in irritation. If he hadn't been pulling the red triangle above the patient's bed, so that the siren went off and the lights flashed, I might have heard him swearing under his breath at the idiot new girl.

What I saw, though, when he turned his head, was a calm face, filled with energy and intelligence. What I heard, as he gave me clear, succinct instructions, was an authoritative voice. 'Dial 2222. Say, "Adult cardiac arrest on the cardiac unit". Go. Now, Holly. And call me Zac.'

What I thought, as he began chest compressions, was how does he know my name? What I noticed, unable to look away, was that the compressions were a kind of violence. The patient's white belly flopped from side to side each time he plunged down on her.

'Go,' he said again. And, at last, I did.

Afterwards, I said, 'Sorry about earlier. I'm still learning how it all works.'

He looked at me carefully. 'It can be overwhelming when you're new. You'll learn quickly. And thank you for passing on the message from the GP.'

It was only then that I properly registered that he was entirely bald, though from his face I'd guessed he wasn't more than forty. I blushed, not simply out of embarrassment for my blundering, but because he had already won me over with his life-saving heroics, his composure under pressure, and his courtesy, which I did not think I deserved.

* * *

Although I didn't get to learn the secrets that working for MI5 would have revealed, I soon understood that the hospital had its secrets too, even if they weren't of national importance.

There was a young woman, a few years younger than me, waiting for a heart transplant. Over coffee, Zac spoke to me about the case in a hushed voice. 'I shouldn't tell you, but I trust you.' Even as my eyes filled with tears to hear that the young woman would almost certainly die, I was imagining how I would write about her in my journal. Zac touched my hand. 'Don't be sad,' he said. There was a tender side to him, despite the swaggering.

When Zac walked through the ward, the eyes of the patients and their families followed him like a flower follows the sun. Zac was a god there, and he knew it. He didn't bother to hide the fact that he revelled in his power. Zac saw everything. When he saw that my eyes followed him too, he strutted even more.

My grandmother had told me again and again that my long-dead father was a hero, and I did not doubt it. He was a pilot, flying search and rescue for the Royal Air Force, so he saved many lives. It wasn't rocket science to see why I would be attracted to a charismatic and commanding older man like Zac, who also saved lives. But self-awareness and self-control are not the same thing. The fact that you know you are acting like a cliché doesn't necessarily stop you from doing it.

I was sitting behind the reception desk. Zac brushed his shoulder against mine as he looked with me at the computer screen. I was working on the notes for an eighteen-year-old

21

male with a heart infection that his mother knew everything about, but a sexually transmitted disease that she knew nothing about. Zac was making sure that both were being taken care of.

'Have dinner with me tonight. I'll cook for you.' He was so full of pent-up energy he seemed ready to vibrate, but he kept himself still, in control. He was like that whatever he said or did, though he displayed an unflappable cool in all of his interactions with patients.

'Your glasses are steamed up.' I noticed because I wanted to sneak a glance at his extraordinary eyes. One was violent blue. The other was the real wonder. It was a half circle of cobalt in the top of the iris, and a half circle of brown in the bottom.

He took the glasses off and handed them to me, an intimacy. 'Is that a yes to dinner?'

'I think so.' I fiddled with his glasses. 'I don't have anything to clean them with.'

He looked at his jacket pocket. I fumbled my hand inside, meeting those bright eyes of his as I did, and found a square of grey microfibre covered in tiny stethoscopes. I wiped the lenses. When I handed them back, he let his skin touch mine and gave me an electric shock.

'You'd better watch for Mr Rowntree's girlfriend. If she turns up during visiting hours while his wife is here, he may arrest again.' Zac was smart enough to make sure nobody heard him say this – it was the kind of talk that could get even a doctor in trouble. A piece of my hair had slipped out of my ponytail. He slid it between his fingers as he walked off to do his ward rounds.

Milly came over. 'You're looking hot.'

'It's extra warm in here.' I tried to tuck my hair into the elastic.

'Not that kind of hot.' She eyed Zac, who was disappearing into the doctors' office. 'Nothing says, *I'm a very important cardiologist doing super-cool interventional things* like a scrub top and smart-casual trousers.'

I laughed so hard I almost snorted, which encouraged Milly to keep going.

'That *I'm looking beautiful but heroics were needed so I threw this top on* outfit is definitely for you. I wish I could dress for impact.' Milly frowned at the purple dress the staff nurses had to wear. 'It's like *The Handmaid's* fucking *Tale* around here, with all this fucked-up colour coding.'

Milly and I kept an incognito blog. We called it *Angel's and Devil's Book Reviews*. Devil found the novels that everyone loved and gave them one star. Angel found the ones everyone hated and gave them five. We had two thousand followers and the most beautiful review blog in the world, because Milly was an artist, so everything about it was visually arresting. She was the most creative person I'd ever met. There was a photo on our 'About Us' page, with both of us wearing superhero eye masks. Mine was white, Milly's red. She had scarlet horns pinned to her blonde hair. I had a white halo. Milly's hatchet job reviews got twenty times more Likes than my attempts at justice for the unfairly spurned.

'Please tell me you're not doing Atwood,' I said.

'I am for sure going to do Atwood.'

'You will make her cry.' I clutched my heart in mock sorrow.

'She doesn't strike me as the crying type.'

I looked down at myself. 'She for sure would if she had to wear this.'

'True. Those white polka dots.' She rolled her eyes. 'Dr Hunter seems into them, though. He'd be perfect for you, except for the fact that he sleeps with everything that moves.'

'If that's true,' Zac said, 'then why haven't I slept with you?'

Milly let out a squeak.

Zac's face was a tight mask. How did he manage to sneak up on us? Normally the sound of his shoes gave him away. Did he change his gait, to avoid the usual noise of the taps on his soles? Or were Milly and I so absorbed in each other we didn't notice? There was no doubting the clip-clop of his walk as he went off to continue his rounds.

Milly wasn't finished, though she was no longer smiling. 'It's so fucking predictable, your falling for this powerful doctor. It's pure fantasy. We're not living in my mum's collection of Disney films. Tell me you at least know that.'

'I do know, yes. But I also know I'm not alone.' I hummed a few lines of the Gaston song from *Beauty and the Beast*, because Gaston was my nickname for Milly's boyfriend.

'You have got to stop calling him Gaston,' she said. 'Why do you?'

'You know why. Because he's so in love with himself. Like the character in the Disney film. They're practically identical.'

'That's true.'

'Remind me of his real name, Milly.'

'You've known it since our first day of school.' She put her hands on her hips. 'Tell me the truth about something.'

'What?'

'You know that love letter you got when we were in Reception? We thought it was from a boy in our class, but we never figured out who . . .'

'We were four. It was twenty years ago, Milly!'

I'd actually written the letter myself. It said, 'I love you, Holly', and the words were surrounded by a heart. It was hardly a work of art, though I suppose it was evidence of how much I loved to write and make things up, even at that age. I'd wanted Milly to think I had a secret admirer. I'd experienced a small sense of triumph that I pulled off that bit of fiction and made someone think it was true. Even then, though, I knew that the fact I *could* fool her didn't mean I *should*. I'd felt a twinge of guilt, too, that it had been so easy.

'Was it Fergus?' she said. 'Do you think he wrote the letter?'

'God. No. I mean, I don't know, but I'm sure it wasn't him.' I still didn't want to confess to Milly that I'd faked the letter. At the age of four, I was already practising my tradecraft as well as my writing. But my strongest motive for tricking Milly was my wish to impress her. I'd wanted my brand-new friend and neighbour to think that other people saw me as special.

I tried to joke. 'Gaston probably wasn't able to write then, so it couldn't have been him. But you and I were very advanced.'

She laughed. 'Again true.'

'I get that you had a crush on him when we were four. I don't get what you see in him now.'

'What I see in *Fergus* is that he's always been in my life. That kind of loyalty matters.'

'Not to him. You shouldn't hold on to someone because they're a habit.'

'Why not? I've held on to you.'

As a joke a couple of years ago, Milly bought a book that

instructed women on all the right things they should do to get a man to fall madly in love with them, and all the wrong things they shouldn't. She read out bits to me and the two of us hooted in derision.

On my first date with Zac, I did two of the biggest wrong things. The first was that I didn't make him take me out to dinner. I went to the house he was renting, nestled in farmland and set a few hundred metres from the coastal path.

After weeks of flirting and brushing past each other, his hands were all over me the instant he closed his front door. I said, 'All those women. Is it true?'

'Not any more.' He was unzipping my dress, sliding it off my shoulders, letting it drop to the floor.

The book put the second wrong thing in a different font, for emphasis. *Do not sleep with a man on the first date. Never ever. No matter what. Just don't.*

Zac was pulling me towards a rug in the centre of his sitting room, pushing me onto my back, and we were making love almost in the same movement.

When we got up to go to make dinner, he asked how I liked my steak, and I said, 'Well done, with horseradish sauce.' He kissed me and sat me at his marble-topped table and told me he would be right back. I heard him climb the stairs, and a minute later, his footsteps drawing near. But instead of returning to the kitchen, there was what I guessed to be the rattle of keys and the creak of the front door opening and closing, then the roar of his car engine.

Half an hour later, I was reading an article that Zac had left the newspaper folded to, which he'd neatly arranged on the corner of the table. The article was about a huge leak of records from a Panama-based law firm, and how the prime minister's own father was on the list of rich people who put their money in offshore tax havens.

When Zac walked into the kitchen he nodded approvingly at the article. 'Impressive thing to pull off.'

I took his hand. 'Whoever leaked that data is a hero.'

'Doubtful that he'll appear on the Honours List.'

I stood and pulled Zac against me. 'I hope they don't catch him.'

'I'm glad you feel that way.' One of his hands was on the small of my back. The other was taking a jar of horseradish sauce from the pocket of his blazer and putting it on the table. 'I want you to have your dinner exactly how you like it.' But we ended up not eating anything.

Zac slept with his body pressed against mine that night, and it was the first time I could remember feeling as if I belonged somewhere. When he went into the bathroom the next morning to get ready for work, I listened carefully for the sound of the water running in the shower, then sat up to peek in the drawer of his bedside table.

There was a photograph of a woman who looked like me, with hair the colour of maple leaves in autumn and eyes the colour of moss. She was on a cushiony reclining chair by a beach with palm trees, sipping from a cocktail glass with carefully arranged edible flowers around the rim. She was wearing a tasselled white cover-up, so filmy I could see her orange bikini beneath it. On her left ankle was an oval mark like a black star sapphire, so distinct I wondered if it was a tattoo. Perhaps it was a birthmark.

'You found my first wife.' Zac's voice came as the quilt slipped from my shoulders, or rather, as he pulled it from me, so it was only when those two things, the words and the movement, happened at once, that I inhaled and looked up to see him standing there, though I could hear that the shower was still on.

'You startled me.'

He sat on the edge of the bed, a towel round his hips. There were drops of water on his shoulders, and he was dripping on me. He drew a wet finger down the centre of my chest and to my belly button, where he left it.

There was no good story to defuse my being caught with the photograph, so I didn't tell one. 'She's very pretty.' It occurred to me that other than the incident of Peggy and the apple tree when I was four, I had never knowingly been caught snooping.

'Not as pretty as you.'

'That was the right thing to say. Was there a second one?'

'A second what?' He pressed one hand over my breast and the other over my throat, tilting me flat again.

'Wife.'

'The divorce of the first only came through at the start of this year, so not yet.' His mouth was against mine. 'The grounds were desertion. She left me.'

'When?'

'Three years ago.'

I thought, but didn't say, that three years ago wasn't a great time for me either, with Maxine and that glass table and the line I was stupidly ready to cross.

'What's her name?'

'Jane.' Zac went on. 'The end of that marriage – it's the worst thing that ever happened to me. If you know that now, it will help you to understand.'

'Understand what?'

'Understand me. The way I am. The care I take, now, to cherish what I value, to make sure I don't lose it.'

'The way you are is perfect.' I pulled him on top of me.

He laughed. 'That was the right thing to say too. And to do.'

'Except for the arrogance thing and the god complex thing.'

'That not so much.'

'I find it hard to imagine any woman wanting to leave you.'

'Good recovery. Smoothly done.' He kissed me into forgetting about his first wife. When I next opened his bedside drawer, the photograph was gone.

Now The Girl with the Two-Coloured Eye

Three years later

Bath, Monday, 1 April 2019

I am at work, based now in the paediatric unit of a hospital in Bath. This place is so different from my old job in Cornwall. I am concentrating hard on inputting patient details, when the sound of a crying child makes my attention waver.

A woman is in a deep knee bend beside a pushchair, fumbling with a manicured hand to pick up a stuffed kitty that the child must have thrown. One of those women who spends her morning in designer activewear, then transforms into a lady who lunches. Her expensively jewelled fingers are tipped with blue-black manicured nails that for most mothers would not be compatible with a toddler. Those fingers curl around a takeaway coffee cup that she is struggling not to spill.

The child's small hand shoots out to grab the edge of the woman's techno-fabric sleeve. Trying to protect the child from the hot drink, the woman loses her balance and falls. The cup lands beside her, the lid pops off, and the steaming coffee splashes onto the linoleum as well as the woman's blossom-print leggings. The child stops screaming, arrested by the spectacle of her mother on the floor.

'Can't she read?' Trudy, who is the ward manager's assistant and senior to me, is hissing from behind her computer screen. 'Tell her. Get out there now, Helen, and tell her about the sign.'

'Isn't it a bit late for that?'

'Go,' Trudy says.

In my cardiology ward clerk job, I wore a dull-red smock with off-white polka dots. The spots on this paediatric smock are mint green. The background is strawberry-wafer pink. I will look like a walking cupcake as I approach the polished woman.

'Okay, okay. I'm going.' I grab the roll of blue paper towels we keep on a nearby shelf for such emergencies, then emerge from the shelter of the curved reception desk.

I squat in front of the woman. 'You're not burnt, I hope?'

She shakes her head no.

I offer her some paper towels and she begins to dab at her clothes while I wipe the floor. Trudy has marched across to direct this little scene and glower at the woman. I wouldn't have imagined that somebody with curlicue hair like Shirley Temple's could be intimidating, but Trudy is, despite being a mere one and a half metres tall. I know about Shirley Temple because my grandmother loves her, and endlessly watched her films.

'No hot drinks allowed in Paediatric Outpatients,' Trudy says. 'Did you not see the signs?'

The woman stands, elegant and willowy beside Trudy. 'I'm sorry. I was desperate for caffeine.'

The child is watching all of this with quiet fascination.

'Children can be scalded by hot drinks. That is why there is a bin by the entrance,' Trudy says.

'I was tired,' the woman says, 'but that's no excuse.'

Trudy softens, but to detect the softening you would need to be accustomed to monitoring every gradient of the human anger scale.

'Come with me,' Trudy says to the woman. 'You need to book your daughter in and have her details checked.'

'Let me grab her first.' The woman moves towards the front of the pushchair to unfasten the child, who immediately begins to squirm.

'Helen will watch her for a minute,' Trudy says.

I am on my knees, mopping coffee. I straighten up, so my shins are resting on linoleum that is printed to resemble a giant jigsaw puzzle, and my bottom is on my heels. The little girl is staring at me, pursing her lips as if she is about to blow out birthday candles. Her hair is the colour of copper, the same shade mine used to be before I soaked it in black dye. It is baby fine, and her mother has arranged the front in a ponytail-spout above her forehead, to keep it out of her eyes. The spout is a white jet, and adorable on this child, though I wonder if her hair colour is a symptom of whatever medical condition has brought her to the paediatric unit today. Her skin is ivory perfect, though perhaps a bit too pale.

I glance at the mum, whose own hair is dark and artfully highlighted. It reaches the bottom of her neck.

She pushes it behind her ears and says to me, 'Is that okay?

'Absolutely,' I say, and she follows Trudy.

The child is frowning, uncertain as she scans for her mother, who is now out of her sightline. I expect her to start to cry again, or scream, or kick. But she doesn't do any of these things. She blinks her eyes several times, so I look more closely at them. They are surrounded by long, red-gold lashes that match my own, though I wear mascara to hide the colour. One eye is four-leaf clover green, again like mine. The other is blue as a dark sky in the top half-circle, and brown as the earth at the bottom. The only other person I have seen with such an eye is Zac. It is one of the most beautiful things about him. Again, though, I wonder if the child's eye is a symptom of something medical, the same as her white forelock.

I fantasise about picking her up and holding her close, pretending that she is mine.

To others, I must appear to be a normal woman. I alone know that I am a creature stitched out of pieces that don't fit and never will, with some of them missing and others stretched too thin and in the wrong shape. My seams show vivid and red like those of Frankenstein's monster.

I say to the child. 'You are very pretty. What's your name?'

She opens her mouth, then smacks her lips together.

I laugh. 'I bet your name is pretty too. Can you tell me how old you are?'

She shakes her head.

'Let me try to guess. Are you two?'

She holds up one finger.

Her mother speaks over her shoulder to me while Trudy enters more details into the system. 'Alice will be two next month.'

'Ah.' I throw a smile of thanks over my own shoulder. 'So you are one right now, but nearly two. That is very big. And you're so clever to count like that.'

She gives me a slow, serious nod of agreement.

'So you are Alice. I knew you'd have an extra-pretty name. Do you come from Wonderland?'

Alice nods yes to this question and holds out the stuffed kitty, stretching both arms in front of her in one decisive move.

'For me?'

Another nod.

I take the kitty and jiggle it until she laughs and snatches it back.

'I love your dress, Alice.' It is sunburst orange with pink and purple daisies.

Alice points to my head, and I remember that I took the white pom-pom from the Christmas hat Katarina gave me last December and tied it around my ponytail this morning. I touch the ball of fluffy yarn. 'Do you like it?'

Alice nods, her eyes wide.

Alice's mum returns, and I show her where she can wait with Alice. It's the nicest part of the paediatric unit, with PVC-upholstered benches for parents and boxes of toys for children. As soon as she is freed from her buggy, Alice toddles off in her bright play dress to the toy oven, to make pretend cups of tea and bake pretend cakes, helped by her mum, who kneels beside her.

Trudy is preoccupied at the other end of the desk. The buzzer goes, signalling the arrival of a new patient. The last thing on Trudy's mind is me – she has way too much to do, hitting the button to release the door lock, then signing in a little boy and answering his parents' anxious questions.

I shouldn't do it. I know it is irrational. But that eye. I have to check. A few keystrokes, and I have Alice's computerised records on the screen. The address is on a very expensive street. When I see that her mother's name is Eliza Wilmot I get an electric shock and my heart starts to beat faster.

Eliza was the name of a woman I glimpsed with Zac in a hotel bar on a horrible night two years ago. I never learned her surname. Is this the same Eliza? And the child. Could she be Zac's? I shake my head at the possibility, then stop myself, self-conscious, though when I look around nobody is paying attention.

When I see that Alice was born on May eighteenth, just a few days after my own baby, I take a short, sharp breath. My throat tightens, and I am in the grip of grief and panic. There is a real risk I will cry. Last year, on May fourteenth, I pulled the comforter over my head and didn't get out of bed at all. I think of my grandmother's photo in the paper. Has Zac managed to find me, and dragged along a child I never knew about? The coincidences are too strong for me to imagine anything else.

I press on through Alice's referral letter and medical notes. She has type 1 Waardenburg syndrome, which is a rare genetic condition that can cause hearing loss as well as changes to the pigmentation of the skin, hair, and eyes. So far, the medical notes say, Alice has three manifestations of the condition. The white forelock, the iris that is segmented into two different colours, and eyes that appear widely spaced, though in Alice the latter manifestation is so subtle I hadn't noticed it. She is new to the area, and today is her initial appointment with the paediatrician who will be monitoring her. Tomorrow, I see, she is going to audiology for a hearing test.

For the first time, it occurs to me that Zac might have this condition, too. Could that be why he shaves his head, morning and night, to hide the white forelock? He led me to think the shaving was an aesthetic choice. That he preferred no hair at all to a bald spot. When I asked him about his eye, he said he was made that way. I try to picture his face. I *think*, though I am not certain, that perhaps his eyes, too, are a little widely spaced. But why would he keep the condition a secret, and try to cover it up, if he did have it? As soon as I silently pose the question, I know the answer. Zac hates anything that makes him appear vulnerable.

A sudden influx of newly arrived parents and children overwhelms me and Trudy. I catch sight of Alice's mother, hovering nearby, handing Alice a biscuit and a sippy cup, then checking her phone. When the queue has finally cleared, she comes over to me. 'Thank you so much for your help earlier.'

I give her an it-was-nothing shrug. Does she know who I am? Did Zac send her here? I can't decide. The appointment is certainly genuine – Alice clearly needs it. I am praying my face isn't drained of colour when I say, 'Your daughter is gorgeous.'

'She is, isn't she?!' Without looking at it, she grabs a flyer about MMR from a pile stacked on the counter, rummages in her bag for a pen, scribbles something on the flyer. 'I'm Eliza. And this is Alice.'

It's as if I have a hot sword running through the centre of my chest to the bottom of my stomach.

'And you're Helen, aren't you?' I nearly jump at her knowing my name, but then she lowers her voice and says, 'The scary woman called you that.'

I manage a laugh. 'Ah. Yes.' I lift the flap in the reception counter to let myself through. I crouch in front of Alice. 'Goodbye, Alice.' I put out my hand, which she takes and shakes, imitating grown-ups. She holds her arms out, so that I lean closer in, and she giggles and tries to slide my glasses from my nose, then giggles some more. This child looks so like Zac, but his strong features are delicate and beautiful in her face.

'I don't normally do this.' Eliza lifts her shoulders in pretend embarrassment. 'I mean, pick up new friends in hospital clinics. But we've not long moved here, and I barely know anyone. Would you like to meet for coffee? I wrote down my name and number.' She offers me the MMR sheet.

I take the sheet. 'Coffee would be lovely.' It is quiet here, a brief lull, and Trudy has gone on a break. Nobody will notice that I do not dutifully tell my would-be friend Eliza that I am not supposed to do this sort of thing with the parents of patients. I smile with what I think is perfect composure, though the fizzing electrical noises that are a constant in this place seem to be bleeping and pinging from inside my own body.

That night, I cannot sleep. I squirm beneath sheets that are sticky with my own sweat, feeling as alone as a lighthouse keeper trapped on a rock island in a storm so terrible no relief boat can get to him. I grab the phone from the floor by my bed and dial Peggy, with my number blocked and the mute button engaged, my heart beating so much faster than the ringtone.

Peggy is still half-asleep, sounding scared, thinking something has happened to Milly, repeating the word 'Hello' over and over, and Milly's name as if it were a question. I can hear James in the background, asking who it is and what has happened. I disconnect, telling myself it was worth it just to hear their voices after almost two years. I feel dreadful that I've frightened them, but tell myself they will soon discover that Milly is fine.

I pull off the quilt and drag myself from the single bed beneath the crypt-like brick archway I'd painted bright yellow. I sit in a rocking chair I'd stained deep teal, and I sew the tiniest of tiny baby clothes for the most premature of premature babies. I am one of a handful of volunteers who make these so that hospitals can keep a few on hand. And though I hope they will never be worn, I know all too well that they will be. I prick my finger with the needle and feel certain that somewhere out in the world a bad thing is happening.

Then Human Asset

Two and a half years earlier

Cornwall, 14 October 2016

It was the Mermaid of Zennor who prompted my move into Zac's rented farmhouse two months after we first slept together. We made the decision when I took him to see her in the village church.

The Mermaid is six centuries old, and carved into the side of a little bench, holding her looking glass and comb. The dark wood is scarred and scratched and discoloured. Some of it is peeling away. She has a rounded belly and breasts that you can't help but want to touch, though countless hands have smoothed her features away through the years.

Zac and I knelt side by side and trailed our fingers over the Mermaid as I told him her story.

What happens to her is nothing like Hans Christian Andersen's version or the Disney film. She is enchanted by the beautiful voice of a local man, drifting out of the church towards the waves. And it is the man who then goes to live with her in the kingdom of the Merpeople. She doesn't need to give up her tail and grow legs to have a life with him on land.

Milly and I had always planned to write a book about her, with my words and her illustrations.

'You're my mermaid,' Zac said, as soon as I finished the story. 'That is what I want to do for you.' He knew I would never want to leave Cornwall, though before he met me he'd viewed his job there as a brief stop on his starry route to someplace else. 'We'll stay here,' he said, 'in your world.' I was moved by that. And in his debt.

That was four months ago. Since then, we'd spent just three nights apart, when he attended a medical congress in Moldova towards the end of the summer. I'd missed him during that trip, despite the fact that living with a man for the first time wasn't entirely easy for me. My grandmother brought me up with a strange mixture of regulation that I didn't miss and freedom that I did. I felt so visible, so watched and accountable, when before I could disappear for what seemed endless stretches of time. But none of that was Zac's fault.

I'd come to my special place to consider all this. It was where I liked to read and think and scribble hospital stories in my secret journal, which I kept hidden from Zac. I was wearing his parka, hugging it around myself, and sipping from the thermos of coffee I brought with me. The bench that I was sitting on was erected by the town soon after my parents died. The tarnished plaque behind my back was engraved with the words, *In Remembrance of Squadron Leader Edward Lawrence and His Wife, Matilda Lawrence.*

The bench sat on a section of the coastal path my parents had often walked together, above a gorge in the cliff that made a kind of waterfall down to the rocks below. Usually the waterfall sounded like thunder, and the sea churned and heaved its foam. On that October day, though, the water-fall was a trickle of gentle music, and the sea was so calm I could see the rocks below its glassy surface. Already it was past the high season. There were few other walkers despite the unseasonally mild autumn morning.

It was a short walk to that isolated stretch of the coastal path and I made it whenever I could, as if in my parents' footsteps. Zac's rented house was a few hundred metres inland. I thought of my bright charity shop clothes, stuffed in his drawers and wardrobe, mixed with the sleek designer wear he organised with military precision. The tall, narrow house I grew up in next door to Milly and James and Peggy was virtually abandoned, but I understood Zac's reluctance to live so close to them.

I pictured my childhood bed in the attic, and its bright pink quilt dotted with red poppies. That bed seemed to fade. Instead, I saw the new one I shared with Zac, the white sheets thrown on the floor, and the two of us in it the night before.

My clothes were off, and Zac's hands seemed to be every-where, and I reached towards the drawer in the bedside table where I kept my diaphragm, and he caught my arm before I could get to it and pinned my wrists above my head and held me down and kissed any words away, and it was impossible to make him wait any longer, though I was uncer-tain about whether I wanted him to, and in a haze of confusion over what had just happened, my head foggy from too much wine, and my body seeming not to be my own.

* * *

There was a noise, coming from the coastal path, and my replay of the night before blew away. A figure was striding towards me, dressed in baggy walking trousers and a sweat-shirt, wearing a small backpack. Her hair was hidden beneath a khaki bush hat, her eyes shielded by dark sunglasses.

I aimed a polite 'Morning' vaguely in her direction, hoping that she would walk on and leave me with my thoughts. Instead, she lowered herself onto the bench beside me. Because I had arranged myself in the middle, she seemed too close. I slid over, until my right side was pressed against the wooden arm. I studied the copy of *Jane Eyre* in my lap, trying to signal that I wasn't interested in talking.

'Good book?' The voice was familiar. I looked up to see the woman remove her sunglasses. There was the same indigo eyeliner, the same thick mascara, the same crimson lipstick. Her hands were gloved, but I was betting the nails were scarlet.

'Yes.' It was a present from Zac, a beautiful old edition, given because he knew how much the novel meant to me.

Maxine perched her sunglasses back on her nose, then extracted a clear plastic bag from her backpack, which contained pastries. 'Croissant?'

I squinted at her. 'No. Thank you.'

'Bottle of water?'

'Again, no. Thank you.'

It had been three and a half years since I crashed out of my final interview for MI5, and her appearance was so unex-pected I wondered if I was dreaming. Why on earth was she seeking me out after all that time, and offering me breakfast?

'I'd like to talk to you.' She seemed to be answering my unspoken question. She looked out at the sea with her usual indifference and took a bite of a croissant. 'Stale,' she said, tossing it behind her without looking.

I stifled a laugh. 'We had to do a role-play exercise, during that residential assessment. We pretended to be agent handlers making an approach to a potential informant. "Always provide amenities." That was part of your script for how to recruit an agent. Are you trying to recruit me, Maxine?'

To my astonishment, she said, 'Yes. I am.'

'You're joking.'

'I'm completely serious. You're in a position to help us. I've come to ask if you will.'

I had fantasised about Maxine seeking me out, Maxine telling me she'd got it wrong, Maxine saying that getting rid of me was the great misjudgement of her career, Maxine confessing that she – that they – needed me.

'Are you offering me a proper job with the Security Service?'

'You have access to intelligence that we need, and we know you're skilful enough to get it for us.'

'No you don't. You don't think that about me at all. I seem to remember that flattery is part of that script for recruiting informants, too.'

'It is, as a matter of fact. But I do think you're skilful – there was only that one critical flaw that ended the possibility of your joining us.'

'Please spare me the flattery. I'd have thought that if you wanted a lab report or a patient's medical record you could reach right in and grab them.'

'That isn't what this is about. But technically speaking, yes, you would be a Covert Human Intelligence Source, or agent – what the cousins call a human asset. I much prefer their term. You already know, Holly, that a human asset collects information for us, then passes it on.'

Her words stabbed away the mad bit of hope I'd somehow conjured. What Maxine wanted – what they wanted – was to use me. I was little more than a drone to them, and would never be properly inside MI5.

'And you would be my handler?'

'Yes. I would have responsibility for your security and welfare. Something we take very seriously.'

'I bet. So you see me the same way you see a drug dealer who gets to stay out of jail if he reports on the bad guys who are above him in the chain. Or a prostitute who you'll pay if she gives you information about her pimp. Or someone working for a company with trade secrets you're after.'

'Those aren't the only kinds of agents we recruit.'

'Nice of you to say. I'd be a rubbish informant, and I don't have access to any intelligence you could possibly be interested in.' I concentrated on the soft slap of the water as it gently rolled in and out.

'You have integrity – the qualities that made you want to join us in the first place.'

'I meant it about skipping the flattery section of your script. You don't think I have a single atom of integrity. You remember why I bombed my MI5 interview.'

She ignored this unseemly reminder with the tact of a hostess managing an awkward guest. 'We are authorised to make arrangements of this nature, Holly, in order to detect or prevent a crime, protect national security, or in the interests of the economic well-being of the UK.'

'Is that some kind of legal document they made you memorise?'

'Again, you are correct.'

'What is this really about, Maxine?'

'Your new boyfriend is Zachary Hunter.'

I was trailing my index finger over the gold lettering on *Jane Eyre's* cover, then tracing the edge of the oval portrait of Charlotte between the title and the author's name. 'You obviously know that he is.'

'So you know about his ex-wife?'

'I know she left him.' I followed a fishing boat with my eyes, a speck whose ghost-shape outline I could still see, imprinted from when it had been closer to land.

'Does he know where she is?'

'Why don't you ask him?'

'It's been tried. The experiment was not successful.'

I shrugged. 'Well why should he know? The fact that she's not in his life is pretty normal, given the circumstances. That's how it is with most people after a relationship ends. Not to mention the fact he divorced her on the grounds of desertion.'

If Maxine were given to expressiveness, I couldn't help but feel that she would be rolling her eyes. 'She's classified as a missing person. Did he tell you that the police questioned him about her disappearance?'

There was a trickle of sweat down my spine. 'The police always question previous partners. There can't have been any evidence against him or they'd have charged and tried him.' Then, the obvious thing, the thing I should have asked first, came to me. 'Why do you care about this?'

'I care about a missing woman.'

'No you don't. Even if you did, it's not the kind of thing MI5 gets involved in.'

'Believe what you like. You know it isn't protocol for us to explain the reasons for what we do to potential informants with no security clearance. Do you know her name?'

'Jane.' I didn't elaborate on my failure to discover her surname. I'd tried a few Internet searches for her under Zac's but found nothing. I hadn't wanted to press him to talk about her, when I could see how painful he found it.

'Jane Miller,' Maxine said, as if she guessed that my know-ledge was limited. 'Let me give you some facts.'

'I don't want your facts.'

'Hear me out. Okay?'

I didn't say yes, but I didn't stop her, either.

'Born August fourth, 1980, in London. Raised there by a single mother. Father was American – died in 2008 – Jane never knew him, unless seeing him as a baby counts. The father moved back to the US after Jane's mother divorced him – their relationship ended before Jane's first birthday. The mother's been dead since 1998.'

I couldn't quell my own curiosity, though I tried to sound bored. 'What was – is – Jane's profession?'

'Social worker.'

'Maybe she pissed somebody off. Maybe you should be looking at that.'

'She stopped working a few years before she disappeared.'

'What was her area?'

'The elderly – not a speciality where she'd be likely to attract a lot of hate.'

'You didn't tell me the names of her parents.' I pulled *Jane Eyre* closer, across my tummy, as if to shield myself.

'Jane's mother was Isabelle Miller. Her father was Philip

Veliko. Philip remarried soon after he returned to the US and had a son with his new wife. Frederick.'

'Would the father's new family have reason to resent Jane?'

'Jane inherited some money from her father, but the second wife predeceased him and Frederick didn't dispute Jane's inheritance – everything was split equally between Frederick and Jane. No known grievances or hostile behaviour from any of them.'

'Was Jane in contact with her brother?' *Jane Eyre* rose and fell as I breathed.

'As far as we can tell, only after their father's death, not before.'

'Well, you should still look at the brother. Most people would be pretty pissed off if some sibling they didn't even know swanned in and took half their inheritance.'

'Listen to me, Holly. Jane Miller is like you. And like your friend in the book.' Briefly, lightly, she tapped *Jane Eyre* with a gloved finger. 'She found herself living with a man whose closets were filled with skeletons. And she found, in the end, that she had to look in them. You are already living the perfect cover story. You don't need to change a thing.'

Round and round my finger went. 'My life isn't a cover story. My life is my life. My life is real.' I shook my head. 'Normally, you ask someone inside a government organisation to betray their country in some way. In my case, you want me to betray my boyfriend, be an informant on my boyfriend. No way. Not happening.'

'There are countless kinds of intelligence targets. You know that. We want any information that can help us find Jane and make sure she's safe.'

47

'Zac doesn't make women unsafe. Zac saves people's lives. Besides which, making sure women are safe is not your core business.'

'Our core business is complicated.'

'Then perhaps you should try explaining it in more detail to your potential agents. You might find they'd cooperate more enthusiastically.'

'You're a little different than most, more informed than is typical, given your history with us. I'm telling you everything I can. More than usual.'

'Flattering and confiding all in one move – you're a master of that recruitment script, but it's not working. Zac wouldn't hurt anybody. He's the most loving, protective, generous man I've ever known.'

'That's a lot of adjectives.'

'I don't need you to critique my language. I finished my English degree.'

'If you're right about him, then looking more closely can only show that.'

I put *Jane Eyre* in my bag, out of her sight and reach. 'Why on earth would I do this for you? What are you even trying to buy me with? I know you normally think of incentives when you're recruiting an agent. What possible incentive would I have?'

She allowed herself a smile. 'Ideological, in your case. I won't patronise you by not admitting that. It's your value system. You'd be protecting other women. Helping Jane. As I said, you'd be helping Zac, too.'

'He wouldn't see it that way. This is a wasted journey for you. There is no way I will do this.'

'Look. Here's another incentive for you, but maybe one

that isn't so easy for you to admit. I'm talking about your curiosity. You are Pandora, Holly. It's in your blood, that impulse to look where you shouldn't. My guess is that you've continued to do it, even without the legitimacy that the job would have given you.'

She was right, but I wasn't about to admit it to her. 'I'm not going to spy on Zac. Not for anybody and certainly not for you.'

'If he's telling you the truth, you've nothing to lose. You'd be helping him, removing him from suspicion. If you're wrong, wouldn't it be better for you to know it? Because if you are wrong, you may be living with a modern-day Bluebeard.'

I shook my head, trying to use reason to fight the tightening in my stomach. 'It doesn't make sense. This isn't the kind of thing the Security Service involves itself in. We aren't talking about national security, here. What aren't you telling me?'

'We work extremely closely with the police on many operations and investigations.'

'That's empty rhetoric and you know it.'

'Do you know what Jane looks like?'

I thought again of the photograph I found of her on the first night I slept with Zac. I'd searched for it several times since, without luck. 'Yes.'

'Then you know you resemble her. Same height and build – you're a couple of centimetres taller, but not much. Same colouring, that unusual strawberry blonde hair you both have. Doesn't that disturb you?'

'Having a preferred type isn't a sign that a man's a psychopath and a murderer.'

'Holly. I need to ask if Zac has ever done anything to hurt you.'

'Of course not.' I tugged Zac's parka down at the wrists. They were slightly red and swollen, from where he'd pinned them above my head the previous night, one of those fine lines that you sometimes crossed during sex, when you were carried away. 'But despite the fact you obviously disagree, rather than rescue me from him you want to send me back in.'

'I'm confident there's nothing I can say or do right now to keep you away from him. You don't want to be rescued. So, given that this is where we find ourselves, it would help us a great deal if you would keep an eye out.'

'No.'

'You don't need to do much. We can start small. If you come across any objects of Jane's, tell us about them in as much detail as you can. Give them to us, if at all possible.'

'It's pointless. Not just because I said no and I mean it. Zac doesn't even have any of her things.'

'You might still stumble on something. We'd like to know of any communications Zac makes, especially if they are connected in any way to Jane. Who are his contacts? How does he get in touch with them? Email? Text? Phone? Laptop? Does he have any social media accounts? Maybe under a user name that people wouldn't link to him? What trips does he make? If he ever happens to leave a device powered on you might be able to look. See if you can guess his password. Pay attention to where he's going, who he's meeting, if anyone ever visits him at work . . .'

'Those are disgusting things to do to someone you care about, someone who's trusted you and let you into their life.'

'Do what you are comfortable with, then. What you can. You understand Zac. You're intimate with him. You see the ins and outs of how he operates in ways we can't.'

'The answer's no.'

'It won't kill you to think about it, and to be gently watchful while you do.'

'Again . . . no.'

'Let me ask you something.'

'What?'

'Did you ever tell Zac you tried to join us?'

'No. Why would I?' My voice cracked. 'It was humiliating. Do you ever consider what it means to someone to work so hard to try to join you, to want to devote herself to that, to protecting her country, and then to discover she's not good enough?' I was surprised by my own honesty, by my naked-ness and exposure.

'I do. And it was wise of you to keep it to yourself. Did you tell anyone else?'

'Only Milly and James and Peggy. As I disclosed when I applied.'

'Again wise – I suggest you keep it that way. But just in case you change your mind about doing this for us, let me explain a bit more about how it can work.'

'I'm not going to change my mind. I've said no so many times in the last few minutes I've lost count. No means no these days.'

'I know that. I respect that. But it won't hurt you to hear me out. It doesn't obligate you to do anything. I've come a long way to see you – you can at least listen.'

'I don't remember guilt and emotional blackmail as part of the recruitment script.'

'Well they are. Can you give me a few more minutes?'

All I gave her was a shrug, but she seized on it with a pleased nod.

'Good,' she said, and though I punctuated her sentences with shakes of my head, she told me that my identity would be protected, and that any written records would not be available except to a small number of those who needed access, and that any information about my own wrongdoing would not be acted upon.

'There is no wrongdoing. Because I haven't done anything wrong.'

'We know that.' But still she went on, telling me about the secret channels through which I could contact her to pass information. And I couldn't help but listen, because the trade-craft she was describing, the basic techniques for surveillance and communications, fascinated me too much to stop her altogether or simply leave. She told me how to speak through classified advertisements, and about a dead letter drop she would set up near the bench where we were sitting. She mentioned a safe house, in case I ever needed to get away quickly.

'You really have wasted your time and wasted your breath,' I said, when she finally stopped.

'We'll see.' Without another word, she got up to retrace her steps along the path, vanishing as suddenly as she appeared. She moved silently, and I realised that the rustle she'd made when she first approached was no accident. Nothing Maxine said or did ever was.

Now The Two Tunnels

Two and a half years later

Bath, Tuesday, 2 April 2019

My head is filled with the little girl who visited the hospital yesterday. Each time I try to explain away her appearance there, I fail. I look over my shoulder, half-expecting to see Zac.

I am on my morning run. The route is already in my bones. My body moves along it without effort, though I barely slept last night. Hearing Peggy and James's voices comforted me, but agitated me too. For so long, I have had to hide myself from the few people in the world I love, all the time fearing that Zac would turn up. Now, there is a high probability that he has, as well as the distinct possibility that he dragged a wife and child along with him.

But I am not going to sit around waiting for them to pop out at me again. Or for him to. I added Eliza to my telephone contacts last night. 'Madam likes to be up early,' she had said, 'and my husband's usually out before the sun, so call any time.' I grab my phone from the pocket in the waistband of my leggings and use a voice command to do just that.

As we speak, Eliza clatters breakfast things and tries not to sound stressed, while Alice chatters in the background. We arrange to meet in the park for a quick coffee tomorrow morning, before I go into work. 'Getting Alice out early into fresh air would be good,' she says. There is a screech from Alice, and a crash of what sounds like glass onto tiles. 'As you can hear.' Eliza breaks off, though she hurriedly promises to bring the coffees.

I put the phone away and speed up. The sun is cutting through the pre-dawn mist and the bluebells are out already. Despite the two miles I have already run, and the call, I am not at all out of breath. I had to work hard to get this strong after it happened.

I turn into the disused railway line, going faster still, then enter the first tunnel. The dimness swallows me. The air seems still and dead, and smells of damp. Soon, though, the motion sensors begin, the flashes and sounds activated by my movement – Milly would love this. A circle of blue light surrounded by a white halo blazes at me from a window-shaped cut-out in the wall of stone, then a blast of violin music that is louder than my breathing as I speed up. But the tunnel is filled with ghosts, as if Eliza and Alice brought them along to the hospital and released them to chase after me.

I emerge into fresh, cool air, and the song of birds. There is the magic glimpse of a kingfisher in the gap between the two tunnels, by the river below. After the one that froze here last Christmas, I want so badly to take it as a good sign, but can't bring myself to.

I enter the second tunnel, leaving the sunshine behind me again. When I come out the other end, I think of a baby's first breaths, gasped in the midst of all that new brightness and noise. I try to envisage a baby's birth as it should be, because the bad outcomes are the exceptions and it is important to keep that in mind.

'Helen.'

I halt as if somebody has jerked me backwards. I know that voice, but I blink several times, as if to be sure of what I am seeing.

There is no doubt. The woman standing before me has stepped straight out of my nightmares.

It's not the right time yet. Getting you out the right way will take time. We need to set things up properly.

It has been almost two years since I've seen her, and Zac is a better candidate for the starring role in my bad dreams. But Maxine is the one who comes to me in the night, just as she did on my last night in hospital, the sheets clinging, cold and damp from my sweat.

Maxine has this way of never seeming to look at anyone or anything, her eyes downcast, her shoulders rounded. She is droopy. That is the word I often think of when I observe her. Your eyes would slide over her as if she were the most uninteresting piece of grey furniture ever made. And that is exactly what she wants your eyes to do.

'It's good,' she says, 'how readily you respond to Helen. Presumably Graham is natural to you too, now?'

'Yes.' I hadn't been out of breath, but now I am.

Maxine's blouse is elegant in midnight-blue silk, but untucked and sloppy. Her loose black trousers disguise how slim and dangerously fit she is. She is slouchy, as ever. Only the unfortunate know what it means when she straightens her back, something she does rarely. I am one of that select group.

'You look different.' That flat flat flatness of her voice. The pretence of indifference, as if I am a neighbour she sees every day, walking up and down the path to the next-door house.

'That's hardly surprising.'

Time seems to spool backwards, speeding past her twilight swoop on me in the hospital almost two years ago – it's too painful to freeze time there. It rushes further back, past her ambush on the cliffs two and a half years ago. Time stops six years ago, on the day I flunked out, sitting in that white-light room with the exposing glass table between us.

You're like that puppy who was too friendly to be a police dog, she'd said. *We don't recruit good-looking people. You need to look like Jane Average, but you're too vain to let yourself look that way.*

She has left the rear door of the car open, the engine purring but the driver invisible behind dark windows and hidden by the partition that keeps his section of the car separate. We both know it is no accident that she has crossed my path. Nothing is ever an accident with Maxine.

'Why are you here?' I channel her flat indifference, though I am pretty sure I can guess. As repellent as she is to me, it is looking as though I am going to need her help.

'Have you done anything to give yourself away?'

The question is a confirmation more than a surprise, but the air still puffs out of my stomach. 'My grandmother . . .' My voice trails off. 'It's possible, yes.'

She starts towards the car, parked where the road ends and the tunnel opens. 'Come with me.' It is as if I'd seen her yesterday, to hear her boss me around.

'Are you having me watched? Is that how you found me this morning?'

'Not necessary. You seem to have forgotten that I already knew where you were.' Do I imagine that there is a flash of something behind her eyes? Maxine opens the car door. 'There's something I need you to see. It's for your protection.'

'Excuse me if my confidence in your ability to protect me isn't great.'

'It's not as if you have anywhere important to go. Or anyone to go to.'

I say nothing. I keep my face indifferent, channelling Maxine herself. But she is right. Other than my grandmother, there is nobody.

'Trust me,' Maxine says.

'I've tried that before. It didn't work out great.'

'As far as I can tell, it still hasn't.'

'Do you have children, Maxine?'

She pretends not to hear.

'I asked you a question.'

'If I answer, will you come?'

'Yes.'

'I have children.'

'How many?'

'I agreed to answer your first question, not a series of them.'

'How many?' I say again.

'Two.' She looks so sorry for me. 'I have two.'

Then The Plague Pit

Two years and five months earlier

Cornwall, 13 November 2016

Since Maxine's failed attempt to recruit me four weeks ago, I'd plugged Jane's name, and her mother's and father's and brother's, into every Internet search engine I could think of. There was no social media for any of them, though I found a record of Jane's birth in London on 4 August 1980 and her marriage to Zac in September 2006.

I also found her father's obituary, which confirmed what Maxine said about his wife pre-deceasing him and his son Frederick surviving him. Two other things struck me when I read it. First, that Philip Veliko had been a property developer, and second, that the obituary didn't mention Jane at all.

The Remembrance Sunday ceremony always started at the outdoor war memorial in the square, then moved into the church. I was getting ready to leave for this, twisting up the front of my hair and fastening it with a jade comb, when Zac slipped his hands beneath my knitted dress. Before I knew it, he was tipping me back onto the bed and I was pulling him on top of me and there was a pile of sea-green wool on the floor.

Afterwards, when I stood in front of the looking glass to try again with my hair, he pressed against me from behind, wrapped his arms around me, and rested his hands on my belly. He whispered that he knew my period was two weeks late and my breasts were bigger, which he loved. I wondered that he could know these things, that he could be watching my body that carefully.

I had loved my brief time of hugging the secret of a pregnancy close and just for me. My breasts had been tingling for the past few days. Little electric sparks shot through them. I'd planned to share the news with him tomorrow, on his birthday.

So I said my period had a tendency to skip around, and my breasts were the same as ever, and it was too early to tell, and he smiled at our reflections and said, 'Then we will see.'

When Zac and I arrived at the war memorial, we found Peggy and James waiting for us close to the Cross of Sacrifice. Peggy invariably got there early on Remembrance Sunday, because she liked to have a good view of the ceremony. She was resplendent in a white fur Cossack hat and scarlet coat.

Zac put his mouth by my ear. 'She looks like a giant poppy,' he said, and I nearly sprayed the mouthful of the takeaway coffee I'd just sipped.

James stood beside Peggy, his silver hair sticking up, straight-backed as ever in his black greatcoat and red scarf. He was his usual quiet self, and gave me his usual kiss on the cheek with his usual near-smile, and made his usual half-joke that he was still waiting for me to come back to the pharmacy to work for him again. Peggy put on a display of exaggerated patience as she allowed James to finish, then threw her arms around me.

Zac reached into his coat pocket and produced a wooden cross. Two names were already written on it, in his precise, perfectly controlled lettering. *Edward Lawrence, RAF. Matilda Lawrence.*

'You are lovely.' I put a hand to his cheek. 'Thank you.'

'That was thoughtful.' Peggy tried to smile at Zac but managed only a stiff movement of the upper corners of her mouth. She beamed warmth democratically on everyone – waiters, people behind supermarket tills, neighbours. Zac was the one person for whom she could muster nothing more than cold politeness.

Zac guided me to the Cross of Sacrifice, and I knelt to place the small cross at its base, among the others, before I rose and stepped backwards.

'What was his rank?' Zac asked.

'Squadron Leader. He was a commissioned officer, but he wasn't born into it. He grew up on my grandparents' dairy farm. He was young when he died. Thirty-three. They both were. Did I tell you he flew search and rescue helicopters?'

'You did. You should be very proud.'

As I honoured my military father and civilian mother, I thought of my grandmother, and what she constantly said about my parents' deaths. She, of course, had a conspiracy theory, and believed that the car accident that killed them wasn't an accident at all but made to look like one because my father knew something he shouldn't. Whenever she dropped her dark hints I tried to quiz her, only for her to clam up. Sometimes, I thought my obsession with joining the Security Service was driven by my wish to get access to whatever hidden information there might be about this. I remembered Maxine's seemingly innocuous questions about their deaths during that awful interview.

Zac put an arm around me, and we slowly walked the few metres to join Peggy and James. Peggy said, 'So you're living above the plague pit, Zac?'

He looked bewildered, which was not a look Zac often wore.

'Didn't Holly tell you?' Peggy said.

'No.' He managed a joke. 'I ought to ask for a discount on the rent.' He turned to me, as if for help. 'Holly?'

'It's just a story,' I said.

'You know it isn't,' Peggy said.

'Are you going to tell me?' Zac's eyes were glittering at mine.

'Hmm. I'm thinking I have to say yes to that.' So I began. 'In the mid-fifteenth century, five hundred people from the town were lost to the plague. The burial records for that period don't survive, and the plague victims aren't in the graveyard.' A paper poppy petal, torn away from the body of the flower, floated above us, lifted by the wind. 'So here is the question. Where were the poor souls put?'

'Souls?' Zac raised an eyebrow.

'The thinking is that the bodies were loaded onto carts and taken along the coffin path. Then they were dumped into a pit. This was three kilometres along the coast, but slightly inland.'

'Where you are.' Peggy was fingering the cross that

dangled from a silvery chain around her neck. 'To rid the town of contagion.' She glanced up at the smoky-blue sky, as if for heavenly support. 'The pit is on the land behind your farmhouse. Your back garden, as a matter of fact. Nobody wants to live there. It's supposed to be unlucky.'

'Sounds like a load of superstitious . . .' Zac paused to find a more polite term than whatever he'd been about to say. 'It's as likely as mermaids.'

Peggy's eyes narrowed. Her nostrils flared. To Peggy, an accusation of superstition was as bad as one of devil worship.

'You know that mermaids are real.' I was trying to tease the tension away. 'I told you. You can't live in St Ives and not believe in mermaids.'

'True.' He pulled my head against his chest. We were both thinking of the rough-hewn and time-scarred Mermaid Bench, the two of us holding hands as we knelt by the Mermaid in a kind of pledge to each other and to her.

'Holly's our little Ariel,' Peggy said.

Zac gave me some serious side-eye at this Disneyfication. I squeezed his hand, trying to communicate silent understanding as well as a plea for him not to start on a critique of the 'sugary sentimentalism' that he detested.

I smiled at Peggy. I knew that she was picturing me and Milly, still tiny girls in pink nightdresses, snuggled against her during one of our countless sleepovers, the three of us eating popcorn and watching the Disney video.

There was room in the world for all kinds of mermaids.

Milly was gesturing for me to join her near the open church door, where she was standing by Gaston, whose hair was slicked into a ponytail. He broke up with her a few months ago, but Milly couldn't get over it. She continued to sleep with him, and whenever they had sex it gave her false hope that he'd changed his mind.

As I looked at Gaston, I was again struck by how strongly he resembled the character from the Disney version of *Beauty and the Beast*, which was another of the films that Milly and I watched with Peggy when we were children. That one was our favourite, because Belle was a passionate reader, like me and Milly.

Again Milly was beckoning me, this time even more frantically, but I shook my head no, not wanting to leave Zac when he was so palpably uncomfortable.

'Milly needs you, sweetheart.' Peggy was tugging at my arm. I looked helplessly at Zac as Peggy prised my hand out of his, deliberately ignoring the don't-you-dare-leave-me-with-them look he was shooting at me. She gave me a push towards Milly that practically sent me flying.

Milly was in tight jeans and sheepskin boots, a cream beanie hat covering her bright hair, seeming to know everyone, kissing old and young alike but making sure all the time that she kept within a metre of Gaston.

I took a lock of her hair between my fingers, to peel off the purple acrylic gloop that had dried on it. 'You've found some time to paint this morning?'

She was glowing when she nodded yes. 'At last. I got up early.' She was so beautiful and cleverly funny that almost every man I ever met would want to go out with her. But she didn't seem to know this.

'I'm glad.' I noticed Zac, pushing through the crowd to get to me.

'Hi, Holly Dolly.' Gaston's voice was so booming that Zac sent a look his way that would vaporise other mortal beings.

'Hello, Gaston.' At least nobody could say I only used the name behind his back. Milly had given up on trying to stop me. I'd known since we were four that he would hurt her. Now that he actually had, I wanted to punch him in his rock-hard gut.

'You know I consider that name a compliment, don't you?' He insisted on kissing me on the cheek, nearly choking me with his aftershave. 'Don't pretend you don't love me.'

'I really don't.'

Zac had reached me at last, and curled an arm tightly around my waist, pulling me close to his side. The gulls were wheeling above our heads.

'The parade's about to start, Holly.' He aimed us in the direction of the War Memorial, but the crowd had grown so thick we couldn't get close to Peggy and James. 'I came here to support you, and you repay me by sneaking off to Milly and her boyfriend.'

'Ex-boyfriend, now.'

'I don't care who he is.'

'I'm sorry. I didn't sneak, I don't need to pay you, I didn't mean to upset you, and I can promise you that talking to Gaston is not fun.'

'Gaston? I hate those Disney names. You're too intelligent for that.'

The increasing decibel level as the marching band approached saved me from the need to say more, because the outdoor part of the ceremony was finally underway, and the buglers were sounding.

They shall grow not old, as we that are left grow old . . .

My voice joined with the others, and I could feel Zac's irritation melting away. He encased both of my hands inside his, and kept them that way through the two-minute silence.

As we walked from the outdoor memorial to the church that towered over it, he whispered, 'I'm sorry, Holly. I feel left out, sometimes, of your life here. You're such a part of things.'

'You are too.'

'Am I?'

'Of course. It matters to me that you want to live here. I know you're doing it for me. I'm moved by that.'

We processed into the packed church together, and slipped into a pew at the rear. The pillars were garlanded in ribbons that had been strung with poppies. Zac did not bow his head for prayers or recite the Act of Penitence or sing any of the hymns, and certainly not 'God Save the Queen'.

After the service, he held my hand as we joined the parade, following the band and swinging our arms back and forth to 'The British Grenadiers'. Zac sang along, and I loved that he knew every word. We were at the tail end, and when I finally glimpsed Milly and Peggy and James again, they were getting further and further ahead as we processed through the town.

I tugged at Zac's arm, smiling. 'Shall we catch them up?'

It was as if I had flicked a switch, turning him from happy to sad. 'Don't you want to be with me?'

'Forever.'

'The three of them are a family. It's the two of us now.' He smiled. 'Or three. Yes?' He put a hand on my tummy. 'We're making our own family. Aren't we?'

'Yes.' I smiled up at him. When I broke his gaze, I realised that I had lost sight of my best friend and my surrogate parents. As far long as I could remember, I had walked with them, and until the last few years, with my grandmother too, claiming James's arm during the Remembrance Sunday commemorations that St Ives did so beautifully.

'Doesn't that make you happy?'

'Yes.' I nodded to confirm it. 'That's a lovely thing. Yes.' It was what I had always wanted. And I could see he was right about my not being a part of the family of three that was Peggy and James and Milly. But to be without them in that place, on that day, was like having a piece of myself cut away.

Now The Backwards House

Two years and five months later

Bath, Tuesday, 2 April 2019

The country lane that Maxine's driver is speeding along is lined with golden daffodils. They flutter and dance and twinkle on their green banks in exactly the way Wordsworth said.

I have the sense that Maxine is watching me, though she is slumped against the cream-coloured leather car seat and seeming to look at her own lap, where her hands are resting. Her nails, as usual, are long and perfectly manicured. The polish is what my grandmother calls dragon-lady red, and matches Maxine's lipstick. I have never seen a chip in that polish.

'Where are we going?'

'Not far.' She answers like a parent. Or at least how I think parents answer, because my own have been dead for too long for me to know this from experience, and I am not a parent myself, however much I try to tell myself that she counted and I am.

The car enters a neighbourhood on the outskirts of Bath. Because the houses here are built on top of old quarries, they get alarming cracks from subsidence, so walls split and ceilings buckle, hurling dark-grey plaster dust and chunks of building into the rooms.

Maxine's driver turns onto a street that is filled with police cars and vans, all clustered near a modern, brick, perfectly square end-of-terrace house. The house is surrounded by police tape. 'Come on,' Maxine says, and I follow her out of the car.

I stand a couple metres away as Maxine speaks to a tall man with dark hair and dark-rimmed glasses, wearing a dark suit and standing outside of the cordon. He looks like the prince of death as he peers at me. I decide he is more likely to be MI5 than police as he nods at Maxine and says, 'Tess's up there. She's expecting you.'

Maxine moves her head to signal that we need to go into the tent that encloses the house's front door. The door has an awning with a strange coating of artificial grass. We are given forensic suits, so that our hair is obscured by white hoods, our mouths and noses covered by white masks, and our shoes enveloped in white foot-wear protectors. I want to hesitate, but I don't let myself. Maxine marches into the house, and I march after her.

'Don't touch or move anything,' she tells me, without turning round.

The carpet inside the entryway is mink-grey and I can see the tracks left by the vacuum, despite the ghost-shapes of old spills that no amount of shampoo will remove. The air is scented with pine and lemon, and window cleaner, plus the lingering hint of something that makes my stomach clench because it reminds me of Zac's soap.

'The burglar alarm wasn't tripped,' Maxine says. 'She

either de-activated it to let someone in, or didn't activate it in the first place. Good chance she knew them.'

'*She*. Who is *she*?'

Maxine is making a performance of looking around too attentively to notice that I have spoken.

The house seems the wrong way round, with the sitting room at the back, spanning the building's entire width. There are no books on the shelves of the fake wood bookcases, and no dust either. There is a single half-drunk cup of strong black tea on the cheap glass coffee table. Not many people drink their tea with no milk. I've known two, and though Milly likes hers weak, and Zac strong, it came as a surprise that she and Zac should share anything other than their mutual hatred.

The kitchen is to the left side of the entry hall. It is also pristinely clean, though far from luxurious with peeling laminate cupboards, a half-size fridge like my own, and cork flooring.

At the bottom of the stairs is a handbag, stiff and upright, the obvious item in any game of odd one out. Tan leather, shiny gold hardware, and the Hermès logo in its cleanly embossed capital letters. Only once before have I come across a designer bag of this ilk.

Maxine answers one of the many questions I haven't voiced. 'It was a two-month holiday let, paid by credit card. They haven't traced the holder of the card, but it didn't belong to the woman who was occupying the house. She moved in a week ago – used a false name.'

We crunch our way up the stairs, along a roll of white paper. I can see on either side of it that the stairs have been sanded and painted.

At the top of the landing, straight in front of us, is an open bedroom door. A tall woman in another moon suit, glasses peeping out of her otherwise-covered face, emerges and squeezes onto the landing with us. 'Hey, Maxine,' the woman says.

'Hey, Tess.' It isn't the forensic drama that brings home the fact that I am being allowed to see another version of Maxine, who is not slouching. It is Maxine's use of the word 'Hey' and its attendant chumminess.

'Needless to say,' says Tess, 'don't touch anything.'

'Sure thing,' Maxine says, in more of the new Maxine language.

Tess does not ask who I am when she motions for us to follow her. There is a frizz of grey hair on her temple, which has escaped the head covering. There are smile lines around her eyes, and my guess is that in the part of her life that doesn't involve space suits and corpses, this woman is restrainedly contented, with wry good humour.

Instead of moving forward when Tess beckons, though, I freeze. My head is telling me to go in, but my body does not seem to want to.

I'd thought the sweat had dried on me in Maxine's car after my run, but I am wet again, beneath my breasts, down my spine. The mask over my mouth is stopping me from breathing. My scalp is itchy and hot beneath the hood.

Maxine puts a hand on my shoulder. The last time she did that I practically chopped it off. She says, 'You don't know the strength of a person until they've been tested.'

I nearly say, *No shit, Sherlock*, which is one of Milly's favourite expressions. Milly loves the word shit. Instead, I manage a more restrained, 'Thanks for your wisdom,' and for the first time in forever, Maxine visibly blanches.

Then The Forgotten Things

Two years and four months earlier

Cornwall, Mid-December 2016

Zac left for London early this morning for a British Cardiovascular Society symposium. Tomorrow he will fly to the Ukraine for a fleeting visit, to do some teaching in a hospital in Kiev. Before he drove away, I leaned into the open car window for a final kiss goodbye, my hair unbrushed and circles under my eyes after a night of endlessly being sick.

I watched the car disappear out of sight, fantasising that I would get out my journal and write. Instead, I wandered through the house nibbling a special ginger biscuit that was supposed to help with nausea but was proving useless. I was ten weeks pregnant but the sickness wasn't getting any better.

Zac hated clutter, but this place was decorated in a romantic style that seemed to invite it. The personal things were all mine – the cardigan thrown over the cabbage roses sofa, the pregnancy magazines covering the distressed coffee table, the pot of lip gloss and ponytail holder on the white-painted chimney piece, the novels on the chintz armchair. Zac was constantly putting them away, then scrubbing the artificially aged surfaces with disinfectant wipes. I was trying to be more orderly, because it was painful to see him so unnerved by what he would call mess and I would call the ordinary chaos of human life.

Since Maxine's ambush on the cliffs two months earlier, I'd stepped up my efforts to search the house for some sign of Jane. I poked my fingers into the toes of Zac's socks when I tossed the clean pairs into the drawer. I ran my hand under the mattress when I made the bed. I examined the seams of his suits when I hung up his shirts from the dry cleaners. I checked his books as I dusted, to see if any were mere shells with cavities for hiding things. So far, I had found nothing. His taste in books, all hardbacks and dust-free, was unsurprising – medical ethics, law, artificial intelligence, and the surveillance state. He especially liked it when these subjects intersected. His current book at bedtime was about the use of technology by a group of anonymous hackers to promote political and social change.

As I closed the lid of a shoebox that lived in his wardrobe – it contained a pair of unworn black Oxfords – I had a flash of Zac loading a new carbon-fibre suitcase onto the passenger seat of his sports car. Everybody saved their old suitcases for packing stuff when they moved, didn't they? Before I had finished this thought I was rushing down the stairs to the cupboard that runs beneath them.

My own suitcases were towards the front. I'd used them to transport my stuff from what I referred to as the brown house. My attic bedroom, with walls that I'd painted all the colours of the rainbow, was the one exception to the law of brown. The rest of the house was filled with brown carpets that my grandmother vacuumed every day, brown tapestry curtains that I was always opening and she was always closing, and brown sofas covered in bobbled brown blankets that I was always tearing off and she was always putting back. 'I don't want my fine furniture destroyed by the sun,' my grandmother would say.

I actually felt a kind of nostalgic affection for the brown house as I started to drag my suitcases from the cupboard beneath Zac's stairs, sliding and pulling them into the wide hallway behind me.

I couldn't help but smile at my grandmother's blue vinyl train case, which was like seeing an old friend. When I once expressed surprise at the pretty colour, she told me my grandfather bought it for her. 'Horribly impractical. See how it scuffs,' she said. But she looked at it with reluctant affection. After all, she'd brought it from their farm to my parents' house when she moved in to look after me. I in turn brought it to Zac's, stuffed with my bathroom things and make-up.

It wouldn't occur to Zac that I'd enter this dank and dusty place, which he avoided, given the germs that must infest it. I had to crawl inside to reach the final suitcases. They were old, made of tan canvas and trimmed with tan fake leather in the corners. The larger of the two was too bulky and heavy to comply with today's airline specifications.

I shone my phone torch over them. Flimsy padlocks linked the zippers. I lifted each of the identification tags. Zac had written his name on both. He'd probably dragged them around the continent during his gap year grand tour, and kept them out of nostalgic fondness.

I tugged Zac's clunky things into the hall, then unfastened my grandmother's train case. Tucked within a silky stretch pocket on its topside was a snap-closing coin purse filled with tiny keys for old suitcase locks. The purse – quilted fabric, and brown, of course – had lived in that pocket for as long as I could remember. I could hear my grandmother's voice. *Brown is a practical colour, Holly. It doesn't show the dirt.* Hurrah for brown. For once, I was glad of my grandmother's fixed habits. In an instant, I spilled the keys onto the stripped floorboards with a clatter.

The good thing about suitcase keys, my grandmother used to say, was that so many of them worked in multiple locks – you just needed to gauge the size by eye. Perhaps my grandmother had a bit of spy in her, too. The third key I tried fitted perfectly into the lock on Zac's larger case. There was a satisfying click and the shackle popped out.

I wasn't sure what I was hoping to find inside when I unzipped it, kneeling on the cold floor. Secret documents? Stacks of cash? Jane's body? My expectations were unreasonably high, so my stomach fell when the lid of the case flopped onto the floor with a puff of dust and I saw that it was empty.

The same key worked on the lock of the medium-sized suitcase, too. 'Oh,' I said out loud. Because there was no way that the suitcase nested inside belonged to Zac.

Despite my grandmother-shaped aversion to brown, the hidden case was quite charming. The diagonal lines of four-petalled flowers and interlocking Ls and Vs processed in their determined order, stamped in muted gold on a brown background. One of my hands floated towards the monogrammed canvas and slid extra-lightly across the PVC coating, surprised by how smooth it was. But I quickly got down to the business of unbuckling the leather tag to check whether there was a name on it.

JM was hot-stamped on the surface. It had to stand for Jane Miller. *Had to.* To my delight, there was a piece of thick cream paper inside the tag, though there was no writing on the front. I took it out and flipped it. On the reverse, in Zac's perfectly regular cursive, it read *Jacinda Molinero.* There was no address or telephone number or email. Just the name. Hardly of any use if the suitcase were to be lost.

My language skills had languished since that final MI5 interview. Practising them hurt like an imperfectly healed wound when you picked off the scab. But there was something about the word Molinero . . . I needed to remember what it meant.

I closed my eyes to try to think. What came to me was the illustrated deck of cards from when I first started to learn Spanish. The teacher thought the cards would help us with the words for different occupations. It was a kind of un-cosy version of *Happy Families*, where the dentists and plumbers and shopkeepers all looked tired and overworked. There was a particular card I was fumbling for, in whatever dark corner of my brain it was filed in.

I squeezed my eyes shut more tightly, and the picture began to form. An old lady scowling in her blue apron and white hat, letting flour fall from her fingers into a huge yellow sack. Behind her was a red-roofed wooden house with a windmill attached to it. *Señora Molinero.* That was what it said beneath her. *Mrs Miller.*

Molinero was Spanish for Miller. Jane Miller. Jacinda Molinero. The first names started with the same letter. Jacinda had to be Jane. Zac's handwriting on the suitcase label seemed to confirm this.

If you come across any objects of Jane's, tell us about them in as much detail as you can. That was what Maxine said to me on the bench by the cliffs. But it wasn't Maxine I wanted this knowledge for. It was me. *Me, myself and I*, as my grandmother used to say, never clear as to whether she thought this emphasis on self was a good or bad thing. I grabbed my phone and typed in the name Jacinda Molinero, but the search engine returned only blanks.

Thankfully, if Jacinda Molinero's uber-designer bag ever had a lock, it was missing. The brass zipper moved with satisfying smoothness, and I laid the two halves of the bag carefully on the floor. Each half was covered by a mesh divider, so I unzipped those too. There was nothing beneath them.

One of the dividers had a small zipped pocket built into it, so I undid this and slipped a hand inside. My fingers bumped against something stiff and square, and came up clutching a black card with silver lettering and a foil edge. *Albert E. Mathieson, International Tax Law*.

I tried another Internet search, this time for Albert E. Mathieson. There were pages of hits, including a link to his business website, multiple articles in professional tax journals, and blog posts that I could see were genuinely informative as well as extremely scary, because they seemed to suggest that it was very easy to be a criminal tax evader and not even know it. He specialised in high-net-worth clients who were in trouble with America's Internal Revenue Service, and though his office was in Malibu he represented clients in more than fifty countries.

'Going somewhere, Holly?'

I screamed, and fell backwards, sitting hard on the floorboards, my stomach plunging even faster than the rest of me.

'Oh my God. I think I had a heart attack.'

'Lucky I'm here then.' Zac held out a hand. I reached for it and he pulled me up. He plucked something from my hair. 'Cobweb.' He brushed my cheek with a finger, frowned and wet it in his mouth, then tried again. 'Dust smear.' He took a miniature bottle of sanitising gel from a pocket and rubbed some on his hands.

'Don't ever sneak up on me like that again.'

'I didn't sneak, Holly. You were clearly absorbed.' His voice, as usual, was ironic and light, but his face was pale, his dual-coloured eye extra bright against his skin.

'You look as though you've seen a ghost.'

He shook his head to deny this absurdity. 'What are you doing?'

I tried to swallow as I thought, but it was difficult. I surprised myself by telling the truth, which was sometimes easier than a lie. 'I – I wanted to know about you. See your things. See your history, who you were. Are.'

He laughed. 'Clearly someone whose taste in suitcases has improved.'

'Why are you here, Zac? You should be on your way to London.'

'Why are you here, Holly? You should be on your way to the hospital.' There was a tension in his lips, as if he was trying not to let them move. But there were still occasional twitches.

'I called in sick. The morning sickness is so bad. I hardly slept last night.'

'My poor Holly. I had to come back because I forgot my phone. I'll still make it – my talk isn't until late this afternoon.' He smiled slowly. 'So we're both here when we should be somewhere else.'

One of my hands rose to his caress his head, which was damp. 'Is it raining?'

'No.'

My heart was still beating fast, but he was sweating. I was struck by how controlled he kept everything in the house, as if in contrast to a body he couldn't perfectly regulate, though he mostly managed to. 'Are you angry at me?' I asked.

'Why would I be?' He pulled me into his arms.

'For looking in your suitcases.' My forehead was against his chest. He smelled soapy and clean and woody and lovely, when the smell of everything else for the past two months had made me want to be sick.

'Were you telling me the truth about what you're doing, Holly?'

I pulled away and looked up at him. He was studying me so intently. 'What do you mean?'

'I mean, if you wanted to see my history, as you say, you could have asked. So I can't help but wonder if you were dragging out those suitcases so you could pack them and run away.'

'No. Of course not.' I was shaking my head at the irony of my telling the truth but not being believed. 'How could you think that?'

'It's happened before.' I could feel him playing with my hair again. 'Dead fly.'

I shuddered. 'Have you got it?'

'Yes.' He walked quickly to the front door to flick it away, then applied more gel to his fingers. 'This is your house too. You can go anywhere you wish. Touch anything you find. Open whatever cupboard or drawer you want. I'd never stop you.'

'Really?'

He took a step away, still with a hand on each of my upper arms, as if needing to evaluate me from different vantage points to make his assessment. 'Really. I have no secrets from you.' He leaned over to lift something from the floor. The tax attorney's card, which I must have dropped when Zac walked in. 'So you found my good friend Al.'

I cleared my throat, feeling caught out again. 'Yes. Who is he?'

'American. We were at UCL together – he read international law. Obsessed with tax but an interesting, funny guy. As smart as they come.' He glanced towards the beautiful suitcase. 'Was Al's card in that?'

'Yes. Did you give the card to Jane?'

'Could have been Al – he visited us in London once, several years ago. Might have been me – hard to remember. Anything else you want to know before I leave?'

'Was the suitcase Jane's?'

'Yes.'

'A gift from you?'

'Yes.'

'Why do you still have it?'

'I didn't know I did. She didn't leave anything behind when she went. Was her suitcase inside one of mine?'

I nodded, then confirmed it with a quiet, 'That one,' as I pointed to his medium-sized suitcase.

'She must have stored it there, so it was a kind of stowaway when I moved here from London – I didn't know she'd done that. Would you like it?'

'Wouldn't that be weird?'

'Why would it be? It should be used.'

'Why does the tag say "Jacinda Molinero"? Molinero's Miller. Right?'

'It was my nickname for her. Did you look up the Spanish on your phone?'

I nodded. I'd never told him about my ability to speak Spanish, probably because I never wanted him to know about my failed aspiration to be a spy, and my language skills were bound up with that.

'Jane loved Spanish.' He looked so fond, even proud, as he talked about her. 'She seemed to be able to learn any language she wanted, as soon as she stepped into a new country. It's a rare gift, but some people have it. She loved to travel.' He had never spoken about her before. So normally. Using her name.

Maxine could fuck off. He wasn't behaving like a man with anything to hide. Tears were running down my cheeks.

'What is it? Holly? – You cry so easily these days.'

I shook my head. 'I don't deserve you.'

'Yes you do.'

'I don't. You should be with someone who's accomplished – some clever doctor or barrister.'

'They're boring. And that would be predictable.'

'A supermodel.'

This made him laugh. 'Even more boring. And I'm already with the most beautiful woman I've ever seen.'

'I'm not.'

'You are to me.'

I pulled him closer, trying to shut out Maxine's voice, which whispered out of my own bones that if I was the most beautiful woman he had ever seen it was only because I bore a likeness to Jane. He looked so pleased when I moved my hands down his back, when I kissed him, when I whispered that I wanted him so much and I couldn't wait until he returned.

'But will you always feel that way?' He moved a hand up my thigh, under my dress, beneath my underwear. 'Are you sure you'll never change your mind?'

'Yes.' I was unfastening his belt. 'I'm sure.'

Now The Woman in the Room

Two years and four months later

Bath, Tuesday, 2 April 2019

At first, I try not to look at the woman who has drawn so many police officers and forensic scientists to this house. I try to look at everything but her. I focus on the room.

The carpet is pale beige. It is clean and soft and probably the last thing she walked on. There is little in the way of furniture. A small pine wardrobe, a television screen attached to the wall, and a four-poster bed of shiny fake wood. The white sheets are so tangled I cannot help but imagine the aftermath of recent sex. It makes me think of another room, and another tempest of a bed, in a faraway house that rests on top of a plague pit by the sea.

'What do you see?' The voice is Maxine's and she is talking to me.

'The bed doesn't go.'

'I mean the woman.'

What I had wanted to say was that the mess of the bed doesn't go with everything else in the superhumanly clean and empty house. 'Nobody could die that neatly, in such a messy bed,' I say.

She is naked, as far as I can tell, though the quilt hides her middle, going from the top of her thighs to the upper edge of her breasts. She is delicate, and probably a few centimetres shorter than I am, though it is difficult to be sure with her lying as she is. Her arms are by her sides, resting above the quilt and curved like parentheses. Her legs are as straight as a ballerina's, though her toes are not pointed. I wonder if she was arranged in this position before her body grew stiff and cold.

I can't look at her face. I put my hand to the side of my right eye to stop myself. I am too afraid, and I do not care if Maxine and Tess know it.

'Were you wanting to say,' Tess asks, 'that the messy bed is out of place in context with the rest of the address?'

'Yes.'

'Be back in two minutes.' Tess hurries from the room.

I crouch by the side of the bed. I long to smooth her hair. But again, I am too frightened that if I do I will see her face. If I were alone, I would tell her how sorry I am that I failed her, that I didn't do enough to help to find her in time.

Where have you been, I silently ask, for the last six years?

My hand curls around hers, an impulse to comfort somebody who is beyond help. Even through the thin blue gloves they made me wear, I can feel that her warmth is gone. She is the temperature of the pine wardrobe. I remember imagining how my baby would pink up, as I fantasised about her birth. What has happened here is the opposite of pinking up. The hand in mine has lost its softness, its human sponginess. There is no give any more. The give, the warmth, the pinking up, that is what makes us human. But this hand is a plastic doll's.

Maxine crouches beside me. 'You can't touch her.'

As I release my grip, I notice the nails. They are well cared for, and though they protrude no more than a few millimetres beyond the tips of her fingers, they are painted pinky-nude. They are not broken – there is no obvious evidence that she fought or struggled.

I want Peggy. I want her to fold me in her arms and let me press myself into her plump softness the way I did as a child.

Tess comes back into the room.

'Can I ask when this happened?' I say.

'The early hours of this morning.'

What I can see of her skin is like a waxwork, but there is a blue tint to the jaundiced-looking yellow.

'Are those pressure marks on the face?' Maxine asks. 'Though they're not very pronounced.'

The question prompts me to look. It is an accident, a reflex, my movements so quick and panicked that everything is blurred. Before I can tear my eyes away, I glimpse skilfully dyed blonde hair. And I see her face. Her nose and mouth, I think, had oozed blood. The skin around them is extra pale, and her tongue sticks out as if she had bitten it. Her cheeks are dotted with red pinpricks that I think must be some kind of bruising.

'Could be from post-mortem postural changes,' Tess says.

What is not pronounced to Tess and Maxine is very pronounced to me.

I have learned too much from Zac. I cannot stop what comes out. 'It's suffocation of some kind, isn't it?' My voice is quiet. I force my eyes upwards, stop them at her neck, quickly close them before turning my head towards her feet. 'I can't see any marks on her neck, so maybe smothering more than strangulation.'

'And you know this how?' Tess says.

'I used to date a cardiologist.' There is a twinge of fear at saying this, as if Zac were in the room, listening. Even now, I imagine how he would bristle at the word *date*, and especially at the words *used to*.

Dating is a word from women's magazines filled with things that rot your brain. It's the worst kind of cultural vulgarity.

We will never be in the past tense, Holly. You and I are forever. You don't go through what we have, invest what we have, only to give up.

This is why I say *date*. This is why I say *used to*.

'Explain what you see, please,' Tess says.

So I try, in a strange blend of Maxine's lack of inflection with Zac's words. What I remember about his saying them to me was his charm, the way he smiled, as if he was telling a dark joke. And that I smiled back, and my face grew flushed, and there were shivers all the way down my arm as he traced a finger over my bare shoulder.

'It's the blue tint to her skin. What happens to the heart, and the skin, if someone dies from a cardiac arrest, it's the same as what happens with suffocation or strangulation. The heart continues to pump blood around the body for at least a couple of beats, but that blood doesn't have as much oxygen, so it's less pink. That's why her skin has the blue tinge – the blood beneath it is deoxygenated.'

Tess nods. 'Correct. Plus, the eyes are bloodshot.' I

nearly ask how she can know this, but realise she must have prised them open to look before we got here.

Maxine says, 'Can Helen see her right ankle, please, Tess? You'll need to go round to the other side of the bed, Helen.'

The oval is there, on the outer side of the lower calf, though I'd already half-glimpsed it. A smoky purple circle the size of a two-pence coin, slightly above the ankle bone. A bruise like a black star sapphire, perfectly cut, and set against the blue-tinted skin.

I am staring at that oval. Maxine is staring at me. 'I'm not expecting you'd recognise her face in the circumstances, but have you seen the mark before?' she says.

I can taste bile. The last time I tasted that was when I woke in hospital after it happened.

'No,' I say.

'You're sure?' she says. 'It doesn't remind you of anything?'

Three years ago, looking at the photo in Zac's bedside table, I'd wondered if it was a tattoo.

'It's a birthmark,' I say. 'A dark circle, that's all.'

'I'd say it's very distinctive,' Maxine says. 'Would you say that too, Tess?'

'I would.'

'Then I will defer to your expertise. Am I free to go?'

My breathing is getting faster. My back is soaked, just as it was during the night sweats after her birth.

'We've come across a photograph,' Maxine says. 'On the hard drive of a laptop that someone took a great deal of trouble to copy for us.'

I know who that someone is. That someone is me, and though I've never been told exactly what was on the drive, I have guessed.

'There were indecent images and video footage on that drive – I can assure you it has all been carefully protected.'

I look at my feet. My eyes are welling up but I am determined not to cry.

'One of the relatively innocuous images is of a woman lounging by a pool. Her birthmark is identical to this one.'

I take a few small steps, unhurriedly, towards the door. 'I asked if I am free to go.' I am practically choking.

'Of course,' Maxine says.

I am out of the room. I am on the landing. I am halfway down the paper-covered stairs.

Maxine is right behind me. 'Tell me the specifics of anything you've done to give yourself away.' Her voice is quiet. 'Contact with anybody from your old life. Any crumb of evidence that could lead Zac to finding you here. Please.'

The image of my grandmother in the newspaper photograph, and the caption with her full name, flashes before me. Maxine's face is expressionless as I tell her. But I leave out the sound of Peggy's voice last night, and James's, both of them flailing in the dark.

There is something else I leave out, too, because it belongs entirely to me, and I genuinely don't think it is why this has happened. It has been over two years since Milly or I reviewed anything on our blog, but it still exists in hyperspace. A straggle of readers occasionally look at it, and every once in a while, a new comment appears.

Last summer, there was a response to a five-star review of *The Tenant of Wildfell Hall* that I'd written several years earlier. Somebody with the username Abandoned Friend had this to say.

> Your review sucks. You don't address how selfish the
> heroine is. Whatever her husband did to her, she doesn't
> stop to think about the worry and grief she caused the
> people she left behind. What about her poor aunt, who
> loved her? She should have found a way to let her
> know she was okay.

I didn't know for sure that Abandoned Friend was Milly.
But it seemed pretty likely that she was, and that she
was talking about Peggy when she mentioned the poor
aunt. So I created a new User Name, Brontë Fan, and
replied to the comment.

> I don't think you are being fair. If she'd let her aunt
> know, that would have increased the risk of being
> discovered, and might also have put her aunt in danger.
> She knew her aunt was wise and would understand,
> and hoped the day would come when they could be
> reunited.

As soon as I posted the message, I felt sick, knowing I
shouldn't have done it.

I haven't revisited the blog since then, fearing that even
the act of opening the page would set off an alert somewhere.

'Holly.' The way Maxine says my name, my real name,
out of anyone's hearing, is almost human. For nearly two
years, my grandmother has been the only one to call me
that.

Despite this, my next words come like an explosion.

'Why don't they just arrest him? You know he's done this.'

'They need evidence first – that's what's happening here right now.'

'Why didn't they arrest him two years ago, once you had the hard drive? She wouldn't be dead if you had.'

'The data wasn't as strong as we'd hoped, back then – it wasn't conclusive. As far as the body in that room—'

'Not "the body". Jane. A human being called Jane.'

'As far as Jane is concerned, we can't go around making arrests for cases that the Crown Prosecution Service would toss in the bin. We need to get this right, so it will stick.'

I press my fists against my eyes. 'He's here. A woman came to the hospital. I think she must be his wife. With a little girl who must be his. Is she? Is she his daughter?'

'Yes. His wife and his child. You've nothing to fear from them.'

'The child is the same age . . .' My voice trails off.

'I know that must be difficult for you.'

'Does the woman know who I am?'

'We think probably not. The little girl's medical condition is real. She needed that clinic appointment.'

'Are they safe? He shouldn't be allowed near a child.'

'There's no evidence he would hurt a child.' She is uncharacteristically thoughtful, even hesitant, before she continues. 'I'd hoped you could put all of this behind you. I wish that could have been true.'

Then *A Quarrel*

Two years and three months earlier

Cornwall, 3 January 2017

Since finding Jane's suitcase two weeks ago, I'd barely thought of anything else. On the third day of January, though, I was thinking about Milly instead. I was on my way to see her, and we were meeting by the harbour.

The sea was boiling. The wind was howling. The waves were moving walls of rock. Milly and I would never take the safer, drier lanes through the town. Like teenagers, we stuck to the path that followed the sea wall. Spray shot out and up, chasing us. We knew we really could be snatched and swallowed. It had happened to others before.

We threw our arms around each other, grabbed hands and ran through a gauntlet of water, screaming and laughing our calls of *Happy New Year*, refusing to worry about slipping, stopping to buy chips at one of the cafes along the harbour. There was a belated rendition of Happy Birthday, sung by Milly to me.

We turned on to the eighteenth-century pier, passing walls of stacked lobster pots, jumbo bags of green rope, and red plastic crates for hauling the dead mackerel from the boats to the land. The smell made me gag, but Milly didn't notice and we walked on to the pier's far end, where the air was clear.

Our feet were soaked, our hair was drenched, and we were shivering. But we were happy, sitting on the stone bench that followed the wall of the pier and doubled as our backrest. We were burning our fingers on the chips.

I scrambled to my feet, standing on the bench to look over the wall, so I could watch the lighthouse winking in the distance. Milly did the same.

'I've missed you,' she said.

I pictured the two of us, dancing together in a nightclub upcountry to celebrate my sixteenth birthday, our arms around each other, tinsel in our hair and swaying in heels too high to walk in, the room and lights spinning from too many bottles of beer, elated that we had pulled it off despite being underage.

'Me too you,' I said.

'My mother says you have a father complex, because of your dad dying and all. She says that's what you see in Zac.'

'Eew. That's not true.' Though a part of me knew it was. Still, I blushed at the idea of Peggy thinking that.

'We're neglecting the blog,' Milly said. 'We'll lose followers.'

'I'll do something this week. *Wuthering Heights* has been getting a lot of hate.'

'Mum will be happy. She's our number one fan. But have I told you lately she is completely insane? We crossed on the stairs, and she closed her eyes and chanted "Avert" and waved her hands about. Honestly, it was the most embarrassing thing.'

'Did she pick that up when we made her read *The Earthsea Quartet*?'

'Yep, but she won't admit she's trying to ward off curses or bad luck. She'd die before she confessed to any superstition about stair crossing.'

'Have I told you lately that I am an orphan, and you are lucky to have a mum?'

'Well you have Lord Voldemort. I can't believe he let you out. Does he make you sleep in a dungeon?'

'Yes – but don't call him that, Milly.'

'I'll see your Lord Voldemort and raise you a Gaston.'

'Fair enough. I deserved that.'

'Looks like Lord Voldemort. Acts like Lord Voldemort. He's even got the bald thing going on. Please tell me he hasn't branded you with the dark mark.'

'Only between my legs.'

She snorted a mouthful of the beer she'd brought out from the pub, the last place in the row of shops and restaurants along the front, and the closest one to the pier. I was drinking spiced tomato juice, and Milly thought this was because I was driving, which was true but not the most important reason.

'You're still in there after all,' she said. 'I was beginning to think he'd replaced you with a Stepford wife. Thank God the two of you aren't married.'

'He wants to.'

'Well don't. Please, promise me you won't.'

My own secret voice was saying, *You're betraying him to sit and listen to this. You should say, How dare you talk about him that way. You should go home right now.*

'You'll never escape him if you do,' she said.

'I don't want to escape him.' I thought of my baby, and how desperately I wanted him – or her – to be raised by two parents. To have what I didn't.

'Has he taken control of your bank accounts yet?'

'No! I wouldn't let him. But he wouldn't try.' As if to protect my baby from what we were saying, my hand started to float towards my tummy, though there wasn't much of a bump yet. I had wanted to tell Milly about the baby several weeks ago, but Zac persuaded me that nobody should share such news until after the magic three-month mark, when the chance of miscarriage was dramatically reduced. The start of January meant I had reached that mark.

Milly looked genuinely surprised. 'No joint accounts?'

'No.'

'Strange. That's not what I'd have predicted. He's not tried to get his name on the deed to your house?'

I was lucky, in that I had the house my parents left me, plus some money from my father's pension. But I was still careful to live off my salary.

'Of course not. He's generous – too generous – but he likes to keep his things and mine legally separate. It's a big thing with him, and it's important to me too, because of my grandmother.'

My grandmother had savings from the sale of the family farm many years ago, and I was using them to fund her care. But the money was being eaten away fast, and it wouldn't be long before I had to take over the cost.

Milly shook her head. Her blonde hair gleamed in the moonlight, then dimmed as a heavy cloud moved in front of the full fat moon again to eclipse it. 'Okay. I have to admit that that stumps me.'

'Why do you hate him so much, Milly?'

'He hates me.'

'He doesn't.' We were back in total darkness, feeling the mist from the sea but unable to see it. 'He wants to get to know you.'

'No he doesn't. Question. Did you tell him we were meeting tonight?'

'He's on nights tonight.'

'I know that, Holly – I saw him going in as I was coming out. That's not an answer. You could have told him yesterday or this morning. Does he know?'

'No.'

'I knew it. That's why we're here. If you'd told him, he'd have got in the way. You know it too. You're just not admitting it to yourself. He's found ten different ways to stop us spending time together over the last few weeks.'

We turned away from the wall, facing the harbour once more. 'It was the time of year, Milly.' I sat down again. 'You said so yourself.'

'I was trying to make it easy for you.' She sat too. 'Do you ever make calls without his being there?'

'All the time.' But I realised this wasn't true. Somehow Zac was invariably nearby when I used my phone.

Milly went on. 'He may not be controlling your money yet, but you *will* get sick of him, and when you try to leave he won't make it easy. Mum and I are frightened. He's cutting you off from us.'

I tried to lighten things. 'Isn't this a bit dramatic? I want to make a family with him. I want to make what you grew up in.'

'And he fucking well knows it. He's playing you. He's saying what you want to hear.'

'He's loving. He cares for me.' I threw up my hands, invisible in the darkness. 'I matter to him.'

'Of course you do. More than anything in the world. I've heard him say it and that's what scares me. He chose you because he thinks you have no one. He thinks you're all alone. But he's wrong. You have us.'

Although I never felt the cold since becoming pregnant, I shivered. 'I know that.'

'Well don't ever forget it.' The light slowly returned as the cloud moved sideways to reveal the moon. Milly pulled away to study me. 'At least you're starting to look more like you again. Your face isn't so thin and pale. And I love what you're wearing.'

'Chosen for you.' I loved what I was wearing too. Green ankle boots, bobbled red wool tights, a short mustard tube skirt, and a fleecy orange jumper to disguise my thickening waist. I unzipped my coat and flashed the full view at Milly.

'And Rainbow Girl is back!' she said. 'Goodbye, Grey Woman. Hello there, Rainbow Girl. We've missed you. I much prefer you in clothes I need to wear sunglasses to look at.'

'Hello.' I zipped up again.

'Oh, don't put it away. I want a pic to show Mum.' Milly's teeth were chattering.

'You won't get a pic out here. Not with the light changing every five seconds.' The moon was flashing at us, off, on, off, on, as a procession of clouds sped past to eclipse and uncover her. She seemed to mirror the lighthouse's lamp. For an instant, I glimpsed a frown that Milly didn't imagine I could see. 'How's Gaston?' I said.

'I hate him so much,' Milly said, 'that I want him to die,

because then I would get over him. But I can't stop fucking him.'

It was my turn to snort my drink.

Milly went on. 'I hate how he puts that fucking gross hairspray on that fucking gross long hair of his, and I wish it would catch fire when he fills that fucking gross old wreck of a car of his with petrol.' She paused. 'Look how – odd – you look.'

'I'm making my disgusted face.' I pulled her close, put an arm around her, tipped her head forward so I could kiss the top. 'Let's not tell anybody about this conversation, because if anything bad does happen to Gaston, they're going to look at you.'

'I love the sex, that's all. Do you think I could be addicted to him sexually?'

'Eww,' I said, for the second time that night. 'Now I'm making my I'm-about-to-be-sick face.'

'Seriously, Holly.'

'I absolutely do think you're addicted, and you're in desperate need of therapy.'

'I can't get over him.' Her voice choked, and she started to cry. She curled up on her side of the bench and put her head in my lap, and I played with her hair. When she sat up again, I took her hand.

'I'm cold,' she said. Her teeth were chattering, and I snuggled her close. Neither of us had remembered to bring mittens.

'There's nothing of you to keep warm. Shall we go in, get another drink? Something hot.'

'Holly?'

'Yes, Milly?'

'I'm really going to try to stop fucking him.'

'Okay,' I said.

'Will you be mad at me if I can't?'

'Of course not.' I gently touched a finger to her cheek, to wipe away a tear that she'd missed. 'But I'll be mad at him no matter what you do.'

The pub was quiet. Milly and I stood at the bar beneath the silver tankards that hung like a string of Christmas decorations. They were entwined with red and green ribbons and strands of gold beads. We got served straightaway, then made our way to the wood fire, where we stripped off our coats and huddled close. I sipped warm apple juice and Milly had mulled wine. The scent of cinnamon and cloves steamed up at us, and I was not feeling at all sick.

This was a quiet place to tell her my news, but I hesitated, when she was so traumatised by Gaston. At the same time, I was scared she'd be hurt that I had waited so long. Not to tell her immediately would make that longer still. Plus, she'd see it as yet more evidence that Zac the Evil was dictating everything I did, and how and when I did it.

I took a deep breath and leaned in close. 'There's something I need to tell you,' I started to say. But before I could go any further, she froze. I turned to look at whatever had struck her with such horror. My words stuck in my throat.

'Hello, beautiful,' Zac said to me. 'Hello, Milly,' he said to Milly.

Milly stood. I made an effort to convert the sadness I was feeling into a cheerful tone, turning the inflection up on the last word. 'Oh no – no – don't go yet.'

'I have to.'

'I was going to drive you home.'

'I'll get a taxi.' Already she was moving away.

I didn't take my eyes from her, and when her shining bright head was gone, I felt as if the light in the room had dimmed, and I wanted to cry.

'You changed your clothes,' Zac said.

'Yes.' I'd been wearing one of the elegant tweed shifts Zac bought for my birthday, along with a silk blouse and cashmere cardigan he'd also stuck in the package.

'Why?'

'I felt like it.'

'I thought you loved the things I chose for you. It pleased me that you did.'

'I do love them. But I love the things I choose for myself, too.'

To my relief, he let it go. 'Your friend hates me.' He sounded hurt.

'She doesn't.'

'Her parents hate me too.' He jutted out his chin, and I saw again why he wanted me to move into his rented house – why he was so passionately averse to living next door to James and Peggy. It seemed fair, too, when he was only staying in Cornwall for me. He went on. 'They're too possessive of you.' His feet were flat on the floor, his elbows on the table.

Since that failed MI5 interview three and a half years ago, I had tried to shut down every bit of tradecraft I ever learned. But just as my Spanish resurfaced with the name Molinero, Zac finding me in the pub pricked at me too. I weighed it alongside something else I'd repressed. The way he turned back from his journey to London and caught me looking through his old suitcases.

I made myself say the difficult thing. I couldn't turn away from it. 'How did you know I was here, Zac?' I watched him carefully as he answered.

He coloured slightly, and flattened the tone and speed of his speech. 'I saw your car. I was worried about you being out on a night like this. I wanted to find you and get you home safely.'

'You were on nights tonight. Milly saw you at the hospital.'

'What? Is she a private detective now?' Though his upper body was still, he was vibrating his knees together.

I didn't understand how he'd got away from the hospital, but all the data was processing through my brain and coming up with one conclusion: he wanted to see what I'd do and where I'd go when I thought he was safely at work.

'I brought this for you.' He held out a card. 'It came to the hospital.'

I studied the envelope. Sent from London, no return address, and obviously opened and then resealed. 'It's addressed to me. Why has it been opened?'

He shrugged. 'Looks like a Christmas card you missed. Hardly top secret.'

'You chased away my friend, my best friend.' I swiped at tears, and realised they were made by rage as much as distress.

'It was her decision to leave.' He stared hard at me. 'Are you going to open that?'

'No.' I shoved it in my bag but he snatched it out, tore away the envelope's flap. 'What is wrong with you? Who are you and what have you done with my boyfriend?'

But he simply displayed the card to me. Mary and Joseph gazing adoringly down at baby Jesus, and the twinkling night sky above. 'Who's Martin?' he said.

I grabbed it from him. Inside, it said, *May we all remember those who love us at this special time of year. Martin.* I stood. 'I'm going home.'

'I asked you who Martin was.' Each word was through gritted teeth.

I had only known one Martin in my life, and he was Maxine's boss at MI5. I would strangle her for this if I could. Had she seriously believed this cryptic message was the way to get me to do what she wanted, despite my saying no? But as furious as I was with her, I was even more furious with Zac.

'A friend,' I said.

'What kind of friend?'

'A friend of my grandmother's. He's about ninety. You should trust me. You shouldn't open my letters.'

'I didn't. It was like that when I picked it up. Must have happened in the post.'

'I'm not an idiot, Zac.'

'How did Martin know to address a letter to you at the hospital?'

'He might have visited my grandmother when she was having a lucid moment, or maybe Peggy ran into him and mentioned what I was doing.' One lie after another. They came easily.

'Let me take you home.'

'I can take myself home.'

I rushed into the house ahead of Zac. He had tailed me the whole way, stalking after me on foot as I stomped from the pub to my car, which must have looked absurd, then following close behind as I drove – he had to run a red light to keep up. I slammed the front door without waiting for him. Let him use his own key.

I went straight to the bathroom and struggled to turn the lock. As ever, it stuck and resisted before scraping loudly when it finally moved. I could hear Zac shouting from downstairs, then bounding up, his voice growing closer.

'Don't walk away from me, Holly. You know I hate that. It's cruel. It's a form of abuse. It's not the way to treat people.'

'I'm getting in the shower,' I said.

'The fault is always on both sides,' he said. 'It isn't all me.'

'Yes it is.' I turned on the water to muffle his voice and began to take off my things, dropping my coat on the floor.

He was banging so hard on the door I jumped with each bash of his fist against the wood.

He was shouting, and rattling the handle to try to break the lock. His face must have been right against the wood. 'What you're doing to me is hateful,' he said.

I took my smartphone from my handbag and examined it. Had he put a tracker on it? Spyware? I couldn't think of any other way for him to find me. It would explain why the battery had been bleeding out lately – I'd been telling myself it was what happened to phones after a few years, to get you to buy a new model. I decided to reinstall the operating system as soon as I could – that should remove anything.

'I'm out here waiting for you.' He had changed tack, using the patient, disappointed voice of a reasonable adult speaking to a toddler in the grip of a tantrum. 'Still here.' I pictured him sitting at the edge of the bed, staring at the bathroom door.

I put the phone away and took off the rest of my clothes, adding them to the messy pile on the floor. I used a towel to clear the mist from the looking glass, then stared at myself, fascinated by the vivid blue veins criss-crossing my breasts like roads on a pale map. I pressed one of them lightly, astonished by how tender and swollen it was. My breasts had grown a whole size.

As I stepped into the shower, something caught my eye. My pale pink underclothes, the last things I took off, were at the top of the pile, and they were spotted red with blood.

After I screamed Zac's name and struggled to get the door unlocked and he crashed into the bathroom to find me completely hysterical. After Zac drove me to the hospital and then used his magic to get them to take me to the closed obstetric clinic to scan me. After we cried to see our baby's beating heart and perfectly human profile where I expected only a blob. After Zac said that it must be a girl because she was beautiful and looked exactly like me. After they told me that bleeding in pregnancy was common, and the baby's heartbeat and size meant that we were statistically likely to have a good outcome. After Zac made me promise not to run around again on dark and stormy nights. After I promised not to fight him, and to let him look after me. After I refused to quit my job but agreed to go part-time. After he promised that he wouldn't let anything happen to our baby, and made me believe him. After all of those things happened, I fell asleep in his arms.

Now *The Excursion*

Two years and three months later

Bath, Tuesday, 2 April 2019

I pause in front of the house where Jane died. Maxine has never told me much about anything. She has merely dropped whatever scraps suited her. But I need to know what she is doing for Jane. I have but one thought, or perhaps it is impulse more than thought. It is to see where Maxine goes and what she does next.

Moving, taking action – that is what will stop me from collapsing in a heap of fear and grief. I resume my run, pulling out my mobile phone after I have turned the corner. It takes me less than a minute to order a taxi.

As I run, I search for a cluster of houses that appear empty and quiet, the occupants likely to be out for the working day. I file away the best available vantage point. My intention is to pass the house I've earmarked without slowing, but a flash of Jane's ruined face overcomes me and I realise that I am crying.

I dash into the front garden, concealing myself behind the hedge as I double over, gripping my knees and putting my head as close to the grass as I can while I am being sick, trying to limit the splash and area covered, silently apologising to the people who live here.

Then I hurry away to meet the taxi behind the parade of local shops, wiping my mouth on my sleeve. As the driver zooms me to a row of garages in the alley behind my flat, I see him watching me in his rear-view mirror. Silently, he passes me a handful of tissues, and I manage to thank him in a squeaky voice.

My tears have dried by the time I pull away in a black hatchback with dusty paintwork that I have deliberately not washed. It is the most inconspicuous model I could find, and I have barely driven it, except for occasionally starting the engine to keep the battery from dying.

I re-enter the neighbourhood where Jane died from the other side, passing a big field where the workhouse poor were buried long ago. Sometimes, I think the whole world is nothing but one huge burial ground, and the plague pit is everywhere.

I return to the house whose garden I was sick in twenty minutes earlier. I park in the driveway and keep my eyes on the junction that Maxine's dark-windowed sedan will have to pass through on its way out of this neighbourhood, though it's possible she's left already.

All the while, I am trying to forget about the taste of vomit in my mouth, and accept the fact that I will have to live with it for the rest of what is likely to be a long day. I try to concentrate on that junction, but when I blink my eyes I see Jane's ankle.

In my early days with Zac, I was jealous of her, my phantom predecessor, my Rebecca. But I should have thought of her as my sister, not my enemy. I squeeze my eyes shut again. When I open them I am astonished to see Maxine's car flash past, on its way to meet the ring road. I am not too late, after all. I wait a few seconds, then pull out.

Cheltenham, Tuesday, 2 April 2019

I keep as far behind as I can and use lorries to shield me. After nearly an hour on the motorway, Maxine's driver takes a slip road to Cheltenham. He drops her off at a Georgian terraced house near the town, on a hill that backs on to fields.

I drive slowly, watching in my rear-view mirror as she starts on the path to the front door with keys in her hand. Is this her house? I consider what to do next. I could knock on the door and ask her to let me in, but I've already learned as much from her today as she is prepared to tell me. I decide it is better to stay hidden and watch.

So I do a U-turn at the top of the hill and head down to the centre of town. I leave the car in a car park, then move quickly through the stalls of an outdoor market. A day that began with spring sunshine has dissolved into mist and showers. I buy a navy rain hat, a pair of cheap wellies, and some gum. Chewing it helps to get rid of the vomit flavour, and I make my way through the whole pack, discarding each piece as soon as the hit of mint is gone, then popping a new one in my mouth.

A stallholder hands over the grey hoodie I have just paid for. 'Looks like we're in for some April showers,' he says.

'I think you're right.' I don't want small talk. I want to get back to that house while she is still there. I want to find out if she lives in it, or if she is meeting somebody there.

'You look – Are you in need of help?' he says.

'No. Thank you.'

'I'm sure I've seen you before, your photograph, I mean.'

'You must be confusing me with someone else.'

'Look.' He takes out his phone. 'This is you, despite the glasses. I'm sure of it. Your hair is different, but I have an eye for faces – I'm a super-recogniser.'

'Can I look more closely?'

He puts his phone in my hand and I peer at the screen. It's a Twitter post, and it's been retweeted thousands of times since it first appeared last summer. When I scroll down, I can see the retweets are from this man's community – people who interact with the public such as stallholders, owners of roadside cafes, motorway service workers.

The text reads, *Help us to find Holly Lawrence*. My photograph appears too, with the words *MISSING from St Ives, Cornwall, since June 2017*, and a confidential telephone number. I remember when Zac took the picture, snapped in his garden in early spring of that year. My hair looks like copper in the sunlight – I'd almost forgotten what it was like before I dyed it, and how long it was. Now, it barely skims my shoulders. Then, it was halfway down my back. The top of my baby bump is visible. I was so happy, knowing she was inside me. So why do I look so sad and haunted in that shot? Nobody else has that image. There is no question that Zac put it on that site.

I smile at the man. 'It's not me. I hope I don't look lost or missing, because I know exactly where I am.'

His response to my feeble joke is a half-hearted smile. 'You're good to be concerned. I hope she's okay and that they find her – if that's what she wants.' I thank him and hand him the phone, then turn and walk quickly away, so his view will be of my retreating back. This should make it difficult for him to take a photo of me, if the idea occurs to him while in the throes of his civic-mindedness.

I cut to the side and out of the crowd of stallholders, rather than pushing through it, as confident as I can be that nobody is paying attention to me. This is the best I can do for now, though as soon as I can, I will get Maxine to take that photo down.

I find a public loo in a near-empty park, where I stuff my black-dyed hair beneath the hat, pull the hoodie over my running shirt, and shove my trainers in my backpack after slipping on the wellies. I study a map of the area before returning to the road where Maxine's driver dropped her. I park one block down the hill from the house she entered.

I watch the rear of the house from the drizzle-damp fields behind it. I'm about to take my binoculars from my backpack and risk a quick look at the windows, but then I work out that they are made of privacy glass. This, more than anything, inclines me to think that she really does live here. Only someone as secretive as Maxine would deliberately blur their view of the Georgian town beyond these fields.

Being still and simply observing is bound to draw

attention, so I cut across the fields, wanting to learn more about Maxine's world. It is working-day, school-day quiet, but for an elderly man out walking a poodle. Whenever I fantasise about having a dog, it is a huge great beast and I have named him Keeper, like Emily Brontë's dog, and Keeper and I are running along the beach with a small child. This impossible picture still comes to me, even now.

The public footpath winds me to a village, hidden in the valley, where I pass a double-fronted brick farmhouse with a large duck pond. The house's front garden ends at the base of a steep hill, which is covered in tombstones.

Stone steps twist their way up through the tombstones, towards an octagonal chapel of rest. As I climb them, I hear the laughter and shrieks of children, coming from the section of the footpath I have already taken, though they are still behind the farmhouse and out of sight.

What comes next is Maxine's voice, scolding one child for pushing the other. I freeze for an instant, stabbed by something I cannot understand. Pain. Jealousy. The two mixed together, probably. I make myself move, and manage to slip behind a pair of mildewed gravestones. They are as close as a husband and wife's pillows, separated by a few centimetres. I crouch on the wet grass and peek through the space between the two stones as Maxine and the children come into view.

Maxine has changed clothes. She is wearing jeans, green wellies, and a navy waterproof jacket. Her hair is in a ponytail. Her face is scrubbed of make-up. She looks a decade younger – late thirties at the most.

She looks pretty, which is normally too frivolous a word to apply to Maxine.

Clinging to each hand is a perfect blond child, one boy and one girl, who look about four years old. Are they twins? It appears she was telling the truth when she said she had two children. The little girl is wearing a red raincoat, while the boy's is olive-green. Their beauty makes my heart squeeze. I am astonished that Maxine managed this. Glinting on her finger, I glimpse a wedding ring. Clearly, she leaves that off when she is working.

A man comes from the other direction, quickly approaching Maxine and the children. He isn't dressed for the countryside. He looks as if he has rushed from the office, not expecting such an outing in his dark grey suit. At first I don't recognise him. Then I realise it is Martin, and that I could not have described him if my life depended on it. It is as if he'd been genetically engineered for the job.

Why is he here? Why are they both here, in Cheltenham? Maxine and Martin are MI5, but Cheltenham is the location of Government Communications Headquarters. Could one or both of them have transferred to GCHQ, or been seconded there? GCHQ specialises in communications intelligence and cyber security, but Maxine is all about human intelligence. I am struggling to see how Jane's death, which was so very domestic – so very Zac – can be of interest to GCHQ.

Martin nods when he and Maxine are a metre apart, and they both stop. The children run to play tag while he and Maxine talk. I am straining to hear them. Martin's words are clear and loud enough for me to catch. Maxine's voice is a quiet, cautious murmur, so different from how she spoke to her children. But I can judge from what Martin is saying that she is telling him about Jane.

I catch a familiar name, so distinctive it makes me pause to try to remember where I've heard it.

Frederick Veliko.

Then it comes to me. Frederick Veliko is the name of Jane's brother. Why has Martin mentioned a brother Jane barely knew, in the context of a discussion about her murder, when it is so clear that Zac is responsible for her death?

Martin gives Maxine a final nod, waves at the children as if he is performing the part of a fond but distant uncle, and sets off, heading in the direction he came. Maxine calls out, and the children run to her side and take her hands. I need to get out of here. I hold my breath, praying they won't climb the steps into the graveyard, as I did. They don't. Instead, they cross the grass towards a neighbouring field. The boy breaks away and runs. Maxine and the little girl shoot off behind him, laughing as they give chase.

I sit back on my heels, my breathing louder in my own ears than it must actually be, waiting for them to be safely out of sight. I can feel my body sag, as if I am a balloon and giant hands have popped me with a pin, so all the air rushes out of me. Slowly, I make my way out of the graveyard, slipping on the wet path and landing smack on my tailbone. The pain seems to spear through me, but my face is wet with rain, not tears.

Then Provocations

Two years and two months earlier

Cornwall, Early February 2017

A month had passed since I bled, and I'd made it to sixteen weeks, though Zac thought I was showing symptoms of anxiety and insisted I needed to take things more gently. Secretly, I checked my underwear multiple times a day, terrified each time I looked that there would be blood. But there hadn't been a single drop more.

The sky was white with snow, a pair of blackcaps landed on my bird feeder, and the hospital ward I used to love was becoming a different world. It was as if the air there had changed, so the oxygen levels were barely enough to keep me going and an excess of carbon dioxide was leaving me struggling to breathe. Or maybe the problem was that I had mutated into an altered life form.

Whenever Zac swaggered past the reception desk, he had another request, made with unimpeachable courtesy.

'Can you do me a favour and find the notes for Mr Hopper, Holly?'

'I'd appreciate it if you'd print me some labels for Mrs Walker.'

'Do you know where the continuation sheets are?'

As I visibly spun from filing cabinet to printer to desk to telephone and back again, Zac said, 'Let me look after you. Even part-time is getting too much. You don't have to do this any more.'

Milly told me that the way to boil a creature alive was to increase the temperature slowly, so they didn't realise what was happening until it was too late to get out. 'You're in too deep,' she said. 'He's got you now – that's why he wanted you pregnant.'

'No.' I crossed my arms.

'You've lost all of your confidence. You're too dependent on him, practically and emotionally. He hates for you to be out of the house. He doesn't like you being in contact with any human being other than him.'

'Stop it, Milly.'

'I used to think not being loved by Fergus was the catastrophe of my life, but it leaves me free. Maybe there's even a part of me that chose that. You make me see that being loved too much is far worse.' And she hurried away before I could continue the argument.

I couldn't think clearly. I was a woman on the moon without a spacesuit to equip her for the new environment.

On the ward, Zac was a useful and benign king, and it made me want to kill him. The nurses were his prime targets. In rare interludes of quiet, he oozed around them, bearing food and drink, which he knew was a valuable currency there.

'Any drug timings which aren't working? Anyone you want reviewed? Any cannulas?' He knew the nurses loved that stuff, but he went further. 'Would you like some tea or coffee? A biscuit?'

'You're pale, Holly. Your face is pinched.' He came behind the counter, into the nurses' station, squeezed my shoulder, and logged on to a staff computer to work on the discharge summaries that went to the patient's GP, outlining why they were admitted, how they were treated, and any changes to medications and actions the hospital wanted the GP to take. When Zac finished the last discharge summary, he double-spun his chair.

'Sorry, Zac.' I quietly put a fresh stack of patient folders in front of him. 'These need discharge summaries too.'

He smiled at me, then turned that beam on two nurses who were walking by. Scarlett and Joanne witnessed his display of courtesy-despite-being-sorely-tried. 'Thank you very much, Holly. I appreciate your keeping me on top of things.'

Joanne flipped her hair and sucked in her stomach and smiled at him. 'I wish all doctors were as nice as you.'

'I aim to please.' Zac watched her walk away as I answered the phone for the twentieth time in ten minutes.

'Cardiac unit. Ward clerk speaking.'

'Hello, Holly.' There was no mistaking Maxine's voice when she wanted you to. 'I wondered if you'd had any further thoughts about the task we discussed.'

'I'm sorry, but I think you have the wrong ward. I am unable to help with that request, but I will put you back to the switchboard, who can assist you.' I redirected the call, then concentrated on my computer screen as if I were working on the most important task in the world.

When Zac finished the second batch of discharge summaries, he turned to me. 'Anything else?' He expected me to say no. Instead, I held out a list of the patients who needed risk assessments for venous thromboembolisms.

His bleeper went off. He didn't take the VTE list. 'Those will have to wait.' He reached beneath a pile of stationery that someone had dumped on the far side of the desk. He pulled out a journal. The cover design was a series of thin vertical lines. They were every shade of orange in the colour spectrum, bleeding from lightest to brightest. He slipped it into my hand. 'I found this in front of the house.'

My face went red. I felt myself trembling, my body vibrating like hummingbird wings.

I'd filled that journal with notes about some of the cases I'd encountered in the hospital. I could be fired, maybe even prosecuted, if anybody at the hospital were to discover that I'd been compiling stories based on the patients' histories. But the worst thing of all was the exposure and the humiliation. The journal was where I practised my observations and information gathering. It was also where I secretly wrote fiction, which I'd been doing since I faked that letter from an admirer when I was four years old.

Thinking about it, I saw that writers really were spies. That, in truth, was why I took the ward clerk job. Because what place could be better than a hospital for finding stories of people at extremity?

Three of the stories in my journal were finished. One was about a young mother having to choose between her own life and her unborn baby's because the treatment she needed would poison a foetus. Another was about a father bringing a court action against the hospital for refusing to operate on his child, because his daughter's case was medically hopeless but he couldn't accept it. The third concerned a young doctor who, for the first time, had to break the news of a death to a family while also broaching the subject of organ donation.

I had been looking in places I shouldn't and documenting what was forbidden and stealing stories that weren't mine to take. Zac had forced me out of the shadows, and though I would never be a real spy, and there was nothing in the journal to reveal my history with MI5 and Maxine, out of the shadows was a place where spies should never be. To get caught, to be so stupid and exposed, to have others read my work when it wasn't yet good enough – I couldn't decide which of those things pained me the most.

Zac gave me his fond look. 'You're blushing. Are you writing about me?'

There was that bright smile of his again. It had never struck me until that moment that it was more of a sneer than a smile. I was certain he knew exactly what I'd been writing about, and that he had read every word. He'd probably made a copy of the whole thing. In fact, I was willing to bet he'd scanned it on to that laptop of his, which went everywhere with him.

My journal was never in front of the house. I always hid it in a gap between the upper kitchen cabinets. That hiding place was completely invisible, unless you climbed onto a high stool and knew to slide a hand in, where I'd hung an open folder to keep the journal within reach and stop it from falling all the way down the crack. You'd only look there if you knew to. So how did he know?

My voice was shaking, though I was trying to appear calm. 'I'm sure I've never taken my journal out of the house.' I felt as though a stranger had ripped off my clothes.

'You know how careless and forgetful you are these days.' He licked his lips. 'It must be – very interesting.'

Harriet the Spy's nanny tells her that if anybody ever finds her secret notebook, she should apologise and lie. I was too angry to apologise but the lies were easy. 'It's a journal of my sex dreams about you. And my descriptions of the actual sex with you.'

'We can act it out later,' he said.

'Good. I'll look forward to tying you up.' There was nothing Zac would hate more than losing control, though he'd once asked to do it to me and I'd said no.

He looked completely panic-stricken. 'You didn't write that.'

He was right. I hadn't written a single word that was directly about him, and nothing explicitly about myself, either. 'How do you know if you didn't read it?'

My sleep was interrupted. I told Zac it was because my bladder kept waking me up, which was supposed to happen when you were four months pregnant. But that wasn't the whole truth. I was frightened by my lapses at work. Medical notes were going astray or ending up by the wrong bed, putting patient confidentiality at risk. Everything I typed seemed to be filled with errors. I was exhausting myself all the more, because I wasn't just double-checking everything I did but triple- and quadruple-checking, too. I was going in early and staying late, and still I was falling further behind.

I was practically drooping in my chair when Zac slid his own beside mine. My chin dropped onto my chest and I cupped my forehead and cheek with my fingertips. 'I don't remember making any of these mistakes.'

'It could be you're suffering from antenatal depression. We should mention it to the midwife, see what she suggests.'

I looked up. 'I'm not depressed.' But was I? I was no longer sure of anything.

'Okay. I don't want you feeling stress about this.' His expression stayed placid. There was no tension anywhere in his body. 'You do know, don't you, that lack of sleep can have a serious impact on physical and emotional well-being.'

'That makes sense.'

'I wonder . . .' He looked around, saw that the others were all busy with patients or in offices. He put one hand on my tummy, the other on my thigh. 'Are you worrying about your journal?' He moved his head close, so I could smell the coffee on his breath.

'Yes.'

His voice was so low it was practically a whisper. 'I won't tell anyone. I'm used to keeping secrets. I expect loyalty, Holly. I won't forgive or forget disloyalty. But I give loyalty too, and my loyalty is fierce.' He pressed his mouth, briefly, against mine, and then he was gone.

A few days later, after hours in front of the screen, my eyelids were growing so heavy I wondered if I was going to fall asleep sitting up. As I updated yet another patient address, and checked the accuracy of yet another transcription from paper to computer, I realised that I needed the loo so badly I couldn't sit for a minute longer.

When I returned, Sister was sitting in my chair. She pointed at the screen, her face tight. 'What is this?'

'I don't understand,' I said.

'What are you doing, looking at this patient's blood results?'

'I'm not. I wasn't.'

'Are you not logged into this computer?'

She could see that I was. 'Yes,' I said.

'Were you not using this computer?'

'I was, yes. I only stepped away for a couple minutes.'

'Are these not Mrs Fielding's results?'

'They are. But I wasn't working on Mrs Fielding's notes. I don't understand how they got on my screen.'

'This is a serious breach of patient confidentiality. You are a ward clerk. You have no business looking at this part of the patient's file.'

I thought again of my bright orange journal and what would happen if Sister got her hands on that. 'But I wasn't. I really wasn't.'

'I won't have this, Holly.'

Milly was hovering nearby. 'It was me.' Her cheeks were red. She was a terrible liar.

Sister was searching Milly's face, guessing that she was covering for me, but she held back from accusing her of this. She shook her head in disbelief, but said, 'Explain yourself.'

'I needed to check Mrs Fielding's INR,' Milly said. 'Holly's computer was still logged in, so I used it to save time.'

'You,' Sister said, looking at Milly, 'had better not use anybody else's log-in again. And you,' she said, looking at me, 'had better be sure to log out when you walk away from your screen in future.' She stomped off to her office.

'I didn't,' I started to say to Milly. The words came out in a stutter.

But Milly just looked at me sadly, as if she didn't believe it either. She put a hand on my cheek. 'Go home, Angel.

You're on a half-day today and your shift finished two hours ago. You need sleep.'

I didn't go to sleep. At least, not immediately. The winter sky was the colour of petrol as I crunched through frozen grass across fields, guided by my torch, then along the path towards my parents' bench. I felt like a witch, walking beneath the cold new moon in Zac's loose dark coat, seeming to engage in a ritual as the wind lifted my hair.

I crouched to extract the leak-proof and airtight container that Maxine had planted in the gorse three and a half months earlier. In my hand was a slip of paper on which I'd written the name Jacinda Molinero as well as Albert E. Mathieson's details. I was so close to slipping it in, but I hesitated.

Again, I looked up at the moon, bone white and lighting my skin with her glow. We were supposed to have an affinity, given that I was pregnant, but there was no magic in that sky. The moon wasn't going to start talking when she never had before.

I rose from my knees. Carefully, I stood, extracted myself from the tangle of bush, and made my way to the cliff edge. I dangled the piece of paper over the heaving sea below. But I didn't let it fall from my fingers. Instead, I snatched my hand back and stepped away. I hurriedly returned to the gorse and Maxine's weather-proof canister.

I hesitated one final time, facing up to the implications of what it would mean to do this. I would be working deliberately against Zac. I would be working with intent for Maxine. I would be changing my emphatic No into an ambivalent Yes.

I thought of Zac and my constant slip-ups at work. I could

no longer repress my suspicion that he was behind them, though he would say it was my paranoia, my anxiety, my antenatal depression, that made me imagine such a mad thing. I thought also of the orange notebook with my hospital stories. There was no doubting that one.

What I wrote in that journal was illicit and embarrassing, and I never wanted to share it with anyone. Though there was the small consolation that there was nothing about spying in the journal, and nothing about Zac himself, I still felt my face go red with shame when I imagined him reading it. He had peered into my head and extracted my fantasies without my consent. Is that why the Goddess Diana was so angry and humiliated when Actaeon caught her bathing, naked and in disarray? Though poor Actaeon stumbled upon Diana accidentally. Zac did this on purpose.

And for the first time he had openly threatened me. There was no doubting that one, either. If I were to do anything he considered a betrayal – and I was clear that his definition of betrayal meant anything he didn't like – then he would expose me. He had a power over me that he gained through trickery.

'No, Zac.' I said this out loud. 'You don't get to play it this way.' I slipped the paper inside, screwed the lid on, and returned the canister to its hiding place. Then I walked home, climbed into bed, and slept the sleep of the dead.

Now Further Warnings

Two years and two months later

Bath, Tuesday, 2 April 2019

When I get back from Cheltenham, I am still wearing the sticky running clothes I put on at dawn. I hurry into my basement flat to shower and brush my teeth. I pull on a pair of faded jeans and a chunky cream jumper, both of which I bought from a charity shop. My hair is wet and there is no time to dry it, so I tie it in a low knot at the nape of my neck and stick a few pins in to hold it there.

I log into an email account Maxine set up for emergency contact when I first moved to Bath. It will alert her as soon as I sign in. I find the Twitter post the stallholder showed me, and copy and paste the link into the body of an email.

But I can't resist looking at it myself. The photograph is bigger on my laptop than the phone, so my baby bump seems more prominent. I close my eyes like a child frightened by a scary film. My breathing is fast and jagged, and I am crying. Quickly, trying to focus on the x in the upper right-hand corner of the screen, I close the window.

I write two short sentences to Maxine. *Make this go*

away. Zac took the pic. Then I save the email to the drafts folder where Maxine will find it.

I plug Frederick Veliko's name into every Internet search engine I can think of, as well as a variety of US government websites, as I did soon after Maxine first told me about him. My searches garnered so little, then. Now, there is nothing at all.

By the time I pull on to the tarmacked parking area in front of my grandmother's nursing home, it is dark. Katarina is on night duty. She is my very favourite of everyone who works here, and my grandmother's favourite, too – as far as my grandmother feels such things.

'You look tired.' Katarina hands me a pen and opens the visitors' book.

'I'm so sorry I'm late.' I squiggle an illegible *Helen Graham.* 'I promised her I'd come.'

'No problem, Helen.' Katarina leads me from the reception area to the day room. 'She's refused to go to bed. A part of her remembered . . .'

'That's good.'

My grandmother pretends not to notice when I come in. She is in her wheelchair, and alone. I drag across one of the straight-backed wing chairs, which match the blue carpet. Before I sit, I kiss her powdery cheek. 'It's great to see you out of bed today, Grandma.'

'Who are you?'

'I'm Holly.'

'You're late.'

'It is so sweet, the way she calls you that,' Katarina says.

'It is.' I don't want to dwell on this. 'Have you been

waiting, Grandma?' I'm filled with hope that she is tracking time.

'Have you brought Princess Anne?' my grandmother says.

'Not today.'

'I want to go home. Why have you forced me upcountry?' My grandmother classes anything above Truro as upcountry.

'To keep you near me. It wasn't safe for you any more in the place you were before.' I touch my grandmother's hand, then toss a smile at Katarina as she slips from the room. 'I miss home, too. I miss the sea.' My grandmother was forever shutting windows and curtains, but maybe it was important to her simply to know the sea was there.

I close my eyes for an instant and I see splodges of indigo and aqua, the view from my bedroom window, high in the attic where my grandmother hardly ever climbed. And the small islands of rock that Milly and I used to imagine invading, living there as two princesses, and Queen Peggy sailing out in a magnificent boat to bring us cakes. And the white torch of the lighthouse, always there to give me my bearings.

But the sea colours change, and I see the livid white around Jane's nose and mouth, the congealing blood, the blue tint to her skin. I can taste sick again. I take a large gulp and it goes down as if I am swallowing a rock.

My grandmother's ankles are extra swollen today, seeming to spill over the openings of the velvet house slippers I bought her. I crouch in front of her to loosen the Velcro, perplexed that somebody who was once so tall and bony could become so puffy.

'Why bother,' she says. 'It's not as if they'll let me walk.'

'But they've got you out of bed. They've even got you taking a few steps with assistance. That's wonderful.'

She throws her head back and moves it from side to side with her eyes closed. 'I am ready to go.' This is a grand announcement, made with such theatricality I am worried she will injure her neck.

'Go where, Grandma?' She and I play out this exchange every time I visit.

'You know where.' She drags out each word, in a sort of dirge. 'Take me now and bury me. Don't let my coffin touch your mother's. I refuse to lie near her for eternity. I will be next to your father when I rot. He was a hero, you know.'

Despite the absurd dark comedy of my Sarah Bernhardt-esque grandmother, the word rot makes me feel as if my heart is throwing in extra beats. Once more I picture Jane's mottled face, the features unrecognisable, and her birthmark like a black star sapphire. Her body will be changing still more in death. I can feel myself shaking with pure fury and absolute hate. I want to destroy Zac for doing this to her.

I pull myself back into the place I am now, into this poor imitation of an elegant room that smells of cabbage and body odour and old people, however many windows they open, however much disinfectant they drench it in.

I can deal with my grandmother by rote. I have heard her graveyard instructions so many times they no longer shock me. By my mid-teens, I got to the point where I could parody them for Milly, and have her laughing so hysterically she would beg me to stop before she wet herself. The silver lining – and it is a vital one – is that Zac found my grandmother so horrible he was never around her enough to hear these instructions too. He met her once, and that was enough.

'Yes,' I say. 'I know he was a hero. And I'll be sure to keep him in the middle.'

'In the family vault.'

'Yes, Grandma.'

'The graveyard's closed to new burials, you know, but not to us.'

'We're lucky to know so many of the dead.'

'It needn't have happened. He'd still be alive. They'd both be alive if your mother hadn't pushed and pushed for them to go that day. She made friends with some other RAF wife, got them invited to that lunch party. Your father didn't want to go. He hated that sort of thing . . .'

'What's so wrong with her making a friend and who was the friend and why didn't my father want to go?' How many times in my life have I asked these questions? But my grandmother merely shakes her head and makes a motion of sealing her lips.

Time and again during my childhood, I searched the house for clues and found nothing. I set up a recorder by the one landline my grandmother had, and monitored her conversations. All I discovered was a litany of complaints about the woes of raising a child in old age, gossip about geriatric infidelity, blackmailing threats to leave her electricity and gas provider for a better deal, and her endless pestering of saintly, patient James about her many prescriptions.

She is beyond any ability to answer these questions now. 'Never mind.' I kiss my grandmother's papery cheek. I put a box on her lap. She attempts to peel off the plastic but gets nowhere, so I do it for her, then lift the lid. 'Peppermint chocolates. Your favourite soft ones. No hard centres, so you won't struggle with your teeth.'

She puts one in her mouth and starts to chew. Zac said that watching her eat had put him off his food for several days – that was probably the thing that helped most to keep him away from her. And the fact that he said she was a cross between a dragon and Cruella de Vil. I take out a tissue to wipe her lips and chin, but she bats away my wrist.

She uses her special whisper for what she says next. It is a whisper so loud I imagine the dolphins can hear. 'You are evil,' she whispers. 'Just like your mother.'

'Please, Grandma—'

'Your mother pushed me out of the way at her wedding. When the photographer was going to take the family portrait, and I was getting up to join them, she pushed me down into a chair by the top of my head. She said, "Not this one. We don't want this one." I cried to your father. He should have put his foot down with her from the start. But you are always on her side. Your father was too. No matter what horrible things she did.'

Nobody as sour as my grandmother can be trusted to impart a fair version of history. I found the wedding photo between the pages of my father's copy of *A Tale of Two Cities*, on a shelf in his study. My grandmother is in it, in her full brown-velvet glory, standing to my father's right. He is in his uniform. My mother is on his left, wearing a halter-neck gown. It is simply cut of ivory silk and falls like water. Her amber hair is sprinkled with tiny white flowers, and drops in a sheet to several centimetres below her shoulders. We are so alike, she could be my twin. My father's arm is around her, and the two of them are smiling on the church steps and leaning into each other. There is a small bump, interrupting the perfect column of my mother's gown, so I am there too.

Perhaps my grandmother is thinking of that photo, not imagining I discovered it and have kept it near ever since, and that is why she comes out with her equivalent of an unexpected left hook. 'What did you do with your baby?' she says.

'There is no baby.' My voice cracks.

'Are you sure?'

'Yes.' But a part of me is not sure at all. It is as if a ghost baby follows me, not as she is in the one photograph I have from the day she was born, but seeming to go through every milestone, so that she is the age she would be now.

Zac's child exactly matches the little girl I keep so close. Madly, I wonder if it was all a mistake, and Alice is mine. These are the thoughts I don't confess to anybody, for fear they will lock me away, and I will have escaped one prison only to find myself in another.

'Was there ever a baby?' my grandmother asks.

I pause, feeling as if I have killed her all over again. 'No.'

'You sent that man again,' my grandmother says. 'He pretended to be nice but he wants to murder me.'

'Nobody wants to murder you, Grandma.'

'He does. The bad man from before. The one who scared me.'

I put my hand on her knee.

'Ouch.' She smacks my hand, hard.

'Sorry.' I loosen my grip. 'What do you mean, the bad man from before?'

'The one with the evil eye, who you brought to see me.' Despite having only paid a single visit to the previous nursing home, Zac clearly made a lasting impression. All the more remarkable when you consider how faulty her memory is. 'I detested him. I told him so. When you went away to talk to the waitress, he said terrible things to me.'

On a better day I might smile at my grandmother's persistent insistence on referring to the director of the previous care home as *the waitress*.

'Grandma, I think you must be talking about the old place, not this one. You can't have had a visitor. No one knows where you are, and the people who work here won't let anyone in to see you unless I've given permission.'

Katarina returns. She puts a light hand on my grandmother's shoulder. 'Are you having a wonderful time with your lovely granddaughter, Mrs Lawrence?'

'No,' my grandmother says.

'My grandmother hasn't had any visitors today, other than me, has she?'

'No. Of course not. You know that cannot happen. Not with our procedures.'

'Has she been alone at all today? I mean, is there any way someone could have slipped in?'

'No.' Katarina shakes her head to emphasise it. 'That is not possible.'

'In the garden this morning,' my grandmother says. 'You are all so stupid. You are always insisting on pushing me out there for air like some big baby put out to nap in a pram. It rained on me. I got wet. I will probably catch pneumonia and die. You are trying to murder me.'

'Can you describe the man, Grandma?'

'I don't need to. I know who he was. That boyfriend of yours. The bald one with the strange eye. I still detest him.'

I manage a nod to acknowledge that she has spoken. I have a new thought, and I cannot decide if it is liberating or suicidal. Perhaps it is both. The thought is that I am too tired to run any more, and I am losing the will to hide. Doing these things didn't save Jane. Doing these things takes every last drop of energy and concentration. Doing these things has taken over my very being. Zac is here, and I need to face that fact.

But there are more mundane things I need to face, too. 'Can you please do something for me, Katarina?'

'Of course.' Katarina slips a black scrunchy from her curly brown hair and re-does the knot at the top of her head, tightening and neatening before fastening it once more.

'Can you get them to dipstick my grandmother's urine? It wouldn't hurt to check . . .' I break off. My grandmother finds it mortifying for such a thing to be discussed, but she gets bladder infections all the time, and they make her memory and general befuddlement even worse.

I don't need to be any more explicit for Katarina to understand. 'That is an excellent idea.' She makes a note in the book she keeps in her pocket.

I am struck by the fact that my grandmother's skin

has a faint blue tinge, like Jane's this morning. I know that the living can get this too, when their hearts aren't at full function, so their blood isn't properly oxygenated. Another piece of knowledge gifted to me by Zac.

'And I think a GP appointment, too, please, Katarina. So that he can have a listen to her heart, and take her blood pressure.'

'I'll arrange it tomorrow.' Katarina makes another note. 'You've been more tired than usual, haven't you, Mrs Lawrence.'

'Nonsense, you silly girl!' my grandmother charmingly says, despite having spent a good deal of time complaining to me of this very thing.

Katarina motions me to the other side of the room, where I rest my head against the chalk-pink wall, tastefully decorated in washable, wipe-able paint.

'Don't talk about me behind my back,' my grandmother says to us, in her whisper.

'Sorry to ask this, but can you please make sure she isn't on her own outside again? And the usual vigilance about no visitors other than me?'

'Of course. It was just for a few minutes. No need to worry. Have you had a hard day?'

I glance across at my grandmother, who is wearing the expression of someone sucking on a sour lemon. 'It can't have been as hard as yours.'

'You do know,' Katarina says, 'it is the condition that makes them act this way. It can make them mean.'

'Thank you,' I say. 'But she's always been like this.'

Then Eavesdropping

Two years and one month earlier

Cornwall, Early March 2017

A month after leaving the canister in the gorse for Maxine, I was beginning to wonder if I would ever hear from her again.

The fleeting pink blossom that I loved so much appeared in Zac's front garden. The blossom, capped thick with snow, made the ornamental cherry tree look as if it was decorated with cupcakes. Flitting brightly among the branches were the crimson faces of goldfinches and the yellow breasts of blue tits. The birds were drawn by the feeders I put out for them.

A package arrived, addressed to me at the hospital. Since Christmas, I had developed a habit of visiting the post room as soon as the internal mail was sorted. Unlike the card that Zac delivered to me personally, the seal on this was intact. I took it into the loo, ripped it open and found a book I hadn't ordered. It was a journal. Each blank page had a different motivational slogan at the top. It seemed that Maxine had not gone quiet after all. It wasn't so much a thank-you present as a message, and I imagined her ordering it with a curled lip on her usually expressionless face.

Do more of what makes you sparkle! That was the extra-special encouragement reserved for the journal's cover. It was Maxine's sardonic version of a pep talk, telling 'sparkly' little me that I had done well to find Jacinda Molinero and Albert E. Mathieson's names. Given that Maxine was Maxine, she wanted me to 'Do more'. Those two words were emphasised in gold shimmer, and while the rest of them were inked in a mere flat silver, the purple 'sparkle' was fittingly glittery too.

At work, the red smock with the ugly white polka dots strained to cover my twenty-weeks-pregnant lump. Milly gave me her usual wry smile, and touched my hand when we passed, or put a brief, protective arm around my shoulder if she found me in the supply cupboard, but there was a new reserve.

Two days after Zac and I discovered that the baby was a girl, Milly passed me a drawing she had done, her own version of the Mermaid of Zennor, honouring the original's folk art style, but with a touch of her own whimsy. 'In case you'd like it for the baby's room,' she said, and I threw my arms around her. Mostly, though, she sneakily watched me, like someone with a crush, hoping not to be caught stealing glimpses.

Whenever the nurses clustered for a group talk, whether in twos or threes or fours, and they saw me approach, there was a hush so obvious it made me blush. On one occasion, I heard Zac's name before they saw me and clammed up.

One of the nurses, Joanne, only wore make-up during Zac's shifts. Crimson lipstick, foundation, a fresh wash of dark brown to hide her grey roots. My guess was that she was ten years older than I was – maybe about thirty-five. She was forever finding excuses to put herself in Zac's path. She laughed loudly at his jokes but no one else's. In fact, she hardly spoke to anyone else. She was constantly touching Zac's arm when she said hello or goodbye, as if to a close friend at a party.

'I hate women like that,' Milly said, taking me by surprise.

One morning, Zac swanned in post-nightshift to check the ward before going off.

'Life,' I heard Joanne saying to him, 'is about dancing, and eating, and making love.' She bounced up and down and threw her arms around while speaking, as if she was so filled with joy she couldn't contain it.

Her back was to me, but Zac saw that I had returned to the desk. I was sorting patient files in order to straighten out the notes trolley.

He was bristling with the worst form of the cocky arrogance that I first found so attractive but had come to find acutely distressing. He did his usual thing of raising an ironic brow. He said something I couldn't hear, and Joanne tossed her head to demonstrate that she was laughing in complete abandonment. The implication was that she did other things in complete abandonment too.

Milly was standing nearby, a hand on her hip, rolling her eyes and glaring at Joanne, and wanting Joanne to see that she was on the verge of getting a slap right across her ecstatic face.

A few days later, when the ward was quiet and I was about to leave, I heard voices in an unoccupied side room. I was careful not to pass the observation window in the centre of the door, where I might have been glimpsed. It was impossible to pick up more than the odd word without literally putting my ear to the door, but I could tell that one voice was Milly's. The other was Scarlett's, a nurse friend of hers. I caught my name, and Zac's. What I did next happened as a kind of reflex.

I went to the metal filing cabinet we kept in the nurses' station, behind the reception desk. The cabinet was a relic, as we transitioned from paper to electronic systems. Hidden inside was an unidentifiable burner phone that I had stashed. To find and extract the phone, I had to rummage through the mess of blank request forms for blood tests and MRIs and X-rays and imaging and CT scans and echocardiograms. There was a second phone in the drawer beneath, as a fallback, buried beneath out-of-date guidelines and thick British National Formulary books.

I was still moving as I opened the professional voice recording app I'd installed. It had an extra-sensitive microphone. Standing to the side of the door jamb, I held the phone as close to it as I dared with my fully extended arm.

My heart was pounding in my ears out of fear that I would be caught. My stomach felt as if a butterfly was flying inside it. The din of machines on the ward was like a motorbike revving in my head.

My other hand floated to my belly. That was when I grasped that what I was feeling was not a psychosomatic response to the nervousness occasioned by my technological eavesdropping. What I was feeling was physical and real. After days of not quite being certain, there was no doubting it. I was feeling my baby kick.

A couple minutes later, the side room door smashed open,

and I turned on my heel, bringing the phone to my ear as if engaged in a conversation. I looked behind me and saw Milly. Her face went bright red, and I knew that she guessed I'd been listening. I knew also that she would never give me away. But her horrified expression made me certain that whatever she and Scarlett had been saying would not be easy for me to hear.

Zac was on nights, no doubt assisted tirelessly by Joanne, whose shift began an hour before mine ended. I glimpsed her trailing after him as I left the hospital, but I still double-locked the front door. If he did somehow come home early, I wanted the extra warning of his loud curses when he realised he needed to undo the second lock.

I had thought some more about Zac's discovery of my orange journal in its kitchen hiding place, trying to quell the mortification and force myself to examine the circumstances clearly. I'd also been replaying the way he came home to find me inspecting his old suitcases – he said he'd forgotten his phone, but I was no longer convinced. I wondered what really made him turn around and come back. The only explanation I could think of was that he somehow saw me dragging the suitcases out of the cupboard. And he saw me hiding my journal.

That is why I brought a new toy home with me, a multi-function sweeper for detecting hidden cameras that I'd stashed at work. My extremely disturbing theory was that Zac had installed some kind of surveillance system. If so, chances were that it recorded onto the cloud, so he could have infinite storage space and be able to check the footage from anywhere. He would want to be able to watch in real time or fast forward through it until he caught something interesting.

Turning the Internet router off was the best way I could think of to kill any cameras, because I certainly didn't want him to see me sweeping the house. My heart was pumping faster as my finger approached the router's off switch. I was crossing my fingers and toes that there wasn't a lens trained on the router.

If there was, then I would casually mention to Zac later that the Internet had been playing up, and wonder aloud if he had had problems too. I would also say that I turned the router off for a few minutes to try to reset it and improve things.

The router sat on a small table on the first-floor landing. I aimed the sweeper at every possible place a camera might be. When it became clear that there was nothing there, I exhaled in relief. Zac might still notice the outage, but everyone's Internet sometimes blipped.

I peered through the flashing red monocle of the camera lens finder, going from room to room, scanning as systematically as I could. I found four tiny red dots. Zac had been spare but targeted, favouring central ceiling positions with the widest vantage points. He had chosen rooms where conversations and activities were most likely to happen, but he had left private spaces, undoubtedly for himself. I was bending my neck to wipe the tops of my cheeks against my arms and blinking hard, angry at myself for crying as the reality hit that he had been using visual surveillance on me.

One camera was tucked in the sitting room's chandelier. It made me remember my first night with him, making love beneath it. As I suspected, another was in the kitchen, in the middle of the track lighting, which confirmed how he watched me hide my orange journal. The third was in the main hallway, which would ensure he saw whoever came in and out of the house, and also took in the cupboard under the stairs – so that was how he'd caught me with the suitcases.

The fourth camera was in the pendant that hung above our bed.

My hand was visibly shaking as I switched the router on again, but my stomach was a tight ball of fury. I tried to calm my breathing as I went to the camera-free zone of the baby's empty room, taking along some scatter cushions from the sitting room. I piled them in a corner and made myself as comfortable as I could.

There was that saying about fighting fire with fire, though I was no longer sure which of us was first to light the flames. I did know he had been spying and me, and I intended to spy right back. I would not sit and weep myself into a crumbling wreck over the camera he'd trained on our bed.

I got to work on the recording, reducing the distortion, sharpening the clarity, fine-tuning still more before finishing off with the amplification tool. I relaxed into the cushions, rested my hands on my lower belly in the hope that I would feel her move again, and listened.

It was Scarlett's voice first, picked up mid-sentence – 'to the police but they didn't want to know.' Scarlett paused. 'Are you going to tell her?'

There was a small gasp and I realised I had inadvertently recorded myself, capturing my elation at feeling my baby kick for the first time.

Milly spoke next, her voice trembling like it always did when she was upset and trying not to show it. 'She's barely recovered from the bleed and the sickness. She's lost so much confidence.'

There was a rustling, somebody moving, and I imagined Scarlett closing in on Milly to offer a gesture of support. A squeezed shoulder. Maybe a hug. 'You're an amazing friend,' Scarlett said, 'but she won't want to hear it. He's got her completely brainwashed. She doesn't sneeze these days without his permission.'

'It's hard to look at,' said Milly. 'It's hard to be around her right now.'

Milly. That was my Milly. Saying those things of me. Feeling that about me.

'Joanne keeps saying she thinks he's charming,' Scarlett said. 'She thinks Holly's lucky he's so protective, that she doesn't appreciate him, doesn't deserve him.'

Milly mumbled something. I played it again and again, but it was impossible to hear it clearly, so I let the recording run forward. 'Did the healthcare assistant make a formal complaint?' Milly asked.

'Yep. Said he pressed up against her.' It was Scarlett's voice again. 'Said he made comments about her breasts.'

Milly groaned. 'What exactly did he say?'

'That they were ripe,' Scarlett said.

'Please excuse me while I puke,' Milly said.

As my heart sped up, listening, my baby seemed to wake up too, and it was the strangest co-existence I had ever known of despair and pure joy. I hit pause for a minute, to wipe my eyes and blow my nose. Then I steeled myself and pressed play again.

Scarlett went on. 'He denied it, of course – it was her word against his. They moved her to Care for the Elderly.'

Milly sighed. It was a sigh I knew well, and one that she got from Peggy, who used it when the state of the world made her sorrowful. 'Don't you love it? He harasses her and she's the one who has to move.'

'I'm so sorry for Holly,' Scarlett said.

The last few seconds of the recording were the creak of the door and my own footsteps as I hurried away, stunned by the expression on Milly's red face.

Now Persistence

Two years and one month later

Bath, Wednesday, 3 April 2019

After the events of yesterday and that grand finale of a late-night visit to my grandmother, I need the stress relief of this morning's trip to the gym more than ever. My heart rate is a steady 135 beats per minute. The speed of the treadmill is held at 10 kilometres per hour. It has taken almost two full years to get this strong. When I first moved here, I wasn't allowed to exercise properly. Once the doctor said I could, I would clasp my side and gasp for breath after one minute of what could barely be described as a slow jog.

The skin where my bump used to be is tight again. *You're young – you'll spring right back.* That's what everybody said. Nobody would guess she ever existed, unless they saw the scar. Work, exercise, good food, fresh air, not shutting yourself away, staying busy. Those are the things the professionals advise.

Working in the paediatric unit helps. We are all different, and for some it would be too painful, but for me, though it hurts, seeing children who can still be saved is a kind of therapy.

I am nearly finished with the five kilometres I routinely do at the gym on working days, when I have to be at the hospital early. Otherwise I'd run for an hour. Maybe I'd run all day, or until I exhausted myself and fell over. So often, when I run, I hear Zac's voice. *You know you're not strong, Holly.* Maybe this used to be true, and that's why he chose me. Or maybe it wasn't true but I let him make it so.

I hear Milly's voice, too. *It's the rejection from MI5 — that's why you let Zac do whatever he wants — you think you don't deserve any better.*

The treadmills are positioned in a row on the first floor, in front of windows that overlook the tiny car park. It fits six cars, so I try to get here a few minutes before the gym opens. That way, I can be in and out super-fast. Already, the car park is full.

I watch a familiar SUV pull in. It belongs to George, who joined the gym a few months after I did. He is smiley and chatty to everyone. He told me once that he worked in computer security, and I remember thinking that he had the vague, civil-service-y profile of a perfect spy. I'd promptly dismissed the idea as ridiculous and chided myself for being paranoid. I was starting to feel stronger, then, and it had been easy to let the thought drift away in the wake of medical appointments and counselling sessions. But given Zac's reappearance, and the fact that this is the first time I've seen George in weeks, I am wondering if I should have taken my initial instinct more seriously.

Instead of finding a space on the street like any normal

person would do when they see the car park is full, George leaves his car right in the middle of it. He blocks me in. He blocks everybody in. My heart rate climbs. 138, 140.

Again I hear Zac's voice. *It isn't safe for you to drive, Holly. I can't let you go, Holly.*

I speed up. I watch George jump out of his car, whistling to himself as if he has done nothing wrong.

I look again at the fitness tracker circling my wrist. My heart rate is climbing so fast I can scarcely believe it. 142, 144. What if I need to get away suddenly? 146, 148.

I can see George's mop of thick blond hair, flopping over his brow. He probably thinks this is a charming look. Dark grey tracksuit bottoms. A loose black T-shirt. Navy trainers. I take all of this in as he dashes from his car and disappears from my sight through the door and into the building.

My heart rate is increasing still more. 150, 152.

It's dangerous to put your heart under strain, Holly.

You can't think of yourself, Holly. You need to think of our baby.

Maybe I'm wearing the tracker too low, so it isn't accurate. I try to push it higher up my wrist but there is nowhere left for it to go. It is snug enough. There is no doubt.

A minute later, George is on the next treadmill, barely a metre between us, foppish hair bouncing. He smiles and nods hello, as if what he did is so normal he has already forgotten it. His eyes are blue. *George blue* should be in the *OED* to signal the brightest blue ever seen in organic human form. They crinkle in the corners as he continues to smile. He puts the speed at 12 kilometres per hour and runs with the ease of someone on a gentle walk.

His mouth moves. I can read his lips. 'Good morning.'

I give him a small nod of acknowledgement, continuing to look in front of me as if my lab-rat motion requires absolute concentration. Despite this, I am still aware of him in my peripheral vision. I grab the hand towel I laid over the console and wipe my forehead. My black-framed spectacles have slipped down. I push them back in place, wondering if I will ever get used to them, and swipe at the sweat beneath them.

George is motioning for me to turn off the sound on my earphones.

I touch my phone to pause the music. 'What?'

He is studying my wrist and looking worried. 'Something wrong, Helen?'

'What could be wrong?'

'Your heart rate's a bit high. Do you think you should slow down? I'm only concerned.'

I'm only concerned, Holly.

I look again at the tracker. 165. The number practically gives me a heart attack. 'My heart rate was fine until you blocked me in with your car.'

'I park like that when there are no spaces – lots of people here do that. I'd move it as soon as you asked.'

'I don't want to ask. I don't want to have to search for some arrogant stranger.'

'Sorry.' His expression manages to be a smile, an embarrassed grimace and an apology all at once.

'I don't want to have to spend time interrupting people – men – during their workouts.'

'Why men?' He ducks his head slightly.

'Because you can bet it's men who do this, not women. I can just hear myself. *Hello. Are you the inconsiderate bastard who blocked me in?* No thank you. And then I'd have to plead with him to move as if he were doing me a favour.' I look behind me, where a handful of men are urging each other on with the weights. 'What if you were with them? I'd have to deal with all of you.'

'But I'm not with them.' The effort of speech doesn't make him breathe any faster.

'I want to get away when I want to get away. I don't want to have to negotiate some kind of treaty to do it.'

Want, want, want. It's always what you want. Why is what you want the only thing that matters?

Is it really so terrible to want?

George jumps his legs to either side of the treadmill belt so he can hop off before the machine slows and stops. A few seconds later I see him striding towards his car, jumping in, driving away. In five minutes he is back on his treadmill, again gesturing for me to turn down my music so I can hear him.

'I'd never want to make anybody uncomfortable. I should have thought.' His balance is perfect, even though he is looking sideways at me. 'Glad to see your heart rate is calming down.'

I glance at the tracker. Already it has fallen to 145, though I can't blame George entirely that it rose in the first place. Jane – what Zac did to her – the fact that he is so near – all of this is a big factor in my increased heart rate. George blocking me in was merely the tipping point.

'Can I buy you a coffee when we're finished here? To apologise for being such an inconsiderate idiot?'

This is unexpected. 'I can't.'

Eliza and Alice will be waiting for me at the little park near the hospital for our early morning date. Eliza has promised to bring flasks of coffee that I am predicting will rival a professional barista's. I will bring nothing but my suspicion, hidden beneath smiles and the new moves of embryonic friendship.

'No worries. We're all busy. I know I am.' He is running at his steady 12 kilometres per hour and there isn't a drop of sweat.

Oh? I think. *What are you busy at*?

My suspicion that George is a spy no longer seems at all ridiculous. In fact, the suspicion has grown so huge that my urge to test it is now irresistible. 'What is it that you do with computers, George? Am I remembering right that it's something to do with security?'

I have an impression that he wipes away all emotion from his face as if he were erasing a chalkboard with one swipe. His voice goes flat, where before it was expressive. 'I work with information systems.'

'Tell me more.' As soon as the words are out, I remember Maxine using them against me.

He manages a half-smile. 'It's boring.'

'Is it cyber-security?'

'You could call it that.'

'Who do you work for?'

'The civil service.'

'Ah. You said.' *Of course you did.* 'Can you find stuff out? Find people?'

He taps his mouth with his index finger. 'Sometimes.'

Workout finished. Congratulations. My treadmill slows, comes to a stop, but the world around me seems to be moving, still, in a funny kind of near-vertigo.

I climb off the treadmill and sling my bag over my shoulder. 'Can I ask you a favour?'

He raises an eyebrow. 'I'm intrigued.'

Push, push, push. Test, test, test. What will you do, George? What will you reveal?

'There's someone I need information about,' I say.

'Mysterious.' He brings two fingers to his chin. There is more tapping.

'Exactly. Because I can't find much.'

'"Curiouser and curiouser." Who?'

I reach into my bag for a pen and paper and sketch a bare-bones version of Jane's family tree. I circle her brother's name and point. 'Him.' I hold the paper in front of George.

He stops his treadmill for a second time, then jumps off and leans against the machine, his arms crossed. 'Why does he matter to you?'

Because I want to know why Maxine and Martin were talking about him the day Jane was killed.

I don't answer this direct question of his. I say, 'I put the other names and details there to help search – for connections to him, maybe, or to narrow down any results. He's American.'

George's voice is gentle, verging on teasing, but what he says is not. 'To do something like this I need to know more. You're going to have to tell me why he matters.'

'I've never met him. I won't understand why I need to know about him until I know it. Does that make sense?'

'It actually does, yes.'

I have estimated Frederick Veliko's age, guessing that he'd be a few years younger than Jane. 'He's probably in his early to mid-thirties, but he's nowhere on social media. I'm not an expert at Internet searches, but I've tried everything a non-specialist can think of.'

'Let's see.' He takes the paper and studies the family tree. 'Frederick Veliko.' He looks hard at me. 'Unusual surname.'

'I suppose it is. I hadn't thought until you said.'

'So his sister's dead, according to your chart and dates. Very recently dead. Sad.' He doesn't sound surprised.

'Yes.'

'She must have been young.'

'Yes.' I watch him carefully.

'Different surname.' His face is again a blank.

'Yes. Jane Miller. Her legal surname was her mother's.' *I'm betting you already know all this, George.* I glance at Zac's name, which I also wrote on the family tree. A few days ago it would have seemed unthinkable to speak or write it. But the sky has since fallen. Zac has found me. He has found Jane. 'Jane was married to this man.' I touch Zac's name and George looks sharply up at me. His guardedness disintegrates. His eyes do not leave my face. 'Jane may have had an affair. If so, I haven't been able to figure out who her lover was.'

'I see.'

'Here's the thing that's bothering me. The first time I searched for Frederick Veliko was a couple years ago. All I got then was an obituary, and that only came up because I plugged his father's name in. I tried again last night. Now, the obituary is gone.'

'Things come and go from the Internet.'

'Yes.' I nod in agreement. 'But there was another weird thing. I tried some birth and death websites, all government records databases in the US. Each time I plugged Frederick Veliko's name in, I got an error message with this long string of numbers, saying there were too many requests. I tried other names and that didn't happen.'

He hesitates, as if he is considering something. 'Leave it with me. No promises, but I'll see if I can find anything.'

'Do you think I'm crazy to think it's as if he never existed? As if someone tried to clean him away but missed the obituary at the first pass. Then they went back and got rid of the crumb they'd overlooked.'

'I'd never think you were crazy.'

'Thank you.' I imitate his mixture of seriousness and teasing.

'It's nice to see you, Helen.' He adds, 'I mean, nice for me. Obviously not nice for you. I was a bastard, blocking in your car. I'm truly sorry. Maybe we can meet for a drink sometime . . .'

It's not a marriage proposal. It's a drink. With a man who is probably spying on me. But if he is, why? 'Maybe,' I say. And whose side is he on?

I arrive at the park ten minutes early. From the car, I can see that the children's play area is still deserted.

While I wait for Eliza and Alice, I take out my phone and find the review blog that Milly and I created. I haven't let myself look at it since last June, when I posted my illicit reply to Abandoned Friend's comment.

She answered me a month later. *The heroine should have trusted more in those she was closest to. It is dangerous not to do that. Love can all too easily turn to hate when you think you've been abandoned.*

Quickly, I type, *Not if it's real love.*

To my astonishment, Abandoned Friend likes my comment almost instantly. She must have set up some kind of alert for whenever I make a reply, since discovering my first. She is out there, in real time, talking to me. It must be her.

My heart is beating so fast. Half a minute later, she replies again to my comment. *There is no doubt that it was*, she says.

I look up, and see Eliza and Alice entering the park from the other side of the children's play area.

I type another reply. One word is all I have time for. One word is all I need. *Was?*

She answers my single word with her own. *Is.*

Then, before my eyes, the review vanishes, and the comments along with it. Is Milly erasing any evidence that could possibly hurt me? Whatever the answer to this question, the contact with her has given me a much-needed boost of strength and heart, but also a reminder of how deeply I miss her.

I drop my phone in my bag and jump out of the car. Eliza waves madly as I walk towards her and Alice. We stand in front of the swings. She punches a juice box with a straw, then hands it to Alice before reaching into a bag she has hung on the handles of the pushchair and producing two flasks of coffee.

She takes a sip, closes her eyes, and sighs. 'Oh, do I ever need this.'

'Me too. Thank you. It's delicious.'

'Good.' She smooths a stray hair from Alice's eyes. 'Madam's had a bad couple of nights. We don't seem to be able to do bedtime without a temper tantrum lately, do we, poppet?' She touches a red mark on her cheek that she must have noticed I'd been staring at.

It makes my stomach drop in worry. 'Alice did that?' Is this a version of the I-walked-into-a-door excuse? Alice herself is holding a little pink pig, which she squeezes so it lets out a squeak and makes her giggle. It doesn't seem the right moment to ask Eliza if her husband has been extra busy stalking his ex-girlfriends and murdering his ex-wives while beating his latest partner in between.

Eliza looks down at the grass as she says, 'Never underestimate the strength of a squirming toddler.'

'Swings,' Alice says, and Eliza bends to release her from the pushchair, kissing the top of her head before plonking her into a toddler swing with safety bars.

While she pushes, I tell Eliza about a make-your-own-pizza restaurant that a patient's father mentioned. 'I thought you and Alice might enjoy it. Sounds fun.'

'Meet us there tomorrow for an early dinner,' she says. 'I could so use the break.'

'Will your husband come along?' How can I get her to talk about Zac?

Eliza doesn't colour or hesitate. 'I wish. I'd love you

to meet him, but he's flying to Edinburgh tomorrow afternoon.'

So I say yes to the make-your-own-pizza dinner, promising to meet them there after I finish work. 'What a shame your husband will miss it.'

Her response is a vague and regretful nod, and I see that yet another of my attempts to introduce Zac into the conversation has led nowhere.

I cannot make up my mind if this is natural or deliberate. Is it normal never to say her husband's name? Probably, I decide, at least at this early stage of friendship. When I glance at my watch and realise I need to be at the hospital in fifteen minutes, I am no closer to working out if Eliza is Zac's co-conspirator, his victim, or oblivious to it all.

Then Concealment

Two years and one month earlier

Cornwall, Early March 2017

The conversation between Milly and Scarlett was running on a loop in my head. Invisible hands seemed to haul me from the bed where I was curled, in a practically catatonic state, hair wet from my bath and in my nightdress. Those hands pushed me into the baby's room, where I had a hiding place, a box stowed under a floorboard that I'd prised up. They pulled me down the stairs and into Zac's ground-floor study. This was another camera-free zone, presumably because he didn't want whatever he did in there to be filmed. They pressed me into his desk chair, where I sat and stared at the rusting latches of his old steamer trunk.

It was a heavy blue rectangle of aluminium, covered in dents. Zac claimed that the key was lost, but it didn't matter, it only contained old notes from medical school, he'd break into it someday when he could be bothered. Like Bluebeard's wife, I had tried every key I could find. Unlike her, I hadn't found one that worked.

In my hands were the objects that I'd removed from my hidden box. An old book on locks and locksmithing that I'd ordered using the local library's computer, and several sizes of flat-edged screwdrivers. I was also holding the burner phone I'd used to record Milly and Scarlett earlier that day, in case I needed its camera.

What I was about to do was an absolute betrayal of trust. It didn't matter what Maxine called it. It didn't matter whether the person was highly placed in British intelligence, or a handler, or a jealous husband, or a lowly human asset on the ground, or a suspicious girlfriend. I was the last two, but spying is spying, and it's a shitty thing to do. I was certainly feeling shitty that Zac had been doing it to me.

Which betrayal was the worst? Zac lying to me? Zac trying to control everything I did? Zac's flirtations with other women, which undoubtedly went further than I yet knew? Zac bullying anyone who he thought was obstructing him – or maybe bullying merely because he enjoyed it and could get away with it? Zac secretly filming me? My breaking into his private things would be a tiny infraction compared to the other options in that ugly game of multiple choice.

The hidden cameras, more than anything, made me see for the first time that I needed to get away from a man I'd thought I loved. They made me recognise that I barely knew him. I took stock of what he had told me.

That his birthday was November fourteenth, and he was forty-one, so sixteen years older than me. That he was an only child, and hated his parents for sending him to boarding school. That his parents lived in Vancouver, where they'd settled at the end of his father's career in the diplomatic service, and he barely spoke to them, rarely saw them.

That he owned a house in Yorkshire which his grand-parents had left him, but he wouldn't take me there, despite my asking to go and saying how nice it would be for red squirrels to be part of what the baby knew. That he was evasive when I asked exactly where the house was, because he said he had painful memories associated with it, and asked me not to press him again on the subject.

That he basked in attention from women as if it were his birthright. That he was controlling, and sexually dangerous, two related things that I had not faced properly, telling myself that the night we conceived our baby and he held me down was an anomaly, a misunderstanding.

And that he had a missing first wife. *Jane*. I said her name in my head again and again. *Jane*. A missing woman. How could I let that go? How could I not try to help to find her, if I could, knowing what I'd learned about Zac? A man who secretly filmed me in bed with him, and probably did that to Jane too.

My head was crowding with practical questions. Was it realistic that I could simply walk out? Or smart to try? If I did, could I ever truly be rid of him? No judge would termi-nate his rights as a father without powerful reasons. Would he try to get custody? Maybe he would say I was unfit and unable to support a child, and that I'd been incompetent and anxious and even mentally ill since I became pregnant.

'No,' I said aloud.

The word made me feel stronger. I would not do anything to make myself and my baby vulnerable. I would not put us at risk. I would not let him steal her from me. There was another good reason not to leave him quite yet. If I did, how could I help Jane? Maxine knew what she was doing when she appealed to my solidarity with a woman in trouble. And she knew of my Pandora-like curiosity.

My baby fluttered like a butterfly, as if to encourage me. Her movements were a gift. 'I'm so in love with you, little baby,' I said. She fluttered again, as if to tell me that she loved me back, and I laughed.

I got up from the chair and carefully lowered myself onto the rug in front of the steamer chest. I was cross-legged, to give my growing belly extra space, and to keep myself steady and grounded. At that moment, I couldn't let myself think about the recording of Milly and Scarlett. And I especially couldn't think about Zac's home-made films. I pushed away my memories of what we did in that bed, what I wore, positions, the sounds I made, the things we said.

I turned my full attention to the steamer chest, and got to work on picking the lock. I inserted the largest of the screwdrivers into the vertical keyhole, but it was way too big. I inserted the middle-sized screwdriver, but it was slightly too big. I inserted the smallest screwdriver, and it was just right and perfectly tight.

I checked what I was doing against the illustration in the open book, but my hand was wet with nervous sweat, and it was hard to concentrate when I was jerking my eyes between the book and the lock. I lost the angle and the screwdriver slipped.

When a spy was *bad* in a novel, it didn't mean they were incompetent. It meant they'd gone rogue. It pissed me off, the way the heroes in those thrillers were portrayed as so hard, so impervious. The way they seemed to do everything right.

I wiped my hands on the Persian rug that Zac put in that room to fight the country house florals the owners had stuck everywhere. I lost count of how many attempts I'd made when, to my amazement, I felt the two pins push in together, and the little locking wedge tabs along with them. I took a deep breath and lifted the lid of the trunk.

Inside were stacks of faded green and pink file pockets. I picked up the nearest few, flicking through the papers inside. Zac had told the truth about his medical school notes. They were organised by topic, and labelled in his ultra-controlled writing. I looked quickly through each of them, arranging them in a careful sequence so that I would be able to put them back exactly as I'd found them.

Radiology was towards the bottom of the last pile. Beneath several pages of anatomical diagrams was a cream envelope, greeting-card sized and made of thick, expensive stationery. The sender was a country hotel in County Cork, whose details were printed in the upper left corner in ornate script. It was addressed to Dr and Mrs Zachary Hunter, and was posted to Thorpe Hall in Yorkshire. Finally, I knew where the Yorkshire house was. I wouldn't forget the address.

The glue on the flap had dried out. Inside was a receipt for a three-night stay from 5–8 April, including a room service dinner with a bottle of champagne. The receipt was dated 10 April 2013, which was shortly before Jane vanished. There was a cover letter, also dated 10 April, on cream stationery that matched the envelope.

Dear Dr and Mrs Hunter,

Thank you for contacting me by telephone to make payment by credit card. Please find enclosed your receipt for €1982.45. We regret the unfortunate circumstances that necessitated your early departure. We are grateful to you for paying in full, and for your understanding of our policy, requiring forty-eight hours' notice of cancellation.

Kind regards,
Mr Patrick Murphy, Manager

I snapped a photo of the letter. What could the 'unfortunate circumstances' have been? A range of possibilities crowded in. Illness? A medical emergency for Zac? It couldn't have been a work crisis for Jane, because Maxine had said that Jane quit her job a couple of years before she disappeared.

Why did Zac leave this there? Did he forget it existed? Doubtful, given that he wasn't a man who forgot much. Maybe he didn't know the letter was in the trunk, and unwittingly brought it along as a stowaway, like he did Jane's beautiful suitcase? Jane herself could have slipped the letter into his medical school notes before she ran away. Then again, why did he keep the trunk locked? I recalled his assertion that the key was lost. Maybe he was telling the truth. Not everything he said could be a lie.

I was so immersed in thinking about this visit to Ireland that I didn't notice the extra light bathing the curtains, or the sound of the car engine, which was barely audible on the other side of the triple-glazed windows. Then I heard the car door close.

'What the fuck?' I said aloud.

I saw him at work. I knew with absolute certainty he was on nights tonight. So how could he be home before his shift finished?

His key turned in the front door as I moved the files into

the steamer chest at speed. There was swearing when he realised I'd double-locked the door and he had to fumble for his second key. I'd bought myself extra time with that move, but he would still be in the entry hall in a few seconds. Had he noticed the Internet outage, and that his cameras had gone blank for a few minutes? Was that what brought him home? What excuse did he give at the hospital to get away?

I shut the lid as softly as I could, then reinserted the screwdriver into the keyhole. To my surprise and relief, it rotated and the lock reengaged with a click.

I was halfway to the over-stuffed armchair in the corner when Zac's footsteps drew near. When he continued on, up the stairs, I let out my breath. Tiptoeing the rest of the way, wincing at a creaking floorboard, I slid the book and the tools and phone under the chair's fat seat cushion, thankful that the owners of the house chose such heavily upholstered furniture. All I could do was hope that I would get a chance to retrieve them soon, without Zac discovering them first.

Already he was calling my name, sounding puzzled not to find me in bed, going through the upstairs rooms to search for me, coming down the stairs again.

When the door to the study opened I was posed in the chair as if I had been waiting for him to come home but couldn't help falling asleep. I'd pulled up the hem of the silky maternity nightdress Zac bought me, so one of my thighs was exposed. I'd slipped a spaghetti strap off my shoulder, though at twenty-weeks pregnant I worried that I looked too lumpy to play that trick. Still, the nightdress had a sheer lace panel at the top of the empire waist, and it didn't take much to seduce Zac. That was one of the things I loved about him.

Used to, I reminded myself. Used to love about him.

I felt him standing in front of the chair, felt him bend, felt his lips against mine, then his fingers brushing my shoulder, slipping beneath the blush-pink fabric he chose when we found out last week that he was right and we were having a girl. Since then, he'd called the baby his mini mermaid, which I loved. I pretended he'd just woken me, when he told me how glad he was to find me, that he couldn't bear to lose me, that he was scared I had left him.

I lifted a hand to the back of his neck, pressed my fingers into the little hollow at the top, which was as smooth as his scalp. 'Why would I want to do that?'

He searched my face but said nothing.

'Is it because Jane did?'

He kissed me so hard I could barely breathe, and I tried to push him away, which he only let me do when he had kept me like that for a few seconds too long.

'I would never do what she did to you, Zac.'

He knelt beside the chair.

'Is that why you're so' – I was about to say possessive, though the right term was *why you're such a sick porn-making fuck* – 'why you worry so much about me?'

He was gripping the arm of the chair so hard his knuckles were going white. 'I worry about you because I love you. I loved her too, but differently from you.'

'Did you used to worry about her working, the way you do with me? It must have exhausted her. Social workers are under so much pressure – she must have been relieved to stop.' But had she wanted to? Or did fighting him over it become too soul-destroying?

He whispered, 'I never told you she was a social worker, Holly. Or that she stopped.'

My heart was thumping faster. I knew this because of Maxine. All I could do was use one of Zac's favourite manoeuvres right back at him. 'Of course you did. It isn't a secret. You've said we have no secrets.'

He looked confused at this, as if he were questioning himself.

'You're home early,' I said. 'How did you get away?'

'Favour for Omar.' Omar is another cardiologist, and Zac's closest friend at work.

'Is Omar okay?'

'You can't tell anybody . . .'

'Of course not. What?'

'He and his wife are having IVF. She needs to have her egg retrieval tomorrow morning but he's supposed to be working. I said I'd cover him, so he's finishing my shift tonight.'

It was plausible, but I realised that it had got to the point where I didn't believe Zac even when the truth was more likely than a lie. Zac knew this was too delicate a subject for me to check with Omar, and I couldn't mention something so private to anyone else.

'I guess his presence is essential.'

'Talk about performance anxiety.' He wiped imaginary sweat from his brow. 'I'm told the fertility clinic has a great collection of porn.'

'I hope it works for them.'

'Yes. We're so lucky.'

'I know.' I pulled his face towards mine. 'I was missing you so much tonight.'

'Is that why you're in my study?'

I nodded.

'You fall asleep everywhere, these days.' This was not

innocent. It was another opportunity for him to press the point that even part-time work was too much for my feeble pregnant self to handle. His hand had left the chair arm. It was moving lower, over my belly. 'You're like a furnace.'

'Your hands are freezing.'

'Then we'll need to think of a way to warm them.'

My smile was real. 'Did you feel that? She's started kicking.'

'Not sure.' His other hand was below the small of my back, lifting me towards him. 'But we need to celebrate.'

That would be the best way to get him away from the steamer chest. 'Shall we go upstairs?'

'Always. But she'll need to close her eyes, because I'm going to do things to you that no child should see.'

As he pulled me into the bedroom, I told myself that one more film hardly mattered, and I could thwart him by dragging the quilt on top of us to block the camera. But he was the one who thwarted me, tearing the quilt away and throwing it on the floor.

Now The Robin

Two years and one month later

Bath, Thursday, 4 April 2019

When I arrive home from work, the black iron stairs that lead from the pavement down to the front door of my flat are slippery from the rain. But I am practised at navigating them quickly, which is what I need to do now, because I'm meeting Eliza and Alice in an hour for the pizza dinner we arranged while we were in the park yesterday morning.

As I approach my front door, my stomach drops the way it does when I skid in the shower and catch myself in the nick of time. There is a robin, lying on his back on the grey stones that pave my basement courtyard. The stones have darkened with water to mirror the grey skies above. He is so vivid against them, with his red chest and splash-of-white lower body. I know he is male, from his size as well as his intensity of colour. Peggy taught me to distinguish.

The robin looks perfect from the front, cradled in his soft brown wings. Tentatively, I roll him, forcing myself past my hesitation to touch him. There is a slash across his back, a gash of inside where only outside should be that makes me queasy. There is another flash of Jane's face, once beautiful – so distorted by what I saw in that sad rented house.

How did the robin get here? Though a cat probably killed him, it couldn't have positioned him so neatly, with no feathers or mess or blood anywhere that I can see. It is likely he was brought here by human hands and left for me. It again makes me think of Jane, carefully arranged in the bed despite the clumped and rumpled quilt.

I look up at the bullet-style security camera I had installed opposite the front door. Whoever did this managed to throw some kind of adhesive-backed cloth across the casing, which drapes over the lens too. It's a low-tech solution but effective. Though I have a faint hope the camera caught him before the lens was covered, the likelihood is that that camera isn't going to tell me anything.

I turn two keys in two different deadlocks, then step inside. The flat always smells slightly of damp, because it actually is damp. I wash my hands in the kitchen sink, then head for the rickety shelf unit I managed to squeeze into the tiny bathroom. I choose a washcloth from the pile of rainbow-bright towels that lives on it, then I return to the robin. Tenderly, I crouch down and wrap him in soft cotton.

As I stand, something catches my eye in the place where the robin was lying. It is a square of silky grey cloth stamped with a repeat pattern of small stethoscopes, and identical to the one Zac favoured when he needed to clean his glasses. The colour blends with the grey paving stone step, so I didn't notice it at first. It is Zac's calling card, and I am not sure if it is this recognition or the sound of a car screeching its brakes on the street above that makes my heart give a painful squeeze. It gives a second squeeze at the recollection that Zac once heard Peggy call me her little robin, because of my red hair. Eliza said he was flying to Edinburgh this afternoon, so he could easily have done this before he left, while I was at work. Later tonight, I will stick the cloth in a ziplock bag for Maxine. Right now, I must look after the poor robin.

There is a way out of the flat at the rear, too, through a door in the sitting room that doubles as my bedroom. I deactivate my wedge-shaped under-door alarm, then walk into the scrubby garden that only I can access. Unlike the other basement flats in this street, where each garden stretches far back and spans the width of the house, mine is the size of a double bed. Years before I moved in, the next-door house managed to increase their own garden by buying most of this one.

But the garden is fine for my needs. It is easy to climb into next door's, then vault their fence into the alley that runs behind the houses. Late at night, several times, I have practised doing exactly this. Right now, though, all I want is the neglected patch of grass. In the last of the day's light, I pick up the rusting trowel that the previous occupants left behind, then kneel on the wet ground to dig. By the time I have finished covering the poor creature with earth, my knees and shins are soaked, and my hair and face are dripping with rain.

I remember a cross that I bought from a charity stall for Remembrance Day. I never used it, because I found it too painful to attend the services in Bath – I was haunted by my happy times in St Ives with Milly and Peggy and James. I run back into the flat and grab the cross from the wicker basket that is filled with the things I have no other place for. I imagine Zac frowning, that seeming concern of his.

Are you sure this is the right thing to do, Holly? Are you sure it isn't disrespectful? I know how prone you are to feeling guilty. You'll upset yourself. You'll agonise about it. You know how fragile you are. That cross was made to remember the soldiers who sacrificed for us. You're really going to put it on the grave of a bird? Not the kind of thing I lose sleep over, but for you it's sacrilege. What about your father?

I picture Zac dissolving in a puff of smoke like a cartoon baddy. I push the cross into the ground that I have tilled, above the robin that he brought me. I have another thought, and run inside again to where I display a precious little vase that Milly made for me. I take out the bunch of forget-me-nots I'd put in it, and lay these on the tiny grave, too.

Then Startling Intelligence

Two years and one month earlier

Cornwall, Early March 2017

Zac's professed kindness to Omar presented me with a perfect opportunity. After what he'd told me the previous night in his study, I was confident that he wasn't going to pop out at me – he *had* to be at the hospital covering Omar's shift.

So I headed for the local library, feeling grateful for once that I'd given in to Zac's demand that I reduce my working hours to three afternoons a week, which he still thought was too much. The library was my favourite place for Internet searches that I didn't want to make on my home laptop or phone. I always chose the desk where the screen was facing the wall and I was facing the room, so nobody could sneak up on me from behind to see what I was doing.

Finding the Blackwater Hotel and Spa where Zac and Jane stayed in Ireland was easy. It was what I expected – super-expensive, with beauty treatments and massages on tap, a gym and swimming pool in the basement, a golf course in the grounds, and the most highly rated restaurant in the region.

I did another search, plugging in the hotel's name and the date that Zac and Jane stayed there. When I considered the drama of their long weekend being curtailed so abruptly, I added the word police, then hit the return key. There was nothing, but then I remembered that in Ireland they said Garda, not police, so I substituted that. The third result down was practically flashing.

Woman Beaten, Gardaí Called to Hotel in County Cork.

I didn't want it to be true, but nothing I could do would change those words. They appeared in a headline from a local newspaper that wasn't putting its articles online four years ago. The paper had gone the way of so many publications and since closed down, so the article wasn't clickable. There was only one way I could think of to get hold of it. In seconds, I was on the British Library website to pre-register for the reader pass that would allow me to access their newspaper archive. Somehow, I was going to have to get to London to read it.

That was my morning's task completed, but I continued to stare at the computer screen, still feeling that I should be doing more. I let my mind wander.

Four years earlier, when I'd tried to join MI5, I'd created an email account using the name Helen Graham. I'd also got hold of a photo ID and credit card to match, thinking even then that I might need them some day.

As I sat in the library, looking at its ocean-blue walls, I considered what I might do to plot my escape and be ready to leave quickly. I felt thankful for that alternative identity as I opened a new online bank account in Helen Graham's name, using an address Maxine had given me to establish residential history.

Then I researched some care homes for my grandmother. The one I liked best was in Bath, which was far enough from Cornwall, and a place where Zac had no known history. Milly and I once took a weekend trip there, and we were so happy, doing all the tourist things like two complete geeks.

I would do everything I could to help Jane, to look for her, as long as I safely could. But if I had to leave quickly, I needed to be able to take care of my baby. I needed to be in a position to act calmly, neatly and completely. I couldn't act rashly. I realised, though, that to do this effectively, I was going to need Maxine's help.

Cornwall, Mid-March 2017

Two weeks later, I saw my London chance. It was a Monday morning and Zac came into the bedroom to say goodbye before leaving for work, mentioning a sudden trip to University College Hospital. He needed to be there on Friday, when he had an afternoon meeting. He would set out early, but didn't want to drive home the same day so he'd stay overnight. That was his usual routine on such occasions.

An hour after Zac left, I phoned Milly. I used a tiny burner phone no bigger than my index and middle finger pressed alongside each other. I'd hidden it in a secret pocket that I sewed into the hem of the curtains I made for the baby's room.

The hidden phone pocket wasn't the only special thing about the curtains. I'd had Milly's drawing of the Mermaid of Zennor digitally printed onto aqua fabric. The figure was stamped in brown ink, because I wanted to honour the original dark wood of the Mermaid Chair. Milly's primitivist design was beautiful in its simplicity. I couldn't wait to show her, but she hated to visit the house when Zac was there.

Milly didn't question me when I asked if she could confirm that Zac was in the building. She said that she'd seen him talking to Sister five minutes earlier, so I headed straight for the local library, leaving my mobile at home to ensure I couldn't be tracked.

I logged into the British Library's online system to make the arrangements, relieved that I'd squeaked through before it was too late. It took a minimum of two days to get a newspaper from the Stores to the Newsroom, but you needed to place an advance order at least four days before you required it. The article about the incident in the Irish hotel would be waiting for me on Friday.

I cooked Zac's favourite dinner. Prime rib so rare the juice ran pink and I could smell iron. It was the smell dirty coins left on your fingers.

When Zac came home, he poured himself a glass of the strong red wine I'd already uncorked. 'I tried to call you this morning.'

'I didn't hear it ring.' I could taste the wine, from his kiss.

'The landline and your mobile.' His colour didn't change.

'Oh.' I licked my lips, wishing I could pour myself a glass too.

'You haven't been yourself lately, Holly.' There wasn't a drop of sweat. His blinking stayed at the same rate. 'It's as if you've gone to another planet.'

'I feel, sometimes, that you're looking for things that I do wrong.'

'You're being paranoid.' He took several sips, with his eyes closed. 'I'm worried. I want to take you to see someone. There are drugs that would calm you. Stop the anxiety and depression. Help you to be more clear-headed. There are safe ones for the baby.'

My own skin reddened, and I couldn't control my rapid blinking, or the feeling that my forehead was suddenly damp.

'I'm fine. I won't take any drug, no matter how safe they claim it is.' And you can fuck off, I added silently. Because I will be so gone if you ever dare to try to make me.

'You will if it's needed. It's not good for her to have a mother who is ill.' He went into the sitting room, returned with my handbag. 'Your mobile's not in here.'

'I must have forgotten it. It's probably still on the bedside table.'

'You shouldn't be without it – that's not safe. The forget-fulness is another sign that your mental health is suffering. You don't need to be afraid to seek help. There's no shame in it.' He rummaged some more in my bag, and pulled out a DVD I'd bought that morning. 'What's this?' He held it up. His face was ashen.

'A present for you. I thought we could watch it together. It's a film about WikiLeaks – it's a few years old but I know you're interested in that stuff. You know, getting the truth to the people despite the personal risk, fighting for justice, stopping the bad guys from keeping dangerous secrets.' I tried to laugh. 'The kind of superhero thing you do every day.'

He swallowed hard, but managed a smile. 'That was thoughtful. You're right. I'd like that. And I haven't seen this one. Thank you.'

'Zac?' My voice was soft.

'What?'

'I don't need help from anyone else when I have you. I don't need medicine when I have you. And I want to come with you to London.'

To my surprise, he said, 'That may actually be a good thing.'

'For you or me?' I meant this as a joke.

'Both.' This was unexpected, too.

'I feel better with you around.' I tried to smile.

'But . . .' He downed the rest of his wine and poured another glass.

'But?'

'I'm worried the drive will exhaust you. Especially when you still insist on working those three afternoons.'

'What if I stop immediately?'

'And never go back?'

'Never. Then I'll have the energy to come with you. I'll be under less strain.' Work didn't matter any more, anyway, when my time there was about to end.

'You promise you will stop now, if I let you come?' It was so easy for him to use the word 'let', to assume he had the right to decide for me.

'Yes.' I tipped some olives into a bowl and pushed it towards him.

'Then okay.'

'Great. It'll be fun.' I bounced a little to demonstrate my enthusiasm.

He studied me. 'You usually hate being dragged away from here.'

'I want to shop. To get some special things for her.'

'I thought you said it was bad luck to buy baby things early. I was surprised you made those curtains. You said Peggy told you not to.'

'Peggy thinks there's a plague pit in our garden. Peggy has to buy twice as much salt as a normal person, because she's always throwing it over her shoulder.'

He gave me his slow smile and picked up an olive. 'You really are relentless, you know.'

I shook my head, and said what I knew he would take as a compliment. 'Not as relentless as you.'

London, Late March 2017

We left St Ives at six on Friday morning and I slept for the entire journey. When I opened my eyes five hours later, Zac was driving into the hotel's forecourt. He handed his keys to the valet, then came round to my side.

Milly referred to Zac's sports car as the Noddy car, though I had spared Zac this knowledge. The Noddy car was so low to the ground that I was grateful when Zac helped me out. It made him laugh, and he seemed so happy that I forgot everything for a minute and felt happy too. He put his hands on my bump and kissed me and said he was going to change the car for something bigger in plenty of time before the baby came. I pictured us in a bubble with our baby, a beautiful little family, but I blinked and the bubble floated away and burst, along with the impossible picture inside.

We took a taxi to a cafe near the shop that I had told Zac I wanted to visit. I'd chosen it because I'd studied the building plans while I was in the library on Monday, looking for a place with a rear exit.

Zac ordered a cooked breakfast of such heart-killing proportions it was staggering to think he was a cardiologist. He ate every bite of his fried eggs and mushrooms and tomatoes, his bacon and sausages, his fried bread and black pudding and baked beans, as well as several pieces of thickly buttered toast with marmalade. His pleasure in eating, his huge appetite, was another of the things I'd loved about him.

I managed a cheese omelette, a few bites of toast, and a glass of orange juice. When we'd finished, Zac walked me to the shop and followed me in.

He fingered a white babygrow with two pink rabbits embroidered on the chest. It was impossibly tiny. 'Do you like this?' He sounded shy, something I'd never heard before.

'I do. She will too, since you chose it.'

'You have great taste,' the shop assistant told him. She was willowy and elegant and I felt like an elephant standing beside her.

Zac looked so pleased with himself it made my heart hurt. I couldn't forget that he was the father of my child, though I sometimes wished I could, however lovely he'd pretended to be the past four days. I reminded myself that this was only because of my absolute compliance with his every wish and command since Monday.

Except for the sex. My compliance with that was not perfect. I pretended to be asleep, but he worked hard to wake me up, moving me over on the bed, probably because he was considering the camera angle. When my avoidance attempts failed, I thought of the woman from the hospital who complained about him. Did he film her too? Or try to? I thought also of Jane, and the likelihood that there was film of her as well. Maybe they had a fight about that, and it led to whatever happened in that Irish hotel.

It wasn't a problem I could solve alone. My best chance of protecting all of us was to extract a promise from Maxine that she would get me and my baby out of this mess and ensure those images reached a dead end. If I could pass on the information she wanted, she would be more likely to. I just wished I knew what the information actually was. And the true reason she wanted it so badly. I wouldn't give up on pressing her, whatever she said about informants not being allowed to know the ins and outs of MI5's motives and methods.

The shop assistant turned to me. 'How far along are you?'

'Five and a half months.' My hand floated to my bump.

'You look gorgeous.'

'She certainly does,' Zac said.

'That's kind.' I could feel myself blushing. 'All pregnant women are beautiful.'

'True. I love your dress, by the way,' she said.

'Thank you.' It was a tight navy sweater dress.

'And you have one adorable bump.'

Zac smiled. 'I need to go. I'll leave you in safe hands.' He kissed me goodbye, and I thought, fleetingly again, that we almost seemed normal. 'Take a taxi back to the hotel.'

'Of course.' And I fully intended to, though not from that shop.

I stood in the curtained window, still clutching the babygrow, peeking over the Moses basket that was displayed front and centre of the glass. The basket had an ivory-spotted cover of quilted voile, edged in lace. I watched Zac walk away in his designer suit and film-star sunglasses, the sun glinting on his scalp. He flagged down a taxi with decisive authority and jumped in.

I shopped quickly, taken by surprise at the joy I felt in choosing baby clothes, despite the circumstances. I kept adding to the small pile of things near the till. The babygrow Zac picked out. A white cellular cot blanket rimmed with yellow daisies. A smocked swaddling wrap. A shawl with an embroidered fawn. A plain white nightdress with pale blue stitching. A peach merino-wool bobble hat.

My phone was switched on, and password protected, though I had let Zac see me tap the code in to unlock it, certain he would look, invited or not. I switched the ringer to off and slid it into a stack of cashmere baby blankets. Because the battery was haemorrhaging again, I was sure he'd reinstalled the spyware and tracker.

I bought the Moses basket from the window display, along with the other things. I arranged for it all to be delivered, but said that I would take the babygrow with me. When I saw that the assistant was distracted by a new customer, I asked to use their loo, which was in sight of the back door. As I'd hoped, a nearby panel indicated that the burglar alarm system wasn't engaged during working hours. Ignoring a sign that said 'staff only' and another which warned that the door locked automatically from outside, I opened it and left.

I cut from the alley to a street that ran parallel to the one with the baby shop. After several blocks, I flagged down a taxi. It took half an hour for the driver to reach the British Library. I went straight to Reader Registration to show my identification and proof of address and get my Reader Pass, then to the Newsroom's Issue Desk.

Twenty-five minutes later, I was sitting in the Reading Room, in front of a huge table made of smooth fake-wood. The article was spread on top of a white blotter pad. I took a deep breath, and read.

Woman Beaten, Gardaí Called to Hotel in County Cork

A man was cautioned for assault and spent the night in Garda cells after detectives were called to the Blackwater Hotel and Spa in the early hours of Saturday morning. An unnamed couple staying in the room next door heard the woman's cries and notified the Garda.

A spokesperson said: Gardaí were called to a hotel in County Cork at 01.33 hours on Saturday following reports of an altercation, and a victim with injuries to her face and body. A thirty-seven-year-old man was arrested on suspicion of common assault. A thirty-two-year-old woman required hospital treatment. The woman chose not to provide a statement, and the man was released without charge.

The letters seemed to be floating off the page, turning in circles, sliding across the paper and mixing themselves up. I blinked several times, but that didn't help. I squeezed my eyes closed for a full minute. When I opened them at last, the letters were finally still.

The man and woman were the right ages, at the right

place, on the right date. It had to be Zac and Jane, and to see this evidence that he'd hurt her so badly she required hospital treatment made me feel absolute despair.

What I did next was a blur. I asked the librarian to make a hard copy of the article, and hardly counted the coins I dropped into her hand to pay for it. I bought a *Harry Potter* stationery set from their shop, grabbing the first suitable thing I laid my hands on. I scrawled Zac's Yorkshire address on the inside of a card with a picture of the Marauder's Map on its front, then stuffed it in a matching envelope that I addressed to Maxine at a Royal Mail Post Office Box, using the agreed name of Mary Greenwood. I slid the photocopied article in, too, before sealing it.

I bought a stamp at a nearby newsagent's and dropped the whole thing into the first postbox I passed on the busy Euston Road. I was too numb to think about what I was doing and too dazed to care. I saw a charity shop ten metres away, so I slipped in, placed the remainder of the *Harry Potter* stationery on the counter, and slipped out. Then I took a taxi to the hotel.

Zac steamed towards me the instant I walked into the lobby. He didn't say a word. Before I'd finished thanking the doorman, his arm was around me and he was hurrying me into the lift and down the hall to our room. He shoved me, roughly, onto the upholstered bench at the foot of the bed.

'You're going to hurt the baby.' My words were a cry more than speech.

'No. You're going to hurt the baby.' I could smell beer on his breath, and I was guessing that he'd had several with his medical friends. I tried to stand but he stopped me. 'Don't move.'

'I need a glass of water. Please. You'll need to get it, Zac, if you want me to stay here.'

He lurched into the bathroom, keeping the door open and looking at me every few seconds, swaying so much I didn't know how he managed to keep standing. I didn't hear the tap running but there was a glass in his hand when he returned. He tripped over my bag, and saved himself from landing on the floor by grabbing the edge of the bed, the water spilling almost entirely, soaking his shirt. He was bent double and growling, while I looked on in horror, as if an enraged bear had stumbled into the room.

A tiny black rectangle fell from his pocket into a small pool of water that the carpet hadn't absorbed. The rectangle was about one and a half centimetres across, a centimetre tall, and no more than a millimetre thick. I was pretty certain it was one of those micro SD cards for storing and transfer-ring data. He shoved the glass at me, then snatched the card from the carpet in what I could only describe as a panic. He was muttering and swearing, wiping the card on his trousers, alarmed that the key had got wet and might be corrupted. Everything he said was interspersed with multiple repetitions of fuck fuck fuck, and he was so drunk and furious and out of control he seemed barely conscious of the fact that he was speaking aloud.

He blinked several times, then turned to me, swallowing hard. 'Drink it.'

I gulped down the few sips left in the glass. My fingers were white from clutching it so tightly. When I'd finished, he took the glass and hurled it at the wall. It shattered. Again, I started to get up and again he pushed me down. He crouched in front of me and put his hands on the velvet bench, beside each of my thighs, ready to stop me if I tried to get away.

His face was fierce red. His words came like an explosion. 'Where the fuck have you been and why the fuck is your phone off and still at the shop and not with you?'

He was too angry to realise he'd slipped up – he knew the phone was at the shop through the spyware he'd put on it, which would tell him where it last pinged. 'Have you been with someone else?'

'No.' My breath was shuddering, coming in gasps. 'Of course not.' A sob came from somewhere, and I realised it was me. I pictured Jane, cowering in the hotel in Ireland, screaming so her cries were heard through the walls. 'You're scaring me.'

When he moved his hands to my shoulders, I saw that he had ripped away one of the buttons on the silver uphol-stery. 'Stop that noise. You don't need to be scared of me. You don't need to cry. You're being over-dramatic.'

'Can you please calm down, Zac?'

'You don't tell me to calm down.'

'It's not good for the baby.'

'You're the one who isn't good for the baby,' he said.

I pressed my eyes into the crook of an arm.

'Look at me.' He pulled my arm away. He knelt on the thick carpet at my feet, blocking me in. He nodded slowly. 'You provoked me. What do you expect if you hide from me all day?'

I played dumb. 'I don't understand.' His hands moved onto my thighs, digging in. 'Can you not hold me so tightly? I want to look in my bag.'

He grabbed the bag from the floor and shoved it at me so hard I nearly toppled backwards. 'Look, then.' He watched as I did.

'My phone isn't here.' My fear of him was so real that it coloured my performance of alarm and surprise, which felt strangely real too.

'I've been calling you all afternoon. My pregnant girlfriend disappears in London and I've been fucking having a heart attack worrying about what might have happened to you.'

'I'm sorry.' I'd repeated those two words so many times I'd lost count. 'It was an accident. I'd never mean to upset you. Please don't be mad at me. I went for a walk, sat in the park, that's all. It was a beautiful day.' I was desperate for him to calm down, for him not to start shouting again, for him not to hurt me and the baby.

'You don't mean it. You're trying to make the problem go away.'

'Are you sure about that?' I pulled his head towards me, kissed him, fought off my gagging reflex at the taste of beer on his mouth, realised that I used to find this alluring, and noticed for the first time I could remember that he didn't respond.

'Everyone around you is fucking terrified about what you'll do next.'

I whispered that it was pregnancy brain, I must have left the phone in the baby shop like he said, and we could ring them in the morning to ask them to send the phone along with the things that would be delivered on Monday.

'Look.' I pulled out the babygrow he chose. 'I managed to remember the most important thing.'

'It's my baby. You don't walk away whenever you choose.'

There was a pulse in his temple. His whole scalp seemed to move with it.

'I'm not. I don't want to walk away.'

'Do you think I'd let you?'

'No.'

'Are you glad of that?'

How could he think anyone would be glad to be a prisoner? The lie was absurd, but I still said it. 'Yes.'

He stood. 'Rest.' His hands were in fists. 'Lie on your left side and get some oxygen and nutrients to the baby. I'm going to the bar. I'll come and collect you for dinner.' He glanced at the wardrobe and I followed his eyes. I hadn't noticed the dress that was hanging from the moulding at the top. 'Wear that. It was supposed to be a present. A surprise to make you happy.'

'It's beautiful. Thank you. I am happy.' Did he buy a dress for Jane, and hang it on their hotel room wardrobe, before he attacked her? Did he accuse her of meeting someone else, as he did me?

I tried to think beyond this. Did he have a reason for wanting us to be seen together at dinner, a happy couple on a weekend break of fun in London before their baby was born? I remembered his saying that my coming with him might help us both. Was I some kind of pretext for his being here? A cover story? This seemed the most likely explanation for his agreeing to take me.

'You can show me how thankful you are later tonight.' He jerked open the bedroom door, stepped from the room, and slammed it shut so hard the walls shook.

*   *   *

I waited fifteen minutes, then levered myself off the bed. I squeezed myself out of the sweater dress and threw it on the floor. I slipped the smoky blue new one over my head. The bodice was lace, the sleeves were sheer, and the skirt was silk. A jewelled crystal belt was encrusted along the empire waist, making my bump look distinct and unquestionable. I glanced longingly at the ballet flats I'd worn all day. Instead, I slid my feet into the heeled gold sandals he'd arranged beneath the dress. His medically informed concern for my pregnancy had once again been defeated by his impulse to dress me like a doll.

It was a hushed room, despite the fact that every full-grain leather chair in it was filled. This was not the kind of place where you stood and ordered your own drink. Attentive waiters glided among the tables before returning to the mahogany bar to murmur the guests' choices of cocktail and champagne and whisky. When one of them headed towards me, I gave a slight no-thank-you shake of my head before stepping back. The man retreated instantly, practised at attending to the tiniest gesture.

It didn't take long for me to see what I was looking for. Zac, and a woman in the chair opposite him. They were both leaning intently towards each other. A shard of her light hair whipped briefly into view, though I couldn't see her features because Zac was in the way. He started to move. Before he could swivel around, I stepped to the side of the door jamb, out of his sightline, then disappeared into the narrow back stairwell I'd discovered earlier. My attempted surveillance had been thwarted within a minute of it having begun.

I was panting by the time I reached the second-floor

landing, and wondering how I would make it all the way up to the fifth. I paused to catch my breath and allow a young woman in a blue housekeeping dress to pass.

'Are you all right?' One of her hands rose, as if she wanted to steady me, but she stopped herself.

'Fine. Thank you.'

'You know that there are lifts?'

'Yes.' I raised a hand to brush my hair out of my eyes.

'And a nicer staircase, for guests?'

'Yes.'

'Can I help you with anything? I'd be happy to see you to your room.'

'No. Thank you.' I began the ascent. I could feel her watching until the stairs twisted round at the next landing, and I was no longer in her view.

I didn't take my dress off, though I slipped my feet out of the shoes before I lowered myself onto the bed and rested on my left side. I would have chosen that position without Zac's instruction. All the pregnancy books told you to do it. I arranged one pillow beneath my bump and another between my thighs and knees. I lay on top of the counterpane, but pulled Zac's side of it over me, so it was like a single slice of bread folded in half with me as the filling in between.

He didn't hesitate to accuse me of secretly meeting someone else, but he did that very thing himself. And became violent – the broken glass was still in shards near the wall. I remembered the black micro card, and his muttering about a key. A key to what, I wondered. Could it be something from his medical meeting at University

College Hospital? The video footage of women that he'd been taking covertly? Something else altogether? I wished he hadn't noticed when it fell out. I wished I could have got hold of it. But he did. And I didn't.

My heart was beating fast and my brain was spinning dizzily and my stomach seemed to be shaking around in my torso despite how crowded it was in there. Nonetheless, my eyes still closed.

I wasn't sure if I was in a dream when Zac knelt by the side of the bed, saying softly that it was nearly nine o'clock and I should rest and not worry about anything, and he'd go down and have dinner on his own. Though I fought hard to look at him, I couldn't wake up.

When I next dragged my eyes open the clock said 1 a.m., and Zac's side of the bed was empty. I felt queasy, but the tiredness was more powerful and I fell asleep once more.

Two hours later Zac returned. I felt him lifting the hem of my dress, his hand on my skin, resting on my bump. 'Holly? My love?' Somehow, he had got the counterpane out from beneath me and opened it fully to cover us both. He was naked, which was how he always slept. He pressed against me, his breath on the nape of my neck as he asked if I was awake, whispering that he'd tried to rouse me for dinner but the colleague he'd hoped to introduce me to cancelled and I'd been in such a deep sleep he didn't have the heart to disturb me. I realised I hadn't dreamt his coming in to talk to me.

'What colleague cancelled?'

'Another cardiologist. It was disappointing, but we'll rearrange.'

'Why was it disappointing?'

185

'There's some research I wanted to share with him.'

I thought again of the micro card. 'Oh. What kind of research?'

'Medical, of course. But you and I have more important things to talk about.'

'Yes.' That was a word he usually liked. I was glad he couldn't see my face, though I wished I could see his.

'I won't be able to sleep if we don't make up,' he said.

'I saw you in the bar, Zac. I came down to look for you, to say sorry again. You were with a woman. I didn't know what to do. I left.'

I braced for him to rage at me for spying on him. To my surprise, he didn't. Instead, his lips were on my shoulder. When I flinched, he said, 'Oh, Holly, I'm so sorry,' then kissed me again. 'I shouldn't have lost control. I got too angry.'

I was stunned that he'd apologised, that he had shown some recognition of what happened. I could feel my heart starting to thaw, and I told myself to keep it frozen.

He went on, and I sensed that he was trying to think aloud, and that what he was saying was difficult for him. 'Did you know, what you experience as anger, as my attacking you, it's actually distress?'

'I didn't know that, no.'

'Does it help you to understand better?'

'Maybe. But the woman. Who is she?'

'An old friend of mine from university. She's making a brief visit to the UK after some time in America. She's expecting her first baby, too.'

'She happened to be here, in this hotel, in the bar?'

'No. She got in touch and we planned a quick drink. She

only had an hour. I went and had dinner on my own after she left, when I couldn't wake you.'

'What's her name?'

'Eliza.'

'Are you lovers?'

'Honestly, Holly. She's six and a half months pregnant!'

'Pregnancy's hardly stopped you wanting me.'

'That's because you're you. I'm pleased by this new jealous side of yours, but no, I've never been attracted to her – Holly?!'

'Did you see the flashing lights?'

'You're overtired.'

'Did you – did you put something in my water earlier?'

'Of course not.' I could hear him trying to temper his response, trying not to sound too furious.

I flung his arm off, sat up as fast as I could and stumbled out of bed towards the bathroom.

I didn't make it to the sink. I'd barely stepped through the door before yesterday's omelette and juice spattered onto the white tiles. I was bent over, my hands on my knees, shaking so much I wasn't sure if it was me who was moving or the floor itself. Zac came from behind and wrapped his arms around me, as if I were in labour.

When I'd finished, when there was nothing left and I was so floppy and exhausted my head felt too heavy for my own neck, he sat me on the edge of the bath, turned on the taps, and peeled the sticky clothes from my body. He got in with me, seeming to fear I would slide under the water and drown if he didn't. Washing the sick from my hair and my skin, washing us both everywhere.

Now The Visit

Two years and one month later

Bath, Friday, 5 April 2019

Eliza's house is early Victorian, and sits low on a hill on one of the most expensive streets in the city. It has to be worth several million. There is a gravelled forecourt big enough for five cars, and black iron gates that are over two metres tall. I really need to find out where all this money comes from.

The gates are locked, so I push a button above an intercom. Eliza's voice greets me as she buzzes me in and the gates swing open. I hate being captured on film. But cameras are what people who live in houses like this insist on, so there is no avoiding them.

I smile as I crunch across the gravel towards Eliza and the open front door. Alice is anaemic. Her doctor wants her on iron straightaway, but Eliza didn't get the blood results until late yesterday, through a voicemail that was left while she was on her way to meet me at the pizza restaurant. She listened to the message in horror as we waited for our wine, so I offered to pick up the prescription and bring it over as soon as I could this morning.

Anaemia is something I know about first-hand but don't like to remember.

'Do you have time for a coffee?' she says.

Knowing that Zac is safely in Edinburgh, I say that I'd love one, then follow her into what appears to be a beautiful mausoleum. The floors are white marble, and the stairs, which go up and down and in all directions in a fair imitation of Hogwarts, are white marble too. Is there a danger of Alice falling? There are no stair gates.

It takes more effort than usual to get my bearings in this seeming labyrinth, as we descend to the basement, where there is a kitchen that is twice the size of my flat. One wall is made entirely of glass, and opens into a huge garden that slopes gently downwards.

I rummage in my bag, then hand her the bottle of iron. 'It's in liquid form. She'll absorb it best if you give her some juice and food with it. Oh – and avoid milk if you can, close to when she takes it. There are instructions on the bottle label.'

'Do you do this for every patient?' Eliza smooths her already-smooth dark hair. I'm struck by her dark eyes, which are huge and lovely but so unlike Alice's.

'Only the special ones. And their mums. But her iron is very low – the doctor wants her started on this.'

'As soon as she finishes her nap.' Eliza's face is radiant. 'Did you know her hearing test was perfect?! We're in the lucky forty per cent. I knew we would be!'

I do know, because I looked up Alice's result, but all I say is, 'That's wonderful news.' And it is, because the majority of those with type 1 Waardenburg syndrome have hearing loss.

'We had so much fun last night, Helen.'

'I think she got more of the toppings on herself than the pizza base.'

'Well, I was so tired. I can't tell you how much that little break meant. Sitting and enjoying a glass of wine while someone else entertained Alice. You absolutely enchanted her. I hope she didn't exhaust you.'

'Not at all.'

While Eliza busies herself with the cafetière, I climb onto a high stool at the breakfast-bar end of a granite-topped island. There is a row of old servants' bells on the wall, with an oval plaque underneath each one to indicate where the call is coming from. North Bedroom. Blue Tapestry Room. Dining Room. Study. Library. The Red Room. The Cabinet Room. Picture Gallery. The Chapel. Grey Dressing Room.

'Most of the rooms those bells rang in are long gone.' Eliza is arranging biscuits on a stoneware plate. 'Our house is the sole surviving wing of a once-grand mansion. The wing was a late nineteenth-century addition.'

'It still seems pretty grand to me.'

She laughs. 'The central building and the other wing burned down in 1904. There was parkland, these huge grounds, but they sold most of it off and built on it. There's a bit of the original garden left.' She points to the right of her own garden, where the tops of several trees are visible on the far side of a tall brick wall. 'Over there. Do you see?'

'Yes.'

'It belongs to the city, now. I love taking Alice there for walks and picnics.' Eliza smiles at the flowered paper bag I've laid on the table. 'What's that?'

'Oh. A little something I thought Alice might enjoy.'

'How kind.' She slips the book out of the bag. '*Horton Hatches the Egg*. I love Dr. Seuss – I don't think I've read this one.'

'It's one of my favourites.' There was a copy among the picture books that were part of my forgotten life with my parents, chosen by them. I kept those books in my childhood room. They are probably still there, alongside my father's edition of *A Tale of Two Cities*, because I can't imagine Milly letting anyone move them.

Eliza takes the chair beside me, gives my hand a squeeze. 'I'm so happy you're here.' Her eyes look wet, as if tears are on the verge of spilling. Even now, a stranger's kindness can sometimes make me cry. Does Eliza have reason to be that raw, too?

'You must be homesick. Bath is much smaller than London – it's lovely, but there's so much we don't have in comparison. When did you move in – I can't remember if you said?'

'I'm not sure I did. A month ago. My husband's idea.'

'It must be hard, being away from your friends.'

'It is. Meeting you helps. I should probably say that I don't usually pick up new friends in hospitals.'

I laugh. 'Me neither.'

She reaches across, squeezes my hand. 'It's just, my husband—' She bites back whatever she was about to say.

'Have you taken Alice to some toddler groups? We have details for loads of them at the hospital. I can grab some flyers for you.'

'I'm not sure I can—' Again she breaks off, leaving me

anxious at this visible sign of a woman censoring herself – it is too familiar.

'It's not easy, moving to a new place, meeting new people.'

She nods vigorous agreement. 'Absolutely. That's what I try to explain to Zac. He travels all the time for his work, so he doesn't understand – he's away in Edinburgh right now – I think I told you. He's away so often.'

There it is at last. Despite my guess about who Eliza was from the day I met her, and Maxine confirming it, to hear her finally use Zac's name punches the air from my stomach.

I study Eliza's beautiful face. She looks so innocent of her effect on me, though in spite of Maxine's assurances to the contrary, I still wonder if Eliza has been cultivating me because Zac wants her to.

'Have you and Zac been married long?' I don't hesitate to say his name. I won't let myself be fearful of speaking it or thinking it. I won't allow him that power.

'Alice was a year old when we got married. I met him at university. I had a big crush on him then. You could probably say I was a bit in awe. But nothing happened. He barely noticed I was alive.'

'I find that hard to believe.'

'We ran into each other, quite by accident, about two and a half years ago . . .' Her face reddens. 'That's when Alice was conceived. I don't usually open up about this, but Alice was a happy accident. Zac didn't tell me until I was pretty far along that he was in a relationship. I thought— Well, until Alice was a few months old, I thought I'd be raising her alone.'

I know all too well how good Zac is at keeping secrets. Did he tell Eliza in that London hotel that he was expecting a baby with his wayward and mad girlfriend, who happened to be asleep in their room upstairs? Maybe he was making this confession as I watched the two of them from the doorway of that hushed bar.

'It's great when things work out.' I am scanning for family pictures. There is nothing in this pristine kitchen, which isn't surprising, given how Zac detests clutter. He isn't someone who would tolerate a fridge that was covered in a child's art or magnet photo frames, as Peggy's used to be. In fact, I cannot see a fridge at all – it must be hidden behind the bespoke cupboards.

Eliza pushes the biscuits towards me. 'And you? I was starting to ask you last night if there's anyone, but then Alice sprinkled you with sweetcorn.'

'I like sweetcorn.' My smile is real, when I remember Alice trying to brush it off me, afterwards. 'There's nobody – I'm good on my own.' I take a rectangle of shortbread, nibble on it. 'Can I use your loo?' I hear how abrupt the question is.

'Of course.' She directs me. 'Don't get lost. Everyone does.'

I laugh too. 'I never get lost.' Though this time I plan to.

I deliberately miss the ground-floor cloakroom that she told me about, instead passing through huge rooms that seem to dissolve into one another. There is nothing personal in any of them. No discarded shoes or toys. No dust anywhere. It is as if this house is a giant hotel, a place straight out of Zac's dreams. My trainers squeak with every step, and I make a quiet note to myself that trainers on marble are not good.

I climb the stairs to the first floor, where I find two master bedrooms, each with its own sitting room and bathroom. They make me think of castles where the king and queen each had their separate quarters, though the king would visit his lady's chambers on occasion. Is this the kind of arrangement Eliza and Zac have? It is difficult to imagine Zac wanting that.

In Eliza's room is a framed collage of photographs, the first intimate thing I have found in this house. It sits on a dressing table that is made entirely of mirrors. I snap a photo of the collage as fast as I can, knowing I will study it more closely later.

For now, I cannot let myself react to what I see. Eliza holding Alice at a few weeks old, looking blissfully pleased with herself, as I would have. They are both wearing white eyelet sundresses, a mother and her mini-me dressed as angels. My heart is pounding, and I press my lips together.

It pounds harder still at the photograph of Zac, holding an older baby Alice at about six months. He does not look happy, though he is standing in a playground, holding his child beneath a maple tree so heavy with red leaves it resembles a firecracker.

I am increasingly disinclined to agree with Maxine that Eliza doesn't know who I am. How can she not? But if she does, why doesn't she say? I shake my head. My thoughts seem to shake with it, in a confused jumble. Again, I ask myself if Eliza engineered that appointment at the hospital. Then I remind myself that Alice's condition is real – Maxine was right to say that the need for her to be examined regularly at that clinic is an absolute.

Given this, did Zac ask Eliza to look for me there, and to try to strike up a friendship with me? It's also possible – no, probable – that Eliza is another of his victims. And this could be true even if he has forced her to collude with him.

Does Zac know I am here now, in this house? All at once, I am consumed by the idea that this is a distinct possibility, despite Eliza saying he was in Edinburgh. I think of the hidden surveillance cameras in the house we shared in Cornwall, and his ability to monitor them in real time using the Internet. He has probably done the same thing here, so he can spy on Eliza and Alice. He could be watching me live, standing in Eliza's bedroom. I am torn between my impulse to run and the intensity of my need to learn more. For myself and for Jane, and maybe for Eliza too. Above all, for Alice. Because how can she be safe with such a father?

I rush from the room, enter a bathroom on the same floor, flush the loo without using it, wash my hands without needing to, splash water on my face, compose myself.

I re-enter the kitchen. 'I did get lost! Your house is beautiful. Very big, and a bit of a labyrinth, but extremely lovely!'

'We like it.'

'Do you mind my asking where you go for your hair? I really love it.' Does she hear the falsity of this over-bright guest voice?

'He's near Pulteney Bridge. I'll give you his card. I used to be blonde, but I wanted a change – you can feel so frumpy when you spend all your hours looking after a child – but Guy is a genius with colour.'

I remember that flash of her long light hair in the hotel bar. Her admission is so open. For most people a change in hair colour isn't a sinister disguise. It is simply what human beings sometimes do.

Eliza tops up my coffee. 'You're wonderful with Alice.'

I smile, trying to keep it light, keep it natural. 'I love children – that's why I love where I work. Alice is especially gorgeous.'

She touches my hand. 'Sometimes you seem rather sad.' She smiles wistfully. 'Sorry to be so personal – I know what it's like.'

'Are you sad, Eliza?'

'Sometimes. It makes me sound spoiled, to say that.' A shadow falls across her face. 'Zac is always saying . . .' She stops herself.

'You don't sound spoiled at all. What is it that Zac is always saying?'

She starts to take a sip of her coffee but stops. Her hands are shaking. 'I'm so lucky to have Alice.'

'Well, Zac is right about that.'

'Oh, no, that isn't what he says. It's what I say.' She hastily adds, 'And lucky to have Zac too, of course. But marriage . . . don't ever let anyone tell you it's easy.'

'I don't think anyone ever has.' I picture my parents' wedding photo. They look so shining and joyful, despite my grandmother's sour presence. Did they find it easy? I will never know. Is that why I am the way I am, always trying to find things out, to compensate for knowledge that is impossibly out of my reach?

Eliza looks down at her own lap, laces and unlaces her fingers. 'Previous relationships, they form you, don't they? Set your behaviours.'

'They do.'

'The things that went wrong with Zac's previous girl-friend have made him' – she searches for the right word – 'extra-protective.' Is she doing this on purpose? If she is, she is a wonderful actress. It isn't lost on me that I could have said this very thing of Jane.

'That must be hard on you both. Did he ever tell you what those things were? That went wrong, I mean.' I'm not a bad actress either. That I can be so calm, so normal-seeming and unreactive, is amazing even to me.

She shakes her head. 'He won't talk about her. He says it's too painful. Won't even speak her name. She – I think she may have killed herself – as best as I can piece it together. I do feel so sorry for her, but – you'll think I'm a horrible person if I tell you this.'

'I'm sure I won't.'

She takes a deep breath. 'It's hard, knowing I'm his second choice.'

'I'm sure you're not, but I've felt that too, before.' Saying this makes me remember my initial jealousy of Jane. I can't let myself harden towards Eliza, who may also be desperate for help. At the same time, I can't trust her, either. How do I remain open, between these two states of mind? 'I'm sure he loves you in your own right.'

She lifts a shoulder in a half-shrug. 'That's what I try to tell myself. I've searched for information about her. All I found was a folder of medical articles. Mostly they were about breaches of electronic patient records – he was enraged by some scandal with that. But a few were about suicide in young women – he admitted he had them because of her, but that's all I've ever got out of him. I've even gone through his drawers – I know it's wrong.'

'You're not the first or last woman to do that.' I know better than anyone how good Zac is at hiding his past. Did she find those articles because he meant her to, or is she playing with me, knowing full well that Zac's supposedly dead ex-girlfriend is sitting in her kitchen? I am in a state of profound uncertainty.

'Have you?'

'Oh yes. With every man I've ever lived with.' Never mind that Zac is the only one.

She laughs. 'Good to know I'm not alone.' She takes a huge breath, then swallows. 'Zac is a wonderful husband. And he's amazing with Alice. I'm – tired today. Alice was up again most of last night. She hasn't been sleeping well lately.'

'Poor Alice. And poor you. Hopefully the iron will help her feel better, so you'll both get more sleep.'

'I'm sure it will. Plus, she's especially unsettled when Zac's away – I think she misses him tucking her in.'

'That's sweet.' I feel as if a knife has twisted in my heart. 'What does Zac do? I meant to ask.'

'Ah. He's a doctor. Cardiology. He's not practising right now. Something went wrong. Honestly, he was in a kind of post-traumatic stress when he and I first got together.' She's giving me so much of the truth I am veering towards thinking she is sincere – that she can't be playing some manipulative game. 'These days, he offers himself as an expert witness in cases of clinical negligence. Basically, he advocates for patients. He's on a kind of mission.'

'It sounds as if he wants to do as much good as he can.' I remember Zac's intercalated BSc was in Medical Ethics and Law.

'He hates oppression, hates it when powerful people do wrong and get to cover it up. The reason he's in Edinburgh is to advise on a case. He works so hard. But do you know, he did the grocery shopping for me and Alice before he left? That's how kind he is – he knew I was tired.'

Positively heroic to buy sprouts and milk, I think, imagining him popping along to my flat to deposit the dead robin before he trundled off to the supermarket and the airport.

'This poor woman in Edinburgh . . .' Eliza tops up my coffee. 'They missed all the signs of her skin cancer. It's criminal.'

'That's awful.'

'Zac won't let them get away with it. He'll expose them. Do you know, pretty much all of the competency reviews in hospitals are cover-ups. Internal stitch-ups. Zac always says, "If a plane crashes, you don't get the pilot to conduct the investigation."'

'If a plane crashes, isn't it rare for the pilot to be around to do that?!'

'Yes, but you get my point.' She tops up her own coffee too. 'External scrutiny is crucial, don't you think?'

'Absolutely. Though it must be incredibly hard to be a doctor. The consequences of making a mistake are so serious.' I wonder, not for the first time, if they could have intervened earlier, got my baby out earlier, if they missed some sign. Although what happened to me wasn't medical negligence. What happened to me was Zac.

'Anyway' – she pushes her coffee cup way – 'he's on his way home now. He'll be able to tell me all about it.'

It is difficult not to jump up and run for the door. I make myself smile. 'I don't want to interrupt his home-coming.'

She looks worried, but her face relaxes when she checks her watch. 'It's eleven. His flight doesn't touch down until midday. He'll have taken a carry-on, and his car's waiting at the airport, so if everything is on time, he should walk through the door at one.'

I would blow out air with relief in other circumstances. At the same time, my stomach clenches to witness this recitation of his minute-by-minute itinerary, remembering how I used to play it out in my own head.

She seems to want to say something, grapples for the right words. 'He can get – a bit – upset, when things are unexpected. I mean, when there are guests here and he's not prepared.'

This could be me, trying as delicately as I could to brief Milly on timings, so she'd be sure to be gone before Zac walked in. Milly always knew exactly what I was doing. Early on, she would call me on it. By the end, she had given up.

There is a long wail from the baby monitor, which sits on top of one of the grey-green kitchen cabinets. The cry seems to echo, except that it grows louder each time instead of fading. I sit as if tranquil.

Eliza stands, straightens her tan suede skirt, checks

that her thin black sweater is properly tucked in. She is dressed for a casual lunch with the Queen, schooled in the Zac Hunter fashion playbook. 'Won't you come up and say hello? Alice would love that.'

'Okay.' I calculate that I still have plenty of time to be cleanly away before Zac walks in the door. Despite my vow to stop running, I am not ready to see him yet. Not like this. Not unprepared. And not behind the closed doors of this house, where his wife might be willing to aid and abet anything he does.

Eliza's court shoes click-clack on the tiles, and I squeak up the stairs behind her, past the ground- and first-floor landings, to the second floor. We pass what appears to be a nanny flat, though empty and unlived in. Then there is Alice's room.

Alice's hands are clutching the top rail of her pale pink cot. She is standing on one foot. The other foot is beside her hands, as if she is planning to climb out. I realise now that the extra-paleness of her skin is from the anaemia. There is a tear, still perfectly formed, below her dual-coloured eye. When she puts her leg down on the mattress and lifts her arms, it's all I can do to stop myself from stepping forwards. Those arms are for Eliza, not me.

'Hello, funny girl.' Eliza picks Alice up. The white forelock is gathered into its usual ponytail-spout. 'Did you wake up grumpy?' Alice nods once. 'Do you feel better now?' Alice nods again. 'Do you want to say hello to Helen?' Alice hides her head against Eliza's chest, peeps at me, then lets out a squeal of laughter.

Eliza looks at the open door of the bathroom, which

is more white marble, from floor to ceiling. She turns to me. 'Would you mind taking her for a minute? I'll be quick.'

'Of course. If she's happy.'

'Little limpet.' Eliza peels Alice away and plonks her in my arms. 'She loves you. She never goes to anyone.'

Alice is so warm, and so light, and slightly damp after her nap. She smells of soap and warm bread. She smells the way my baby would smell. 'Hello, mermaid.' I sink into a rocking chair and settle her on my lap.

Alice puts a hand on my face, caresses it with her fat fingers. 'Tear,' she says, touching my cheek. 'Tear,' she says again, proud of herself.

I blink several times, very hard, and swipe at my eyes with a sleeve before the bathroom door opens and Eliza emerges.

'Tear,' Alice says again.

Eliza looks puzzled.

'This has been so lovely, Eliza.' I tickle Alice beneath the chin and she giggles. 'Thank you for having me. I wish I could stay longer, but I'm working this afternoon.'

'Thank you for the book. You must come back soon. Or meet me and Alice in the park again. Won't you?'

'Of course.' Alice is playing with my hair.

'We can do it when Zac's next away.'

'Whatever works best for you.'

Eliza lets out a little gasp and visibly jumps at the sound of the door opening downstairs. Then, there is a voice. 'Eliza?' It is a voice I haven't heard in two years, and hoped never to hear again.

Eliza's face has drained of colour. I can feel that mine

has too. If I weren't sitting, I might fall. She shouts down to him, 'Up in Alice's room.'

Alice climbs off me. She is practically dancing. 'Daddy!' She is laughing and smiling. 'Want Daddy.'

Daddy. He gets to be Daddy. I am nothing. I have no name. Even the one I was born with has been stripped away. My heart is thudding so violently I imagine it would be visible if I looked down at my own breast. I stand, amazed my legs don't simply fold at my own weight, though my fingers are tight on the arm of the rocking chair. I can hear him coming up the stairs, up and up the stairs, his footfall still in my bones.

'You get to meet Zac sooner than expected.' Eliza attempts a smile, but it falters.

He calls, 'I changed to the early flight.'

Eliza's distress at Zac's seemingly unexpected early return has me convinced that she doesn't know who I am. If she does, she deserves an Academy Award. If she does, then she and Zac have planned this with chilling care, including the charade that he was in Edinburgh.

But I don't think this is a charade. She found out about Alice's need for iron late yesterday. I know that was genuine, and by then she'd already said he was away. She isn't handing me to Zac on a plate. More likely she doesn't want him to catch her with a friend, or to imagine she has made any. He is doing to her exactly what he did to me all the time. Pretending to go away. Or actually going but returning ahead of schedule for a surprise ambush.

Eliza's hands are trembling. I nearly clasp them in my own to try to calm her, but she moves before I get the chance.

'Daddy!' Alice toddles off towards the door, and Eliza scoops her up. 'Daddy now!' Alice cries. She is squirming so furiously I don't know how Eliza manages to keep hold of her. I can make sense, now, of how Eliza got the red mark on her cheek a couple days ago. 'Want Daddy!'

The footsteps pause on the first-floor landing. He calls up. 'I wanted to see the two of you before my afternoon appointment. Let me take a quick shower, first.'

'Daddy!' Alice is screaming. She is pounding her fists against Eliza's shoulders and arms.

'Be right there, sweet girl,' he says. There is the sound of a door closing.

Thank God he is still germicidal. He can't bear to fly without washing the air travel away as soon as he walks in the door, before touching anything or anyone.

'Don't worry,' Eliza says. 'Daddy just wants to get all clean for us, after the aeroplane. While we're waiting for Daddy, how about we go and try some of the special new medicine Helen brought you? We can have it with some juice. Shall we try apple?'

'I'll slip out, Eliza. Leave you time alone with your family.'

Relief washes over her face. 'Are you sure? I don't want you to feel unwelcome.'

'You've made me very welcome.'

'He's so – concerned – about my having friends. I think – I get the feeling maybe his previous girlfriend had friends who came between them. I know he wants the best for me and Alice.' She is ten years older than I am, but suddenly looks ten years younger, and so vulnerable.

'Daddy, Daddy, Daddy.' Now the words are a happy chant, a game, each one stabbing me in the chest.

'I'm sure he does.' I kiss Eliza's cheek, then the wriggling Alice's, and make my voice light. 'I'll meet Zac when the time is right. I can see myself out – you have your hands full.'

I practically fly down the stairs, cursing my shoes for squeaking, my heart pounding each time a foot hits the marble. When I get to the heavy front door, I can't figure out how to unlock it, and I struggle for what seems like minutes but is probably seconds, my hands slippery with sweat, so this feels even more nightmarish, and my breathing comes still faster. At last, miraculously, the knob turns and I jerk the door noisily open, taking a quick look over my shoulder as I step into the sunlight, half-expecting a monster to be chasing me. But there is nothing.

I rush along the gravelled drive, only to find that the black iron gates are closed. I let out a cry of despair, and decide I have no alternative but to climb them. I have both feet on the horizontal rail that runs a metre above the ground, linking the posts, and I'm trying to work out how I will manage to clear the spearheads that decorate the top, when there is a click and the gates start to swing open with me clinging on. Eliza must have realised I'd be trapped here, and pushed a magic button somewhere inside. I jump down, stepping quickly out of the path of the slow-moving gate. Then I slip through the gap and walk away as fast as I can without drawing attention to myself, though what I want to do is run.

Then *A Meeting*

Two years and one month earlier

Cornwall, Late March 2017

The day we returned from London, I placed an announcement in the 'In Memoriam' section of the newspaper. I typed it all out on a burner phone with Internet access that I'd hidden behind the air vent in the bathroom. I named my fictional dear-departed Heidi Keyes Greenwood. My message read, *I miss you every day. All I want is to see you again.*

Two days later, I found an announcement in the 'Birthdays' section, placed by Max Parkinson. *HAPPY SECOND BIRTHDAY to Hillier Parkinson, with love from all the family. Xxx.* It was not a hard code to crack. 'Max' was a version of Maxine's already-probably-fake name. 'Second' meant in two days. 'Hillier Parkinson' was the park on top of the hill. 'Xxx' signalled 3 p.m.

Two days later, at three in the afternoon, I walked through a small park at the top of a short hill. Few people came to this quiet place. Although close to the centre of town, it was hidden from view and not on a direct path to anywhere the tourists would want to get.

The park was in the shape of an octagon, bounded by ornamental trees and shrubs. A gravelled path skirted the perimeter, with offshoots leading towards the centre, which was laid with tiles. The tiles were painted with botanical designs.

At the park's outer edge were benches. I aimed myself towards one and sat down on what was essentially a slab of concrete supported by blue bricks, putting the bag of delicatessen treats I'd bought a few minutes earlier onto the seat beside me. There were honey-roasted cashews; a salad of olives, sun-dried tomatoes and pasteurised feta; sourdough bread with fresh herbs; and chocolates stuffed with hazelnut praline.

I was still waiting for my heart to slow down from the effort of walking up the hill, when an old woman entered the park from the opposite side. She hobbled slowly until she reached my bench, then lowered herself onto the other end.

I'd brought my phone, not wanting to draw Zac's attention by leaving it behind again, and banking on the fact that there was nothing about a shopping trip and stroll through the centre of town to alarm him when he checked whatever tracking alerts he'd installed.

I was about to say a polite and neutral hello to the old woman, to test a theory that she might not be an old woman at all, when my phone rang. I was not surprised to see Zac's name flash across the screen. I hit accept and said hello.

'Where are you?'

As if you didn't know. I made an effort at hypercheerfulness and told him the truth. 'I'm sitting in the park. The sky is all clean and washed by spring, the primroses are out, and your baby girl is doing somersaults.' I'd checked with Milly before I left, and she confirmed he was at the hospital. 'Everything okay at work?'

'Fine. How did you get there?'

'I walked. Even pregnant women need regular air and exercise. As a doctor, you know that.' I was very aware of the old woman, though she was studiously ignoring me.

'You shouldn't tire yourself.'

'I can take a taxi home. I wanted to get a few things from the deli. I don't feel like cooking tonight.'

The old woman took an already-segmented orange from a plastic tub and put a piece in her mouth, leaving me in no doubt about her identity. Oranges were the recognition signal Maxine and I had decided on.

'Glad to know I'm worth so much effort,' Zac said.

'I'll pick up some steaks.'

'Don't bother. I need to go to London tonight.' The line went dead.

Good, I thought. Now I can eat my chocolate pralines without your fake-concerned comments about my putting on too much baby weight, and your pretend worries that I'll be distressed when my body doesn't snap back after she is born.

The old woman had finished chewing her orange segment. 'Nice afternoon.' She didn't change her voice.

I let my eyes slide over her. The make-up and clothes and posture were so good she could be my grandmother's best friend.

'Yes. Isn't it.' I switched the phone off and slid the handset beneath me so that I was sitting on it. If he'd installed a bug app, then this would thwart him – a counter-measure I felt amused by.

'Heidi Keyes,' Maxine said. 'Clever. What kind of hidden key?'

'Something fell out of his pocket while we were in London a few days ago. We were in our hotel room. I think it was one of those micro SD cards. SD is Secure Digital, isn't it?'

'Yes.'

'I only glimpsed it. He was drunk and furious. Not in control. He muttered about a key – I'm not sure what he meant – it was an upsetting time.'

'Upsetting how?'

My face went hot when I thought of how he behaved in our room after my return from the British Library. 'He—' I broke off, and gave her a different truth. 'He was anxious that the card might have been corrupted, because it got wet.'

'*Very* slight possibility, but water damage would be unlikely,' she said. 'Those things are pretty protected and robust.'

'What do you think he's doing, Maxine?'

'We need to see. But it's useful to know about that card. You've done well. Any chance he still has it?'

'I don't think so. He was supposed to meet someone for dinner that night, to pass on some research. I think it was probably on that card.' I felt a wave of the pregnancy nausea I'd thought was finally in the past, wondering again if the encrypted material was film footage he'd taken of me, remembering also how sick I'd been in London.

'Did he say who this person was?'

'A medical colleague. He said the man cancelled. I'm not sure he did, though. I fell asleep early that night – I wasn't feeling well – and Zac was out until very late.'

'You're better now, I hope?'

'Yes. Thank you. I checked his pockets when he was in the shower the next morning.' I didn't think she needed to know that it was his second shower since I'd been sick. 'The card wasn't there, but it's so small he could easily have hidden it somewhere else.'

'Any other contacts in London?'

'Supposedly a lunchtime meeting at UCH, but I can't be sure that's where he actually went. I did see him meet an old friend in the hotel bar early that evening. A woman called Eliza who he knew at university. He said she left after an hour. I was – watching them, but I couldn't for very long. He returned to our room for a few minutes sometime after that and said he was going to dinner alone, but he could have lied – I was too tired to wake up properly.'

'We'll check the hotel CCTV, see if there's any sign of a brush pass.'

'He could have given the woman that micro card, or planted it on her for someone to retrieve without her knowing. He said she's pregnant, though – I can't imagine a pregnant woman wanting anything to do with what he has on that card.'

'What do you think that is, Holly?'

My face went red again – the pregnancy made my body temperature spike in response to my emotions. I still couldn't get the words out. About the way he'd behaved in the hotel room. About his video surveillance in our bedroom. I managed to say, 'I'll come to that.' I considered some more. 'Maybe he crunched up the card and flushed it down the men's loo. I can't make sense of it. This is only an instinct, but I think he wanted me in London because he was doing something wrong or dangerous and having me there would make everything appear normal and domestic.'

'Instinct is important.'

'Did you know about what he did to Jane in Ireland? I thought you probably did know about the Yorkshire address, but I wrote it down in case.'

'We knew about both, but thank you for taking the trouble to copy that article.'

'It might be nice if you told me what you do know, so I can gauge what's important. Have you considered being specific about what I should look for?'

'You seem to be figuring that out pretty well on your own, but that's why I'm here now.'

'What about the name Jacinda Molinero? Did you know Jane used it?'

'We didn't. We're looking at that – again, well done. It's a dead end so far but we'll keep at it.'

'And that tax attorney?'

'We're following it up – it might be useful – thank you.'

'You could have told me that Zac assaulted Jane.' I pulled a bottle of water from my bag. Gulped half of it. 'It happened shortly before she left him, didn't it?'

'She disappeared a week after their return from Ireland.'

'What aren't you telling me, Maxine? What's the real reason you're so interested in her? And Zac.'

She didn't reply.

Finally, I had to say it. The words fell out of my mouth as if I were being sick. I couldn't keep them in. 'He's getting dangerous. He was violent towards me in London, in our hotel room. As he was to Jane.'

'Did he hit you?'

'He held me down. He – I don't know how to say it. He forced me to sit, took me by the arm, loomed over me. He was so angry. I can't get a minute alone. There's barely a second when he isn't watching me or tracking me. Have you thought how much harder it makes it for me to search the house? For me to find things?'

'I have. I'm impressed – we all are.' It was rare to catch her looking, but her eyes skimmed over my bump. At nearly six months, it finally looked like a distinct ball instead of a misshapen lump.

'I was so tired, that night in London. The most tired I can ever remember being. I was sick, when he came back to our room. I wondered if he'd given me something to make me sleep, to try to keep me out of it, and I had some kind of reaction. Then again, I can't bring myself to believe that of him. He's a doctor. He cares so much about the baby. It's more likely I had food poisoning, or that the trip and the pressure of it all proved too much.'

'I agree he wouldn't be likely to drug you, but I'm uneasy about the rest of it.'

'You have a duty of care towards me.'

'Yes. And we'll make sure you're somewhere safe. But we can't move you straightaway so please keep your eyes open for a while longer, for your sake and Jane's. I can see you care about whatever has happened to her.'

'I do, yes. But I don't want it to happen to me too.' The baby punched my bladder with an elbow or foot, and I had to stop myself from crying out. What was she trying to tell me? 'If you won't help me now, then probably the best thing is for me to go to a refuge. Maybe he can be prosecuted for coercive control.' My voice caught. 'He won't let me get away easily.'

'There are some encouraging signs. Arrests for coercive control are up, with roughly one in six resulting in charges. It's going in the right direction, but for now it's quicker and cleaner for us to get you out. Less to go wrong.'

'Fine. Do it then. But don't make me wait.'

'Listen to me, Holly, because you need to keep your head clear. You need to think and act calmly. And we need to get everything right for you. There are documents to arrange, housing, a job, doctors for you and the baby. We want you in a sustainable life, a life that's close enough to your own for you not to break down and give yourself away. You enjoy hospital work, yes?'

'Yes.'

'Anything else?'

Writing, I thought. Or I did until Zac stole my journal. But I didn't want to share that with her. So I shared a different but also very true thing. 'Children.'

'Good. That shouldn't be hard to arrange. Have you given any other thought to your escape plans? We try to let people choose the location themselves, as long as they choose wisely, but we can choose for you if you prefer.'

'I found a good care home in Bath for my grandmother. I'll be telling Zac that she died.'

'We can move her for you.'

I let a crumpled supermarket receipt fall onto the bench between us, as if accidentally. On it, I'd scribbled some essential details.

'We can help to pay for it,' she said. 'We'd be happy to do that for you.'

This offer made me even more frightened. Because it showed how bad she thought things had got, and that whatever she'd involved me in was more serious than I'd ever imagined. But I didn't want her to have the kind of claim on me that money would buy. 'No. Thank you. I've been preparing for this, for her care, since before I ever met you.' Then I said the thing I most needed to say, the hardest thing. 'He's installed a camera in our bedroom. Do you know about that?'

She didn't answer.

'I'm taking your silence as a yes.' My voice faltered. 'Are you monitoring what he stores on the cloud?' Her continued silence made me say, 'I'm taking that as a yes too. It's bad enough that that footage exists, that he has done this to me. I'd lose my mind if it ended up going viral – there's probably some fetish group who are into pregnant women, with Zac as their president.'

I had been waiting for the right moment to broach this, but she was at her most blank. My face was going red. All I could be was blunt. 'You need to promise me you'll destroy those materials if you get your hands on them. If he did pass on that micro card in London, it was probably filled with his home-made porn.'

At last, she reacted. 'I know this must be difficult for you. I promise that any footage of you will be safe with us – it ends with us.'

I interrupted. 'There may be other women. Maybe Jane is one. If there are, you need to protect them, too.'

'We will.' She adjusted her position and the receipt disappeared.

'Use Helen Graham – I already set up bank accounts and a credit card in that name.'

'We can get you some clerical work in a hospital, arrange the paperwork showing you have no criminal record. Practise thinking of yourself as Helen Graham.'

'I already am.'

'Whatever happens, we'll get you out in plenty of time before your baby is born.'

Maxine stood and hobbled slowly past me, using the cane heavily and looking at the ground. She whispered as she moved, her lips as still as a ventriloquist's. 'A final word. As comfortable as we will try to make you – you will never be properly you again. All of this. Everyone here you love. It never works if you try to keep those connections. You can't be half-in, half-out.' She made me think of a spurned godmother or wicked stepmother reciting an impossible task, or cursing a fairy-tale princess.

But I was no princess. And Zac was no prince. When she reached the nearest gap in the plants that enclosed the park, a man appeared, aiming his laser beam eyes at me, as if expecting to discover me with someone else. There was a flicker of surprise when he did not. Did he imagine I'd heaved my six-months-pregnant self to the park to meet a lover?

He made a show of his courtesy in stepping to the side for an old woman, leaning towards the trunk of a sweet chestnut tree but keeping his eyes on me. She passed him with a stiff nod of gratitude, as if it hurt her neck to do it.

As soon as she was gone, he stormed along the path until he was glowering over me.

'Get up, Holly.'

'No.'

'What?' He was amazed I'd used the word.

'I said no.'

He changed tack. He shook his head wearily. 'You forget things. You make yourself ill. But you walk two miles when you don't have to. Are you trying to kill our baby?'

The last sentence made me catch my breath. 'How can you say that?'

'Isn't it obvious?'

'No. Why are you here? You're supposed to be at work.'

'I was. And I should have gone straight to London from the hospital, but you made me come here first to look after you.'

'I didn't make you do anything, and I don't need looking after.'

Another sad, disappointed shake of the head. 'If you won't trust me as your partner, trust me as a doctor. You aren't looking well.'

This got to me. 'Why? What's wrong?'

'Your face is pinched. You're pale. If your body has to fight to keep you going, it's going to be depleting resources for the baby. You need to be home. Not here.' He put out a hand. 'Please.'

I waited for several seconds. Still he held it out. It was too uncomfortable to leave it hanging there. I was too frightened that he was right. Was I hurting the baby? I needed to be careful to remember that not everything he said was without truth or reason. Slowly, I put my hand in his and allowed him to pull me up.

He led me to his car, to the front door, to the sitting room, to a chair, where he lifted my feet onto a low stool. All the time he looked as hurt as a man who'd found his lover in bed with someone else rather than simply sitting on a park bench, alone.

He put a cushion behind my back, then knelt at my feet and rested his ear on my bump. 'I don't think I'll go to London after all.'

'Good. I like it best when you're here.' I was wearing my *radiating love and delight* face, though every step I took with him at my side made me feel as though I were wearing invisible handcuffs.

Now *An Assault*

Two years and one month later

Bath, Saturday, 6 April 2019

The day after my visit to Eliza and near-collision with Zac, I begin my morning by climbing back into bed with coffee and my laptop, still wearing the oversized T-shirt I slept in. It is easy to find Eliza's house on the Land Registry website, where I buy copies of the Title Register and Title Plan. The first tells me the property was registered in Eliza's sole name in late February, which isn't surprising given that Zac always avoided doing anything financial in joint names. The second tells me more about the property's boundaries and surroundings. It might, I think, be possible to get in – or out – through the parkland that touches one side of their garden – I remember Eliza drawing my attention to it.

I take a long shower, then head to the hospital for a supposed catch-up on admin on my own time. Paediatric Outpatients is a ghost clinic, eerily quiet, with no one else there. Genuine admin is mostly what I do, in order to disguise the small part that is not genuine. My search history will show that I've been rooting around in places

I don't belong on a day I shouldn't be in, though it's unlikely anyone will have the time or inclination to look.

I dig deeper into Alice's records. She was referred to our clinic by a paediatrician in London, but I can only trace her medical files back a year. Why is there nothing earlier? Is this evidence that there is something odd about the circumstances of her birth?

I close my eyes and shake my head until my neck hurts. Even so, I continue shaking my head like a madwoman, as if doing this will force enlightenment into my brain. It doesn't work. For now, I must move on. In any case, I am in a position to know how dramatically hospitals in the UK vary in their progress with migrating to electronic records. Some are fully there, some are still using paper, and some are in the messy hinterlands in between.

I don't leave the empty clinic immediately. Instead, I turn off the hospital computer and switch on my laptop, which I've brought with me. I find out that Eliza studied Art History at University College, London, which is where Zac went to medical school. The circumstances fit, as well as the minimal truth Zac told about it the night I glimpsed her with him in that London hotel. They graduated from UCL the same year. Her degree would have taken three years, whilst his was six preceded by a gap year for European travel, like an eighteenth-century gentleman's grand tour.

Zac is forty-three now, and Eliza half a decade younger than he is. If she spent all that time with a crush on him, and then they finally got together, she may be all the more in his thrall – and under his control.

I learn also that she comes from an extremely rich family, with a financier father, and is an only child. Her family money explains how she bought the surviving wing of that once-magnificent but still-stupendous house. She worked at a New York art gallery for five years – Zac had told me in London that she'd returned to the UK after a spell in the US.

Finally, I find the barest snippet of a report about Jane, referring to the as-yet-unidentified body of a woman thought to be in her mid to late thirties discovered on Tuesday morning. The cause of death is suspicious, and police are urging members of the public to come forward with information.

Early that evening, it seems a good idea to go to the pub. After starting my second glass of wine, it seems a good idea to phone George. Twenty minutes after the phone call, a pack of salt and vinegar crisps appears on the table in front of me, along with a pint and a third glass of red wine, so it seems a good idea to look up and see who the bearer of these wonderful things is. George is standing there, smiling and hooking out the chair beside me. Our knees almost touch, because the pub is crowded. And because it is too noisy in the pub to talk, and that third glass of wine is too much for me, and George only just saves it from spilling when I knock it over but he catches it and a little sloshes onto his hand, it seems a good idea to leave, and take a walk by the river.

The clouds are giant sculptured angels, white and floating, processing slowly over the weir, and there is a slivered crescent of moon in the night sky. The clouds are calm, but the weir is angry, hissing like a blow torch, the water thundering down the sides to the boiling centre. The weir is hungry like the sea.

When I first moved to Bath, I was so close to letting myself fall in. I thought all the time of feeding myself to the weir, letting it grab me and suck me under and tumble me round and round as if I were trapped in a washing machine's drum.

'It soothes me.' I begin to sway forwards, towards the water, rising on my toes. George reaches out, as if to make sure I don't step off.

He laughs. 'Well that's scary. I think it's time to get you away from here.' His fingers close around mine. It is the first time he has touched me in a way that couldn't possibly be construed as accidental, the first time any man other than a doctor has done this since Zac, and I stiffen.

'Sorry.' He releases my hand.

I shake my head. 'It's okay. I just wasn't expecting . . .' I take his hand, feel how warm his fingers are, loose in mine. I curl my own around his.

Gently, he curls back. 'Okay?'

'Yes.'

We are still for a minute. 'Nice?' He leans sideways, drawing closer, but not touching.

'More than nice.' I squeeze his hand.

'Shall we find somewhere quieter?'

I am not going to let what happened freeze me forever. In the throes of my tipsiness, my appreciation of the difference between George and Zac makes me turn to George and look up at his face.

I have yet to conclude whether George is a good spy or a bad one. He may, in fact, not be a spy at all, though I think this is the least likely option. Whatever he is, my hand is floating to the side of his head, my palm on his neck, my thumb in front of his ear and my other fingers cupping his head behind it.

Somehow, one of his hands is on my shoulder, and the other on my waist.

'You're much faster with those hands than I guessed, Mr Markham.'

'I like to think I'm full of surprises, Miss Graham. You certainly are.' He pulls me closer. 'You've drunk quite a lot, haven't you?' Those bright blue eyes of his, those fluttering lids, the way he dips his chin.

'Three glasses isn't that much, is it?'

'Well, you can still count, so that's a good sign, and a bit of that third glass did escape.' He is so gentle. The way he dresses reminds me of a schoolboy. Grey trousers, blue jumper. As if he never learned to do it any other way. He is the anti-Zac, as far as his fashion conscious-ness goes, or rather, his lack of it. I find it endearing. 'I won't take advantage of the fact that you are a lightweight.'

'That's a shame.' To my astonishment, I am flirting. My skin is so alive the sleeves of my thin sweater are filled with static. 'Do you know?' I say.

'Know what?'

'That I nearly didn't come out tonight. And I probably wouldn't have phoned you if I hadn't had that wine. But I'm glad I did.'

'I'm glad too.'

I shake my head very quickly, several times, from side

to side, then stop suddenly, and open my eyes wide to look in his. *Test, test, test.* 'Have you found anything about Frederick Veliko?'

'There's something I want to double-check. Give me a bit more time.'

'You can't get in trouble, can you? Are you searching on the Deep Web? Or is it the Dark Web? I get them confused.'

He laughs. 'I use a VPN.'

'A what?'

'A virtual private network. No risk of trouble.'

Push, push, push. 'That's good. But how do you know how to do this stuff, George?'

'Practice.'

Even drunk, I can't help myself. 'Isn't it unusual to be able to find that sort of thing? I mean, stuff that normal people can't?'

'They could if they took the time to figure it out.'

'Hmm,' I say. 'You have very nice eyes, you know.'

'What?'

'You heard me. A friend of mine says men always do that.'

'Do what?'

'Pretend not to hear when you give them a compliment, so you have to repeat it. She says a man can never hear a compliment too many times.'

'Very wise. What friend is this?'

I want to say Milly's name, in the way that unfaithful wives want to drop the names of their lovers into the conversation, despite knowing it is dangerous. Instead, I go onto my tiptoes and kiss George, quickly and lightly, then fall back on my heels, wobbling. He is so tall, I realise, compared to Zac. He must be 1.9 metres.

He steadies me. 'As distraction tactics go, that was – excellent. So effective I can't remember what it was I asked you.'

He holds out his hand again, and I take it as we descend steps to the lower path that skirts more closely along the black cord of river. To our right is the water, dotted with narrow boats. To our left is the sloping wall of rock. Above that wall, and parallel to us, is the higher path we were on a minute ago, studded with benches. Beyond that is grass, then a brick wall fronted with trees.

The weir soon becomes a distant hum. The air is steamy, by this quieter water, and warmer than it was during the day.

George aims us towards a stubby bollard and invites me to sit down on it as if it were a throne.

I burst out laughing.

He kneels beside me. 'It's good to see you laugh. There's something so sad, sometimes, that comes over you. Seeing you light up . . . I could spend a lot of time trying to do that.'

'Oh. That might be nice.'

He clears his throat. 'When you phoned me tonight, why did you block your number?'

'Did I do that?'

'You know you did.'

'Can't you use your mega-Deep Dark Web skills to find it?'

'Let's say I could . . . doesn't mean I should.'

'I like that answer.'

'Tell me something important about yourself.' He looks so earnest.

'My parents are both dead.'

'I'm very sorry to hear that. But extremely glad that you've finally told me something meaningful.'

I am imagining how George would look naked, realising I haven't imagined this about any man since Zac.

George tips his head to the side, resting it on mine, and we watch the water. It is so peaceful. There is a whoosh from the path above us. Almost in the same instant, there is a thump, then a splash. George's head jerks forward, and his body follows after. It is all so fast I only just manage to stop him from smashing forehead-first onto the concrete. My wrist is practically dislocated, my own body slams sideways off the bollard, and I land half on top of him.

'George?'

He is terrifyingly silent.

I get him onto his left side, in the recovery position, then stand. I am no longer tipsy, as I look above the rocky slope. A dark figure is rushing across the grass and into the shadows, climbing one of the trees that grows beside the brick wall, then vaulting over the top and into the fields on the other side. I will never catch him. And whatever he threw at George has sunk into the water.

I lower myself beside George. His body is limp. My bag has fallen to the ground. I strain to reach for it without moving him, grapple for my phone, and dial 999 just as his lids begin to flutter, his eyes open, and he is sick in my lap.

* * *

While George is having a CT scan, the A&E doctor fires questions at me about what happened, how long he was unconscious, how many times he vomited, how hard the blow to the head was.

A&E is filled with police officers, parading up and down with drunken brawlers who need checks before they are thrown into the cells for the night. Two officers manage to escape their escort duties to take a written statement from me in an empty examination room, and I am subjected to another quick-fire session of questions and answers.

Did I see the person who did it? *From behind, as they ran away.*

Any idea of the height? *About 1.8 metres, maybe a centimetre or two more.*

Male or female? *Male.*

How certain are you of this? *99.9 per cent.*

Had I any sense that we were being followed? *None.*

At this one, I blush at myself for my own failure. I'd been so distracted by George, and hazy with wine, I hadn't been looking.

I try to remember the sequence of events. George tipped his head sideways, over mine, and we'd been still for a moment or two before the impact. The point is that they waited until we stopped moving before they threw, so I'm pretty sure George was the target, not me.

Milly and I spent our childhood by the sea, skimming stones. James used to tease us that we were good enough for the world championships. Did James guess how much time I spent secretly practising, so I could refine my aim and control the force I used? I'd wanted to impress him.

I understand at first hand the skill of the person who hit George.

Zac played cricket at school and at UCL. He was a bowler. He was very good. The two of us used to have contests on the beach, laughing as we skimmed stones. We always drew.

However many questions I ask myself, I come back to the same answer. It is one word, three letters, and starts with a big fat Z.

George is resting on a paper-covered table, in a bay whose blue curtains are drawn at the sides but not the front. In the facing bay, a man with a bloody nose is lying on a gurney. Another hulking police officer is standing beside him. There is so much in the news about how there aren't enough police officers. Clearly it's because they are all in this hospital. Invisible on the other side of the curtain to George's left, a woman is swearing loudly, and I wonder how long it will be before the police officer across the way goes to look in on her too.

Bits of sick are congealing on George's jumper. He puts his hand, lightly, to the back of his head, near the top, and winces. 'I seem to have grown an egg here.'

'I heard them telling you your CT scan looks good. No sign of brain injury so far.' He is so pale. I continue to count the ways he has passed his medical tests. 'You seem to be good in your verbal responses and physical movements.'

'I like to think I excel in those areas.'

'The doctor doesn't want you alone for the next twenty-four hours.'

'You mean to make sure fluid doesn't start streaming out of my nose and ears? It does that most days.'

'That's not funny.'

'Are you trying to invite yourself over, Helen?'

'Unless you'd rather call someone else to babysit you, I suppose I am.'

Bath, Sunday, 7 April 2019

When I open my eyes the next morning, I don't recognise the white T-shirt I'm wearing, or understand why I am lying on top of a strange quilt, covered by a velvety throw.

There is a wooden stool, draped with my skirt and sweater. The sight makes me remember sponging George's sick from my clothes, and where I got the T-shirt. I'd taken it from his chest of drawers under his direction. Now I know where I am, and why I am here.

As carefully as I can, I turn and face the middle of the bed. The curtains are open, and George looks ghostly in the pre-dawn light. His eyes are closed, his legs are beneath the quilt, and the rim of his boxer shorts is visible just above it. His stomach is exposed, and I can't help but think it is beautiful, though worryingly statue-like, so that the resemblance to Michelangelo's *David* isn't entirely a good thing. I wonder so intensely about how it would feel to trail my fingers and lips from the centre of his chest to his belly button that I picture myself doing it.

But I don't. Instead, I hitch myself up, pull my hair

out of the way and hover an ear over his heart to listen. He is definitely breathing. It is there, soft but even, the rhythm of someone deeply asleep. To the best of my judgement, it is the kind of sleep-breathing that is hard to fake.

I slip off the bed and step onto the cold wood, sweeping my clothes from the chair and my shoes and bag from the floor as I move. The door gives a small creak as I open it, but George doesn't stir. I wince when it creaks again as I close it behind me and enter the sitting room.

I look around me as I dress. Given my impromptu invitation to the pub, and the unplanned blow to the head, George clearly didn't have time to prepare for a guest. The utter mess in this flat is endearing, compared to Zac's hyper-ordered ways.

The sitting room sofa is covered in a mix of discarded coats, carrier bags that haven't been unpacked, and two laptops, both closed. The floor is a gauntlet of books, piled so high any of them could tip at a puff of air. If one of these books is a fake shell for storing things, finding it would be as easy as locating a specific grain of sand on an endless beach. I step carefully between the piles, in dread of the crash that would come if one were to topple.

My ever-persistent secret voice is saying, *Stop it, Holly. You like him. He's searching the Deep Dark Web for you with his VPN. Even if you are suspicious of his ability to do this, not every man is a Zac.* But a louder secret voice is saying, *Then he has nothing to worry about. It doesn't hurt to be cautious. And you've learned the danger of not being.*

I examine the spines of some of the books. Dickens . . . Hardy . . . the Brontës. Is it a coincidence that George has so many of my favourites? Mixed in among these are odd volumes in other languages. I pick out French, Italian, Spanish, German, Chinese, and Russian. The last two make me even more certain that this man is no ordinary computer geek.

I don't have any equipment with me, but I have a basic app on my phone for detecting hidden cameras. I aim it at the most obvious places – television, computer, light fixtures, the thermostat knob, a wall clock, even the pens scattered across his desk and the car-lock remote mixed up in them. Nothing pings the sweeper app, but if George is British intelligence, his surveillance tools are likely to be immune to any detector of mine.

I am growing more certain that George's presence in my life is not an accident. What was his job title, again? Something like Information Systems Security Officer. People with his kind of expertise don't fall out of the sky. But he isn't behaving as someone from the Security Service normally would. I may be his target, but his interest in me seems real. And that isn't how it's supposed to work. What's more, if I am his target, why?

There is a desk, facing another paned Georgian window, and a third laptop, this one large and open, the screen dead. The desk is heaped with papers. George's office chair is the only clear surface, so I sit down, my back to the room in the pose of a relaxed innocent who doesn't worry about who is coming. In any case, I can already hear him approach.

He slowly spins the chair to face him, kneels in front

of me, and says good morning. 'Sorry about the mess.'

'What mess?'

He puts his hands around my waist. 'Is this okay?'

'Yes.'

'You only have to say if it isn't.'

My hand floats to his back. 'I'm glad you survived the night. How are you feeling?'

He touches his hair, winces. 'Like I've been hit on the head.'

'Very funny.' I put the tips of my fingers to his cheek, thinking again about how I'd imagined trailing them down the centre of his stomach.

'That tickles.'

'Sorry.' I take my hand away.

He puts it back. 'Don't be. I like it.'

'Will you be okay for work tomorrow?' I touch his blond hair. It is soft, despite its thickness, and surprising after Zac's smooth scalp.

'No worse than a bad hangover.'

'Who is it you work for, again?'

He looks me straight in the eye and repeats the dutiful lie he fed me on Wednesday morning. 'The civil service.'

'Hmmm. Isn't that a cliché of a cover job, George?'

He squints. 'I don't know what you mean.'

'What does an Information Systems Security Officer do?'

'Impressive for you to remember that mouthful.' He turns my hand over in his and studies my palm as if he is about to tell my fortune. 'Boring stuff. Business analysis.'

'Business analysis?'

'You should have been called Echo instead of Helen.' He brings my hand to his mouth, presses a kiss on it, and I can feel that my heart is beating faster.

'So what does that mean? Business analysis?'

His pupils have grown huge and startling, leaving a narrow rim of bright blue. 'Another of my job titles is Solutions Consultant, if that helps?'

I am leaning closer towards him, so my chest is against his. 'What solutions do you offer? Do your employers consult you on the mysteries of the nineteenth-century novel, knowing that your ability to speak multiple languages and penetrate the Deep Web will give you an edge on those pesky Victorians?'

His answer is a kiss. 'Is that okay?'

'Very okay. Which of those job titles is the true one?'

'All of them. Are you a trained interrogator?'

'How many languages do you speak, George? I found books in six so far, but I haven't examined them all.'

This elicits a modest mumble of syllables with no meaning, followed by an it's-nothing, best-not-to-mention-it shrug.

'Is it six?'

He gives me another modest shrug.

'Ah. More than six.' Lightly, I try that experiment I'd fantasised earlier, or at least part of it. I slip a hand beneath the T-shirt he put on before emerging from the bedroom and run my index finger from the centre of his chest and down, stopping above his belly button.

He inhales. 'Maybe a few more than six.'

His persona of self-effacing guilelessness and charm is one of the best I've seen, but if I had a shred of doubt that he has been targeting me, it is now gone. 'Are you a spy, George?'

He turns red.

'Are you spying on me?' I withdraw my hand from the inside of his T-shirt. 'I think you may need a refresher course on controlling your physical stress responses.'

'Only around you.' He circles my wrist, wanting to keep my hand near.

I break his grip, and it is like resisting a magnet. 'Is that an admission?'

'Helen . . .'

'Tell me the truth. If any of this is real – if you actually do like me – you need to tell me the truth.'

'It's complicated.'

'You might also consider reviewing your evasion techniques.' I stand and grab my bag. My heart is pounding – there is no denying my attraction to him, but also my fear, and anger, too.

'Don't go.'

'Your death isn't imminent and I need to leave.' I move towards the door.

He shuffles back and forth on his heels. 'I want to keep seeing you.'

'Only because of the role.'

He looks down, so his hair flops over his brow. 'That's not the reason,' he says to the floor.

'So you admit what you are?'

'Helen . . .'

'Admit it.'

'I can't . . .'

'Admit it now. Last chance.'

'Please . . .'

'None of this is real, and you know it.' I blink away tears. 'Not even my name.'

I am clear about why I am so furious. It is because he is habituated to lying, even when his cover has been broken. The intelligence officer in him – even if it is a force for good – will always trump everything else. It has become a part of his DNA, so that it is impossible to disentangle the role from any true feelings he may have. That line of Maxine's is too blurry to see – you can't even tell when you're crossing it.

I shake my head so wildly my hair flies and slaps me in the face. 'I'm done with men who spy on me. And lie about it.' I open the door and walk through it without looking back.

Then April Fool

Two years earlier

Cornwall, 1 April 2017

Eight days after I met Maxine in the park, two things appeared in the canister in the gorse. Both were the very opposite of what I'd hoped to find.

The first thing was a typed report outlining what the hotel's CCTV revealed. It was the first classified document Maxine had ever shared with me, the sort of thing I used to dream about being trusted with, but it left me feeling sick rather than triumphant.

Upon entering the hotel, the pregnant woman went straight into the bar. She arrived at the same time as Zac, and they were then escorted to a table. They kissed on the cheek when they greeted each other and when they parted. No other physical contact between them was observed. Their hands were visible at all times during these interactions. Informant A – me, presumably – came briefly into the frame. The woman exited the bar and hotel directly, after spending one hour and fifty-five minutes with Zac. She didn't stop or touch anything on her way in or out, and was not deemed to be a person of interest.

After the woman left the hotel, Zac walked through the lobby. There, he bumped into an unidentified man in what had a high probability of being a brush pass, though this was clumsily executed by Zac, who appeared not to be experienced at tradecraft. They were not able to trace or identify this man, and the facial recognition software did not produce a match. The possibility that the man had used heavy make-up could not be discounted. After a brief visit to his room at 9 p.m., Zac ate dinner alone in the hotel's Michelin-starred restaurant, looking at his phone and reading a book before returning to the room shortly before 2 a.m. He didn't leave the hotel at all that evening.

I considered the fact that Zac had lied to me about how long he spent in the bar with the woman. He said an hour, but the CCTV said it was twice that. The report juddered in my hand, because I was trembling at the hard evidence that Zac had given someone that micro SD card, probably with his home-made pornography on it.

The second thing in the canister resembled a micro memory stick. It was wrapped in a note from Maxine that she'd secured with an ordinary elastic band. *Plug this portable drive into his laptop for half an hour. It needn't be turned on. V important. Do it ASAP. M.*

Absolutely no word about getting me out of there. I shook my head in a kind of fury as I tore up the report and Maxine's note, then dropped them into the sea. I'd hoped to find preparations for my escape in the canister, rather than Maxine's never-ending to-do list. I sucked at being a spy, and I hated it. It wasn't lost on me that the thing I'd always wanted to do and be had become a burden, even in this diminished version that had somehow swallowed me up and seemed ready to spit me out in small and bloody pieces.

Zac phoned to say he was going to have a drink with Omar after work tonight, and he would be late because Omar's wife was not pregnant and Omar was feeling extremely low. This presented me with an unexpected opportunity, so I decided to spend some time in the garden, a place where I wouldn't be filmed or recorded.

I made myself comfortable on a white-painted iron chair, putting a cushion down before I sat and trying not to be sidetracked by the curses against Maxine that had been going round and round in my head since opening the canister that morning.

The new moon was barely visible in the early evening light. I wanted to follow up on a detail that had been prickling at me since I read the newspaper article in the British Library, though I was prepared to abandon my plan if Zac made one of his surprise early returns. In my lap was a burner phone which I would stash beneath a nearby rose bush if I heard his car.

My first step was to phone the Blackwater Hotel – with my own number blocked, of course. I asked to speak to the manager, Mr Murphy, but the receptionist told me he'd since left. That was welcome news, though I'd known there was a good chance of it, given how many years had passed since Zac and Jane's visit to Ireland. She connected me instead to the new manager, Mr Byrne.

I gushed breathlessly, barely allowing Mr Byrne to cut in as I explained that our stay back in 2013 had been spoiled by an assault on the woman in the room next door. I wove

237

in every detail that wasn't in the public domain. Zac and Jane's names, the date of the incident on 5 April, the fact that my husband and I had alerted the police ourselves and gone to Mrs Hunter's aid. I told him that Mr Murphy had promised us two free nights at the hotel to compensate for the upset and inconvenience, but that the written confirmation of this had never arrived. Finally, I said I'd had a life-threatening disease the last few years, which was why we hadn't followed it up, but we wanted to plan a new trip to Ireland to celebrate my recovery.

'I'm very sorry about our error, Mrs Hopwell,' Mr Byrne said, 'and especially sorry to hear about your trials, but I'm glad to know you are looking forward to better times.'

Hopwell. I scribbled the name.

He continued. 'I have our incident log open for the fifth and sixth of April 2013, and I can see Mr Murphy's detailed notes of what occurred. You will remember, I'm sure, that you weren't charged for your stay, in light of the sad incident. Mr Murphy made no remark in the log regarding two additional free nights, but we are happy to honour that. We pride ourselves on our customer care, and we want to ensure you have a stay with us you can enjoy. You were clearly deprived of that the last time by circumstances beyond our control.'

'I appreciate that, Mr Byrne. I wonder – Maybe you don't have our correct address and that's why Mr Murphy's written confirmation never arrived. Can you read back what you have on file, so I can check? We don't want the letter to get lost again.'

'Of course.' He recited an address in Austin, Texas, and I jotted it down nearly as fast as he spoke, hoping that my

English accent hadn't set off any alarm bells. But I reassured myself that it wasn't unheard of for people to move countries.

'That's right,' I said. 'Can you also confirm that you've got the right spelling of Hopwell, and our full names?'

'Norman and Belinda Hopwell. H-O-P-W-E-L-L.'

'Perfect.' I felt like the Wolf tricking Little Red Riding Hood – the version where she fell into every trap he laid and didn't get rescued. 'Can you read back our phone number too, just to be extra-safe that you have everything exactly right?'

'Good idea.'

I scribbled that down as well. He apologised once more for what happened, and I promised to keep his letter in a safe place once it arrived, and make our reservation early next year.

The instant Mr Byrne and I disconnected, I phoned the number he read out to me.

A woman answered.

'Is this Mrs Belinda Hopwell?'

'Yes.' She drew out the word in a way that I found charming. It was a proper Texas accent. I nearly sighed with relief that it was her, and the number was still current.

'I'm Sergeant Lynch, from the Garda.' I was doing the best I could to sound Irish. I'd never have fooled someone who genuinely was.

'Garda?'

'The police in Ireland.'

'Oh yes. I love Ireland. How can I help?'

'I'm closing some old cases.' I reached for the whiteboard I'd written her name and number on. Peggy had given it to me for kitchen notes, and it normally lived on the fridge with the wipe-able pen that came with it, stuck there by magnets. Zac hated that whiteboard. His revenge, which did often make me laugh, was to use it to leave me messages about what he wanted to do in bed. 'I need to double-check a few details you and your husband provided us in April, 2013. If that's okay?'

'My husband's gone to Jesus.'

'I'm sorry to hear that, Mrs Hopwell.' I picked up the erasable pen, holding it like a cigarette.

'I miss him every day.'

'It must be very difficult.' I drew a simple circle with dots for eyes and a frown.

'It is, but he's in a better place.'

I drew a daisy beside her name. 'I wanted to talk about your stay at the Blackwater Hotel in County Cork. You may remember. A woman was assaulted.'

'That poor girl. We were horrified.' I heard the clink of what sounded like ice in a glass. 'You don't mind if I take some refreshment while we speak?'

'Please do.'

'We did everything we could.' I could hear the tinkle of liquid. 'I like my iced tea in the afternoon.'

'Me too,' I said, though I had never even tried iced tea. 'If you're happy to assist, I want to make sure all the details we have on your statement are correct, before we archive the file. Can you remind me of exactly what you saw?'

'As I said when we gave our statement, we were in the room next door. Those walls were thin, for such a nice hotel.' She sniffled.

'I know it must have been upsetting for you. Can you tell me what you heard?'

'A woman, screaming in terror. A man, shouting. His language wasn't Christian. You'll forgive me if I don't repeat it?'

'Perhaps you can paraphrase?' I tapped the pen on the iron table.

'He called her stupid and evil and selfish. He said she'd ruined their lives, and what was she thinking, meeting him.'

'Him?' I sat up straighter. 'Did you hear anything to indicate who this was? A name?'

'Sorry, but no.'

Tap tap tap went the pen, leaving black pinpricks on the whiteboard like a photographic negative of stars in the night.

'We called the police then and there,' she said.

'It could have been much worse if you hadn't alerted us so quickly.' Round and round the pen went, swirling and swirling. What looked like a snail emerged, though I hadn't meant it to.

'Norman went and fetched the hotel manager. I can't recall the man's name.'

'Patrick Murphy.' I was pleased that the letter from the steamer chest had allowed me to use this detail twice in the last hour.

'That was it. Mr Murphy. Well, Mr Murphy used the master key to unlock the door. I could see the woman on the bed, wearing nothing but a slip. The shoulder strap was torn and the man was holding her down. My husband and Mr Murphy went right in there and pulled him off her. She was sobbing. There were red marks on her arms and her mouth was bleeding. Her eye was swollen.'

'Can you describe this couple?' I drew a heart. A tiny gift for Zac.

'Oh yes. She was pretty, even though she was very distressed. Red hair, pale, skinny little thing. The husband was bald, with a strange eye. I can't say he was handsome, but ugly is as ugly does.'

'I find that to be true, in my line of work.' Inside the heart, I sketched two stick figures, a man and a woman in bed together.

'I told the man, I said to him, "You're a monster for taking a hand to your wife. Even if she did meet another man, that's no excuse." Don't you agree?'

'I do.' I pulled a tissue from the pocket of my cardigan.

'The wife wanted her husband out of her sight, so Mr Murphy and Norman marched him out into the corridor. The husband wasn't a large man, but he was strong and angry. It wasn't easy, holding him until the police arrived and took him away. I did my best to comfort his wife while we waited for the ambulance.'

'She must have been glad to have such caring people near her.' I scrubbed away Mrs Hopwell's name.

'I hope so. Does that confirm everything you need for your records?'

'It does, Mrs Hopwell. Thank you. And again, I'm very sorry for your loss.'

I rubbed out her telephone number. The only doodle I left on the whiteboard was Zac's heart, and the stick figures inside it.

It was two in the morning when Zac returned from his drink with Omar. I heard his car engine revving while he parked, the bumper scraping against a bush, then the house door slamming and his grunts as he made his way upstairs. He clearly shouldn't have been driving. He staggered into the bedroom, bringing the reek of whisky with him as soon as he opened the door. He dropped something heavy before he stepped into the room, swore loudly, and let the door slam behind him.

I thought about the fact that it was Milly's birthday, and couldn't help but feel a pang. The first day of April always used to be so happy.

'Holly?' Zac said. 'You awake, Holly?'

I murmured in pretend sleep. In truth, I'd been in a state of high alert since he texted that he'd be home late. I'd even turned off the Internet router in readiness. This was not a trick I could play often, but it was worth risking again that night to ensure the bedroom was a camera-free zone, and I wanted to get Maxine's task out of the way.

He tossed himself onto the bed, shoes and suit still on, as if he had jumped down onto it from a great height. 'Holly? Want you, Holly.' He grabbed my deliberately limp hand, put it between his legs. I let it fall away. I sighed as if I were having a lovely dream.

'Never mind.' This was a slurred ramble. 'In the morning.' More slurred ramble. He kissed me wetly on the lips, then threw himself onto his pillow so heavily the whole bed shook. He squirmed his hand beneath my nightdress and cupped my breast. He was snoring a few seconds later. His arm was a great weight, though thankfully his fingers had lost their grip on my nipple.

As gently as I could, I manoeuvred his hand off my chest and rested his arm straight by his side. I opened my eyes. The moon had cast the faintest light through the filmy curtains, which were patterned in more of the shabby chic florals the owners of the house were mad about. There was a sickly mix of rose and baby powder wafting from Zac's shirt, and I recognised Joanne's overwhelmingly sweet scent. Despite everything, a shock of hurt and jealousy speared through me.

And rage. There was a lot of that, too. In London, he accused me of meeting someone else. In Ireland, according to Mrs Hopwell, he accused Jane. The way he behaved, I wouldn't blame Jane if she'd fucked another man's brains out. In fact, I hoped she had. What I hoped even more was that I could figure out who the man was.

By the bedroom door was Zac's laptop case. It was pretty much always in whatever room he was in. I listened as his snoring deepened. My heart was beating fast, counting time. He was so floppy he couldn't be faking. Could he? Softly, mindful of the fact that my body occupied space differently, I slipped out of bed, wiggled my fingers beneath the mattress on my side, and retrieved the portable drive from where I'd stowed it. This would have been a terrible long-term hiding place, but it was useful for immediate access.

Padding across the carpet as lightly as I could, I swept up the laptop case, glided into the bathroom, turned the knob so it didn't click when I shut the door, then released it with care, all the time listening to Zac snoring away on the other side of the wood. Quickly, I plugged the drive into the laptop without even removing the machine from the case. I let the towel drop from the rail so it draped over the whole of it.

Something new occurred to me. In all of my anxiety about the films Zac made, I hadn't considered the likelihood that his laptop contained scanned copies of my incriminating hospital journal. For others to get access to the secret world that existed in my own head, for Maxine to know that my compulsion to write was bigger than my discretion, for MI5 to learn that I'd broken countless data protection and privacy laws with my stories – all of these things together made me feel faint with panic and humiliation.

There will be no adverse consequences to you from anything we discover as a result of your assistance. That was what Maxine said. I had no choice but to trust that she would protect me, and any other women, from whatever was on Zac's machine.

Twenty minutes had passed since I plugged the memory stick into the laptop. I was still in the bathroom, sitting on the loo even though for once I didn't need it. All I wanted was to drag my six-months-pregnant self back into bed to sleep. The door was halfway open before I could stop it – I hadn't turned the lock because no amount of oil stopped it from making a grinding noise that would have woken Zac. 'I'm peeing, Zac.' I stretched out a leg to try to kick the door closed, but he pushed it open anyway. 'Honestly.' My voice was a high-pitched squeak. 'Get out.'

But he staggered in. Within seconds of my managing to heave myself up, he moved in front of me and lifted the seat. His peeing seemed to go on and on and on, as I stood with my back to the sink, my hands on my bump, feeling a series of rhythmic little punches that I thought might be hiccoughs, as if she had just woken and been shocked into them, fired by the adrenaline that must have been pumping through my veins and into hers. My nightdress was hitched up, falling crookedly, halfway to my thighs. Zac moved towards me, faced me straight on, a hand on each side of the sink, his mouth on mine. 'Want you,' he said.

'Me too.' I let my arms come up until one hand rested on the back of his head, the other on his neck. What I really wanted was to keep his attention on me and not the laptop case on the floor beneath the towel, to the right of his feet.

'You know what they say.' He was still slurring his words.

'What do they say?' I whispered.

'They say sex is better for a woman when she's pregnant.'

I sucked on his lower lip. 'Is that medically evidenced?'

'We can add to the research.' Even drunk, Zac was a germophobe. He stayed where he was, pressing harder against me, or trying to, anyway, with my bump in the way. He turned the taps on, fumbled for the bar of lavender-scented soap he'd bought me, and washed his hands. He was reaching towards the towel rail, flailing when he saw the towel wasn't there, spotting the heap of white cloth on the floor, bending to pick it up.

My bump went rock hard, and though it didn't hurt, though I knew from everything I'd read that it had to be a Braxton Hicks contraction, I couldn't move.

'What the hell?' He suddenly seemed a lot more sober.

I managed to look confused. 'What's wrong?'

'Look.' He pointed at the laptop case and I followed his hand with my eyes.

'Did you bring it in here with you when you got home?' I didn't feel even a tiny pang of guilt at gaslighting him, but I did feel huge amounts of terror at the idea of his examining the laptop and finding the portable drive I'd stuck in it.

'I don't think so.'

I looked him straight in the eye, traced a finger over his lips. 'You must have.' I put my mouth close to his again, inhaled. I marvelled that the technique for distracting him had such a high success rate. Maxine knew this when she kicked me out. She knew it when she ambushed and recruited me later. 'Whisky. You know how sexy I find that, especially when I can't have any myself.'

I started to pull him after me, leading him into the bedroom, and he let me. Few circumstances would make Zac resist sex. His fury in the aftermath of my London disappearance was the one time he ever had. He grabbed the laptop on the way out.

'When you said we could conduct some research. I didn't realise you were talking about the kind you do on that.'

He laughed and put the laptop down by his side of the bed. 'Definitely not.'

Afterwards, all I could think was, please let him go and wash as usual. And he did go. I felt tender towards him for that. Some things about Zac were so predictable.

According to the clock on the night table, thirty-five minutes had passed since I'd installed the portable drive. As soon as Zac was in the bathroom, splashing at the sink with the door half-open, I rolled to his side of the bed, letting my arm hang off so I could unzip the case one-handed, snatch the portable drive out of the laptop, and stuff it under the mattress. When he returned a few seconds later, I whispered, 'It's true, what they say about pregnant women.'

'I could tell.' He pulled my head into the hollow beneath his shoulder. Already, I was sliding into sleep, as if the adrenaline had drained away all at once, leaving me with nothing to keep going. 'That's what I love about you, Holly. You can never hide anything. Your body, your words, your face – they always give you away.'

Now An Ambush

Two years later

Cheltenham, Monday, 8 April 2019

Within minutes of George's blow to the head on Saturday night, I'd made the decision to visit Maxine again. As I walk up the path to her front door, I think some more about George. I think about why I met him on Saturday night, despite the horror of the previous week, and how lonely I've been, and what it was like to kiss him once I got past the flashbacks from two years ago, and how soft his kisses were compared to every kiss I ever had with Zac.

Then I think about the fact that George is no different than the rest of them, targeting me and lying about it, and I can feel my mouth set into a grimace. Not that it matters – given the fact I've blown his cover, he will almost certainly vanish.

I don't park out of sight in my secret-stash car. I leave the Mini I drive everyday smack in front of Maxine's Georgian terraced house. My hair is down. I haven't bothered with the prescription-less spectacles. Nothing says *I am as serious and pissed off as Cat Woman* like black jeans and a black shirt and black ankle boots, and that is exactly what I am wearing. It is 8 a.m. when I knock on the door.

A man opens it, hair wet from the shower, white towel around his hips, his face wanting to twist in irritation but too well-controlled to allow it to. From deep in the house, children are squabbling. There is Maxine's voice, trying to calm things, though her words are too far away for me to make out what she is saying.

The man looks at my hands, as if expecting a parcel delivery, but sees they are empty. 'Yes?'

'I need to speak to your wife.' I am assuming she is his wife. I know I shouldn't assume anything, but the wedding ring I glimpsed last time, the children, everything about this set-up makes me think that she is.

The man is square-jawed, brown-haired, and clean-shaven. A perfect specimen of perfect dismissive politeness. 'That won't be possible.' A child's shriek pierces the air. He doesn't react. He is clearly a man who owns the room chairing board meetings.

'Wait – Please.' He is closing the door as I speak. 'Tell her Jane Miller is here.' The door clicks shut a second after my last word.

I cross my arms, lean against the black iron railings that border the steps to the front door, and sip the coffee I bought at a cafe on the outskirts of the town. I evaluate the paned windows on the house's ground floor. The wooden shutters are drawn in the lower half of each of them, so I can't see in, though the upper halves are open, to let in the light.

Fifteen minutes later, the door opens and the man

steps out, flanked by the boy and girl I saw when I spied on Maxine the last time I was here. He must be doing the nursery drop-off on his way to work. He passes me as if I were a ghost. He looks straight ahead, though unhurried and confident, while the children stare over their shoulders.

'Who is that lady, Daddy?' the little girl says.

'A friend of Mummy's,' he says.

'Then why didn't you let her in?' the little boy says.

Good question, I think, but if the boy's father has an answer to this one, by the time he gives it they are too far away for me to hear.

I sit down on the lowest step to wait it out, the cold concrete seeping through my clothes and into my skin. My phone rings, taking me by surprise. *No Caller ID*. I hesitate, but tap the green circle. 'Hello?'

There is only silence, though I can tell someone is at the other end of the line, listening. Those who have the number can be counted on one hand. The care home, my GP's practice, the agency who manage my rented flat, work. Maxine is likely to have the number, too, though I never gave it to her. For an instant, I wonder if it is her, but why would she call when she is on the other side of the door? She will either come out, or she will completely ignore me.

I don't know what makes me say his name. Probably the knowledge that he has caught up with me. Whatever mysterious computations are processing through my brain, I am left with a one-word question. 'Zac?' The line goes dead.

There is a change in the air, and I glance behind me.

'Hello, Holly.' She is wearing beetle-blue cropped leggings and a loose black sweatshirt, and carrying a gym bag. 'There's no point my calling you Helen here, is there, when there is no one around to hear? Unless you'd prefer me to?'

I stand. 'Are you worried I found you? It was easy, in case you were wondering.'

She looks faintly amused, as far as Maxine ever allows herself any visible expression. All at once, I realise she must have wanted me to follow her after she showed me Jane's body. That is why I didn't miss her that day, despite my worry that I was too late.

Does she know I was hiding in the graveyard? And that I saw her talking to Martin? Even if she does, she may not realise that I was able to overhear snatches of their conversation, including Frederick Veliko's name. I certainly won't be telling her now.

'I saw your children this morning. They're beautiful.'

'I'm good with that. You'd only ever protect and help a child.'

I swallow hard. I start to say, 'Don't . . .'

She sighs. I'm not sure I have seen her sigh before. 'Why did you follow me on Tuesday, Holly?'

'Why did you want me to?'

'I wanted you invested in what happened to Jane. But you . . . what were you hoping to achieve? What were your thoughts about that?'

'I wanted to see what you did next. What you were doing for her.'

'I thought as much. By the way, Zac's Missing Persons ad has been removed.'

I stand, not rushing, and cross my arms. 'You know for a fact he's here. You know for a fact he's found me – I just got a silent call from a withheld number that was probably him. You know for a fact he killed Jane. But he's still running around, throwing stones at people's heads.'

'He's a suspect in a murder. I can promise you he's not roaming free, unwatched.'

'Are you telling me he is under surveillance every minute?'

'There was a glitch on Saturday night with the local police.'

'Great.'

'If this is the sum total of what you came to talk about, then I can only say that I've done what I can for you. You know what you need to know to protect yourself, so stay aware. What you did with that blog wasn't smart.' She has her car keys in her hand, and steps past me, on her way out.

I grab her arm, twist her around so fast she nearly loses her balance. 'What?'

'Don't try that again.' A normal person would hiss this. In Maxine's flat register the words are chilling.

'What do you mean about the blog?'

'It's been deleted. Milly will have received an official-seeming message that the domain has expired. I warned you two years ago you couldn't make contact with your old life. Do you think your coded messages to Milly are going to achieve anything other than fucking with her head? Not to mention your own?'

'You had no right.' I feel as if I have lost Milly all over again. 'You're not God.'

'We had every right. It's the deal you made.'

'No I didn't.' I straighten my slumped shoulders. 'I never made any deal with you. Do you know what happened to me at the weekend? The man I was with could have been killed.'

'Is that why you came today? Because of this man? George, isn't it?'

'*Isn't it?*' I practically snort. 'You know it is. Partly that's why I came, yes.'

'I suggest then that you believe exactly what he told you. A man from your gym. A business analyst or solutions consultant.'

I realise George has probably told her that I asked him to search for information about Frederick Veliko. 'Why is he spying on me?'

'Keeping an eye. Protecting. Though it seems you protected him on Saturday night.'

'You reject me from MI5 because you think I'd sleep with someone for the role, but you promote others for doing exactly that.'

'That is never part of any plan. It's not supposed to happen. Not sanctioned.'

I shake my head. 'You've been keeping things from me from the start. Asking me to help you but not giving me enough information to do it.'

'I've given you as much as you need.'

'Why didn't you simply tell me that Jane had been murdered? Why drag me to that house to make me look at her?'

'I needed to impress on you the seriousness of what we are dealing with.'

'Do you think I didn't already know that?'

'Look. It boils down to this. I thought you had a right to know. I thought you were owed that much. *I* owed you that much.'

'Did you know all along she was alive? Even when you first asked me to spy on Zac?'

'It seemed probable. We needed to find her.'

'All that concern about her disappearance, about my being in danger. That was all fake.'

'The concern for you was real.'

'I don't believe you. It never made sense that the Security Service would be so interested in a missing woman. You don't care about an individual case of domestic abuse. Tell me why you're so interested in her. I've asked you this a million times – you never tell me the truth.'

'I could see Zac was hurting you. And I do believe he's dangerous. That's why I got you out. That's why I wanted you to see what happened to Jane.'

'No.' I hold up a hand, as if to ward her off. 'That's why you put me in.'

'You put yourself in.' I notice she hasn't bothered to take off the wedding ring.

'If I'd left sooner . . .' My voice chokes. Two years later, and it still chokes. 'You made me wait.'

'It wasn't—' She stops herself. 'It's possible it would have been different. No use pretending otherwise.' She puts a hand on my arm. Almost no physical contact since we first met six years ago, and now she's tried it twice in a week. 'I wish it had been.'

I jerk away. I think of Eliza's real fear when Zac came

home early. 'Zac may be doing the same thing to his new wife that he did to me.'

'And this matters why?'

'Are you going to protect her?'

'Why would we? She'll be safe from him soon. He isn't likely to be free much longer.'

'What about the little girl? She's the same age – their birthdays are a few days apart. She can't be mine, can she? Can Zac have somehow got my baby away?'

'This is your real reason for coming here today.'

I don't respond.

'Holly.' Maxine's voice is so gentle for a minute I think it isn't her. 'That isn't possible. You know, deep down, that the whole world didn't conspire with Zac to steal your child. Think about it. If it were true, he'd be hiding from you. Putting as many miles between you and that child as he could. He wouldn't be placing missing persons ads and combing newspapers to find you. He wouldn't be chasing you to Bath. He'd have happily believed you were dead.'

I stare at my feet.

'Holly,' Maxine says again in that un-Maxine voice. 'Alice has a mother. She isn't you.'

'She brought Alice to the hospital where I work. Was Zac behind that?'

'Alice has a genetic condition that requires specialist paediatric care. You work in the one place she can get it. I told you that before. It was inevitable you'd meet. If you worked in a Columbian cafe and his wife especially liked South American coffee, you'd have met there.'

255

I squeeze my eyes tightly. 'What about the fact that Jane was having an affair before she left Zac?'

'Who told you that?' Maxine asks this with her usual flatness, the flash of her humanness already so deeply erased you wouldn't think it possible that it ever existed.

I'm in no mood to fill her in about Mrs Hopwell and the telephone calls to Ireland and Texas I made two years ago. 'Tell me who the man was, Maxine.'

'Let me promise you this. I will explore how much more you can be told. That is my best offer for now.'

'Whatever deficiencies I have, you know you can trust me. You know I keep secrets.'

'True and noted. But there is nothing further I can tell you right now.'

'Fine. Then I want to talk to Martin. Tell me where to find him. Give me that much and I'll take it from there.'

'Not possible.'

'Is he in Cheltenham? Are you GCHQ now? Along with George.'

She blinks several times, something I can't remember seeing her do before. 'Martin is still in London.'

I continue to press. 'What department?'

She smiles, as if telling a joke. 'Covert Financial Enquiries.'

'Did Jane commit some kind of financial crime?'

She does her usual trick of pretending not to hear the question, which makes me think the answer is yes. I remember that business card, emblazoned with the words *Albert E. Mathieson, International Tax Law*. Maxine said two years ago that she was following it up. Was she telling me the truth? I ask the question aloud.

'Of course,' she says. 'It was useful.'

'That's vague. In what way was it useful?'

Again this is met with the silence she so often uses when I press her directly.

'Hasn't it got beyond you keeping things from me? You've shown me Jane's body. You took away her privacy and dignity when you did that, when you turned her into a circus after such a horrible death. You intruded me on her. And her on me.'

'It was my call. I stand by it.'

'So why did she turn up where I'm living? Why did she die there?'

'Now you're asking the right questions.' She considers. 'I think I can say that you seem to be the catalyst in all of this. Maybe not the only one, but a key element.'

'You're saying I made someone kill Jane?'

'Of course I'm not saying that. We think Zac found you. And she found him.'

'Well, here is another right question for you, Maxine. Why would she want to?'

Then *The Handkerchief Tree*

Two years earlier

Cornwall, Mid-April 2017

Zac was sitting beneath the handkerchief tree on a white wicker chair, in exactly the place I'd been two weeks earlier when I phoned the Blackwater Hotel and Mrs Hopwell. In his hand was a cup of lapsang souchong. The tea was black and strong, the way he liked it. There was a hardback book on the white iron table. From the cover, I could see it was written by a lawyer who raises asylum claims for whistle-blowers.

Zac was so passionately on the side of those who fought for individual freedoms and stood up to authority, yet so against the people closest to him having any freedom themselves. It occurred to me that such a paradox wasn't unusual. Sometimes when you knew too much about how a thing worked, even if you thought it was wrong in principle, or that it should only be used for a larger good, you still couldn't help trying it yourself. And then it became a habit. Wasn't I guilty of this too?

Beside the book was a laptop, a new machine, I noticed, that Zac switched to sleep mode as I kissed him. Propped against the scrolled table leg was a laptop case with built-in combination locks. The case was silver and new, and appeared to be made of some kind of high-security metal. Was he spooked that night two weeks ago, when he found the laptop in the bathroom?

He tipped his head to look at the new green leaves fluttering above him. 'We have another month before it flowers. I know you can't wait.'

'True.' I calculated. I was twenty-six weeks pregnant. In one month I would be thirty weeks. In one month I would be gone. One month seemed forever, but Maxine insisted it wasn't, like a mother telling a child, *Be patient, the journey will be over before you know it*. In the meantime, I had my own part to play in preparing for my escape. This mostly meant trying to keep things as calm with Zac as I possibly could.

I wrinkled my nose. 'Stinky tea?' It was an old tease between me and Zac that I hated the smell of lapsang. I was using my *I'm trying to be brave against all odds* voice.

He put the mug down, stood, folded me into his arms, whispered into my hair, 'What is it? What's wrong?'

My mobile was a prop, held by a hand that was seemingly too distracted to realise it was there. It wasn't difficult to make myself cry. The pregnancy hormones helped with that.

Zac's face was frozen in horror. 'Is it the baby?'

For him to believe I was distressed hurt him. The realisation came with a stab of guilt that made me dizzy. It should have occurred to me he would think that. It seemed too terrible a thing to do to him, despite everything.

Still, I pushed myself on. I let the phone fall from my hand onto the daisy-covered grass. 'It's my grandmother. The care

259

home just called.' Saying this made the fake tears flow harder, because I knew there would come a day when this would happen for real.

Zac did exactly what I knew he would. He picked up the phone, accidentally twisting out a dandelion as he lifted it. He checked the recent call log, saw that the care home had in fact called me a few minutes ago, and the duration was five minutes. Maxine was behind the call.

'What did they want?'

'She passed away early this morning. In her sleep.'

'Died, not passed away.' He corrected me in exactly the way I expected.

I accepted his correction. 'She died this morning.' Thanks to Maxine, my grandmother had already vacated the building. I felt a twinge that the lovely women who looked after her had been told this lie, too.

The small exchange was part of a private game I secretly played. I had a toy as a child. Because it was from my parents, I kept that toy long after I outgrew it. It was a large plastic ball covered in coloured shapes. The shapes were buttons. If you pushed the orange triangle, there would be a squeak. If you pushed the green square, it would sound a bell. The blue oval resulted in a moo.

Zac had buttons too, and I needed to push them sometimes, to check that the consequence was as predicted. It was like tossing a coin into the air to make sure that gravity still worked – the basic material conditions of the universe that I shared with Zac remained the same, and I must not doubt this. I must not doubt myself.

'I'm sorry about your grandmother, Holly.' Zac turned me around, gently sat me down in the other wicker chair, pulled his own up close, with his legs splayed partly open and mine between them, so the insides of his thighs were against the outsides of mine.

'She'll never meet her great granddaughter. Everyone in my family is gone.'

Under the eaves, something caught my eye. A flash of blue-black, and the red forehead and throat. It was a swallow, leaving its nest. 'Look, Zac. Quick. Do you see it?' I pointed. 'It must have just arrived. The first. Something beautiful, on such a sad day.'

'Their droppings are a health hazard. It's dangerous for you and the baby. We should destroy any nests.'

'I'm hardly going to lick the droppings. Anyway, they're protected – you can't destroy a swallow's nest.'

'Don't change the subject, Holly. You're always doing that. You don't like it when I get grumpy but no matter how many times I tell you . . .'

'Sorry,' I said, having pushed the purple *Change the Subject* rectangle and satisfied myself that Zac's response was what I anticipated. I would keep testing, to make sure I was being fair.

'I can see what a strain this puts you under.' My phone was still in his hand. He scrolled through my text messages. '"Your order has been delivered. Thank you for your business."' He smiled, playing at indulgence. 'More shopping?'

I had known since that text arrived that he would find an excuse to question me about it. The shape was a red octagon, and I called it the *Check the Phone Log* button.

'Oh. That must be the towels for the baby. I think you were at the hospital when they came.' The message was another of Maxine's; she'd used a spoof parcel service to confirm the portable drive had been retrieved from the canister in the gorse.

Whenever I thought of that drive, and the micro SD card, I shook with rage. So I tried to push the thought away. Rage was what I couldn't afford to show and therefore couldn't let myself feel.

'You shouldn't be alone at a time like this. I can cancel my trip.'

Zac was about to depart for a medical conference in Toronto. He would be away for a week, and this made my one-month countdown until departure day more bearable. Looked at this way, I had three weeks to get through with him – not four.

'You've been talking about this conference for a month. I couldn't let you do that.' I pressed my lips against his. 'You taste all smoky.'

'You hate it.'

'Not on you.' I straightened his wire-rimmed glasses. 'Will you see your parents?'

'Vancouver's a four-hour flight in the wrong direction. So no. Not that I'd want to, even if it were five minutes away. What I do want is to be here with you.'

'Me too you.' Compliance was so difficult, even when it was faked. And fake compliance was dangerous, because it could feel so real I was no longer sure of the difference. I sniffled, took the napkin Zac brought out from beneath his mug, wiped my eyes, blew my nose. 'One week isn't long. But I'll miss you so much.'

His face visibly relaxed. 'Next time I'll take you with me.'

'How about New York? I'd love that. I've never been to America.' I was thinking of Mrs Hopwell, and how sweet she seemed, despite the horrible circumstances of that call and the grief she'd suffered.

He scrunched his nose as if there were a bad smell. 'Think of another country. Somewhere special for the three of us.' He moved his chair so he could bend forward and press the side of his head to my bump. He sang a bit of Brahms' Lullaby.

I laughed. 'She liked that.'

'We need to concentrate on the good things.'

I cupped a hand over his ear. 'Absolutely.'

An hour later, he left for the airport, his shiny new laptop and his suitcase squeezed on the front passenger seat. I walked with the car as he slowly reversed out of the drive, then I stood in the road, in the shade of a magnolia tree that was exploding with its creamy goblet flowers. I put a hand to my mouth to blow him a goodbye kiss, waiting until the car curved round a bend and I lost sight of him before I returned to the house. I did not doubt that objects still fell when I threw them.

I had seen Zac's name listed as a speaker for several of the sessions at the medical conference – I'd checked online in the library. Nonetheless, each day at noon UK time, which was 7 a.m. Toronto time, I used our landline to ring Zac at his hotel to say good morning. I had promised to act as his daily wake-up call. When he picked up his room telephone I knew he really was in Canada, and probably as glad to have my whereabouts confirmed with the call as I was his.

The time on my own was happy, with walks in the spring sunshine, and coffees and lunches and shopping trips and dinners with Milly, who had taken the week off work. With

Zac safely out of the way, we returned easily to our previous closeness. The distance that had grown between us over the previous few months seemed to be a part of another life.

I made feeble attempts at prenatal yoga, and imagined the baby was laughing at me. Milly certainly did. The two of us watched old Audrey Hepburn films, eating popcorn for dinner and ice cream for dessert straight from the tub. When Milly finally saw the Mermaid of Zennor curtains, with her design repeating across the fabric, she was so touched and surprised she cried.

There was one frustration, and it was this. The owners of the house stipulated that the garage was off limits because they needed it to store their things. They even put a clause in Zac's tenancy agreement to this effect. I wasn't sure if Zac had managed to get in there, but I wanted to look round, just in case.

Each day, as soon as my call with Zac finished, I made a failed bid to break into the garage. My attempts went like this. Step one was to create a gap between the centre top of the door and the trim that framed it. I did this by climbing onto a ladder and inserting a wedge-shaped piece of wood a few centimetres to the right of where I wanted the gap to be. This was surprisingly quick and easy.

Step two was where it invariably went wrong. I retrieved a long coat hanger made of thick wire, which I'd bent into a hook at one end and a handle at the other. I poked this rod through the gap and began fishing. What I wanted to catch was the pull rope that dangled inside. But I never did. After trying and trying, imagining the hook flailing aimlessly on the other side, I had to admit defeat once more.

On the seventh and final day of Zac's absence I was twenty-seven-weeks pregnant and ready to try one last time with the garage. I thought about the fisherman who spent so long hunting a legendary beast he began to doubt it even existed, and that was when I finally hooked the pull rope.

I hardly drew breath as I slid the hook down the rope until it hit the knob at the rope's end. Sweat dripped into my eyes but I didn't dare break my grip to wipe it away. I climbed off the ladder, careful not to disturb the hanger's position as I moved, then tugged it straight down. To my amazement, I could feel the lock release. I stepped aside, grabbed the handle, and shouted the word 'Yeah!' as the door lifted. I jumped up and down in triumph, forgetting for a second about my bump, then whispered, 'Sorry, little baby.'

I left the garage door open to let in the April sunshine as I checked for cameras. I kept it open even after I discovered there were none. I needed light and air. I didn't want that dark space to close in on me as I circled round it, taking a mental inventory of what was inside. Paint tins. A wooden work bench and tools. The carcasses of dead flies sprinkled across surfaces. If he had ever been in there, Zac would have shuddered at the dirt. In fact, that was exactly why this would be his perfect hiding place – anybody who knew him would discount it.

I lifted dust covers to see what was beneath them, tensing like a child who was frightened she would find a monster hiding inside, or a body. But all I found was an old bookcase with the wood splitting along one of the shelves, and an upholstered chair, covered in the obligatory ditsy fabric, with stuffing spilling out of the seat cushion.

There was nothing in there that could possibly belong to Zac. I rested my hands on the small of my back, tipped my head to stretch my neck, and closed my eyes. When I opened them, they were trained on a square shelf that hung from the centre of the garage ceiling, suspended by four short chains that were attached to each corner.

I grabbed the step ladder. A minute later I was examining the contents of the shelf, thankful the garage ceiling wasn't high. It looked as if the owners had used the shelf to store their linens, which were packaged in clear plastic bags. I manoeuvred one sideways, to check if there was anything behind it.

At first, I was uncertain of what I was seeing, not comprehending what it was about the bag that made it seem familiar. It was the size of an extra-fat laptop case, and made of tan canvas that was trimmed with tan fake leather. My heart started to beat faster as I realised that this was a companion piece to Zac's old suitcase set.

I set my feet more firmly on the ladder's rung and pulled the bag towards me. It was heavier than I expected. The safest way I could think to get the bag down was to let it fall to the ground. Hoping nothing inside was breakable, I moved the bag as far to my right as I could, so it wouldn't knock the ladder on descent, and tipped it over the edge.

The bag smacked the concrete floor with an explosion of dust as my stomach dropped and the ladder gave a great shake. I grabbed the shelf, which rocked on its chains but stopped me from falling. Still trembling, I climbed down, trying to catch my breath. I stood there, my back slick with the sweat of panic, then scolded myself for being pathetic and made myself move again.

I dragged the bag outside by the strap, onto the grass, and lowered myself beside it to inspect the contents. Before I did, I wiped my hands on my faded maternity jeans. When I looked down at myself, I saw that the pintucks covering the chest of my floaty white blouse were splodged with dirt, and my bare arms were streaked with it too.

The zipper went round one of the bag's sides like a horse-shoe. I lifted the flap of tan canvas and felt as if a pair of hands had grabbed my throat. I was looking at the cover of a magazine. Beneath it were a dozen more. They were from the 1990s. Photographs of women. The things that were being done to them, the marks on their skin and expressions on their faces, the poses. I started to cry, and quickly turned the magazines upside down, their covers facing the grass. Could Zac really want to look at this? Want to do this? All of the bad I ever imagined of him never conjured anything close.

There was one magazine in the pile that didn't make me physically sick, which had somehow got mixed in. A special issue of a political magazine from June 2013 with a photograph of Edward Snowden on the front. The odd one out didn't surprise me, given how interested Zac was in surveillance culture and data theft and the threat to individual privacy that algorithms posed.

It took me several minutes before I was calm enough to continue examining the bag's contents. At the bottom was a black cloth, folded into a parcel, with lumps and bumps inside. I unwrapped the cloth and let the things inside it roll onto the grass. A blindfold, a gag, and several coils of rope that seemed to come right out of the world of those maga-zines. They were not the flimsy toys of a high street lingerie

267

shop. I rested my mouth and nose against my fist. Could he have used them on Jane? I shook my head, no. He wasn't stupid – he wouldn't keep the evidence, however well-hidden, if he had done something terrible with it.

Still, I needed to send those things to Maxine for testing. I calculated the risk of Zac discovering they were missing before I'd got away. It was small. In three weeks I'd be gone. Three weeks was soon. I could get through three little weeks. People did much harder things than that.

I stuffed the magazines and other things in Zac's old bag, trying not to look at them as I did. I couldn't possibly lift the bag onto that shelf. The risk to me and the baby was too great. Instead, I dragged it to our recycling bin, which was due to be collected tomorrow, wrestled it in, and covered it with old newspapers. I'd get a message to Maxine that the bag was there and trust her to take care of it.

I triple-checked that everything was in its place in the garage, then closed the door. Maybe, I thought, despite the seriousness of the objects, they were from a phase when Zac was into that, and he put them away because he knew that I was not. But I also knew how interested he was in pornography, with his secret films. Those magazines were on that same spectrum, but more extreme than anything I'd imagined.

I was so absorbed in puzzling all this out that I didn't hear the rumble of the car's engine until it was nearly at the end of the long drive to the house. Though I'd phoned Zac in Canada only two hours earlier, I still thought of the young wife in 'Bluebeard', terrified that her husband would come for her with his knife before her brothers reached her. What I saw was Milly, her face lit and smiling, so that despite everything, I could feel my own face lighting up too.

Now The Doors With No Knobs

Two years later

London, Monday, 8 April 2019

I'm back from Cheltenham by 11 a.m. but I don't go into my flat. I leave the car on my street and walk quickly to the station. Forty-five minutes later, I am sitting on the train to London, trying to make myself relax in the hope that if I do then the identity of the man Jane met will come to me. I close my eyes, but open them with a jerk when my telephone vibrates.

It is the hospital's number, so it will almost certainly be Trudy on the other end of the line. She pretty much runs Paediatric Outpatients. I nearly ignore the call, given that the train is ten minutes outside of Paddington and I have slept nearly the entire journey away, but something makes me answer.

Trudy launches straight in. 'Sorry to bother you – I know you've taken today as sick-leave – Are you feeling better? – I hope you're resting. Is that – Is someone on a loudspeaker? – Are you on a train, Helen?'

'I'm on my way to a clinic in Wimpole Street. Trying

some stuff to boost my immune system. I get too many colds.' The lies come easily.

'Really,' Trudy says, meaning, Do you *really* think I'm an idiot? 'Will you be in work tomorrow?' She is asking this despite knowing very well that I don't work on Tuesdays.

'I don't work on Tuesdays,' I say, with extra sweetness.

'Wednesday, then?'

'If I'm better. Sorry, Trudy – my train's about to pull in.'

Trudy gets to the point. 'You know that little girl with Waardenburg syndrome, Alice Wilmot . . .'

My heart is thumping. 'Yes.'

'Her mum's trying to reach you. She sounded pretty upset.'

'Oh.' I inhale. 'Did she say what was wrong?'

'Only that she's having some sort of family emergency. Not the child, the mother. I explained I couldn't give her your number, but I promised to pass the message on.'

The metal cylinder of the tube train is shaking me and shaking me and shaking me some more as it hurtles along beneath London. There is a pleasure in giving myself over to its rhythms, my neck loose, my head jerking from side to side, as if I am hypnotised, for once abandoning control and not fighting, not stiffening myself against these external forces.

The hot, burnt-smelling wind of the tunnels slaps me in the face and chases me up the escalators, though it seems to be under a spell that traps it within the station's boundaries. It cannot pursue me when I emerge into still air and bright sunshine, blinking, my eyes watering.

I walk along the river, dazzled, and clasp my hands to my ears like a child as plane after plane screams above me, the river their flight path. The London Eye glints a mile away, on the opposite side, its pods revolving so slowly I cannot see them move.

At the start of the next two-minute lull between the planes, I unblock my number before putting my phone to my ear. The blood is pounding in my head while I wait for Eliza to answer. She doesn't. It goes to voicemail.

'Hello, Eliza,' I say. 'It's Helen. Trudy passed on your message. I hope you and Alice are okay. I'm glad you got in touch.' I give her my number before adding, 'I can't believe you don't have it – I'm so sorry about that. I'm about to go into an appointment, so I'll have to turn my phone off for a while, but I'll put it on again as soon as I finish. Bye for now.'

The building rises up like an ugly stone fortress, and I aim myself straight at it. I am startled by how unguarded it seems, with no wall to surround it, and how huge it is in reality, the size of a large block.

The main entrance looms before me. Marble steps pass beneath a massive archway that leads to three sets of double doors. I am stumped. Do I dare walk under the archway? Which set of doors do I try? I really haven't thought this through. The place where real spies go, and I am clueless.

Two armed police officers glance in my direction. Meanwhile, the statues of Britannia and St George are looking at me from far above, down their noses. A carved face hangs like a portrait, front and centre of the archway's exterior. The face seems to be watching me too, despite its blindfold, as are a multitude of deliberately visible cameras.

To the right of the archway is another set of double doors. These are more modest than the others. They are brown. They would be brown. Of course they are brown. On both sides of the doors are duplicate plaques. *Visitors Entrance*, they say. *I am an idiot*, I think.

Slowly, I approach. I study the doors, searching for a bell, a door knob, some way to push or pull them open. There is nothing. The doors are a blank, despite their elaborate mouldings and beautiful panelling. I raise my hand and knock three times, as firmly as I can, though I am shaky. My fist on the ornate carving results only in dull thuds.

There is a tap on my shoulder and a voice in my ear. 'Hello there. Can we help you?'

I spin round, and find myself facing the two police officers. 'Hello,' I say.

The young, handsome one smiles so warmly I find it difficult to believe he knows how to use the assault rifle that he is holding across his body with the casual relaxedness of an athlete carrying a tennis racket. 'Do you have a reason for being here?'

'Yes. To see somebody.'

He nods, as if this explains everything. 'You see, they know when you're coming. If they expect you, the door opens.' He and I both stare hopefully at the wood. Nothing happens. 'It's not looking good, is it?'

'I suppose it isn't.'

'Do you have an appointment?'

I shake my head, slightly, as if the diminished quality of the gesture will make it less true.

His partner, who I am already thinking of as Bad Cop because of his glower, rakes a hand across his salt-and-pepper head. The hair is so short I think he must use a mini-strimmer around his cap of baldness. 'Would you like to move on to elsewhere?' Bad Cop says.

No I would not fucking like to move on to elsewhere. 'If I can just explain to someone inside . . .'

'I appreciate that, but you need to move away from the door.' Bad Cop points to the other side of the road.

Good Cop is looking at me with sad concern, the kind of eye-narrowing, head-nodding understanding people show each other at funerals. If he weren't holding a gun he'd be thoughtfully resting his chin on his hand as he nodded.

'You are committing a criminal offence,' Bad Cop says.

I turn to Good Cop, as if he is my only means of rescue. 'How is that even possible?'

'This has been designated a protective site under the Serious Organised Crime and Police Act.' Good Cop must practise his gentle solemnity in front of a looking glass.

'The criminal offence,' says Bad Cop, 'is that you crossed the outer boundary without permission. The boundary includes the pavement you're standing on.'

I never really thought Martin would simply invite me in and then confess all of his official secrets, though I can't pretend I haven't had that fantasy. But my real reason for coming here is more modest than that. To get his attention, to leave a kind of calling card so he knows I am done with being quiet and invisible, and to press them to rethink what they are willing to share with me. It is the same message I gave Maxine earlier today. And George before that. These are not people who welcome noise. And I am no longer a person who can refrain from making it.

'The man I need to see goes by the name of Martin,' I say.

'And you are?' says Bad Cop.

I fumble for an instant, but what I say next comes out strong, because it occurs to me that whatever happens, I am reclaiming myself, reclaiming my own life. My chest loosens a little when I say my real name. 'Holly Lawrence.'

'I'm going to ask you one final time to move elsewhere,' Bad Cop says.

'Come on now.' Good Cop gives me another bright smile. 'We wouldn't want to have to arrest you.'

I look at the black lamp, high up and to the side of the door. I am in no doubt that it encases a surveillance camera. I make sure my face is in clear view. Up until this point, I have taken care to speak every word as distinctly as I can, certain that whatever I say can be listened to later, if it isn't already being monitored in real time. It occurs to me there is one final thing to get across. 'Martin is in Covert Financial Enquiries.'

'You don't belong here,' says Bad Cop.

'We're going to escort you onto public space,' says Good Cop.

I move away with the two police officers, who keep

me between them. As soon as we round the corner, Good Cop says, 'Goodbye.'

I halt as if a ghost has grabbed hold of me.

'You go on your way then,' Bad Cop says after a few seconds.

But I seem to have run into an invisible wall, and my mind has emptied.

'As I was saying to your good self, you need to be out of this area,' Bad Cop says, clearly thinking that I am not at all good. 'Now,' he says. 'I said to walk on.'

My feet have stopped moving, as if they are telling me they have come so far, and cannot take another step. Somehow, though, as if I am a robot, one foot lifts, and then the other, and I do.

Then *A Misadventure*

One year and eleven months earlier

Cornwall, Early May 2017

It wasn't long before Maxine got a message to me that there were no traces of blood or bodily fluids on the items from Zac's bag, so it was unlikely they'd been used on Jane or on anyone else. Whenever I thought about those magazines, I was overwhelmed with desolation that the things in those photographs had been done. Over a week had passed since I'd seen them, and the images had rooted in the landscape of my nightmares.

I tried not to think about them, and to concentrate instead on good things. One very good thing was that I had reached the magic twenty-eight-weeks mark. All the books said that even if she were to be born at this stage, she had a reasonable chance of being well and healthy, though we'd have to navigate the trauma of premature delivery and the special care baby unit. I tried not to dwell on the exceptions – the babies who were not okay, despite reaching twenty-eight weeks. I clung to the statistics that were on my side and blanked out the ones that were not.

My next milestone was to get to thirty weeks, when we

would disappear. That was two weeks away. We could get through that. Things had been calm since Zac's return from Canada. In fact, he'd been so lovely the last six days that I fleetingly wondered if this new Zac was the real one, rather than the porn-making control freak I'd lived with for the last few months.

But on the seventh day, he left me in no doubt about the true Zac. I was standing at the kitchen sink peeling carrots and he was trying to pull my clothes off.

'I don't feel like it.' The baby swam and rolled, as if to tell me she was in agreement.

'You never feel like it any more. I love you, Holly.' Was he saying this because he sensed how profoundly I had withdrawn from him? I'd tried so hard to disguise it. I'd thought my performance was Oscar winning.

I gave him my most loving, melting look. 'Me too.' What I secretly meant was, I love me too, but not you, and not your magazine collection or your toys and hidden cameras and micro SD cards.

'I need you so much. You're all I have. The two of you.'

My stomach lurched as if I were in a boat being tossed by waves. He turned me around, so my spine was against the edge of the granite counter. I tried to move my lips into the right expression, tried to make my face look warm and happy.

'I have a surprise,' he said.

'What?'

'I made an appointment at the Registry Office. Six weeks from today. It's best for her if we're married before she's born.' He pressed his lips against mine, slipped a ring onto my finger, lifted my hand so we could both look at it. 'What do you think?'

The diamond was square, with a small round stone on each side. 'I think it's perfect.' I slid it up and down, because it felt tight, though it appeared that it was not.

'Just four of us in that room. You, me, the baby, and the registrar. That's how it should be. You agree, don't you?'

It wasn't as if I intended to go through with it, but somehow I heard myself speaking as if I did. 'Don't we need two witnesses? So won't that be six in the room?'

The way his cheeks moved up and his brow moved down was so subtle that even if you knew him well you'd have to look closely to realise his face had tightened. 'I'll take care of the witnesses.' I understood what this meant. He didn't want Peggy and James and Milly at our fantasy wedding. 'So is that a yes?'

I would do nothing to wind him up. Peace was the one thing I wanted, for those last two weeks. 'Yes. A very happy yes.' I kissed my hand, then touched his head with it, surprised to find the faintest trace of a five o'clock shadow on his scalp. He normally shaved it twice a day – the omission must have been a sign that he was under pressure.

My mobile rang. Zac picked it up from the tiled counter where I'd left it. I stepped towards him as he held it up. Milly's name was flashing across the screen, decorated with the flower and heart emojis I'd attached to it. *Calling Milly Pulsating Heart Cherry Blossom*, the phone said aloud, whenever I instructed it to dial her number. 'More like *Milly Stake-Through-the-Heart Bloodflower*,' Zac once said, making me laugh even though I tried not to.

'You don't want to talk to her now,' Zac said.

'Yes I do.' I reached for the phone. 'I can't ignore her. Please, Zac. She's going through a bad time.'

'It's an intrusion.'

'Give me my phone.' His jaw stiffened. I'd blown the *Do not do anything to upset him* rule. 'Please,' I said again.

Slowly, he extended his arm, but with a look that made it clear the subject wasn't closed, that he certainly wasn't going to leave the kitchen so I could talk to her alone, and that if I exited the room he would follow me.

I pressed the green button to accept the call as I lowered myself into a chair. As soon as I did, there was the sound of uncontrollable sobbing. Zac rolled his eyes.

I could hear Milly slapping her head with her own hand, as I begged her to stop, to tell me what was wrong, as I tried not to panic, asking if something had happened to James or Peggy. She managed to get out the word Fergus, and at first I thought Gaston must have died. But between sobs she explained that he had a new girlfriend, and though she'd only now found out, it had been going on for weeks, and he'd been sleeping with both of them, and he still wanted to sleep with Milly but to keep it a secret from the girlfriend, and Milly had finally said no more but she thought her heart was broken forever and please could I come over. That undeserving man, that Gaston, had brought my warrior, my Milly, to this.

As soon as I said, 'I'm on my way,' Zac grabbed the phone and ended the call.

'You can't be serious about leaving now.' His hands were on my shoulders. 'We have something to celebrate. You can't go out when you're this tired. It's after dark. I don't want you driving. You're not just putting yourself in danger, you're putting our baby in danger.'

I had to work hard to make my voice soft and loving,

because every impulse I had was pressing me towards shrill shrieking. 'Pregnant women drive all the time. I'll be fine. I won't be gone for long and we'll celebrate when I get home. We'll celebrate for the rest of our lives. Milly's in crisis. You wouldn't want me to ignore her – don't you love me because I couldn't do that? She's proud, Zac. It was hard for her to ask for help.'

'Think of what happened to your parents.' He released his grip on me and grabbed my bag.

'What are you doing?'

My car keys were in his hand. 'Taking these.'

'You can't.'

'It appears that I can, and I have.'

I was struggling not to stomp to the rage that was coursing through me. Instead, I managed to say, 'Then drive me yourself. I can't not go to her.'

'No.' He was looming over me, making the kitchen seem darker, despite the bright ceiling lights.

'Fine. I'll call a taxi.'

'You won't be able to get out of the house. I've locked the doors.'

'You can't do that.'

'Again, it appears that I can and have.'

'Unlock them. Right this fucking minute.'

'You're not leaving. If you can't act responsibly then it's my job to make you.' He pounded his fist so hard against the fridge he shook his hand in pain. 'See what you made me do? I thought we'd be cracking open the champagne by now.'

I rushed to the front door, then the back, but both were double-locked. I had lost all ability to maintain the charade of loving compliance. I was screaming, my heart was racing, and the blood was in my ears. I ran at Zac. 'Let me out.' I was hitting his chest. 'I can't breathe in here.'

'I knew I couldn't trust you. I've locked us in every night since I got back from Canada.' He was leaning against the fridge, a beer bottle in one hand, the other holding me off.

'Give. Me. My. Keys.'

'You're not going anywhere.'

'Give. Me. My. Phone.'

'No.'

'No wonder Jane left you. The only way you can get a woman to stay with you is to force her.'

He glanced at the kitchen window, which overlooked the driveway, and I saw that he had blocked my car in with his own. 'You're not fit to go out. You're fucking psycho. I'll have you certified before I let you.'

I tore the ring from my finger, hurled it at the floor. 'I'm leaving you. I hate you. You're a monster – you're actually evil. I'm going now. Tonight.'

'You're the one who's evil. What you are doing to our baby, to our family – for you even to consider breaking us apart – that's true evil.'

I launched myself at him again, trying to grab at my keys when he held them out of reach. He thrust me away and I lost my footing, stumbling forward, only partly breaking my fall with my own arms. The front of my stomach smacked so hard against the edge of the marble tabletop I felt as if I had been stabbed. My cry of despair shattered the air, and I clutched my bump.

Zac was kneeling at my feet, his arms around my lower back, and he was crying too, and saying, 'Oh my God, Oh my God, Oh my God. I swore I'd never let anything like this happen again. I'm sorry, I'm sorry, I'm sorry, I'm so sorry. Oh Jane,' he said, not noticing he had called me by her name, 'I am so sorry.'

I didn't forget about Milly. Even in my absolute stricken hysteria I didn't do that. As Zac sped the car to hospital for me to be checked, I phoned Peggy to ask her to go to Milly, trying not to panic her too much about her daughter or about me. It was the one thing I could think to do, and though I was terrified Milly wouldn't forgive me for sending her mother, I was even more terrified of what might happen if she were left alone.

The doctor told me that I wasn't injured, and it was very unlikely the baby had come to harm. She told me that my uterus was thick and strong, and designed to keep my baby safe. She told me that pregnant women bumped their bumps all the time. Those were the things that I would remember later. The things I still remember.

There was no bleeding. There were no contractions. There was no leak of amniotic fluid. My bump was sore, but probably because I was extra-conscious of it. My perception of the severity of the blow to the abdomen was probably amplified by fear.

Those were all good signs. But I was not reassured enough, so the doctor put me on a bed and wrapped a belt with sensors around my bump, and told me the reading was looking good, and I should take things very gently over the next few days because a spell of bed rest never did an anxious pregnant woman any harm.

When the doctor asked how it had happened, Zac told

her I fell, which was technically true. He played the loving expectant father, and tried to hold my hand but I shoved it away with so much force it hit the corner of the metal bedside table and drew blood. Still, he sat beside me and cried as we watched the needle move up and down the roll of paper, tracking her beautiful beating heart.

Now *A Misdemeanour*

One year and eleven months later

London and Bath, Monday, 8 April 2019

I sink onto the train's scratchy blue seat, utterly deflated since the two police officers escorted me from the building. When we are a few minutes out of Paddington I ring Eliza. Again it goes to voicemail. I remind myself that Trudy said Alice was okay, but the attempt to comfort myself fails and the knot in my stomach tightens. I picture Zac, looming over Eliza, making her apologise ten times in a row for some infraction or slight. I picture him doing far worse than this to her, too, though he is too smart and controlled to kill two women in the same week.

With a pang, I recall Alice's pure joy when she heard Zac's voice. Would he deliberately hurt a child? At the very least, a child could end up as collateral damage.

I try to concentrate on other things, so I close my eyes and open my mind to any possible loose end. It is easy to let time open, too, because since Jane died, the borders between my life with Zac in St Ives and my life alone in Bath have dissolved.

The outline of the card I found in Jacinda Molinero's dainty suitcase, sitting in a corner of my brain, fills with colour and grows clear. I can picture the silver lettering over black, and the foil edging. *Albert E. Mathieson, International Tax Law.* Zac's old friend. Maxine said earlier today that when she followed this up two years ago, the information was useful. But she refused to give me the details. Why?

I make a second phone call as the train speeds through the darkening landscape. Close to the tracks are sacks of cement and the skeletons of tractors. Fifty metres beyond are some tumbledown farm buildings roofed with corrugated iron. As I look into the distance, at a field planted with rows of wooden sticks, Albert E. Mathieson's personal assistant explains that Albert can meet with me by video link, and charges a consultation fee of $800 an hour for a minimum of two hours of his time, payable in advance and not refundable. In addition, she explains, I am in great luck, because although there is normally a wait for space in Albert's extremely busy diary, he happens to be free today at 5 p.m. local time, which is 1 a.m. for me.

A ribbon of river winds its way around shadowy churches and castle turrets as I try to quell my panic at the thought of sticking $1,600 on my credit card to buy two hours of Albert E. Mathieson's time. But his assistant cheerfully instructs me on how to complete and sign some engagement documents and forms, including my payment details, and reassures me that for my convenience these can all be emailed.

As I walk home from the train station, I dial Eliza's mobile again, but there is still no answer. I leave another message. I tell her that although I know Alice must be asleep and she herself must be exhausted by now, she can phone me any time, no matter how late. I promise to ring her again first thing tomorrow. I try her landline, too, and recite the same message there, despite my fear that Zac is likely to hear it and recognise my voice. As an afterthought, I say I will come to the house to check on them in the morning if we haven't spoken by then.

It is 8.15 when I reach the basement courtyard of my flat, the phone still in my hand. The night is coming quickly. As I make my usual checks, the silhouettes of the recycling bins look sinister. When I see a male figure sitting on the step in the shadows of my front door, I let out a startled cry.

'Hello, Helen.' George is statue-like in his stillness, as if he fears that to twitch even a finger will startle me more. 'I didn't mean to frighten you.'

I take a step back. 'Why are you here? How did you find me?'

'You're not going to like the answer. A couple weeks ago – after the gym – I – kind of – followed you.'

'You're lying.' I look at the bullet-style security camera trained on my door. He hasn't covered it up or deactivated it in any way that I can see, though I suppose he could reach right in and get rid of anything he doesn't want, anyway.

He sees me looking. 'I'm not bothered about that. I wouldn't interfere with your set-up.'

'Am I supposed to be grateful?'

'No. Of course not.'

'Because you've clearly got big respect for my personal privacy. So you've found me, George. Now you can go. Would you prefer to hear that in Russian or Portuguese? I can try one of the trillion other languages you seem to speak. Chinese, maybe?'

'Helen, I like you so much. I thought . . .'

'It probably took you less than five seconds to find out where I live.'

'I'm sorry.'

'So you know where I live and you've clearly known it all along. Now I can tell you something you might not know. Being spied on is one of the things I hate most in the whole world. And here is another thing. I liked you too. But I don't any more. I know people meet in all kinds of weird ways, and spies have relationships too, but you could have told me the truth. I asked you straight out on Sunday morning and you didn't.'

'You took me by surprise.'

'You could have called instead of ambushing me on my doorstep.'

One corner of his mouth stretches down, bemused. 'You still haven't given me your number.'

'Don't pretend you don't have it already.'

He pushes his floppy hair up from his forehead. 'Okay. I'm sorry again. I do. It's a habit. But I didn't call because it felt wrong when the information didn't come from you.'

I can feel myself softening towards him, though I don't want to. 'I didn't expect to see you again. I thought the tradition was for you to disappear when your cover was blown.'

'Not in this case.'

'Don't lie to me about a single other thing. Tell me why you're here. If you're not prepared to do that, leave now and stop wasting my time.'

'I'm here because you've been busy today. Visiting old friends, knocking on doors.'

'They sent you?'

'Yes. Will you please let me in for a coffee? Maybe something stronger?'

'No.'

'We can talk, Helen. We can work this out.'

'Is that what they want you to do?'

'Yes. But I want that too. And they know I'm involved with you. I've disclosed it.'

'You're not involved with me.'

'Okay, okay. That was presumptuous.'

'The fact that you know so much about me, and I know so little about you, makes this impossible.'

'That can change. I can tell you more about me.' He tries to smile.

'No, you can't. And you know it.'

'Look. I have information to share — it will interest you. Will you give me a few minutes?'

'A few. No more than a few.'

'Before I tell you the thing I've come to tell you, there's something you should know.'

It is as if I am looking through a peephole. 'What?'

'I saw the photo your ex-boyfriend put on the missing person's website. And I know it was probably him by the river on Saturday night. I know about Jane, too.' He pauses.

Everything in the world except that tiny circle has gone black. 'You know what happened to me in St Ives, don't you?'

'Yes.'

My face reddens. My heart starts to race. All I can see is George's face, which is pale.

'I wanted you to know that I knew.' He rests his brow on his fingers and his chin on his thumb.

'Is that what they sent you to say?'

'No. That was all me. What they sent me to say – what I sent myself to say, actually – is about Frederick Veliko.'

I lean against my front door. I cross my arms. I try to collect myself. I blink, knowing the tunnel vision is a stress symptom – it happened to me all the time during my first few months in Bath. 'So tell me.' My voice is quiet. My voice is weak.

'You were right to be suspicious that your searches kept closing down. There's no human way you'd have found him. The United States government would like very much to talk to Mr Veliko, who is one of its citizens. So for that matter would we. But Mr Veliko is not making himself available.'

All at once, I think about what Mrs Hopwell said two years ago. She'd been paraphrasing Zac. *What was she thinking, meeting him?* I'd assumed Zac was accusing Jane of seeing another man, but I realise he must have been talking about Frederick Veliko. 'Jane met her brother. Didn't she? After he did whatever it was you think he did?'

George stares at me. 'I'll come to what that was, but how do you know they met?'

I don't answer. I think again about the conversation I had with Mrs Hopwell as I sat beneath the handkerchief tree, doodling for Zac on my whiteboard. I didn't feel like confiding it to Maxine this morning and I don't feel like confiding it to George now. They have spent years refusing to answer the questions I put to them. Why should I answer theirs?

George seems to guess this, and goes on. 'There is strong circumstantial evidence that Jane and Veliko met, yes. And that your former partner met him too.'

'And that matters why?'

'Because Veliko did some very bad things, and Jane and Hunter are implicated through their contact with him. There is also a likelihood of more recent contact between Hunter and Veliko.'

'Why would Zac do that?'

'It appears Veliko and his ex-brother-in-law share some of the same interests.'

'Well, they shared Jane.'

'Yes, but more than that.'

'And you and Maxine and Martin are finally admitting this to me why?'

'Because you're figuring it out. Because you deserve to know. Because I've been authorised to tell you.'

I shake my head. 'No. No way. That isn't it. That isn't why you do anything. You want something from me. You don't give information if it doesn't suit you to.'

'Perhaps . . . At some point . . . Premature to discuss it now . . .'

'Whatever it is, it doesn't matter. I won't do anything for the Security Service ever again.'

'Understood.' He looks straight at me, no bashful ducks of the head, no floppy-haired charm. 'What made you get interested in Veliko, Helen? What made you ask me to find him?'

I don't answer this either. Why should I? I'm not going to tell him I overheard Martin mention Veliko's name while I was crouching on wet grass above the dead. Instead, I ask a question of my own. 'What is it that you think Frederick Veliko did?'

'You know Edward Snowden,' he says.

'Not personally.'

He allows himself a smile. 'What Veliko did is similar to what Snowden did.'

I think again about the one non-pornographic item I found in Zac's old bag two years ago. That special-issue political magazine about Snowden's revelations. Gruesome details about how the British and American intelligence services were intercepting our private information. It was no surprise to find that magazine mixed with Zac's hard-core porn. Two of his great passions all in one compact container. Taboo sex, and information theft. Naked women in impossible poses, and the rights of human beings to control their own data.

'You know what's weird?' I say.

'What?'

'Zac was forever reading books about how our future is being attacked by algorithms. He was completely fascinated by WikiLeaks. Anything to do with surveillance and privacy and data control, he was into that. Panama Papers, yes. Activist hackers, yes. Whistle-blowers, yes. Snowden, yes, yes, yes. But he was hardly alone. To read about that stuff, to talk about it, isn't a crime. If Zac was doing something illegal, if he was involved in some Snowden-type conspiracy, why would he be so open about those interests? He's not going to document it all for you. He's not going to leave evidence against himself.'

'Hunter buying and owning publicly available material is not going to get him a one-way trip on Rendition Airlines. That's all open-source information.' George avoids calling Zac by his first name. He is *Hunter*, or *your former partner*, or Frederick Veliko's *ex-brother-in-law*. Jane, on the other hand, is Jane.

I think some more about Zac's passion for this subject. Is it akin to my own secret obsession with anything I can find about babies who supposedly died but in reality were stolen, then given or sold to someone else? I found cases of babies who were swapped at birth, so the mothers were told their babies had died but they hadn't. Such things have happened.

George continues. 'Hunter needed to understand the risks and nature of what he was involved in as deeply as he could without getting in trouble, without touching anything that was directly incriminating.'

'One man's cyber-terrorism is another man's heroics.' That was something Zac said to me once, but I don't attribute the quote.

'True.' George pats the empty space beside him on the

step, inviting me to sit. 'Do you want me to tell you more about Veliko?'

I nod. My legs are wobbling. I quietly lower myself beside George, and notice that his cheeks redden. I'm careful to keep half a metre between us.

'Veliko's professional career was similar to Snowden's, but he's much more skilled. He was a senior advisor for the CIA with privileged access. They farmed him out as a telecommunications systems officer for private companies. What the companies didn't know was that he was embedding the work he did with mechanisms for harvesting all that data. Think about the things you do every day, Helen.' George has the excitement of a man who has discovered the key to immortality. 'Your texts and emails, the websites you visit, your bank passwords and records, the videos you watch, the books you read, the Internet searches you make, everyone you communicate with, the communications themselves. All of these things are stored and searchable, so you can be tracked in real time.'

'Without a warrant, George. Without cause. Without my consent.'

'Yes.'

'For our governments to do that is criminal. Snowden thought that too – that's why he leaked that data and told us what they were doing. Presumably Frederick Veliko felt the same. Though you clearly think it's a good thing for every person on the planet to be under constant surveillance.'

'I think it's a complex thing.'

'A necessary evil. Is that what you'd say?'

'Yes, if you like.'

'Well, it's ironic, because the stuff Veliko and Snowden got up to doesn't sound too different from the kind of stuff you do. What is it they say? You can scale any wall – that's it. In your case helped by the fact that you've studded the bricks with hidden toe-holds only you can see. To save the world you need to be able to invade it. You're all the same.'

'I'm not a whistle-blower. I wouldn't jeopardise the security of our country. I wouldn't turn traitor. I wouldn't put lives in danger.'

'You really are one of them through and through, aren't you?'

'Aren't you too? You've helped us.'

I straighten my legs, point my toes. 'I'm an outsider. My motives aren't the same as yours. MI5 knew what it was doing when they rejected me. I never thought I'd come to feel this, but I'm glad of it now. Some would say the Snowdens of this world make us safer. Zac would probably say that and I agree with him for once. They would say the ones who secretly spy on masses of innocent people, who take away our privacy, they're the traitors.' Again, I am struck by the contradiction in Zac, that he should care so much about protecting people from this, but do it to me. 'We shouldn't use the word traitor so easily.'

'I agree. And you're right about how Frederick Veliko sees things. It's probably a view he persuaded your former partner to share. Because here's the thing. Some of the leaks that have been attributed to Snowden – they had to come from a different source.'

'You think Frederick Veliko was the source.'

'We're certain he was. Those error messages when you plugged Veliko's name into US government registers?'

'Yes.'

'Your searches pinged an alert, Helen. They knew you were making them – it got back to us. Veliko's been missing since early 2012. That's a year and a half before Snowden made his disclosures. The US and the UK need to find him. The hope was that Jane could tell us. And Hunter.'

From the start, I pressed Maxine to tell me the real reason why they were so interested in Jane. And Zac. Now, at last, I know.

'Is it GCHQ, George? Is that who you work for?'

'Yes.'

'What's the real reason they decided to tell me about Frederick Veliko after all this time? And you – why have you finally admitted what you are? Two questions, but I think they have the same answer.'

'Partly as I said – you've been pushing buttons everywhere. And partly because everything changed when Jane died. Her ex-husband is our last hope now of getting Veliko. But it's difficult to say whether the fact that he killed Jane is going to make him more or less cooperative. We think he's been in contact with Veliko again – it started a few months before Jane came to Bath.' A fourth alternative name for Zac. Jane's *ex-husband*.

'That makes no sense. Whatever you think he did for Frederick Veliko, Zac's clearly got away with it for a few years. You haven't been able to prove anything, and I know better than anyone how hard you've been trying. So why would Zac take such a risk now? Why would he do something to mess it all up? His killing Jane, that was personal. But getting in touch with her brother again would be too dangerous – Zac isn't stupid.'

'He may have felt he had no choice. If Veliko wanted something, and Hunter said no, Veliko could make things extremely unpleasant for him. Once you cross the line as Hunter did, it's hard to go back. We think the micro SD card you saw in London a couple of years ago was probably from Veliko, and Hunter was part of a chain passing it on.

'It's also fair to say that Veliko played on Hunter's vanity – he'd have made him think they shared the same cause, that he had a unique role to play with his medical background, his understanding of data, his concern with the human condition and bettering it. Hunter's a real believer, a zealot. Veliko would have seen that. And there are the personal links, the family links with Jane and her brother – we never underestimate those.'

'So what do they think Jane and Zac did, exactly? Transported data for Frederick, the way Zac did with the micro SD card? Helped him to flee?'

'Probably both.'

I think some more about Zac's interest in all this. It is certainly true that he's so good at surveillance culture he could write his own book on it, but I'd assumed that talent of his for tracking me was an entirely personal one. Something else occurs to me. 'Could it have been Zac who encouraged the relationship between Jane and her brother? Could he have been the driving force behind whatever help they gave Frederick?'

'That's something we were trying to establish, but we've

struggled to find conclusive evidence. Our hope was that Hunter might lead us to Veliko, probably through Jane, possibly directly.'

'That's why Maxine recruited me, isn't it? It's why you were sent to target me after I moved to Bath.'

He nods. 'Yes, but you should understand I wasn't sent to target you – I sent myself. I've been involved in hunting Veliko since he first stole that data and ran. There was a possibility your ex-partner would find you, and do something to give himself and Veliko away. I needed to be in position in case that happened.'

'Why didn't Maxine tell me all this at the start? I might have made a better job of things.'

'You didn't do too badly.'

'Yes I did.'

'The thinking was you'd be more effective the less you knew. That a genuinely innocent girlfriend working on intuition was far less likely to arouse the suspicion of her target than someone more knowing and self-conscious. And it isn't information we're fond of sharing.'

'I've heard that before.'

'No doubt.'

'So many decisions I've made. The reasons why I made them were all wrong.' My voice trails off, choked. 'The consequences of those decisions, they're hard to live with.'

He puts a hand on mine. 'New information doesn't necessarily mean what you knew before was untrue or irrelevant. Your reasons could have been sound, even if the picture you had was incomplete.'

He knows enough about me to guess how lonely and alone I've been. Is he exploiting this deliberately? Doing exactly what Maxine rejected me for? Maybe he's genuinely attracted to me, but in some sick way, because of what happened in St Ives.

'You're not just a job for me,' he says. 'At first you were. You're certainly not now.'

I hesitate, but lightly, quickly, I curl my fingers round his, then let go and stand up. 'I need to think. I have to be alone.'

He nods. 'Okay. But call if you need anything. Don't hesitate. And Helen?'

'Yes?'

'Do you still want me to call you Helen?'

'It doesn't matter any more, does it?'

'Maybe not. But I need to tell you something that does.'

'What?'

'That I know the meaning of no.'

Then *The Studio*

One year and eleven months earlier

Cornwall, Early May 2017

I had to get through a full week of bed rest before I was able to leave the house to visit Milly. Her bedsit was in a soulless development ten miles inland. Like so many people in St Ives, she'd been driven away by the rising house prices, unable to afford anything close to the sea on her nurse's salary.

The first four times I rang the bell Milly ignored me. Between rings, I phoned her mobile and left a series of voicemails.

'I know you're in there.'

'I'm not going away, Milly.'

'I need the loo and if I have an accident on your street it will be your fault.'

'I'm calling your mother if you don't let me in now.'

It was the last one that did it. There was a hiss as she buzzed me in, but I was too slow and I missed my chance and had to press the bell again.

By the time I'd climbed both flights of stairs, dragging myself up by the handrail and huffing and puffing, pausing every few seconds to catch my breath, Milly was standing on the landing, one hand on a hip. 'Tell me you haven't gone into labour. Because you're breathing as if you have.'

'I'm twenty-nine weeks – I breathe like this all the time these days.'

She wrinkled her nose in disgust. 'You're on your own?' She narrowed her eyes as if expecting to see Zac pop out from behind me.

'I made a steak sandwich for Zac's lunch and surprised him with it at work before I came here. He's definitely at the hospital.'

'Cunning.'

'Yes. That *Girlfriend of the Year* award is sure to be mine. He was deeply touched, given the fact that I've barely spoken to him lately, but way too busy to stop and eat it.'

'Did you get lots of attention from all the nurses?' She looked as if she wanted to smile as she pictured this, but wouldn't let herself.

'They were lovely, and happy for me, and probably extremely relieved that I'm no longer working there and messing things up. Scarlett made me sit down and put my feet up and she fed me chocolates – can I come in, Milly? I need a glass of water. I've been on bed rest the last week and this is my first day out.'

She appeared to think about it, then she turned her back on me and walked through her door, leaving it open so I could follow her in.

The floor was protected by a plaster-powdered and paint-spattered tarpaulin. There was a ramshackle collection of tables and carts of different shapes and sizes, covered in works in progress and tools of varying degrees of sharpness. Beneath the tables were tubes of acrylic, jars of brushes, buckets of sand, tubs of glue, and plastic boxes overflowing with fluffy pom-poms and wires. A blob of grey clay on a pottery wheel matched the smear on Milly's cheek.

The one comfortable piece of furniture was a single bed. It was covered in a bright patchwork quilt that I'd made for Milly on her sixteenth birthday. Along the side of the bed that was pushed against the wall she'd arranged cushions to form a kind of makeshift sofa. The cushions were taken from her childhood room.

'Can I sit down?'

'I thought you needed to pee.'

'I lied so you'd let me in.'

She shot me a glare and flipped her hand towards the bed, presenting it. At the foot was a three-tiered trolley with a hot plate and kettle on top, and a hodgepodge assortment of mismatched crockery and cutlery and tea bags and biscuits on the shelves below – the entirety of her kitchen. She disappeared into what I guessed was the bathroom before she returned with a glass of water and put it in my hand.

She crossed her arms. 'What?'

'I haven't said anything.'

'I know it's a dump. I want a proper artist's studio but this is what I can afford.'

'I think it's wonderful. I think you're wonderful.'

'Don't patronise me, Holly.'

'I'm not. You know I never would. This is me, Milly. I wish you'd let me come before.'

'It's not as if Lord Voldemort would have let you out of the dungeon.'

'Probably true.'

One of the tables was covered in her finished work. Tiny humanoid creatures with strange bulges and psychedelic protrusions were dribbled with neon violet. There was a primitively beautiful model of entwined lovers, hewn from a block of black stone. I put the glass on the floor by the bed and started to heave myself up to look more closely. Milly extended an arm to pull me, and I took it.

Interspersed with her sculptures were numerous abandoned mugs of weak black tea, most of them half-finished. She carried them away so my view of her creations was unimpeded.

'When do you do all this?'

'Nights. Weekends. Whenever I can between shifts.'

I pointed to a sculpture whose head was topped with the greased lavender tail she'd cut from a My Little Pony and tied with a pink ribbon. It had a cotton ball she'd dyed fuchsia for a bottom. The shoulders and chest were absurdly large compared to the rest. 'Gaston?'

'Glad to know that much is clear.'

It had been stabbed in the stomach with a miniature dart, which was surrounded by a red target to highlight the bullseye. 'Is it a voodoo doll?'

'I hate his fucking guts. I hope he dies. And that it's painful.'

'Me too.'

'Even more than I used to. And his fucking ugly new girlfriend too.'

'Me too.'

'I don't want a penis near me ever again,' she said.

'Me too.' I touched a tiny vase, so perfect in scale it would hold only a pinch of the most delicate wild flowers. It was in waves of grey and blue, shades of the sea, sandy and rough outside and smooth inside. 'I prefer your non-Gaston period.'

It was her turn to say, 'Me too.' She waved at the vase. 'Would you like it?'

'I love it so much. But I can't take it. You can sell it – you need the money.'

'There's something – I have something – you must promise not to refuse it,' she said. 'I think – I can't help but feel – I want you to have a small piece of me, something portable. A talisman, to protect you.'

I swallowed hard. She knew. Even without my saying a word she knew I would soon be gone. I was exactly one week away from vanishing. She was crying, and trying harder to cover it up than I was not to notice. I'd never told her about the contents of the bag in the garage, but it would only confirm what she already knew in her bones about Zac.

I tried to speak lightly. 'Talisman, Milly? Are you catching your mum's superstition?'

'Maybe I am.' She reached into the pocket of her dusty cardigan and pulled out a stone.

I blinked, and saw the stone as it was twenty years ago when I found it in the tide pools Milly and I had been exploring.

Then, it was shark-grey and prehistoric as a dinosaur, with a collection of small pits, the tiniest as if pricked by a pin, the largest as if by a pen's nib. It was flat and smooth on the bottom, so it sat like a perfect paperweight, though several chalky scratches ran across it. The top was rounded gently. I pressed it against Milly's palm and curved her fingers around it. 'Paint this,' I'd said.

She repeated my own gesture of all those years ago, putting the stone against my palm, curving my own fingers around it. 'You remember it,' she said. 'I can see that you do.'

She'd enamelled it in a shimmering paint the colour of lapis lazuli. The flaws no longer showed. In her delicate strokes, as exact as the tiny brush of a portrait artist who specialises in miniatures, was a mother holding her baby. Their skin was bare, and seemed lit from within. The mother's hair was a coating of amber, like mine, and matched her child's.

'Keep it with you,' Milly said.

I kissed the stone. 'Have you forgiven me for last week?'

'Having a baby emergency is just about acceptable as an excuse. But sending my mother . . .'

I gulped. She retrieved the water and I drank the rest.

'I might forgive you someday,' she said.

'At least I have something to aim for.' I rested my head on her shoulder.

'I'm sorry I didn't answer your calls,' she said. 'I couldn't talk to anyone. I'd been crying and crying. People caring made it worse. I hate how pathetic I've been about that total prick. I should have picked up when I saw it was you.'

'That's okay. I know you. I know that's how you work.'

She stroked my hair. 'Baby girl is okay?'

I nodded. My eyes filled with tears. 'I saw the midwife yesterday. I'd read that my bump measurement should match the number of weeks, so I had a bit of a freak-out that the number was 27.5 centimetres and not 29.'

'There must be a range of error.'

I nod. 'She said give or take a couple of centimetres either side was fine.'

'You see? You're in range, then. Plus you're slight to begin with. Are you resting enough?'

'All the time. I'm going straight to bed when I get home.'

'Good. Is Lord Voldemort behaving?'

I told her the truth. 'No. He isn't.'

'What can I do?'

'You can move into my house. It's empty and it's going to stay empty. You can live there and look after it for me and save up for your studio by not having to pay for this place. You can eradicate everything brown.'

'May she rest in peace, but everything your grandmother chose was a different shade of shit.'

'True.' I hated lying to Milly about my grandmother's death, but I still didn't confess the truth. 'So treat the walls as your canvas.'

'I'm not a charity case, Holly.'

'No. You're my sister. You're the only one I'll ever have.' I pressed an envelope into Milly's hand. The papers inside were prepared by one of Maxine's people, another of Maxine's many proofs that doing this calmly and methodically, that taking enough time to set everything up before fleeing, was the right course of action. 'This makes the arrangement legal. In case I'm not here. Any eventualities – it's all you need.'

She put the envelope down without opening it. She was wrapping the tiny vase in bubble wrap. 'Only if you take this too,' she said. So I did.

Now *Further Intelligence*

One year and eleven months later

Bath, Tuesday, 9 April 2019

The night has fully set in by the time George leaves the basement courtyard where we have been talking for the last hour. I enter my flat and sit in the dark, thinking about how intimate his knowledge of my past life is. Did he see what happened that night? Did Zac film it? The specifics of this make my chest go tight and my head pound. My heart starts to thump so hard I can barely catch my breath.

What I make myself think about instead is Jane's missing brother, a whistle-blower like Snowden, but one who managed to stay in the shadows. There is absolutely nothing in the public domain about Frederick Veliko. I have no idea what he even looks like. Somebody cleaned away every trace. Was it GCHQ and the NSA, to try to limit the damage by making him invisible? Or did he erase himself, to make it easier to hide, to keep himself safe?

On one of the few occasions that I lulled Zac into talking about Jane, he said it would have been pointless for him to search for her. She loved travelling, he said.

China was among the many places she visited in the years before she left him. He sometimes went with her, if he could get away from work. He certainly travelled a lot during the time we lived together. Doing this reduced his ability to watch me, so the incentive must have been high. Fleeing via China would be perfect for somebody who wanted a route that flew over countries without extradition to the US or the UK. George said that after he escaped the US, Frederick met Zac and Jane. China seems to me to be a likely place for that.

I can understand why Jane would want to help Frederick. No real family apart from Zac. As an only child myself, with no living parent, I know how eagerly I would have seized on the sudden and unexpected gift of a brother, and how seriously I would have taken my loyalty to him. Maxine said when she found me on the cliffs all that time ago that Jane hadn't known about Frederick's existence until after their father died. They must have started to get close soon after that, but before Frederick released those secrets and ran. And Zac must have got close to Frederick along with her.

I try to imagine more about how it all looked to the intelligence agencies. Presumably they reasoned that Jane couldn't have stayed under the radar as perfectly as she did without exceptional help. And Frederick had the ability to provide that help. *He makes Snowden look like an amateur.* That was what George had said. They wanted to find Jane – and put pressure on Zac – because they thought that was their best route to Frederick.

But why did things become so intolerable for Jane that she had to flee, while Zac was able to stay and live a relatively normal life after she left? Perhaps they had more evidence against Jane than they did Zac? Then again, not everything is about international surveillance. I know better than anyone what living with Zac entailed. That, on its own, would be enough to explain why she ran.

I consider again Maxine's desperation to copy the contents of Zac's laptop. She must have thought there was evidence of what Zac was doing on it, and perhaps of where Jane and Frederick were. I think also about the micro SD card he dropped in London. I know now that I'd been wrong to assume it contained the films he'd taken of me and other women. It is more likely he was using it to pass on some of Frederick's data, or at least a code for locating or unlocking it. That would also explain why he was more tense than usual in that London hotel, and why he exploded into drunken violence.

What would have happened if I'd somehow managed to get that micro SD card to Maxine? Would they have arrested Zac then and there? This question hurts so much I can't swallow. The answer hurts even more. *If they had, then everything would have been different.* I sniffle. I work hard to make my throat move. *What If* is too unbearable.

There is a huge *What If* for Jane, too. *What If* she hadn't come out of hiding? The answer is that she would probably still be alive. So why did she risk it? And why now, after six years of perfect invisibility? These are the questions I still can't answer, but I know it is crucial that I do.

Albert E. Mathieson's beautiful blonde personal assistant is so shiny smooth and professional I am convinced that she is an aspiring actress playing the role of beautiful blonde personal assistant. She bends over an executive table, adjusting a glass tumbler, a bottle of mineral water, and pens and paper. Behind her is a huge expanse of window. Through it, I can see sparkling blue sea dotted with boats, as if the room extended over the Pacific Ocean.

'Albert's on his way.' She smiles up at the camera, plays with the settings on a tablet to zoom in on the black leather chair where Albert will soon be sitting. 'Just to reassure you, the video conferencing software I had you download uses end-to-end encryption. Everything you and Albert discuss will be absolutely secure and confidential.'

'That's so important these days.' I say this with real feeling. 'Thank you.'

'It's my pleasure. Here comes Albert. You have a beautiful day now.'

Albert E. Mathieson has the mega-watt smile of a superstar visiting Earth from Mount Olympus. He is in his early forties, like Zac, and every move he makes is made with a snap. 'Hey, Helen,' he says, snapping on a smile as he snaps open his briefcase. 'Great to meet you.'

'Great to meet you too. I'm really curious about what the E stands for.'

'Ernest, my grandfather's name. I do my best to live up to it.' He laughs. 'So,' he says, leafing through the forms I emailed earlier and his assistant clearly printed. 'Your US citizen father and British mother divorced when you were a baby, and you were born and raised in the UK. My main tip is for you to remain calm and not panic as you explore your next steps.'

Is this the kind of tip you charge $1,600 for? 'Panic about what, Mr Mathieson?'

'Call me Albert, please. Your discovery of your US citizenship, and the tax obligations it brings.'

'I see. Am I right in thinking you knew Jane Miller? Zac Hunter's wife.'

'Yes. I know her. Did Jane give you my name?'

Yes, but not in the way you mean. I am thinking of the card she left in her suitcase. 'The information for your forms,' I say. 'My place and year of birth, the countries I've lived in, my parents' citizenship – those weren't my own facts. They were Jane's.' I'd been surprised by how much Maxine had told me about Jane, when it came to it.

'That was an odd thing for you to do.' The smile is gone from his face. 'Why?'

'I'm sorry. I wanted to see what issues Jane's circumstances raised for you. And I was worried you wouldn't talk to me if you knew my real name – it's Holly Lawrence.'

There is a spark of a near-visible charge. 'Zac's spoken of you. We were friends in college – but you must know that.'

'Yes. Do you mind picking up your tablet for a minute? I'd like to show you something.' I direct him to the article about Jane's body being found, watch him quickly read it. 'They say it's an unknown woman. It's not. It's Jane. She was smothered.'

He swallows hard. 'God.' He shakes his head. 'How awful. Zac must be devastated.'

'I'm not sure how devastated the police think he is. Did you advise Jane?'

'No. Zac wanted me to, but no. She wasn't interested. I did advise Zac, after she left him.' He sits back. 'Zac gave me permission to talk to you – said nothing was off limits.'

'Wow. When did he do that?'

'He wrote to me' – he checks his phone – 'August, 2017.' So, two months after I ran away. 'He wanted me to let him know if you got in touch. Said you'd come across my card. He also said you were missing, presumed dead, but he didn't believe you were.'

'Well, he knows now that I'm not. Have you heard from him since?'

'Not a word since that letter.' He pushes the tablet and papers away. 'Do you know about Jane's inheritance from her father? The fourteen-million dollars?'

I don't bother to mask my shock. 'Not that it was so much.'

'When he left her that money he might as well have pushed a red button telling the IRS there was an American cash cow in the next field. She wasn't filing US tax returns and she wasn't reporting her offshore accounts, so she was breaking multiple US laws.'

'But she was a social worker. She wasn't a sex trafficker or a terrorist hiding money. Those "offshore" accounts were local to her.'

'She didn't even know she was a US citizen until the IRS got in touch. Had no idea she needed to obey our tax laws. But boy did they ever go after her. It took me by surprise.'

It doesn't take me by surprise at all. I am betting Jane would never have been on the IRS's radar if the Maxines of this world hadn't put her there. The US taxes were merely a weapon they used against her, because of her missing brother and his Snowden-esque secrets.

'Incidentally, Jane put two million in a joint savings account with Zac that she failed to report to the US Treasury, so the tax compliance problems affected him too.'

I remember Milly's astonishment that Zac never insisted our bank accounts should be joint. She couldn't fathom why he would bypass such a sure way of getting even more control over me. Now I understand.

'I've seen this stuff break up marriages,' Albert says. 'You won't be surprised if I tell you Zac was pretty enraged. They were on vacation in Ireland. Apparently his temper got the better of him. He was violent. Jane ran away, along with most of her funds.'

'Do you think Zac knew where the money went?'

'No way. Plus, Jane left the joint account alone – I had Zac make it over to the IRS. He also undertook to pay the capital gains tax on his house in Yorkshire, once he sells it – did I mention that he put Jane's name on the deed, so Uncle Sam gets a piece of that too?'

'No.' I see now why Jane had to flee and go into hiding, but Zac didn't. There was no clear evidence of their involvement with Frederick, but there was irrefutable evidence of tax crime against Jane that they could use as a convenient excuse to pursue and pressurise her.

Albert sighs. 'It's all so sad. I ought to let Zac know you got in touch, but I won't, given the circumstances. I don't want to do anything to put you at risk.'

I want Zac to know I'm not sitting passively by. And I have said nothing to Albert that would betray a knowledge beyond what Zac would expect of me. 'No, Albert.' My head snaps up. 'I appreciate the thought. But please do tell Zac we spoke.'

Then The Spin Out

One year and eleven months earlier

Cornwall, 13 May 2017

'Hello, beautiful.' It was Zac's voice, dragging me out of sleep. He kissed my bump. 'Hello, other beautiful.' He slipped a hand under the back of my neck.

I was in the sitting room, on one of the fat floral sofas Zac would never have chosen for himself. I was still half in a dream as I pressed my hands against his chest, trying to push him away.

'Please, Holly. I love you so much.'

How should I respond to this? I was thirty weeks pregnant and everything was ready. Maxine had followed through at her end. Tomorrow was the day my baby and I would disappear. I would stretch out in the back seat of the car and trust Maxine's driver to get us to Bath safely. If I didn't return Zac's *I love you* with my own there was the potential for a raging fight that could ruin everything.

'I love you too,' I said.

'It makes me so happy to hear that.' He traced a finger over my lips. 'Have you moved from this spot since I left this morning?'

Gently, I took his hand, which covered the fact that I didn't want him to touch me that way. 'Barely.'

'Good. It's good that you're resting.'

'She kicks more when I lie down. I'm worrying she isn't moving so much. I've been trying to keep track of her kicks, but I was so tired I couldn't concentrate.'

Zac put both hands on my bump. 'Well, she has definitely said hello to her daddy. Did you feel that?'

'I'm not sure.'

'I am. So trust me. I'm a doctor.'

I tried to smile.

'Let me show you how much I love you.' He was pulling open the wraparound maternity dress I was wearing. I tried to grab his wrist to stop him, but my arms were caught up somehow, in my partly undone dress, from the way he'd tugged at the fabric and fiddled with the ties. He was lifting my hair from my neck. His mouth was against my skin.

'I don't feel like it, Zac.' I'd got a hand free. It was against his chest, trying to hold him away.

There was that flash in his eyes, that tightening of his jaw and jutting of his chin, and the familiar pulse that vibrated out of his temple to his scalp. I thought again of my car keys held out of reach, of his magazines and objects. He had promised never to lock me in again, never to take away my phone or my keys again, never to block my car in again, though the last promise would have been easy for him to make given the likelihood that he'd put a tracker on it. Could I trust him to honour all of this, tomorrow of all days?

'There's been no bleeding since the end of the first trimester. We haven't made love since April.' He tried to joke.

'But who's keeping track? The midwife told you that inter-course is perfectly safe.'

I saw the midwife a week ago, the day before my visit to Milly, and Zac wasn't fully quoting what she said. *Safe if you feel like it* were her exact words.

'I need to know everything is okay between us. You need to show me that. Come back to our bedroom. You can't sleep in the guest room forever. It's been two weeks of not having you with me at night and I hate it. The baby needs to see her parents properly together. We love each other, Holly. We need to fix things before she's here.' He'd got me into a sitting position. I was seeing stars. 'Do you remember the first time we made love? In this room?'

I wanted to shove him the fuck off me. But if I did that there would be an argument, and it would never end. It would go on all night and into the morning, and he might disrupt his routine tomorrow to continue it. Milly checked and double-checked the doctors' rota for me, choking back tears while she did it, guessing why I was asking but knowing better than to say. It was absolutely certain that he needed to be at work for handover tomorrow morning. Could I take the risk of wrecking that?

I had only today to get through. I could go to the antenatal clinic in Bath to check on her tomorrow, as soon as I got there. Just one more day, and one more time, to keep us both safe.

He was sliding the dress from my shoulders and down my arms. He was unhooking my bra. Did one last time matter? Would it kill me, once more, to do the very thing Maxine wanted me for? My real value, as far as she was concerned. The thought made me want to cry. Already he was slipping off my underwear. He was planting kisses over my neck, my breasts, growing more intense with each one, his breath coming faster.

He was pulling the cushions from the sofa onto the floor, and me along with them, manoeuvring me onto my side because of my bump, and I told myself that this really would be the last time, though my body tried to move despite my willing it not to, and then I was panicking and he was holding me and the dress was a tangle and my balance was off and I couldn't get loose or get up or stop him.

Cornwall, 14 May 2017

'Say goodbye to me properly.' Zac was trying to kiss me and I was straining my head away because I was scared that if he put his mouth on mine I was going to be sick.

Go, I told him silently. Please, please go. Please go. You need to go. If you don't go, then I can't either.

I didn't want to tell him that I wasn't feeling well, and my bump was hurting. If I did, he might stay. If I told him that I might never get away.

His arms were around me, propping me up. My feet were bare. The flagstones were icy, and I realised that that was different. Since my pregnancy, I had been so warm I didn't usually notice the chill below.

The grandfather clock was no longer in its place. It was sliding sideways.

'You're pale, Holly,' he said. 'Holly?'

The walls were moving and Zac and the clock were moving with them. It was hard to keep his face in focus, but

I thought he was frowning. He was squinting, and saying the word pallor, and blue, and something about listening to my heart, and running bloods. He was saying shock, too, going into shock, and I wondered why he was shocked.

I was no longer in our entry hall. I was with Milly and we were at an amusement park. We were on a ride. It was called The Spin Out. We stayed in one place, standing with our backs to a post and our feet locked down and a belt around our waists, but the circular room turned round and round, twirling us faster and faster as the floor dropped.

'Holly? Holly, Holly, Holly. Holly, look at me. Can you look at me, Holly? Look at me.'

The walls were spinning and spinning and spinning some more, and the floor was dropping further. There was only air beneath my feet.

My legs seemed to have lost their bones. Something stabbed me, low down in my belly, and ripped away inside. A rush of hot liquid streamed down my thighs. My brain seemed to be spinning, too, inside my own head.

Now Illegal Entry

One year and eleven months later

Bath, Tuesday, 9 April 2019

I fall into bed after ending the video call with Albert E. Mathieson, but my head is too full to sleep. It was data that drove all this, I think. Financial data. Security data. Personal data. Text and numbers and codes. But behind it all were real bodies, messy bodies, with blood and flesh and damaged hearts filled with grief and jealousy and longing and despair and fear, and sometimes love. That is what gets lost in it all. That is what Maxine and her friends don't pay enough attention to. That is why they make mistakes. Why we all do.

I am haunted by Jane and how she was hunted by Maxine and the intelligence agencies of at least two countries, then hunted by the IRS at their behest. All the time I thought I was trying to save Jane, I was working against her. I was feeding information to the very people she had run from. Every scrap I found made them more likely to catch her. And if it weren't for my presence in Bath, she and Zac might not have collided. She might still be alive. Why was she here? The question won't leave me alone.

Around 5 a.m. my eyes slip shut, but they open again with the early morning sun. By 7 a.m. I am standing in the shower, trying to wake myself up under a stream of water that is as hot as I can bear. I think of Alice, and put on the most non-grim thing I can find, a midnight blue T-shirt dress dotted in tiny white crescent moons. It is long-sleeved and A-line, with hidden pockets. I wear black trainers. Shoes that I can run in are a constant necessity.

I down two strong coffees, take a bite of a stale croissant, and make myself wait until 8 a.m. to try Eliza again. There is still no answer, so I put my still-damp hair in a quick ponytail, sling my bag over my shoulder and head straight out the door.

The black iron gates are closed. There is no car in Eliza's driveway and the curtains at the front of the house haven't been opened. On the gravel drive is a picture book. *Horton Hatches the Egg*. My first thought is that the book was dropped by Alice as she was carried hurriedly away. My second is that it was left there by Eliza, staged as some sort of cry for help.

When I press the buzzer I have the sensation that someone is watching me, though the only evidence I have of this is my own paranoid instinct. Still, I think of Zac. Is he in there? Are Alice and Eliza with him, not allowed to open the door? Fuck you, Zac, I think, though it is easy to be brave when he isn't in my face. I rattle the gate, but it is firmly locked. I could climb it. I nearly did the last time I was here, though that was to get out rather than in. But I was desperate enough then to risk being seen by a passing car or neighbour, and I really don't want that right now, so I walk up the road and turn left at the corner, to the parkland that touches the side of Eliza's garden.

The parkland is a botanical paradise. Butterflies flicker through clumpy bushes of purple wallflowers. Bees flit through hyacinths and crab apple and crocuses. The blackbirds are singing and the air is already warm, scented with sweet violet and roses. There is a mix of peach and apple and cherry trees, as well as a medlar, which makes me think of the jelly my grandmother used to make each autumn. In the centre of it all is a huge cedar of Lebanon.

The area that borders Eliza's garden is bounded by a wall. This is covered in clematis and jasmine, though they are not yet in flower. Near the wall is a tulip tree with a trunk that splits a metre and a half above ground. Each segment is knotted and twisted and perfect for climbing. I look around me. There is a rock garden, where a mother and her little girl are sitting, the mother sipping coffee from a takeaway cup, the child eating some sort of muffin. On a path that circles a duck pond filled with lily pads, an elderly man is taking his spaniel for a walk. Nobody is paying attention to me.

Thirty seconds later, I am sitting on one of the tulip tree's thick branches, a third of a metre beneath the top of the brick wall. I have a perfect view of Eliza's garden, and the rear of the house. The curtains and blinds are drawn on the upper floors, but the basement wall of glass that is her kitchen is uncovered. The sun is glinting too brightly for me to see inside.

I shift myself onto the wall. I don't have time to think about the two-and-a-half-metre drop. The grass on the other side will be soft, and my arms are strong from the gym. I slip my bag from my shoulder and release my grip. My bag hits the ground with a soft thud, and makes me think of when I dropped Zac's bag from the garage shelf in St Ives two years ago. All in one move, before I can change my mind, I lower myself, dangling from the top, my palms burning as I cling on, my knees stinging from being scraped and banged on the bricks. This move is the hardest part.

The rest isn't so scary. With my arms and body length getting me a good way there, the distance to the ground isn't as much as I'd imagined. I land squarely on my feet, my legs wobbling in a kind of shock that I have done this and managed it without breaking any bones. I wipe my hands on my dress, grab my bag, and move towards the house, skirting the side of the brick wall.

I am startled to see that there is a crack-sized opening in the sliding glass doors that lead out of the kitchen and into this sloping garden. I'm certain they were completely shut when I studied them from the top of the wall. There is no way to hide if I want to approach the house. My best option is to veer away from the wall and walk straight up to the doors. So this is what I do. When I reach them, I peer in.

Standing by the island where I sat with Eliza on Friday morning is a man. His hair is military short and white-grey, and he is wearing jeans and a charcoal shirt, untucked. His arms are crossed and the small of his back is resting against the countertop.

'Hello, Holly,' he says.

There is only a metre and a half between us. The pose is cool, but his face is flushed.

'The cameras picked you up. I'd have buzzed you in from the front but I knew you'd flee if I spoke to you on the intercom.' He shakes his head. 'I'd have tried to persuade you, but I've been waiting for the police. They'll be banging on the door soon. It was hard, watching you leave. But here you are, anyway.'

I'd forgotten the impact of that eye of his. The blue half over the brown half is like the sky over the earth. It goes right through me.

'I heard the message you left for Eliza. Even with the false name, I'd know your voice anywhere.'

I am trembling so violently the room seems to be shaking.

'I knew you weren't dead. I always knew. I never stopped looking.' He is staring at my knee. 'You're bleeding.'

I stare with him. It is badly scraped from when I dropped from the top of the wall, and dripping blood.

'Let me get something to clean it.'

I open my mouth to say No, but nothing comes out.

'Come in, Holly. I mean – please come in.'

I glance quickly behind me, into the garden. There is no tree near the wall on this side, no chink in the bricks to get a foot up, no way of gaining the height I need to scale the wall and get away from him. Even if there were, I couldn't do it at speed, and he would catch me. I stifle a sob.

'I'm not going to harm you or trap you. You can come

through the house and leave through the front door any time you want. But it would help us both to talk and there isn't a lot of time – the police will be here in a few minutes.'

He is the same medium height and trim build, but he looks so different with hair. You'd barely notice the white forelock, because it blends with the grey-white everywhere else, but it's there if you look carefully. He doesn't have even a tiny speck of scalp showing. Whenever I looked over my shoulder it was for a bald man – I didn't factor in the possibility that he would have changed his appearance just as I had.

'What have you done to Eliza and Alice?' These are my first words to him in nearly two years. My voice is so tiny. My mouth is so dry.

'That's what made you power forward, isn't it? I guessed as much. They're in Yorkshire.'

I have to reach for the bottle of water in my bag and take several sips before I can get any words out. 'You wouldn't allow them to go.'

'Not as I was with you, no. But Eliza's had the address and key from the start. I don't imagine she'll stay long, once she sees what it's like there – I tried to warn her.'

'Everything you say is a lie.' My chest is so tight. 'Why are they in Yorkshire?'

'Look, please come in and sit down – you're not looking well.' He is backing away from me, towards the centre of the room.

My breathing is so fast it is hard to talk. 'Because you fucking terrify me.' I am tapping my fingers in the air, which makes me catch sight of my wrist. It is blotchy red and bumped with hives.

'You don't need to be terrified any more. Listen to me, Holly. Open the sliding glass wider – make your potential exit bigger.' He places an ancient, iron key on the marble floor, then kicks it so it lands at the edge of the room. 'This opens a door in the wall you jumped. It's camouflaged by the jasmine, quite near to where you went over. I use it all the time – the police still haven't figured out it's there.'

He moves to a small screen attached to the wall, presses a button, and I see the live video image of the front of the house, with the iron gates opening. 'So you can get out that way too, if you choose.' He returns to the table, hooks out a stool, sits down. 'There'll be three metres of breakfast bar between us. If I even breathe wrong, if I look as though I'm even thinking about standing, you can run. I won't come after you.'

'So you say.'

'I mean it.'

Slowly, I pass the threshold from outside to in, bending to scoop up the key as I move but not taking my eyes from him. I am a metre away from the open door. His expensive cabinetry is between us, as if we were at opposite ends of a long boardroom table.

'Why did you stop shaving your head?'

'For Alice. I'm trying to be the best father I can. I wanted her to have someone around who looks like her.'

You will never be that pretty, I think. But I don't say this. The idea of the two of us bonding over her makes me sick. 'You have Waardenburg syndrome too.'

'Yes. All that time I was shaving so nobody would notice. I thought the white streak was too much of a giveaway on top of my eye.' He shrugs at the irony. 'When I finally wanted the forelock to show, I found every hair on my head had turned white.'

'Tell me why they aren't here,' I say.

'Because yesterday I told Eliza about Jane's death, and that I slept with her. She was going to find out anyway, and I wanted her to hear it from me.'

He waits for me to react, but gives up when I don't.

'She was upset, to put it mildly. And angry. She didn't even pack. She grabbed Alice and left.'

'You made it that easy?'

'I know you have good reason to find that amazing, but yes, that's exactly what I did. I'm in enough trouble without dragging them into it any further than I already have.'

'You never told me about the women you slept with, Eliza included. Don't say you're a changed man.'

'What I'm going to say is that the police will find my semen in Jane's body and my saliva on the mug I used while I was in her house.'

'You raped her.'

'I didn't. What happened to you – I mean, what I did to you – it wasn't true of Jane.'

'Yes it was. I know what happened in that hotel in Ireland.'

'Ah – my good friend Al, yes?'

'Yes.'

'He told me the two of you spoke. What happened in that hotel was a performance. The show was for Al too, so I could tell him about it.'

'I don't believe you.'

'Al explained to you about Jane's US taxes. It was hopeless for her. She was trapped and they were threatening to charge her with financial crimes she hadn't even known she was committing. She wanted me free of it. We needed them to think we'd broken up irretrievably, that there was no link between us. Our life together had been ruined.'

I shake my head. 'No. You're lying. You hurt her. When you – my keys – when I bumped the table.' It is so hard even now to say the words. 'You called me Jane that night. You were crying. You said you'd sworn never to let anything like that happen again. It wasn't a show.'

'Holly. The night before she was born. In the sitting room. I know what I did to you. I'm so sorry. I wish I could undo it.'

My hand flies up to stop him talking. My head is vibrating from side to side, not in my control. Nobody knows. I have told no one. I do not like to hear it or think about it or say it. I press my palms hard against my temples then backwards across my scalp.

He waits a minute. 'I'm sorry. I'm so sorry.' His voice is quiet. 'I promise you. Nothing like that ever happened with Jane. She and I planned it, we staged it as I said. The fight we had, we wanted it to be heard – we waited for the couple in the room next door to come back before we started. We were deliberate about the things we said. But I still did those things to her – we had to make it convincing. What happened with you, when you fell against the table that night, it triggered memories of—'

'No. You're lying. You always lie.'

327

He moves towards me and I let out a cry. He freezes and swallows hard. 'I never hurt Jane.'

'No more of this. No more.'

'Okay.'

I rest my hands on my knees and lean over, as if I have been running hard and can finally stop to catch my breath.

'Listen,' he says, when he sees I am calmer. 'I could have whistle-blown on Jane and got a reward from the IRS – a big cut on whatever they recovered. Believe me, they made that clear. They have laws that allow and encourage that. But I didn't. I wouldn't.'

'So you know where her money is, from the other accounts.'

'Whatever I did or didn't know, I didn't share it, despite Al recommending strongly that I should.'

Something new occurs to me about the IRS's involvement. One of the aims of this must also have been to drive a wedge between Zac and Jane, to give him an incentive to betray her, and in doing so, to betray Frederick too.

'Look, Holly. My fingerprints are all over the house Jane was renting. I'm guessing the only reason I'm still here is that they've been waiting for the forensic results. They want to make sure they have all their ducks lined up before they arrest me and the twenty-four-hour custody clock starts to tick. That will happen any minute. I wanted to spare Alice and Eliza seeing them come for me.'

'If you wanted to spare them, you might have refrained from sleeping with your ex-wife behind your new wife's back. For starters.'

'I've been in counselling, since you left. Since before you left. I check in weekly with a specialist service for men who want to stop their abusive behaviour. I didn't hurt Jane, despite the evidence. I'm sad to say you're the only one I did that to. You paid the price for what happened before we ever met.'

'No. No, no, no, no, no. You've been bullying and controlling Eliza, the same way you did to me. You have her too scared to make friends.'

He looks so puzzled and hurt I'd be tempted to believe him if I didn't already know what a good actor he was. 'No, Holly. I haven't been. As I said, I did do that to you, but not to Eliza.'

'That's what you'd have said if anyone confronted you about me.'

'Yes. I would have then. And I'd have believed my own lies. I wouldn't now.'

'I suppose you'd say you weren't abusing Eliza in other ways, too.'

'I haven't abused her. I regret what I did to you. I understand now how important it is for you to be believed. I also understand it might not be something you want to talk about with anyone.'

I can't look at him. I can't speak for a minute, and he can't either. At last I say, 'Eliza and I were pregnant at the same time. When did you learn about Alice?'

'Eliza turned up with Alice when she was four months old. That was the first time I ever saw her. I didn't know she was mine until then.'

This isn't how Eliza described it. *Zac didn't tell me until I was pretty far along that he was with someone else.*

Isn't that what she said? The implication was that Zac knew about the baby during Eliza's pregnancy, and it was only the existence of his previous girlfriend – me – who stopped their being together. 'She says you did know.'

He shakes his head. 'I didn't.'

'One of you is lying, unless you decided together you'd tell different stories about this. Why did you wait another eight months to get married? Eliza said Alice was a year old when you finally did.'

'Because of you. Because I couldn't move on without you. I only ever wanted to marry you, after Jane. I didn't want to marry Eliza, but I wanted to try to support her. Mostly I wanted to give Alice the closest thing to a real family I could.'

'You're playing mind games. With me and with Eliza. It's what you do.'

'I'm not. I don't do that any more.'

'Does Eliza know who I am?'

'She didn't until yesterday. I told her as she was leaving.'

'Why was Jane in Bath?'

He closes his eyes, takes what seems a long time to open them again. Is he thinking about how to answer? 'Because of me. She was still – powerful to me. As you are.' He shakes his head, slowly. 'It's upsetting to Eliza, but I never lied to her about my feelings.'

'Jane was here because of you, and you, because of me?'

'Yes.'

'Why couldn't you just leave me alone?'

'Because I needed to know you were okay. Deep down,

I'd always known that no matter how desolate you were, you'd never kill yourself – your impulse to live is too strong. But I needed it confirmed. I needed to tell you how sorry I was, though I worried that if you found out I was in Bath you'd disappear again. That's why I hesitated – I didn't want to lose the chance to be near you, to watch over you like a guardian angel. God, Holly – don't look at me that way. I thought, maybe someday, circumstances would let me be with you again.'

I shake my head. 'How can you imagine even for a moment that would be possible?'

'I'm trying to be a better man.'

'Was it the photograph of my grandmother with Princess Anne that led you here?'

'Yes.'

'You visited her care home. You frightened her.'

He nods. 'I'm sorry. I didn't mean to. I left quickly. I was glad to learn she wasn't dead, incidentally.'

'By the river on Saturday night – you could have killed the man I was with.'

'I was upset when I saw you with him. I didn't mean to hit him, I was just trying to shock you apart.'

'You were a bowler, Zac. You knew exactly what you were doing.'

'All right, yes. I lost control. Is he your boyfriend?'

'None of your business. It's attempted murder. To add to the actual murder. Great way to demonstrate how much you've changed. Was the robin meant to do that, too?'

'What robin?'

'The dead one you left on my doorstep on Thursday.'

'I didn't do that. I'm concerned to know who did.'

'I don't need or want your concern. And I don't believe you. I don't believe anything you say. It was creepy as fuck.'

There is the hint of his familiar ironic smile. 'Since when do you swear so much, Holly?'

'Since you. If I tell the police you were responsible for George's head injury—'

'George?' Clearly he is the same obsessive, controlling, jealous Zac I remember. 'His name is George?'

'It doesn't matter what his name is. It matters that you assaulted him. Will you deny it?'

'No. I'll plead guilty to that or anything relating to you that you want to report.'

'Even though it may mean you losing Alice? When you admit to your history of abusive behaviour?'

I watch his face tighten. 'I can't lose Alice.' He works his jaw back and forth. He shakes his head, as if to shake himself out of it.

'See. Easy for you to say. Your words are empty.'

He says, 'You know, Holly, when people change, they don't change perfectly. They have setbacks. They still make mistakes. Throwing that rock was one. And watching you that night by the river.'

'Some mistakes are bigger than others – some are too big to forgive.'

'Yes. They are, though I wish that weren't true.'

I am so close to asking him about Frederick Veliko and his own involvement in that, but I stop myself. Even now, I never want Zac to guess at the kind of help I've had, the kind of people I know, the kind of searches I did when we were together, and might still do. He has never imagined any of this about me. Not my failed attempt to join Maxine, and not my pale imitation of work for her at the edges as a lowly informant.

'Oh, Holly,' he starts to say, 'you'll never—'

There is the sound of a firm knock on the front door. 'Zac.' It is a male voice, loud and insistent, and very, very serious.

The two of us turn to the screen, but it has gone blank.

The voice comes again, preceded by another batch of knocks, then followed by several more. 'It's the police, Zac. We need to talk to you.'

Zac crosses to the screen, taps in various codes, presses buttons, but the screen remains blank. They have somehow deactivated it.

'We've run out of time.' He smiles that sad smile again. 'So little, after so long. There are a few things I wanted to give you, but I guess that will have to wait. At least I've been able to tell you I'm sorry. And that I still love you. There hasn't been anybody like you for me.'

'Thank God for that.'

'Zac,' the voice says again. 'We need you to open the door.'

He nods slowly and walks out of the room. He climbs the criss-cross of stairs that go every which way, moving towards the front door. 'Coming,' he says.

'Good man,' the police officer says.

I am behind Zac, keeping enough distance between us to shoot out of his reach if he suddenly lurches at me.

He turns and catches my eye. 'I'd rather you didn't see this. No reason why you should give me that, but still . . .'

So I pass him. For a second the distance between us narrows to half a metre. He could grab me if he chose to, but he doesn't. I keep going. I think – but can't be sure – that there is the lightest touch of his fingers through my ponytail as I fly by. My trainers squeak the way they did the last time I took these stairs, up to Eliza's room on the first floor, where I have been before.

Below, I can hear the police officer's voice. 'Hiya.'

Hiya, I think. Who says *Hiya* in these circumstances? Clearly, this police officer, who continues to speak. 'Zac Hunter, the time is 09.27 and I am arresting you on suspicion of the murder of Jane Miller. You do not have to say anything, but it may harm your defence if you do not mention . . .'

I strain to listen. Zac does nothing to alert the police that I am here, but I know I have a couple of minutes at best before the house is swarming with detectives.

I try to look at the room as Eliza would. The first thing I notice is that the collage of photographs from her dressing table is gone. One of her precious things, and she seems to have taken it, despite Zac saying she didn't pack before leaving last night. There is nothing interesting or personal in her drawers, which are filled with cashmere and silk.

At the bottom of her wardrobe is a small, fireproof deed box. I heave it onto her bed. It's locked, but it's the kind of flimsy thing meant to stop it from popping open in a fire rather than to deter thieves or a husband. I grab the battery-operated lock pick gun from my bag. After a few seconds of vibrating buzz, I have the lock open.

When I lift the lid, the first thing I am faced with is

a photograph of Zac holding Alice. She is about six months old, and Zac is looking sideways at her, solemnly, while she giggles at the photographer. Alice is so like the newborn picture of my baby. My baby, wrapped in Milly's blanket, with her copper hair and its beautiful streak of white. If they used age progression technology on the photo I have of her and stopped at six months, it would be identical to this one. I slip the photo into my bag. I will cut Zac out later.

The other thing in the deed box is an A4-sized plastic wallet. It is labelled 'Alice – Important Identity Documents'. It isn't Zac's writing, so it must be Eliza's. I stash the folder in my bag, too. As I do, something makes me turn towards the bedroom door.

Standing in the opening is a man. 'Hello, Holly,' he says.

He is slight of build and a little below average height, with metal-framed glasses he probably doesn't need and nondescript brown hair. He is wearing dark trousers, a white shirt, and a navy tie with white dots. You would not notice him in a crowd. He blends in like a serial killer.

'Hello, Martin,' I say.

'Your message reached me. Well played. You certainly caught my attention.' He waits, as if expecting me to thank him for the compliment. When I say nothing, he goes on. 'I'd planned to talk to you today, but not quite so soon.' He is looking at my bag. He smiles. 'I will need to take the item you just placed in there.'

'No.' I lift my toes and begin to rock, then stop myself.

He looks stunned, clearly not used to hearing that word. 'What?'

'I need it.'

'My preference would be for you and me to handle this alone.'

'I don't see how a folder of notes about a small child can be relevant to Jane's death.' I stare at him with a coolness that would make even Maxine proud.

'Maxine didn't want to play your final interview the way we did, you know. My playbook, not hers. I thought you'd hold up better, but Maxine predicted that little vulnerability of yours.'

I have always blamed Maxine for that interview in the white room with the glass table.

He goes on. 'When we learned you were living with Hunter, she didn't want to recruit you, said we'd messed your life up enough already. I forced the issue.'

I have always blamed Maxine for everything.

'She was even more insistent on getting you out of there when she discovered you were pregnant.'

I have always thought he was for me, and she was not.

'We needed you to copy his hard drive. She didn't want you to, but once we learned about that micro SD card slipping through our fingers . . .'

I'd got it the wrong way round.

'I pressed it, said you were tough, that it was what you'd wanted, that she wouldn't be doing you a favour to cut you loose. Was I right?'

He is so casual. For two whole years I have hated Maxine for what happened, for putting me in that position and keeping me there. But it was never her. It was this man. Always, every step, it was him.

'You were not right.' I say this with a blankness I do not feel. Maxine's gift.

'That's surprising. Well, I was sorry to hear how it played out for you.'

How many times has he used the word *play*? The expression *played out*? *Playbook* too. As if all this is a game to him.

He comes closer. 'I'll have that document wallet now, Holly.'

There is no choice but to take it from my bag and hold it out.

He flicks through the contents quickly. 'Tedious.' He tosses it onto the bed. 'Irrelevant, as you said.'

My eyes follow it, though I don't move even a milli-metre. Is he going to ask for the photograph too? Perhaps I'd slipped it into my bag before he arrived, so he didn't see.

'You were right about how Jane Miller died, by the way. Smothering, you told Maxine and Tess. Well done.'

Well done?

'There was bruising on her chest and upper extremi-ties. Looks as though he crouched on her upper body, with his knees digging in and his feet splayed out over her arms. Probably held them against the sides of her torso so she couldn't fight him off while he pressed a pillow against her face. Afterwards, he arranged her in that pose.'

As if he didn't have the courage to look at her while he did it. There is something un-Zac-like about that. He prefers to watch, so he can study the effects of what he does to you, and how you respond. He likes to see your face move between pain and pleasure and fear. I swallow hard. 'Was she raped?'

'Sexual intercourse took place before she died. I'm told there was no vaginal bruising or bleeding, but you can't infer force from the presence of those signs, or infer that there wasn't force from a lack of them.'

Is Martin glad Jane is dead? And that she died so horribly? This supposed traitor they have chased for years? If he is sorry, it is probably because he didn't manage to get his hands on her first.

He goes on. 'There's more in the forensic pathologist's report, but that's the gist of it — Maxine can let you have a look. And I gather our friend George has been briefing you.'

'When can I see the report?'

'Maxine will talk to you. Good to run into you, Holly. I'm sure we'll meet again.' And he walks out of the room.

I grab the document wallet, slide it into my bag for the second time, and hurry down the stairs. Zac is gone. Martin is talking quietly to the same tall detective with dark hair and dark-rimmed glasses who stood outside the cordon of the house where Jane died. He looks exactly as he did then. The prince of death in a dark suit. Martin puts a light hand on the man's arm, to stop him from questioning me. I head straight through the open front door. When I crunch across the gravel drive, I see that *Horton Hatches the Egg* is gone.

Then The Memory Box

One year and eleven months earlier

Cornwall, Late May 2017

Somebody has taken my baby out, but I find her in a little basket by my bed, and though she is bone-white and made of plastic, though she is only a doll, there is a zipper at the bottom of my belly, so I slide it open and put my baby back inside, then seal it up again so I can keep her safe. Now she will turn soft once more, and she will pink up and grow, so the next time she comes out she will be ready.

I opened my eyes. I was in a tight white bed in a small white room with a needle on top of each hand, kept in place with tape that had tubes snaking out from beneath it. Bags of fluid floated above metal posts like deflating balloons.

I crept a hand under the sheet. My skin burned with the tug of the needle. I let my hand hover above my belly, and told myself this was a nightmare and I would wake up. I lowered my hand. My belly wobbled like jelly. The firm bump was gone. Lower down, my skin was covered in papery fabric that I couldn't pull away.

I opened my mouth to cry out. No sound came. But then

I tried again, and when I started to scream, and I saw that Zac was sleeping in the chair, and he jumped up as nurses rushed in, I knew it wasn't a nightmare at all. And I screamed and screamed, and tried to tear the needles from my arm, and shouted at them to give me my baby. I kicked and thrashed and tried to stand, but they were holding me down and stabbing something into the top of my arm, and I fell back, crying softly, begging them to tell me where she was as my eyes closed again.

I was in the same white room, in the tight white bed. Peggy was sitting by my side in the hard chair where Zac used to be. She leaned over and smoothed my hair from my face. There were tears running down her cheeks.

'Why are you crying, Peggy?'

'Because you have been so ill, and we thought we'd lose you. You bled so much you nearly died.'

'How long have I been here?'

'A week.' She hesitated. 'Do you – do you want to see Zac?'

I closed my eyes. I shook my head.

'He was desperate for me to ask you. They've told him to stay away – it upsets you too much, when he's near.'

'I want my baby.'

She took my hand in hers. 'Holly, you've said goodbye to her.'

'Bring her.'

She opened her mouth to speak, but nothing came out. She tried again. 'Your baby is with the angels. She's grown wings.'

'No.' I took in several shuddering breaths. 'No. She's not. No.'

'You held her, my darling. You said goodbye. She's gone.'

'No. No. I didn't.'

She pushed my hair from my forehead. 'Your baby died. I know you don't want to remember. She's a little angel, now.'

'Stop saying that about angels. It isn't true. I want my baby.'

'Holly, my love. I am so sorry. But it is true.'

'Make them bring her.'

'I need you not to go far away from me, even though you want to.' She reached down, and came up with a pale pink box decorated with white butterflies. 'Do you remember? We talked about the memory box.'

I stared at the white sheets. There was a spot of dried blood at the top.

Peggy moved to the edge of the bed, helped me to sit up, put an arm over my shoulder, let my weight fall sideways onto her soft, solid body. She lifted the lid of the box and pulled a photograph out. 'We'll look together.'

She was wrapped in a pale pink blanket, and surrounded by white lace pillows. On each side of her was a matching stuffed teddy bear, ivory and no bigger than my own hand. 'See how beautiful she is,' Peggy said.

'Why haven't they dressed her? Why isn't she wearing proper baby clothes?'

'I asked them about that. They said they didn't have anything small enough to fit. She – her growth wasn't what it should have been, they think for the last couple weeks. I brought the blanket in for her, while you were still in the intensive care unit. It was Milly's.'

Her eyes were closed. Her mouth was a perfect rosebud in her pale face. She had so much hair, for someone so tiny.

I imagined myself brushing that hair. It was the same copper as mine, but it was light, almost white, in the centre.

There was a cry coming from somewhere, a sob that repeated again and again, and at first I thought it was a baby. I wasn't sure how long the noise had gone on before I realised that the sound was coming out of me.

And then I understood the important thing. My mouth shaped itself into a smile, though it was tremulous, uncertain as a child's when they couldn't decide if they should be happy or sad. 'It's okay. Peggy, it's okay. It isn't true. She's not dead. She's sleeping.'

'Holly,' she said. 'Zac told me – the nurse told him – when you, when you kissed her, you said your kisses would make her warm again. It didn't work, my love. They told him you became so distressed, when it didn't work. They wanted to take her away then, but you wouldn't let them. You had her with you for hours. You kept refusing to let them take her away. You had her with you for as long as you could. You're such a good mum.'

'That never happened. Zac is lying. Did you see her yourself?'

'I wanted to, but she'd been out for as long as she could. Even Zac barely had time with her. He felt that time – her, her being out – needed to be yours.'

'Why not longer? What do you mean, as long as she could?'

Peggy didn't answer. 'I – I tried to get a cuddle cot, but the hospital doesn't have them yet.'

'What's a cuddle cot?'

She took a deep breath. 'It keeps baby cool, so they can stay with you for longer. I was phoning everywhere, trying to get one. But I couldn't. I'm so sorry.'

There was a cry, thin and insistent, coming from somewhere nearby.

'I can hear her. Listen, please listen. Don't you hear? She needs me.'

Peggy was crying too. 'It's someone else's baby.'

'Make them bring me mine. Please make them.'

Peggy was sobbing so hard she was choking. 'I'm so sorry. Milly made me promise not to do this.' She gulped water. 'You've had a trauma, Holly. That's why you don't remember. There are so many people who love you. We're going to get you all the help you need.'

'The help I need is to see her. I want her with me.'

'Holly my love, it's been too many days. After you cuddled her, they had to take her away. Do you understand?'

'No. No. No I don't.'

She reached into the pale pink box. She retrieved a tiny white teddy bear and held it up. It was identical to the ones in the photo. 'This is for you to keep. The other one stayed with her – the two were made as a pair.'

I did not answer. I did not move. At last, I said, 'I don't want a stuffed toy. I want my baby.'

Peggy returned the teddy bear to the box, but pulled out something else. 'The nurses took her footprint for you. They used a special ink, so they could wipe it off, afterwards. Look.' She offered it to me. When I refused to take it, she laid a framed display card on top of the bedclothes.

The foot that made that print was no bigger than a doll's. I was shaking my head again. 'That isn't hers. That could be any baby's.'

Peggy took the paper as if it were something holy and returned it to the box.

'I want to take care of her.' I pushed the bedclothes away. 'I want to show her how much I love her.'

'It will be too upsetting for you. She – her little body – it deteriorates. You had her with you as long as you could.'

'No.' I was on my feet, starting for the door, and I was screaming, and though Peggy's arms went around me, I couldn't stop screaming. My screams were interspersed with Zac's name, and the word bastard, then he was in the room too, pushing Peggy out of the way, begging me to lie down, telling me the wound would open and I was going to hurt myself and the lines were being torn out, trying to guide me back to the bed but not daring to apply force, managing to pull the red triangle and set off the lights and alarms while I pounded on his chest, telling him that I hated him, that I would hate him forever, that he killed my baby and I would kill him, and that I wanted to die. All the while, his voice was overpowering mine, telling Peggy and the nurses that I didn't mean it, that we loved each other and it was his job to take care of me, and he was crying, too. I thought of the thing I could say that would hurt him most, the one thing I could think of that would make him hate me as much as I hated him, so he would leave me alone, so I screamed that the baby wasn't his anyway, but he only said, 'There is no doubt that she was mine, Holly,' and then I screamed some more.

It was a severe placental abruption. The placenta was the organ that my body made to nourish her, to give her oxygen, to keep her blood clean and protect her from infection. The placenta was what attached the two of us. The placenta was what tore us apart, ripping away from the wall of my uterus and at the same time ripping my world into shreds.

They said it wasn't my fault, but I know it was. I hurled myself at Zac and grabbed for the keys and fell forward, straight onto my belly, smacking it against the edge of that marble table. A blow, even weeks earlier, even months, can cause it.

They had no choice, they said, but to do a hysterectomy and multiple blood transfusions. They said I would have died if they hadn't, and I said I wished they'd let me and not dragged me back and forced the lost blood into my body. They said, as if they had performed a miracle, that they managed to save my ovaries, so I would still make eggs, and I wouldn't need hormone treatment. But what good did that do when there was nowhere for those eggs to go, and mere indifference on my part to the fact that they existed at all?

The things that I learned, and did, and had done to me, were a blur. It was so hard to put them in the right order. I knew that I'd lost time, but I wasn't sure how much. Peggy acted as my translator, mediating between me and the world of the living, which no longer made any sense to me.

Two weeks. That was how long I'd been in the hospital, Peggy told me, coming every day and trying to help me count. They would not let me leave, because of secondary complications. An infection that I needed intravenous anti-biotics for. Severe anaemia due to blood loss – evidenced by lab reports and by the bruises in varying shades of red and blue and purple and yellow and green that covered my body.

Peggy asked me if I wanted them to do a post-mortem.

'Why? We still can't be sure she is dead.' As I said this, I thought of a tombstone in the graveyard where my parents were buried. The birth and death dates on it were the same. *Born sleeping.* I had a habit of pausing over it.

'Oh, Holly.' Peggy looked so stricken.

So I said that I did not want them to cut her open, and it was pointless, since we knew why it happened, since she was perfect except for the fact that she had a mother who failed her. This made Peggy cry and say I was wrong, but I knew I was not. And then I said, But am I a mother, Peggy? And she said yes, you are, nothing can change that, and she cried some more.

There was talk about cremation, the hospital arranging it to make things easier, and promising it could be done individually instead of with other babies, and I said yes to that, because I couldn't manage it myself, and the less I had to discuss with Zac, the better. Peggy told me we would get the baby's ashes back, and we could bury them or scatter them or even make them into jewellery that I could wear every day.

'I do not want any of those things, Peggy,' I said. 'I want my baby to be alive.'

She told me Father Bill could do a funeral, if I would like him to, and the church was raising money for a cuddle cot in my baby's honour, and Zac would agree to anything I wanted and refuse whatever I didn't.

Zac filled in forms, Peggy put them in front of me, and I signed without taking in a single word.

The nurses asked me what my baby's name was. I remembered that Zac wanted to call her Alexandra Mary, after his grandmother, and I wanted to call her Charlotte, after Charlotte Brontë. I tried to say that her name was Charlotte, but the words would not come out.

One morning, I noticed something that I hadn't absorbed before. On the wall of my little side room was a poster of a smiling mother propped in bed with her nightdress unbuttoned and her newborn baby held to her chest. *Breast is Best*, it said. I pointed to the poster. I couldn't speak. A nurse moved towards it and I scrunched my eyes shut. When I opened them, the poster was gone.

Now *The Choice*

One year and eleven months later

Bath, Tuesday, 9 April 2019

I don't drive far from Eliza's before I pull over on one of the most peaceful streets in the city to try to calm down. It is a circle of Georgian houses surrounding a grass island with trees in the middle. This arrangement is supposed to represent the sun. Just a street away is a crescent of houses that mimics the shape of the moon. The stonework on these houses is decorated with serpents and acorns and sculptured roses, and I can hear birds chirping as I sit in my car.

My hands are shaking as I look through Alice's identity documents. The first thing I come to is her birth certificate. Now I understand why her NHS records are so scanty. According to this, she was born in Montenegro. The certificate is in what I think must be Montenegrin, with an approved translation of the document into English, paperclipped to the original. The birth was registered when Alice was five days old, on 23 May. That was nine days after my own baby was born. Eliza Wilmot is named as the mother, and Zachary Hunter as the father.

The next thing in the pile is a photocopy of an Application to Register an Overseas Birth of a British Citizen. Eliza and Zac did this when Alice was a year old. The section about the Child's Parents' Marital Status shows that Eliza and Zac got married the week before they signed the form. There are copies of their own birth certificates, and one of their marriage certificate too.

There are three receipts. The first is for tracking the application to the Overseas Registration Unit in Milton Keynes. The second is for paying the registration fee. The third is for the purchase of four copies of the birth registration certificate, one of which is in the document wallet. To most people this would seem like overkill, but Zac knew from Jane what a mess citizenship could cause. It isn't surprising that he and Eliza should take a great deal of trouble to document something so important for Alice, then keep it all in a fireproof box.

The last thing in the document wallet is a photocopy of Alice's British passport, issued five weeks after the date on the certified registration. It seems they applied for the passport the first instant they could. Maybe Eliza has the actual passport with her, which is why she didn't bother grabbing this folder of identity documents before she left. It makes me wonder if she is planning to leave the country with Alice.

I check the time on my phone. 11.15. I open my contacts and dial George. 'It's Holly,' I say.

'You used your real name.'

'Yes.' I circle Alice's photocopied passport photo with my finger. 'There isn't much point in not using it now. Are you at work, George?'

'You didn't block your number.'

'Again, would there be any point?' Carefully, I slide the papers back into the wallet.

'No,' he says, after a slight delay.

'But I didn't want to.' I press on the wallet's snap closure. There is a pleasing click.

'Good.'

'I need to access some medical data.' I turn the wallet upside down and lay it on the passenger seat. 'Will you help me?'

'I asked you to call if you needed anything – I meant that. I can meet you at my flat at twelve forty-five.'

A split second after ending the call, my phone rings again. It's the care home. They say, as gently but firmly as such a thing can be said, that I should come as soon as possible.

I practically fly there, kissing my grandmother's papery cheek, whispering in her ear that I love her and she'd better wake up soon and start complaining or I will stick her right next to my mother. But even this doesn't make her respond.

'She's been sleepy the past few days.' Katarina's voice is hushed. 'She has taken no food, and very little water. Do you understand?'

'I think so.'

'The GP saw her this morning. She seems peaceful. It is, how do you say, a natural process? She is very tired.'

I hold my grandmother's hand as gently I would an egg, because already it feels as fragile as a shell. 'Is it another chest infection?'

'That is what the doctor said, yes. We are giving her things to help with the breathlessness, and for pain. She is comfortable.'

'Can we just let her sleep, then, as long as she isn't distressed?'

'I think that would be best.'

I look up at Katarina. 'She is going to die soon, isn't she? She isn't going to wake up.'

'I think that is probable.'

Katarina has arranged my grandmother's white hair on the white pillow, and applied salve to keep her lips from drying out. She has dressed her in the lavender nightgown I bought for Christmas. 'You are so good, Katarina,' I say.

I climb onto the bed and lie beside my grandmother, my head next to hers. I tuck the sheets around her more carefully. The gesture triggers a memory of something my grandmother used to do when I was little. Every night after my bath, she would snuggle me into a towel that she'd warmed on the radiator. I drape my arm over her. She seems even more shrunken. I turn my eyes towards Katarina, who is standing on the other side of the bed, radiating sympathy and kindness. 'I don't know what to do,' I say. 'There's something urgent I need to take care of but I don't want to leave her. How can I?'

Katarina smiles. 'Your grandmother knows you are with her. She knows this even if you are not in the room. You must live. She told me to tell you that. But you look puzzled, Helen. Am I not making sense with my English?'

I decide to believe Katarina, though I know she may

be making this up to be kind. 'Your English is beautiful.' I give my grandmother a kiss, and another and another. I get halfway to the door, then run back to give her one more, knowing that it is likely to be the last.

George's flat is as messy as ever. I think it must be that his head is too full and his life is too busy to be able to cope with cleaning, and this is a position I respect. George is calm in himself but chaotic all around, the reverse of Zac.

While George hurriedly transfers piles of clothes and paper and assorted objects from the sofa to the floor so I can sit, I catch a glimpse of myself in the mirror above his cluttered chimney piece. There is grass in my hair, which is straggling out of a rat's nest ponytail. My cheeks are dusty, but with snail trail streaks that I think must be from tears. The bottom of my dress has ripped, so it dangles jaggedly beneath what used to be the hem.

'Which is the real you?' I ask him. 'The spy or the man?'

'Whichever you like best. Which is the real you? Now, or then?'

'Both.' As I say this very true thing, I see that there is no division between my past and my present, between who I was and who I now am, whatever my name may be.

'Can I change my answer to "both" too?' George is trying to stop the contents of an overstuffed carrier bag from spilling out. 'I prefer that answer.'

Before we can say any more, there is the buzz of his doorbell. George doesn't bother to ask who it is before he gives up on the bag and presses the button to let them into the building. A minute later, Maxine is in the room, wearing jeans and a T-shirt, her hair in a low knot at her neck, her face make-up free and so exposed it makes me blink.

The first words out of her mouth are, 'George, get something to clean Holly's leg.'

I follow their eyes to my knee, which is covered in dried blood that snakes down to my shoe. Zac had noticed it too, I remember.

As soon as George has disappeared into the bathroom, I say, 'Are you MI5, Maxine, or GCHQ like George?'

'MI5, but this is an area where the two agencies are providing mutual assistance. We're more likely to get a result in this case by cooperating and pooling our collection efforts.'

The blood-red hate I felt for her has vanished. Martin is a more deserving target, but the impulse to hate or blame any of them has gone flat. 'What do you want from me? You must want something, to be confiding in me after all this time.'

'It's not what we want from you. It's what we can do for you.'

'Really . . .' I say, obviously unconvinced.

She allows herself a small smile. 'We can help you back into your old life – your contact with Milly shows you can't continue like this. Not to mention the fact that your set-up in Bath has fallen apart.'

'I'd noticed.'

'And yes, since you mention it, there's something you might be able to help us with, depending on whether they keep Zac. Your hold on him has clearly not diminished.'

'You can't seriously think he'll be out any time soon?'

'Doubtful. But we don't need to talk details yet.'

'We don't need to talk details ever. I will never have anything to do with Zac again. I certainly won't be asking him to put me on his prison visitors' list.'

'Let's deal with what you need from us right now.' She goes on. 'George is a genius at getting us into the places we want to visit, and exiting with no trace.'

'So I gather.'

George walks in, clutching a bottle of antiseptic and a handful of cotton wool. He kneels at my feet, dabbing my knee with antiseptic.

'Thank you.' My voice is so soft I am taken by surprise. When he's finished, I say, 'Can you get into some medical databases? I need to find a baby girl who was born in Montenegro – in Podgorica. The birthday is May eighteenth, 2017.'

'I need the parents' names, Holly.' He sits in his desk chair. 'By the way, I like saying your real name.'

'So do I. The parents are Eliza Wilmot and Zachary Hunter.'

He is tapping away on the keyboard. 'Would you two perhaps be more comfortable on the sofa? Maybe have a little chat together?'

'Are you trying to say you're not enjoying having us look over your shoulder, George?' Maxine says.

'No. Of course not. It is a pure delight to have you doing that.'

Maxine pulls me away. 'You look on the verge of collapse. When did you last sleep?'

'Last night.'

'For about two minutes, I'm guessing. Lie down on the sofa. Close your eyes for two more. When you open them again, he may have found something.'

I curl up on my side with my back to the room. When I open my eyes again, it is to the smell of coffee. I sit up too quickly, so my head spins. 'How long have I been asleep?'

Maxine puts a mug in my hand. 'Twenty-five minutes.'

'Anything?' The mug is plain white, and chipped. The heat is comforting.

'He's found her.'

'It was a private hospital.' George is flipping between multiple windows, all of them in Serbian or Montenegrin. 'Hunter wasn't present for the birth, but his name is on the records.'

'He was in the UK at the time.' Maxine is speaking to George, but looking at me.

Something occurs to me. 'Can you access any CCTV for the hospital during that period?'

'The CCTV from all the main entrances is stored on secure servers in the cloud. I got in, but there's a gap. Look.' George switches screens and points to a long list of clickable date entries. 'There's nothing from the first of March until the thirtieth of June that year.'

'That can't be a coincidence.' The coffee is too bitter to drink. 'It's the sort of thing you could do, George.'

'Except that I didn't,' he says.

'Not this time, anyway,' Maxine says. The two of them look so pleased by this bit of spy humour I half-expect them to high-five each other.

I abandon the mug on the floor by the sofa. 'Inside those four months of no footage there are dates that somebody didn't want us to notice. We need to find them. When did Eliza return to the UK with Alice?'

'Twenty-fifth of May. The baby was a week old,' George says.

I tap my head, as if to help myself think. 'Why didn't Eliza tell Zac that Alice was his until she was several months old? Is it possible Alice wasn't born in Montenegro? That Eliza and Zac made it look that way, somehow?'

'That would be extremely difficult,' Maxine says.

'What about the doctor?' I am rapping my fingers on George's desk. 'I want to try to talk to him. See if he remembers the birth.'

'Her.' George gently covers my hand with his, to still it. 'I've made a note of her name but you're not likely to get far. Patient confidentiality isn't an exclusively British thing. Plus, do you speak Serbian? Montenegrin?'

'No. But I'm guessing you do.'

He grabs a phone from his desk, dials, and speaks rapidly in a language that doesn't sound remotely like any of the ones I know. He cuts off the call and shakes his head. 'The doctor left a few days in advance of the Easter holidays with her family. Won't return until the twenty-second of April.'

'Fuck,' I say.

'And I thought you only spoke English,' he says.

'Very funny. When did Eliza go to Podgorica?' I sip from a bottle of water that is somehow in my hand, without remembering how it got there.

George changes to yet another window. 'She flew in on March twenty-first.'

'Inside the dates with no CCTV.' I am calculating. 'So two months before Alice was born. Why not remain in the UK? Why make a deliberate decision to give birth in Montenegro? Have you found a record of where she was staying?'

'Not so far.'

I come close to him, peer at the screen. 'Can you bring up her medical notes?'

His index and middle finger are scrolling down the trackpad.

'Is that Serbian?' I say.

'Yes. I'm no expert on maternity care, but it seems Eliza made one antenatal visit – it was a week before Alice was born.'

'Just one medical appointment?' I say. 'And so late? Are you sure about that?'

'There's only one in the notes. They recorded her weight, tested her urine. There are measurements for the baby's growth. Everything was normal.'

My stomach is tight, remembering how much I loved having those tests, but also remembering that last midwife appointment, when my bump measured on the small side of the normal range. I turn to Maxine. 'One visit isn't enough at that stage of pregnancy. Is it?'

Maxine puts her hand on my shoulder. Her voice is quiet, as if she is being forced against her will to talk about death with someone who is about to die. 'It's every two weeks after twenty-eight weeks, then every week in the last month. But . . .'

'But what?' My knees feel as if they are made of water, as if they can no longer hold my weight.

'There's something called confirmation bias. It's when you make the evidence fit the story you want. Is that what you're doing here?'

'Don't you see this is all off, Maxine? That something isn't right?'

I cannot shake my instinct that my baby didn't die, and they lied to me. I still can't remember ever seeing her and holding her and spending time with her, despite all of them telling me that I did. Did Zac somehow get her smuggled into Montenegro, then out again?

'Holly?' George puts a hand on my waist, as if he thinks I will buckle without support. 'Do you need to sit down?'

I am trying to remember if I ever saw any paperwork to prove that my baby died. I have no recollection of any, but everything was a blur, then, and Zac dealt with all the forms.

I shake my head. 'I'm tired, that's all.'

I try so hard to re-live the feel of her tiny shape and weight in my arms, and her cold body, with no pink, hard like wood, hard like Jane's body was. But no matter how I try, there is nothing. If it were true, surely there would be at least a faint shadow of a memory?

'You're shaking, Holly.' Somehow, he has given me to Maxine, whose hand is on my arm. 'Maxine, can you take her in the kitchen? Maybe find her something to eat?'

'Your kitchen is disgusting, George,' Maxine says. 'You will probably poison us both.'

'You go,' I say to her. I am fed up with being told what to do. 'I'll be right there.'

Maxine gives me a look, but she sits me on the edge

of George's desk and I soon hear her opening the fridge, searching through cupboards, banging things onto the counters.

George reaches up, pushes a stray lock of hair from my face as I peer at the screen. 'You okay?'

'Yes. But look here: "1.6 metapa."' I point. 'Is that Serbian for metres? Is it for Eliza's height?'

He nods.

'Is it some sort of mistake?'

'No mistake, unless the doctor or nurse who wrote it down made it.'

'Well, it's wrong. Eliza has to be at least 1.7 metres – she's four or five centimetres taller than I am.'

A new thought occurs to me. It is something that started in a tiny corner of my brain when I said that deleting the hospital's CCTV from the cloud was the sort of thing George could do. Such an action is also in Frederick Veliko's skill set. 'Can you see if there's any record of Jane Miller in Montenegro at the same time? Try Jacinda Molinero too.'

'We looked for Jacinda Molinero when you gave us the name a couple years ago. We found nothing, then.'

'It wouldn't hurt to try again now. She may have used it since. She would have felt safe with that name. She would have thought it low risk that anyone would be looking for it.'

'Why would Jacinda – Jane – be in Podgorica?' He says this like a teacher who already knows the answer, and is trying to find out if I do too.

To help Zac steal my baby, I think, though I don't quite understand how, or why they needed to be in Montenegro. 'It's just an instinct,' I say.

'It's as if I've been hit on the head since I met you.'

'If GCHQ ever fires you, you can write comedy.'

'Go get something to eat, Holly. I'll see what I can find.'

When Maxine and I come out of the kitchen half an hour later, George is sitting on one side of the sofa. I take the place on the other end, and Maxine wheels his desk chair across.

'Okay,' he says. 'I found three more things. First, Holly, your instinct about Jacinda Molinero was right. Somebody checked into a five-star hotel in Podgorica under that name. It was a two-room, two-bath suite, and they stayed for ten weeks. Arrived on the eleventh of March, departed on the twenty-sixth of May.'

'Again, all inside the March-through-June dates when the CCTV was blocked,' I say.

'Yep. And the second thing is that there's no CCTV for the hotel for those four months – same as the hospital. And here's the third thing.' He takes a piece of paper from the sofa arm beside him, then hands it to me. 'I printed this for you.'

I turn it over. 'Oh.' It is a photograph. 'Oh my God.'

The three of them are so young, so happy looking and beautiful and uncomplicated.

Zac, before Jane ran away from him.

Jane, before she ever knew she had a brother.

Eliza, before Zac broke her heart, then changed his mind and married her.

'It was 1999, the UCL Summer Ball,' George says. 'From the university archives.'

Zac, twenty-four years old, is standing in the middle. One of his arms is around Jane, the other around Eliza.

The two women look like film stars, in their shimmering gowns, with their upswept hair.

'We knew all three of them were at UCL at the same time,' he says. 'But I thought if I showed you the connection, it might help you to understand why Jane was with Eliza in Podgorica. They were old friends. They met in halls in their first year. Jane must have been supporting Eliza for the birth.'

'That partly makes sense,' I say, 'but it's also weird. Don't you think? I mean, Jane supporting a woman who's having her ex-husband's baby? It's not exactly the basis for a thriving friendship.'

'Perhaps Eliza didn't tell her who the father was,' Maxine says.

My cheeks lift and my eyes squeeze in doubt. 'That doesn't sound right.'

Maxine stands. 'Holly, it's been a difficult day for you.'

'Yes.' George reaches across and squeezes my hand. 'I'm so sorry about your grandmother.'

There is a kind of time delay before I manage to speak. 'It has.' Do I sound like a robot to them? 'Thank you. I think I need to go home now. I need to sleep, and then see my grandmother.'

I drive away from George's flat, but I don't go home. I head for the botanical gardens in the middle of the town. I park under some hydrangeas, where pink and blue flowers are growing from the same bush, as if through some kind of genetic magic. I roll down the car window, in need of fresh air.

I think back to my nightmare time in hospital, and

immediately afterward. They all told me I'd held my baby. That I spent hours with her. But I haven't even a sliver of a memory of it. I think back to my certainty that she wasn't dead, that she couldn't be. They all thought it was my grief, the total mental collapse I was having, then.

I am trembling at the thought that I was right, and Zac somehow stole my baby, and bullied and blackmailed Eliza and Jane into helping him. Zac knows the medical world. He knows how hospitals work. He knows Frederick, who can manipulate data and documents and records. Is it possible that Zac could have pulled off such a thing? And that he and Jane persuaded her brother to delete any evidence that she was ever there? Given how much they sacrificed and suffered to help Frederick, it was hardly a big ask.

Even so, I still can't fully understand why Jane would take such a risk. Love for Zac? Guilt about what she brought upon him? Fear, despite having escaped him? Montenegro isn't a Category 1 country for extradition, which must have been Jane's reason for choosing it, but it still would have been extremely dangerous for her to be discovered there.

I start the engine. I do not return to my grandmother. I whisper a small prayer of apology, a plea for under-standing even though I know it won't reach her. I head up to the motorway, towards Yorkshire.

Then The Drowning Place

One year and ten months earlier

Cornwall, June 2017

My eyes were tightly closed against the grief that hit me like a tsunami and tossed me so far and deep I couldn't fight it. I opened them to see a shadow figure, sitting by the bed, watching me. She'd arrived in silence, and at first I thought she was a ghost, or part of the bad dream that continued whether I was asleep or awake.

'Holly,' she said. 'I didn't want to wake you. I thought I'd wait.'

It was like being in a nightmare where you wanted to speak but nothing would come out. I shook my head. I looked at the door. I pointed at it. Go, my body was trying to tell her. Leave at once. Get out of my sight.

'I don't want to upset you,' she said.

I closed my eyes again. When I opened them she was still there.

'I hear you're being discharged tomorrow. I wanted to talk to you before then.'

The tears were sliding down my cheeks. I thought they would never stop.

'I wanted to say how sorry I am.'

I turned onto my side, my back to her.

'Do you still want to get away from him?' Her voice was very quiet. It was almost gentle. It was not a tone I imagined she was capable of.

I tented my face with the blanket, so she couldn't see me.

'We know it will be hard, but it will work best if you let him take you back to his house. My understanding is that they won't discharge you if you're alone.'

'No.' I let the blanket fall, so the air could no longer circulate around my nose.

She lifted it away. 'I'm worried you can't breathe.'

'No,' I said again. The word was a whisper.

'Holly, if you go to Peggy's you will find it much more difficult to take the necessary steps. You won't have to stay with him for long.'

'I can't be near him. You don't understand.'

'Tell me. Help me to understand.'

'Just go.'

'Listen to me. We'll get you out quickly, but it's important to convince him you've really gone, so he won't look for you.' Her hand was on my shoulder and I cringed away so violently she gasped.

'He'll never stop,' I said.

'The plans we already put in place are good ones. Let us at least do this for you. We'll have the medical care set up, and the other support you'll need. Plus a job, when you are stronger. I want to help you,' she says.

'You? You want to help?'

'Yes. All of us. But me especially.'

My voice was raspy and low. 'I don't want your help.'

'I know you don't,' she said, 'but you need it.'

I let Zac take me back to his house the next day, numb and dumb as a piece of wood except for when he touched my hand to help me out of the car and I screamed. But in the end, I decided it was better there than Peggy's. Peggy would want to drag me back to life. Zac wouldn't dare to try. He was relieved I had gone with him, and grateful. He kept saying so again and again. He was timid-seeming, perhaps even frightened, though I was certain the old Zac was still in there, ready to strike at any time. I would never let myself forget that.

The nursery was empty. The Moses basket was gone. I was ambushed by a pang for him, picturing him carrying it from the house, imagining him driving away from the hospital with her empty car seat, which he'd set up in the Range Rover that arrived the day after he returned from Canada. But he did not deserve my compassion.

He had removed the white-painted cot, and the mobile with brightly coloured birds that I'd attached to it. There were empty spaces where the changing table and rocking chair had been. The Mermaid of Zennor curtains I sewed for her, started before I was certain we would have to flee, were no longer hanging in the windows.

I'd lovingly furnished that room, even though I'd known that my baby and I would never occupy it. That proved true, but not in the way I'd imagined. The room was empty. The room was like me.

My nipples tingled and leaked. My body was mocking me. It wanted to remind me again and again of how I'd failed, of what I lacked. My stitches itched and pulled.

Going up the stairs was like climbing a mountain. I had to sit down halfway up. My breath came in gasps, as if I had been running for hours. My forehead was beaded with sweat from the pain in my lower abdomen, my back soaked.

Morning, noon, and night, Zac fed me a kaleidoscope of pills to wake me up and keep me calm and put me to bed. He let Milly and Peggy come and sit with me. He even brought them cups of tea. He actually seemed to want them there. I needed them, so he needed them too.

They said little. They held my hand. They put their arms around me as if they wished the pain could go out of me and into them, as if they wanted to share it. When I winced, they winced too. I saw Zac watching, as if longingly, because they could touch me but he could not.

Zac spoke quietly to the doctor who visited me at home. Their voices were a hum of babble from far away. There was only one thing in all of it that I could understand, a noise that came like a bomb, but was quickly suppressed. The noise was from Zac. It was a loud, racking sob that he seemed to choke on.

One morning, when the post came, I caught him swooping it up, panic in his face. But it was not his usual jealousy and control. It was that the catalogues of baby and new mother products were continuing to arrive, and he was trying to clear them away to make sure I didn't stumble on them.

He bought me a lined journal covered in Far Away Tree fabric, a Liberty print he knew I loved. He said, 'You used to love to write. Maybe it will help.' His voice went quieter when he continued. 'I will never read it.' As he put the new one in my lap, I thought of the orange journal he used against me. 'You have good reason not to believe me, but I won't. I did read the hospital stories you wrote. I'm sorry. I shouldn't have. But they were beautiful, Holly – I couldn't tell you that then because it would have meant admitting the scale of what I'd done.'

For him to say this to me – I couldn't – I hardly knew how to speak. 'You found my old journal because you'd installed hidden cameras.'

'Holly—'

'It's the only explanation. Did you or did you not?'

'I did.'

'Are the cameras gone?'

'Yes.'

'Where were they?'

He didn't answer.

'Was there one in our bedroom? Tell me, Zac.'

'No, there wasn't.'

'You're lying. I know it.'

'Okay. Yes. There was one there, yes. But not for the reason you think. I was worried they might secretly search the house, because of my ex-wife.'

'Don't dehumanise her by calling her your ex-wife. Call her by her name. Call her Jane.'

He looked down. He swallowed hard but said nothing.

'Why would they search the house?'

'They thought I had something to do with Jane's disappearance. I didn't.'

'Did you catch anybody – I mean, did you see anyone come in the house?'

'No. I know I shouldn't have put that camera in the bedroom. I know there's no excuse for subjecting you to that.'

'So there was film of me. Film of the things you did to me.'

'Yes.'

'Because obviously you needed to capture our bed to guard against potential intruders. Did you watch it?'

He hesitated. 'I want to lie and say no, but I don't want to lie to you any more. They say – I've been going – I've been getting help. So yes, I did sometimes watch.'

'Did anybody else see it?'

'No! Never! Of course not.'

'You didn't give the footage to anyone?'

'I promise. The answer's no. All the footage has been wiped.'

'You wiped it?'

'It's gone.'

'So filming me was a secondary motive to the primary motive of making sure you weren't being spied on?'

'Filming you wasn't a motive at all.'

'More like collateral damage.'

'More like an unexpected benefit.' I could see he regretted the words as soon as they were out of his mouth. 'God, Holly. Fuck. I know how wrong that sounded.'

'Why? It's what you think. There's no way anything about any of this can sound anything other than wrong. I found your magazines in the garage. And the things you kept in the bag with them.'

'How did you get in the garage, Holly?'

'Why does it matter?'

'How?'

He had been so compliant, until that moment. So filled with sorrow.

Since it happened, his remorse had made him quell every flash of his usual anger. It made him quash his normal insistence on getting his way about everything. I'd known those things were still there, though. I had been waiting for them.

I felt myself tense with the usual fear. 'Milly broke in when you were in Canada.' He wouldn't dream of talking to Milly about this, so I was in no danger of discovery that way. In any case, he would believe that almost anyone we knew was more capable of doing such a thing than I was.

The colour drained from his face. 'Did Milly see?'

'No. It was bad enough that I did. She left before I opened the bag. I'm glad she hasn't had to have those images in her head, too.'

'I'm ashamed of them.' He was biting his lip. 'I don't look at material like that any more.'

'It's what you wanted to do to me all along.'

'It wasn't, Holly.'

'It's what you did do.' I stood, trying not to wince, because I was secretly weaning myself off the painkillers that dulled me. The Far Away Tree journal fell to the floor. I did not pick it up. 'I put your bag and its contents out with the rubbish where it belonged. I didn't want it near me.'

At bedtime, I found the Far Away Tree journal on my bedside table, beside the pink memory box. I did not touch either of them.

The next morning, he sat with me at breakfast, but I did not eat the toast he had made me. 'You took my baby,' I said. 'Tell me where she is.'

'Holly, our baby died.' He looked so sad I would have believed him if I didn't know him better. He blinked so fast the two colours of his eye blended into one. 'You saw her,' he said. 'You cried over her while you held her.'

'You're lying.' The hair on my arms was standing on end. 'I'd remember. That never happened.'

'It's called dissociative amnesia. There are a range of symptoms, but in your case, you've suppressed your memory of a specific traumatic event.' He wiped a hand over his head so hard his scalp blanched.

'You're constantly telling me there's something wrong with my mental health when what I'm saying isn't to your liking. If she were really dead, holding her would have been the most precious thing in my whole life. I would want to remember. I'd never let myself forget a single second with her.'

I got up to leave the room. When I reached the kitchen door and turned to look back at him, his elbows were on the table and his head was in his hands and his whole body was shaking, but he wasn't making a sound.

I spent as much time as I could in the garden, lying on the grass beneath the handkerchief tree, which was in flower. Above me, the white petals fluttered like doves. Below me, the skeletons in the plague pit reached out their arms, and I pressed myself into the earth to be closer to them, wanting to be swallowed too. I imagined my hair, twining into the grass, tangling with the roots below, pinning me down and pulling me in, until I was more soil than person and I couldn't see or be seen.

I only ate if Zac put a plate in front of me. I only drank if he poured water into a glass and put it in my hand, his fingers careful not to brush mine. I cried all the time. I never seemed not to be crying. The blood seemed not to stop.

All I wanted was for it to stop. Every drop reminded me. I thought it would never stop.

Zac murmured that he loved me, that he would always love me, that I would come back to him in time, that he would look after me, that he would change, he *was* changing and getting help, that he would do whatever it took to earn my forgiveness, that we would have another baby, there were ways, surrogacy, and Milly had told him she would do that for me, and we could still use my eggs. This was a new and different Zac. This was not the Zac I knew. But my heart was hard, forever hard, to him.

'I don't want another baby,' I said. 'I want my baby.' My arms were so empty.

'You are too young, and too hurt, to know what you want,' he said.

I slept in the guest room. Even with a wall between me and Zac, I tamped the quilt into the mattress around me. I was in a quilt bubble. I was like a pill in a blister pack. It was the best I could do, because they had removed all the locks from the doors, not trusting me. Once, I woke in the night, and caught him kneeling by the side of my bed with his hand in my hair. I screamed and knocked it away and he flew from the room, telling me he was sorry, promising never to do it again.

One afternoon, about two weeks after I left hospital, I was sitting on the red velvet cushion of the window seat that overlooked the back garden. My knees were drawn up, and I'd pulled the flowered curtains closed to make a cocoon for myself. I heard the rustle of fabric and lifted my head to see Zac standing near, clutching a cup of chamomile tea in one hand and folds of chintz in the other. His knuckles were white, as if he'd been in dread of what he would find behind the curtain.

'The cowslips are over,' he said, handing me the tea and looking through the window. 'Remember when you told me their leaves were like tongues? I love how you see things, Holly. I'm sorry' – his voice was thick – 'I'm sorry you missed the cowslips.'

I said that I was feeling a bit better, and watched his face light up as if it really mattered to him that I had glanced at the fields behind the house to look for the wildflowers that were no longer there.

During dinner that night, when he left the dining room to get himself another beer, I tipped the contents of two of my sedative capsules into his beef casserole and stirred it in. My own dinner was untouched, the elderflower he had poured me hardly sipped, and it was a measure of how he tiptoed around me that he said nothing.

Early the next morning, before the sun was up, I slipped out of bed. It was a summer storm. The air was so heavy with rain that I couldn't see the lighthouse lamp, however hard I squinted, and this felt like another blow, another goodbye that had been stolen from me. The wind noise and the sea noise were one noise, and I couldn't disentangle them.

I knew what Zac would find, when he woke from his pill-induced sleep, and what he would do. He would find the house abandoned, but I had left a trail for him. He would track me to a little-known, hard-to-access section of the cliffs.

It was a place where I once took him blackberrying. He

hated it there, with the waves so fierce the spray reached us six metres up. He'd covered his face, but I turned mine to the water and lifted it to the sky in exhilaration while Zac said I was mad, half-jokingly, but also half in pride. The cliff jutted out over a section of the ocean where fishing boats had been lost, the currents ensuring that those who drowned there were never found.

Every step Zac took along the path to that cliff would be in dread. He would stumble upon my phone and clothes and shoes, beneath a tree that was bent by the fierce wind that had blasted it for a century. At the very edge, he would find the memory box, with the teddy bear still inside, left for him, but the photograph and footprint gone. He would think that I had taken them with me, into the sea, going where he could not follow.

Now *Thorpe Hall*

One year and ten months later

Yorkshire, Tuesday, 9 April 2019

It is 7 p.m. and I have been off the motorway for fifteen minutes when my mobile begins to ring. George's name is flashing on the display, which is set up for hands-free and clamped into a cheap plastic holder that clips into an air vent. I press accept, hit the speaker-phone button, and say hello.

'I thought you were going home,' he says.

'How do you know I'm not?' Windmills are rising above a valley that is lined with dark brick houses.

'Lucky guess.' There is the tap of fingers on a keyboard. 'I discovered something you might find interesting.'

'What?' I am leaving the rows of houses behind. To my left is a small lake, which channels itself into tiny streams, criss-crossing through fields of deep green.

'Eliza was working at the Museum of Modern Art in New York. She was there from January 2012 until March 2017, flying back and forth between the US and Europe as part of the job.'

Zac said in that London hotel that Eliza had been in

the US for a few years, and I'd found something along those lines a few days ago, when I did an Internet search on her.

'Here's the thing,' he says. 'I found some medical records for her in the US.'

'What kind of records?' The fields are dotted with new lambs, chasing their mothers. I am not sure why, but I am holding my breath for his answer.

'She was seeing a reproductive endocrinologist soon after she arrived there. She was only thirty-two, but the diagnosis was premature ovarian failure.'

The scenery outside my car window seems to mock what George is talking about. It takes me a few seconds to form the words. 'Eliza was already in full menopause?'

'Not my area of expertise, but as far as I can understand it, yes.'

I'm racing through the implications of this, trying to be calm and rational and drive safely when my heart is pounding so hard it seems to be echoing in my own ears.

If Eliza Wilmot was menopausal before Alice was born, she cannot be her biological mother. She could have used a donor egg, but that makes no sense, given that there's little doubt that Zac is Alice's father. It is one thing to believe he accidentally got Eliza pregnant during an affair while he was with me, quite another to imagine he actively participated in her fertility treatment in the way a partner would – though I can't entirely discount the possibility.

Was Eliza ever really pregnant? Could Alice – must she – be mine? Those stories I'd found of stillborn babies swapped with living ones, and forced adoption, and the kidnapping of newborn babies. I'd tried to tell myself it was part of my mad grief, my wish for it not to be true that my baby was gone, my inability to accept it. I don't know what all of this might mean for Alice. Until I do, I don't want her put at risk by having it known. 'Have you kept any records of this, George?'

'No.'

'Do you feel you need to?'

He pauses. 'Do you feel I should feel I need to?'

I laugh, astonishing myself that I still can. 'I'm not sure yet.'

'Then neither am I.'

'Why are you doing this for me?'

'Because when you tried to help us, you got badly hurt. It's the least we – I – can do.'

'What do you want from me?'

'Me, nothing. Maxine—' Do I imagine that he chokes back whatever he'd been about to say? 'As she said, she'll speak to you later. Where are you, Holly?'

'Visiting an old friend.'

'Tell me where you are. Please.'

'It's not as if you can't figure it out, George. Uh-oh. I seem to be losing the signal.' And I cut off the call.

It is dark by the time I reach Thorpe Hall, which sits below the main road in a little valley. I leave my car at the top of the narrow lane that leads to it, then walk down, lighting the way with my phone torch, which I switch off when I am close.

The ground is boggy, presumably from the run-off that must come from above. It looks as if the whole decaying house is about to be swallowed in a huge, quick-sanded gulp. I know from the map that behind the house is moorland, which ends at the cliffs about half a kilometre from the back garden.

Two withered pear trees, their branches entwining, stand in front of the house, silhouetted in the faint moonlight. There is a central portico. Latticed windows like small eyes, sunken in more of the dark Yorkshire brick, seem to study me, though there don't appear to be any lamps behind them. Eliza and Alice are probably asleep, or at the back of the house.

It is too late to knock on the door unannounced. If I were Eliza, I would not open it at such an hour. In any case, I am practically falling over with exhaustion, and in no condition to act. I return to my car and retrace the route I took earlier, stopping at a crumbling old hotel that I earmarked along the way. Through the window of my room, I can see the shadowy ruins of an old abbey. I strip off my filthy clothes and take a shower. When I finally collapse on the bed, wrapped in a towel and with my hair still wet, I am so tired I feel as if drugs are coursing through my veins. I want to think about Alice, but I fall asleep the instant my eyes are closed, unable to think about anything at all.

Yorkshire, Wednesday, 10 April 2019

It is 9.30 in the morning when I stand at the door, gathering courage after coming so far. I take a deep breath and grab the knocker, which is in the shape of a lion's head. I smooth the midnight blue dress with tiny moons, which I'm wearing again. I'd repaired what I could using the sewing kit in my hotel room plus a few extra that I'd taken from a stray housekeeping trolley. Then I'd brushed away the worst of the dirt. I am about to knock a second time when I hear footsteps approaching and the lock turning.

Eliza is wearing jeans and a grey sweatshirt, trainers on her feet, and her hair in a short ponytail. Behind her, I can hear Alice crying, and it is as if I am in hospital again, when those cries I thought were coming from somewhere else were actually coming from me.

'Oh, Helen.' Eliza bursts into tears and falls into my arms.

'I was worried about you.' I am craning my neck to look behind her shoulder. 'Is Alice okay?'

She pulls away, wipes her face with an elbow. 'I'm scared that maybe the iron supplement isn't working fast enough – she's so sleepy after the journey. And extra cranky. It's since we got here – I'd never have brought her otherwise.'

I feel a cramp low in my belly, where my womb used to be, like the twitch of a phantom limb. 'We can take her to A and E.'

She nods. 'I was thinking I would. How did you find us?'

'I went to your house. Your husband – Zac – told me.'

'I see.'

'I didn't want you to be alone.'

'That's kind.' She clears her throat. 'How was he?'

'The police came while I was there.'

'They arrested him?'

'Yes.'

She closes her eyes tightly. 'Alice has stopped crying. She's probably fallen asleep again.' Eliza puts the door on the latch, makes extra sure by grabbing a key from a hook and slipping it in her pocket, then steps outside and pulls the door shut behind her. 'Just in case – I don't want her to hear me upset.'

'It must be so hard, with a little one, to protect them.'

She takes a deep breath. 'Zac told me who you are. Do you know, he wouldn't even speak your name before? I thought – I imagined I'd hate you. But you're just like me. Another of his victims. He might have smothered you too. He might have smothered me. How can I resent Jane for sleeping with him, when she suffered as she did? We were friends once, you know. Good friends. Am I an idiot?'

I shake my head. 'Of course not. I'm so sorry, Eliza.' And though I truly am sorry, I'm not sure exactly what I am apologising for. Is it that I will somehow take my child back, and leave Eliza heartbroken? That the thought of Eliza losing a child she clearly loves makes me feel sick in the pit of my stomach, despite the fact that she may have done this very thing to me? That I cannot decide whether she is innocent in all of this, perhaps believing she has adopted Alice legitimately, or if she has conspired with Zac to steal my baby? That I don't understand why she has stayed with Zac if she sees herself as a victim? That beneath my gentle expression, I am anything but?

'Were you going to tell me who you are?' she says.

'Yes, though I'd been wondering if you already knew.'

She shakes her head. 'No. No idea until he told me yesterday. I would have said.'

Again, I'm struck by the thought that if Eliza is lying she is the best actress I've ever seen, and she would definitely pass a final interview with Maxine. 'That's what I thought. I'm not sure which of us was more terrified when he came home early on Friday.'

She puffs out a sad half-laugh. 'I don't even know which of your names I should use.'

'Whichever you prefer.'

'"A rose by any other name . . ."' She puts out her hand and I clasp it in mine. It is clammy. 'We must help each other. You and I seem to be the only surviving members of a horrible club.' Eliza turns away to unlock the front door. 'I need to check on Alice.'

We step into the silence of a dim entry hall that opens into a long corridor through the centre of the house. The doors that branch off it are all closed. I bump my elbow on a heavy cabinet as I hurry after Eliza. 'Where is Alice?'

'The room at the end. It's where we've been sleeping. Upstairs the paper's peeling from the walls – it's wet to the touch, the damp's so bad.' She manages a grim smile. 'I can't tell you how many dead spiders were in the bathtub. I had to boil kettles and saucepans for hot water. The house is for sale, but Zac seems to be letting it rot.'

I think of the capital gains tax that Albert mentioned. At this rate of depreciation, Zac will owe practically nothing. Or perhaps he is hoping that the whole thing will fall into the sea – I can imagine his pleasure at such a revenge. Only a few miles away, in the middle of the nineteenth century, a small village tipped over the cliffs and was lost.

Eliza sighs. 'I hadn't wanted to run to my father. I was too humiliated. I think I'm going to take a little trip with Alice, after she's seen a doctor – Are you okay, Helen? You're not saying much.'

'I'm just worried for you and Alice.'

'I've been in such shock and grief since we got here, but this place is impossible.' She lets out a half-laugh. 'Plus, our supply of crackers and juice boxes is running thin.'

We have paused outside a heavy door. 'Where will you go?' I can't let her take Alice away.

'No idea yet.' She pushes the door open.

Inside, there is a faded velvet sofa that probably used to be crimson, with the scrolled arms lowered on both sides to convert it into a bed. It is made up with a quilt and pillows that Eliza must have brought with her. The portraits in this room would be perfect for a haunted house. There is a woman who looks like the bride of Death, and a trio who make me think of an executioner, a condemned man, and the priest who will officiate at the burial, though I'm not sure the artist intended the resemblance.

'Alice? Where are you hiding?' Eliza moves quickly to the sofa, hurls the bedding onto the buckling floorboards. There is no Alice beneath it. Maybe the glowering paintings frightened her.

I feel like a fire swallower as I watch Eliza rush to the other side of the sofa, searching behind it.

'Are you playing hide and seek, poppet?' The faint

echo of Eliza's voice plays back to us like a ghost's whisper.

My chest is burning, my stomach turning into a lump. There is a mahogany sideboard against the far wall, the wood peeling. I am terrified that Alice is trapped in it, starved of air. I yank open the doors so violently that the collage photo frame, which Eliza has brought with her from Bath, falls to the floor with a shatter of glass. The space inside the sideboard is empty.

I am calculating the amount of time Eliza and I were talking outside. Probably about fifteen minutes. Unlike the high lattices at the front of the house, there are sash windows in this room, large and low. Both are open.

Eliza is shaking her head, watching me take this in. 'No. Oh no.' The words come out in a squeak. 'It was so stuffy in here, and damp-smelling. We needed air.'

We are running together to the window. About three metres away from the house, dropped in the high grass, is the stuffed kitty I remember Alice playing with on her first visit to the Paediatric Unit.

'Is there any way that could have got there other than by Alice dropping it?'

Eliza is struggling to get her breath. 'No. We came in through the front. We've barely left this room. I've been – frozen – since Zac told me he'd been with Jane. And Alice was so lethargic. She seemed not to want to move, so we snuggled while I read to her.'

'Can Alice climb?'

She gulps. 'We can't keep her in her cot any more. She's ready for a proper bed.'

Before Eliza has finished the sentence, I am opening

the window wider and climbing out. 'Call 999. She can't have got far.'

'I'll go. I'm her mother.'

What I think is, *No you're not*. But this isn't the time for that fight. 'I grew up in this sort of landscape. I can find her faster.'

'I told her I'd take her to the cliffs to see the puffins.'

I manage a nod. Already I am turning away from her, though I hear her shouting that she can't get a signal so she's going to run up the lane to the main road to try for one.

My first instinct is simply to scream Alice's name. Instead, I make myself crouch down, trying to see the world from her height, trying to imagine the steps she would take.

If I were nearly two years old, and searching for puffins, I would zero in on where the grown-up pointed. Sure enough, when I look closely, there is a line where the grass bends slightly outwards on both sides, showing the path Alice must have made by trampling through it. The line is like a faint arrow, aimed at the cliff. Slowly, I follow it.

The sun is bright. The cliff edge lies beyond a wall of gorse. There is a breeze, carrying the heavy coconut scent, making the air seem malignant, and so intense I can almost taste it. The yellow flowers are too abundant, the bushes too dense.

I squint. Again, I crouch low, trying to see the world from Alice's perspective. There is a natural break in the gorse. I crawl through it, partly to stop myself from a rushed panic that will make me lose Alice's trail, partly to maintain her vantage point. Above, there is the deep-throated cry of a gull, the dark tips of its wings visible. I want it to shut up, so I can listen for Alice, who must be near.

My progress is so slow, but the crucial thing is to follow accurately, rather than risk going in the wrong direction and losing her. A metre ahead, caught on a thorny branch, is a scrap of white and pink jersey. It must have come from Alice, so I am likely to be close. I rise, stumble through the last of the gorse, and come out the other end.

Now *The Miniature*

Yorkshire, Wednesday, 10 April 2019

It is as if I have stepped through a tear between two worlds. After the silence, the sea seems to roar at me from below. The grass is so green and unexpected that its proximity to the salty water is impossible to take in. Crumpled beside a large rock to my right is a little girl. She is wearing white pyjamas sprinkled with pink fairies, and her feet are bare and bleeding. She is a metre and a half from the cliff edge.

She isn't moving. I stifle a cry, smacking my hand against my mouth, and twist myself into a change of direction, towards her. There is the sound of a pop, from deep inside my own body. I hurtle downwards, breaking my fall with both hands. I lift my leg. My foot is dangling, as if whatever internal strings that attached it to the rest of me have broken. It ignores the signals my brain is sending to try to operate it. My ankle is tingling as if the worst case of pins and needles I've ever had has been multiplied a million-fold.

It happened in a heartbeat, a fluke because I turned too fast, at the wrong angle at the worst possible time. I have to bite down hard not to scream, because I don't want to startle Alice. Did she see how close she was to the edge, and know enough to pull back from it?

I cannot walk. I consider standing on one foot, to hop, but it is too difficult when my head is about to explode. Instead, I drag my body across the grass as if I were a serpent, barely noticing as I scrape my legs on fragments of rocks. By the time I reach Alice I am breathing so heavily I cannot discern anything when I put my ear to her chest. After a minute, when I have finally stopped panting, I am certain that she is breathing too.

All my life, I have dreamed of the dead coming back. Matilda in the book. My parents, in the world I go to when I sleep. And now it has happened. I pull her onto my lap. She is my true miracle. My own child, returned to me. I bend over her, putting my lips to her cheek, which is startlingly cool, despite the hot sun. As carefully as I can, I examine her.

Other than her feet, there are no cuts, but when I push up her torn pyjama bottoms I can see that there are several new bruises on her legs, ranging from red to blue, and an older green one too. Her anaemia has been diagnosed, and these livid blotches are identical to the ones that covered me after she was born. How did Zac miss this? Was he too distracted? Or did her condition deteriorate precipitously over the past few days, when he saw little of her?

I can't be sure if she is asleep, or if she has somehow fallen and hit her head on that rock. I can't see any sign that she has. I remember that the anaemia made it so hard to do anything but sleep, as if I were in a kind of coma I couldn't wake from, but I'd thought then it was an escape from a life I couldn't bear to be conscious in. She is so light, as I cradle her in my arms, and terrifyingly pale. But for the bruises, she is nearly as white as the background colour of her pyjamas. I hold her hand in mine. The palm is pale, too, and icy cold like her cheek. Her nail beds and lips have the faintest tint of pink. I reach into my pocket for my phone. As Eliza said, there is no signal.

Again I bend my ear to her chest. She is breathing, but not peacefully. I study her some more. The skin at the base of her neck is inflating and deflating, instead of her stomach, and she is wheezing. I pull up her pyjama top. The skin over her ribs is drawing in when she inhales, making them look prominent to a degree that cannot be right.

Keeping Alice in one arm and draped over my lap, I use my other arm, and the one foot that is still working, to slide backwards and away from the cliff and closer to help. Beyond the point where the grass ends and the world drops, the sea is endlessly before me, dazzling and interminable and blue. I cannot let myself calculate how long it will take me to get Alice to the house this way. I have barely moved us a couple metres, and want to cry in relief when there is a crashing noise that makes me look over my shoulder to see Eliza burst through the gorse.

She falls on her knees beside us, weeping. 'Thank God you've found her.' She is touching Alice's hair.

'I can't wake her,' I say. 'I can't see any cuts other than

on her feet, but she's struggling with her breathing and she has several new bruises. She's very pale. She's too cold.'

Eliza shifts to look. 'Oh my God.'

'I can't walk, Eliza – I've done something – I don't know what – my foot's dangling, so I can't help.'

She puts a hand on my shoulder. 'You're in pain – I'm sorry. I've called 999 but it's going to take them a while. The house is so remote. Then they'll have to find us out here.'

What I say next is against my every impulse, because I never want to let Alice go. But I do say it. 'Carry her. Run. If the paramedics aren't in sight, then throw her in the car and drive to the nearest hospital or doctor's surgery.'

Eliza nods. 'Okay. I'll make sure to send them for you.' She bends to take Alice, her face so close I worry that Alice's breathing will be impeded. With that thought, something catches in the corner of my foggy brain. It cuts through my terror for Alice and the pain that is throbbing through the place above my heel so acutely it seems to pierce my skull too. Exhaustion made me fail to see it earlier.

'Eliza?' My left hand is ready to protect Alice.

Eliza straightens and looks up, a question on her face.

'How did you know Jane was smothered?' My right hand is ready to move.

The skin around Eliza's eyes blanches. 'What?'

'You couldn't have known that.' I am bracing myself, my stomach muscles tightening, preparing to balance from this sitting position if I need to strike at Eliza.

'I don't understand. I don't know what you mean.' But

I can see from the way she is biting her lip that she does.

She moves to take Alice from my lap and I try to push her away, but my movements are feeble and I am finding it more difficult than I imagined to keep myself from tipping.

Almost immediately, she straightens up. 'What do you think you're doing, Holly?'

She has used my real name for the first time. I do not like my name in her voice. My answer is to bend forwards, using as much of my upper body as I can to shield Alice.

'Give her to me.' Eliza's jaw is clenched. 'If you make me wrestle you for her, all three of us might end up going over. It will be your fault if something happens to her.'

I gather Alice in more tightly, trying to bundle her into a concentrated mass. 'It's the judgement of Solomon. I would never do anything to put her in danger. You're not her real mother.'

Her hand flies to her mouth. 'Oh, Holly. Oh no.' She looks so deeply horrified and shocked. 'You think Alice is yours.'

Alice makes a small whimper. A strand of copper hair has stuck to her cheek. I smooth it away. 'I know she is. You know it too.'

And then the world lurches. Or rather, I do, because Eliza digs a hand into each of my shoulders, pushing my upper body from my child's with every atom of force she has and not stopping until my head smashes into the edge of a rock and I am flat on my back. I am too dazed to prevent Eliza from snatching up Alice, who is sprawled across my chest.

Eliza stands, holding Alice against her as if she were

burping a baby, and looks down at me. 'She's not yours.'

It is too hard to focus on the two of them. My head is too heavy to raise from the grass. I try to make my brain tell my body to move, but all of the signals seem to have short-circuited. My eyes drift away. They drift up, to the sky. The sky is full of stars, even though it is bleached blue. The sun is a huge orange ball in a child's picture. I decide that staying here is the best thing I can do. I am too tired. I cannot fight any more. And if Alice isn't mine, what is there left to fight for? Now, I will let the grass grow above me. I will let the soil swallow me. I will become part of the huge burial ground that is the earth. The plague pit is here too. It is everywhere. It has been waiting to pull me in. I am finally ready to let it.

The back of my head is sticky and wet as it rolls to the side, where I can see Eliza. Tenderly, she puts Alice down, then tears off the grey sweatshirt she has tied around her own waist, which she makes a pillow of and places beneath Alice's floppy head. Alice is so, so far away. Our time together was too short, but I am ready to let go, at last.

I am six metres from the cliff edge. My eyes fall shut, and I can hear a shuffling noise. When I open them again, Eliza is sitting on the ground beside me. Her feet are braced against my hips, her knees bent. She is crying. 'I don't want to do this. I don't want to hurt you, Holly. But I can't do anything else. You know what I've done.'

When she straightens her knees, the movement slides me a few centimetres. She is like an accordion, contracting and expanding her legs, shuffling forwards, her feet moving up and down the side of my body to continue to manoeuvre me closer to the edge, but stopping again and again, crying all the while. I am too limp, and my head is hurting so much, as if it is filling with blood, and growing so heavy with the weight of all that liquid.

Eliza is becoming more and more breathless, by my side. 'I'm so sorry. Oh God, I'm so sorry.' She looks up at the sky, seeming to talk to it. 'Help me. Tell me what to do.' She pulls her feet away from me and curls into a ball. 'I can't. I can't I can't I can't.'

She is hugging her knees and rocking. 'I'm sorry. I'm sorry. I'm so sorry. I know about your baby,' she says, 'and I'm so sorry. I know you don't believe she died, but she did. Oh God. Oh God Oh God. You're one of the few people who would understand.'

My head is making me so dizzy, and so tired, and I must be careful not to give any dangerous things away, because my judgement is all gone. Maxine would know what to say and do. Maxine knows everything, and she is always right. What was the term she used? *Confirmation bias.* The truth was unfolding right in front of my eyes, but I twisted the evidence to tell the story I wanted instead of the one that happened.

'Why?' That is a good word, and one Maxine might use, too.

'I couldn't love Alice any more than I do. I can't lose her now. Not because of you.'

I snatch another glimpse of Alice, who is curled like a kitten, and my friends from the plague pit loosen their grip. I hear them whispering from below. *Not yet*, they say. *You cannot come to us yet. You must stay among the living for now.*

Eliza's pupils have shrunk. 'You see I have no choice, don't you? Please say yes.'

'No,' I say.

Her eyes are circles of white, with a small dark dot in each. 'Do you understand what Jane and I did, Holly? Do you know about Zac going to Moldova?'

I don't want it to be true, but I do remember. That medical conference Zac went to a couple months before he made me pregnant. Did he meet Jane there? It would have been a relatively safe place for her. Like Montenegro, it doesn't extradite as easily as EU countries. That must have been when Zac and Jane conceived Alice. 'Yes.'

I glimpse a spider moving through the grass. I think of how a spider carries her silken egg sac beneath her belly. What determination must a spider have to drag something so much bigger than she is? If she can do that, I can do this. I force my head into movement once more, to watch Eliza, to convey sympathy. 'You loved Jane.' There is a hammer in my skull.

'I did.' Eliza begins to sob. 'She knew I couldn't have a child.'

'She loved you too.'

'Yes. Yes, she did. She was going through so much herself with her marriage. And the IRS. I wanted to die when I found out I couldn't have a baby, but Jane helped me through.'

It is as if I have a kaleidoscope behind my eyes, and each time I manage to alight on a distinct picture, it dissolves into mess. But I see the pact Eliza and Jane must have made, with Eliza faking a pregnancy and Jane hiding her own. They had to trust each other. They each had so much to lose.

Eliza hits the top of her left wrist with the fingers of her right hand, again and again, a series of sharp smacks that seem to be slapping away inside my own head. 'Jane didn't want Zac to have Alice when she found out he was expecting a baby with you.'

I remember a trip Zac made when I was ten weeks pregnant. That was to the Ukraine, another country that is a lighter touch than most when it comes to extradition, especially when Jane had her brother's help with altering databases and interfering with surveillance measures. Did Zac meet Jane there to break the news about me and our baby? Was that when she decided to keep Alice a secret from him, and give her baby away? She must have been starting to show by then, a couple months ahead of me, but she was so slight – she could have covered it up.

I realise Eliza must have been wearing a prosthetic bump when she met Zac in that London hotel. She deliberately led him to think she'd been abandoned by her partner. Zac had no clue that he had two babies on the way, then. I'm struggling to make my brain compute this new reality – Zac had told me the truth about Eliza and Alice. He'd just omitted the pact Eliza and Jane had made, which he'd discovered when Eliza turned up on his doorstep with Alice.

'You're my friend, Eliza.' I try again to flex my bad foot, testing, but it does absolutely nothing.

'Don't. Don't say that.' She covers her eyes with her

hands and sobs. 'You're the reason Zac made us move to Bath.'

When Eliza brought Alice to the hospital that first time, she must have guessed who I was before I'd even started to mop up her spilled coffee.

She is clenching and unclenching her jaw. 'It's your fault. It's your fault Jane went there. It's your fault she's dead. I wouldn't have had to do it if it weren't for you. I didn't mean to. I didn't want to. And now I have to do this too.'

'You don't.'

'Zac didn't know I knew.' She is shaking her head, her eyes tightly shut. She sounds like a child chanting a nursery rhyme. 'Not about you. He didn't know I knew.'

When he came back early from his Edinburgh trip, Eliza wasn't pretending to be terrified he'd find me there. The terror was real. But it wasn't because she lived in fear of him. It was because she didn't want him to discover the extent of what she knew about me. Perhaps Eliza is the best spy of us all.

I try again to lift my head, and I manage an inch or two, but it thwacks back onto the ground, rattling my brain against my skull. I drag my eyes to Alice. She hasn't moved.

'I don't want to hurt you. I don't I don't I don't. Oh God. I don't.'

'You don't have to.'

'I do. Zac would want to be with you. I'd lose Alice.'

'Not to me.' I see how terrifying it must have been for Eliza, imagining having to share Alice with a woman Zac loved more than her, though she couldn't let herself see that there was zero chance of my ever wanting to be that woman.

She shakes her head again. 'No. No no no no no. I was right. I was so angry when I phoned you on Monday and you said Zac's name. You were expecting his call. You two were already talking behind my back, weren't you?'

I remember Zac saying he didn't leave the robin in front of my front door. He must have been telling the truth about that, too. It must have been Eliza, wanting me to hate him. She'd made a point of telling me Zac had been in Bath before he travelled to Edinburgh later that same day. She'd wanted me to realise he'd had the opportunity to leave me the robin.

She digs her shoe into my hip and the pain shakes me and shakes me and shakes me some more, jetting up into my head and down to my ankle. But it wakes me too.

'We weren't,' I say. 'I'm your friend.'

'You aren't. You avoided giving me your number until two days ago. But I know how to defeat a phone passcode. I've broken into Zac's so many times.'

I try to think when she could have done this. I must have left my phone in my bag when I pretended to go to the loo so I could snoop around her house. That was how she got my number and dialled it while I waited in front of Maxine's house in Cheltenham.

I am grappling to remember something important I wanted to ask her. 'Frederick.'

She looks genuinely confused. 'Who's Frederick?'

'My head.' My brain is like a sheet of glass, spiderwebbing before it shatters.

'For the best? Is that what you said?'

'Yes.'

'I did. I made the best decision I could. I'd always loved Zac. And he was Alice's father. I was able to give him his child. That was the right thing to do, once you were gone. I told him what Jane and I had done – he immediately understood why.'

Something pings for me, and I work hard to form another thought through the haze. The thought is that Eliza doesn't know about Frederick. Jane told her some of the truth, but probably only the IRS part of it. She didn't talk about her brother and what he did, or what she and Zac helped him to do. Eliza doesn't know the real reason Jane was in hiding.

'Family. You gave. Alice.' My words are no longer coming in the right order.

'Zac was still in mourning for you and your baby – he was so lost.' A shadow passes over her face. 'I wanted my marriage with Zac to be a real marriage.' What she says next comes out strangled. 'We were one hundred per cent together when it came to Alice, but he wouldn't even sleep with me – he said it wouldn't be fair. That was the deal.'

She lied that he hurt her. She pretended to fear him.

'No better way to get a man to love you forever than to run away from him.' She wipes her eyes. 'I was too late to that lesson, but you and Jane were born knowing it.'

At last, I understand why Jane took such a huge risk in returning to the UK. It was her longing for Alice. She couldn't live with the choice she'd made.

'I don't. You. Blame.'

'Jane can't just change her mind like that and ask for Alice, can she?'

'No.' This is an easy word.

'She wanted to take them both. My child and my husband.' She flutters her hands. 'It was too much. All in one day. You that morning. Her that night. I followed him there, you see.' Eliza takes a shuddering breath and I picture what happened. Zac slipping out of Jane's house, then Eliza sneaking in.

Eliza gulps. 'Zac wouldn't touch me, but he'd left her smiling in her sleep. I hadn't planned to do it, but that smile . . . I thought she wouldn't wake, you see, but it was so hard.' I recall the red mark on Eliza's cheek. She'd said Alice did it. But it must have been Jane, fighting back. Eliza's voice goes flat. 'I left the pillow on her face, so I didn't have to look.'

The pillow was gone by the time I arrived, and nobody mentioned it until yesterday. Was its removal part of the forensic processes? Or had Maxine wanted to make sure I saw Jane, that I had no choice but to look? Had Maxine known that by forcing me to see, I would care all the more about what had happened to her? That I wouldn't be able to let it go?

I wanted you invested in what happened to Jane. That was what Maxine said on Monday when I asked why she'd let me follow her to Cheltenham.

'I tried to make her arms and legs pretty.' Eliza is like a child seeking praise. 'I covered her – Zac had left her naked – I didn't want others to see that.' She looks behind her, then up, into a sky that is so blue it makes my eyes hurt. 'They'll be here soon, from when I called 999. You need to go away, Holly, before they arrive.'

I cannot walk, and my head has broken into pieces, but I manage to slip a hand into the pocket of my dress. I concentrate with every shred of brain I have left, as if trying to levitate an impossible object. The force of my mind, my body, my fingers, all going in one direction.

Eliza moves closer, and raises herself, so just her shins are on the grass, her profile to the cliff edge. She is still near my feet, but there are two of her, and I cannot decide which one is the real Eliza because my eyes are playing tricks on me.

'If you don't leave, they'll take Alice away. You'll tell them what I did to Jane. You want to help me, don't you?'

'No tell.'

'But you will.' The two Elizas smile, though their smiles are so sad as they squeeze my bad foot, making me cry out, but showing me that the Eliza who is touching me is the real one, and the double by her side is the spectre. 'Please. Can you roll? You'll feel such peace. You'll be with your baby. Can you do it yourself, so I don't have to? I don't want to do it, but I will. Please don't make me. Not again.'

Milly's talisman, the skimming stone she painted with the miniature portrait of me and my baby, is in my palm. I have kept it close every day, since I ran away. My eyes are on Eliza's forehead. All in one movement, I throw. Blood snakes down her temple. Her eyes are open, and roll back like a doll's, so the whites show, and she wobbles, as if in slow motion, before she crashes straight onto her face, lying alongside me.

The only way to get to Alice is to drag myself there. First, I have to climb over Eliza, and my own grunts and pain make it impossible for me to check for any signs that she is breathing. Milly's stone is on the grass beside her. A part of me wonders if I should throw it off the cliff, but I don't. I slip it back in my pocket. Somewhere far away, I have the thought that Eliza is probably dead, and I should try to be certain, in case there is something I can do for her, but it is more important to help Alice so I just leave Eliza where she fell.

I don't know how long it takes, but I need to pause often, because each movement I make jabs me in the head. When I finally reach Alice, I manage to curve an arm around her, and my good leg, because I must somehow hold her where she is, and I don't think I can keep awake much longer to do that.

The sea is no longer roaring. The sea loves me. It has always loved me. There is the sound of shouts and crunching feet, of my name and Alice's and Eliza's. But I am so, so tired, and cannot answer. I haven't been this tired since my pregnancy, with this special kind of tiredness that is blissful to surrender to. I listen to the song of the sea, inhaling and exhaling, slapping forward at the rocks before it is sucked back, lulling me to sleep.

Now The Present

Bath, Saturday, 18 May 2019

At first I don't recognise him. Though I saw him that one time since he stopped shaving his head, my muscle memory defaults to seeking out a bald man. Alice is standing beside him, holding his hand as they wait for me near the entrance to the park.

Her hair is loose, and almost to her shoulders. She is radiant, in a white dress printed with ink-blue roses. There is a faint bloom in her cheeks. The bruises are gone.

I say hello to Zac, but my smile is for her, so wide it makes my face ache. 'Happy birthday, Alice!'

She starts to hum the birthday song, and I sing along, which puts her in fits of giggles. When we are finished, she comes closer to me, shyly putting out her hand to touch the bulky orthopaedic boot that goes from below my knee to the tips of my toes.

'This,' she says, opening her mouth wide. 'Ouch.'

When the surgeon first sewed the two pieces of my ruptured Achilles Tendon into one, I had to keep my foot entirely off the ground. Now, I am allowed to put a little weight on it, with some of the burden taken by the crutches. I demonstrate this for Alice's benefit. 'It doesn't hurt. See?' I move her attention away from the subject. 'Let's go have fun. Would you like to draw a picture for me later?'

'Yes! Yes, yes.' She clasps a handful of my dress in her small fist. The fabric is black, and covered in tiny flowers of vibrant green. 'Pretty. Pretty, pretty.'

'Thank you! Thank you, Thank you.' This makes her laugh. I look ahead of us, along the path that curls through the park. 'Shall we find the swings?'

She nods slowly and decisively, her eyes huge and startling as she looks at me. She toddles along in the sunshine, still holding onto my dress as if it were my hand. Then she chooses a bench inside the children's play area, in the half-shade of an apple tree whose pinky-white blossom scents the air. She carefully props my crutches before running to the swings, chased by Zac. He lifts her on and pushes while she wiggles her legs in a charmingly inept attempt at pumping.

I elevate my leg onto the bench to stop it from swelling. As Zac plays a counting game with Alice, I think of Jane. Alice marked her in every way. Even Jane's body was changed by her. Maxine let me see the forensic pathologist's report. The examination of Jane's pelvis showed she had given birth.

Zac soon settles Alice close by, in the sand pit. He approaches the bench, but pauses a metre away. 'May I?'

The orthopaedic boot will be a kind of wall between us. 'Of course.'

He lowers himself at the opposite end. Together, we watch Alice with her bucket and spade and moulds. She is shaping mermaids and seahorses and starfish. She is entirely absorbed, despite the fact that her figurines keep disintegrating.

'She looks so much better,' I say.

'She's had several sessions of intravenous iron therapy – like you did, after . . .' He trails off. 'It seems to be working.'

'I'm glad.'

'If I believed in God, I'd thank him for helping you to find her. How did you do it?'

Even now, he doesn't imagine that I discovered the address of the Yorkshire house by breaking into his steamer trunk over two years ago. It is a secret, along with many others, that I intend to keep. I say something true, though it isn't what he is after. 'I just tried to see the world as Alice does.'

He nods. 'You understand her so well. There's something special between the two of you.' Then he presses the question he really wants answered. 'But how did you find the Yorkshire house?'

I knew he wouldn't let it go. I still need to test his responses by pushing on those coloured shapes. There are fewer of them than there used to be, but gravity is still gravity.

I tell a plausible lie. 'Eliza mentioned it.'

He hesitates. 'You won't tell anyone who Alice's birth mother is?'

'Never.'

'Thank you.' He ruffles his grey-white hair, as if he

still isn't used to finding it there. 'They aren't blaming you for what happened? You had good legal advice?' He looks so worried.

Martin sent a lawyer to my hospital bed, along with firm instructions that I wasn't to speak to anyone without her there.

'Excellent legal advice. I told the truth. It must have been consistent with the evidence of what Eliza did to Jane.' My voice is low, to ensure Alice cannot overhear. 'I said she was jealous of Jane because of your affair with her, and jealous of me when she figured out I was your supposedly dead ex-girlfriend.'

'Wasn't that a problem for you? Their knowing about your pretend death?'

'I told them all of that. They took their notes, but they were only interested in Eliza and Jane. I'm not the first woman to run away from an abusive relationship.'

He looks down. 'I'm sorry,' he says to the ground.

'I said I threw the stone in self-defence because she was going to push me off the cliff, but that I didn't anticipate it would result in her death.'

'We both know your aim is deadly.' He is picturing the two of us skimming stones across the water. 'Do you remember how we laughed, Holly? How we'd always end up soaked? Then, afterwards, how we couldn't wait to get home . . .'

'Yes.' I stare at my lap while he stares at me. At last, I continue. 'I told them I was anxious to get medical treatment for her little girl – that was the only mention I made of Alice.'

'You spoke to Al last night, didn't you?'

'Briefly.'

I had wanted to check – hypothetically – if a child born on non-US soil to somebody like Jane would be a US citizen. Apparently not, since Jane hadn't lived the qualifying years in the US. 'But,' Albert said, 'the IRS problems get passed to the heirs, whatever their nationality. The IRS always follows the money.' So that was another thing Jane was shielding Alice from.

Was Frederick with Jane, somehow, after Eliza left Montenegro with Alice, so that Jane wasn't alone? I hope so. Perhaps he spirited Jane to wherever he was, probably Russia, so he could try to comfort her. Jane's milk would have come in, like mine did. Her arms would have been empty, like mine were. A mother with no baby, like I was.

'Al likes you a lot,' Zac says. Again, the note of jealousy, this time of his old friend, a man who lives five thousand miles away. 'What did the two of you talk about?'

I tell him, though I omit the baby sea lion Albert zoomed in on as he walked along the beach in Malibu, a world away and talking to me by encrypted video link on his phone. The sea lion was black and shiny, flattened and face down as if it were embracing the world.

Zac swallows hard. 'I wish I could do everything again, Holly. Do it all differently.'

Alice is holding up her arms. 'Daddy,' she says, and Zac gets up to retrieve her. The two of them smooth a red tartan blanket on the grass in front of the bench, then arrange an assortment of drinks and cakes and napkins and paper plates decorated with unicorns. Alice offers me a cinnamon bun.

'I remembered you liked them,' Zac says.

'I do. Thank you.' I take a bite. 'This is delicious, Alice.' I fumble in my tote bag for her present. The wrapping paper is a forest of trees. Little girls in bright dresses are climbing the branches. 'Do you like the paper? The little girls remind me of you.'

Again, I am rewarded with that big-eyed serious nod. She bursts into giggles and points to one with red hair. 'Me!'

'Yes!' I say.

Zac offers to help her unwrap the present, but she shakes her head and tears it open herself. 'Dollies,' she cries, delighted.

'Those are wonderful,' Zac says.

They look like paper dolls, but they are made of smooth wood instead. There is a boy and a girl, with an assortment of vividly coloured felt dresses and skirts and trousers and tops that stick to both figures. Alice spreads them out, and is immediately, deeply fascinated. I am elated that she seems to love them so much.

'Tuesday was another important birthday. I never forget – I have to live with what I did to you. To her.'

I am not a saint. I think, *So do I*, but I don't say it.

Beside him is the large jute bag he'd carried the picnic in. 'I have something for you.' He pulls out a familiar box. My baby's memory box. 'I've been adding to it, since you left. It's all been for you, but it helped me, too, to do it. I'll understand if you don't want it, but I brought it along just in case.'

'Can I look?'

He passes the box over and I settle it on my lap. Slowly, I lift the lid.

405

The teddy bear is still there, but there are other things too. At the top is a birth certificate. I take it out. *Charlotte Alexandra Mary*.

'You were right about Charlotte.' He clears his throat.

There is a pale green envelope. I pick that up next.

'I wish I'd known about that before you ran away,' he says. 'One of the nurses took it. I wasn't in the room, when you were with her. You didn't want me anywhere near you. The hospital got in touch a couple months after you were gone, to see if I wanted it.'

I start to lift the flap.

'Wait, Holly – shall I tell you what it is, first, so you can decide? You might need to prepare yourself. I've been in counselling – she told me to make you aware—'

'No. Thank you.'

I slip my fingers into the envelope and pull out a photograph. I bite my bottom lip as I look at it. The photograph does not bring the memory back, but it proves it happened. They weren't lying to me.

I am in that tight white hospital bed, propped with pillows and clearly not able to sit up unaided. I am almost as white as the sheets. My hair is long, and tangled, and mixes with hers, which is the same shade of amber, but for the white forelock. She is wrapped in Milly's blanket and propped on pillows, because I am visibly too weak to hold a baby even as light as she was, and the tubes are snaking out of my hands and into the bags of fluid attached to the metal sticks above me. My head is bent, to study her. My eyes are filled with tears. I am bathing her face with them. She is so beautiful, but her lids are closed. Her lids were always closed. If she'd inherited

Zac's dual-coloured eye, would it have showed so early? Whatever colours her eyes were, she took that secret with her. My heart swells with love and grief, so big I can feel them pressing against the inside of my chest.

I blink hard, as Alice climbs onto my lap. She smells of baby shampoo.

Zac moves her shoe away from my unwieldy boot. 'Careful of Holly's foot, Alice.'

She looks confused, and I realise it is because of my real name. She is used to my being Helen. But I decide it is easier not to explain. She is so clever and flexible. She will catch on. 'It's okay. My foot is well protected.'

Zac gently takes the photo from my hand, to avoid it getting bent or damaged. 'It's for you to keep.' I can see how expert Alice has made him at doing multiple things at once. He puts the photo safely away, then moves the box to the end of the bench, so she can't accidentally knock it. 'I have copies of everything. I hope you don't mind.'

I shake my head.

'Picture,' Alice says. 'Draw,' she says. 'Promise,' she says.

'Oh yes.' I pull a sketch pad and some crayons from my bag, and Alice gets to work.

While she is distracted, Zac reaches into the box again. This time, he pulls out the Liberty journal, covered in the Far Away Tree fabric. Two years ago, I refused to touch it.

'Don't say anything. Please. I'm ashamed of what we talked about when I first tried to give this to you. But I kept it. I thought you might tell her story. Tell yours. Tell any story you like.' He holds it out. When I don't take it, he says, 'I understand,' and returns it to the box.

I think about the Liberty book, and that it might be empowering for me to write in it someday. At first, I tell myself that this is pure fantasy, because what I plan to do is not something I could ever commit to paper. But then I wonder. *Neither confirm nor deny.* That is the only comment they'd ever make, the only action they'd ever take. They'd treat it as they would any other spy novel. I could change names and places, alter events and timelines, and make up a few things too. Isn't that what fiction is? Lying? And haven't I always been good at doing that? Besides, I have never been a proper employee of the Security Service. There is no signed contract. Nobody ever notified me that I was bound by the Official Secrets Act. I could even use a penname, like the Brontës.

For the first time since Zac found my orange journal, and since Charlotte's death, I am feeling that urge to pick up my pen. Already, the thought of telling this story is gripping me. Unlike the stories I stole for the orange journal, this one is mine to tell.

Alice is engrossed in her art. There is a great deal of scribble, but there are also three wobbly circles, one small, one medium, and one large, that I think are meant to be a mother, father, and child, with a wobbly yellow sun above them.

'Finished, Alice?' Zac says.

'Yes, Daddy.' She opens her mouth in a huge yawn.

'It's beautiful, Alice,' I say. 'Thank you. I will feel happy every time I look at it.'

She and I make a game of putting the sketch pad and crayons away, then Zac scoops her into his arms. She is so delicate and light. She rests her head on his shoulder and snuggles against him, sticking her thumb in her mouth and closing her eyes.

'There's one other thing.' He balances Alice with one hand and rummages in the box with the other. He holds out a pouch of quilted ivory silk, tied with a matching ribbon. 'Please.'

Inside is a charm bracelet, made of some kind of white metal. The charms alternate between white and yellow gold. One bead is engraved with a tiny angel, another with a butterfly, and still another with a miniature pair of footprints. There are hearts too, near solid but for a small tunnel that the bracelet passes through.

'The hearts each have a tiny chamber in them. I put some of her ashes inside. The one with her initials has a strand of her hair.' He hesitates. 'If you don't want it, I'll understand.'

It makes me think of eighteenth-century novels, and the endless list of funeral jewellery and rings made of hair that dead characters bequeath to those who survive them.

'That is so macabre,' Milly used to say, whenever I went on about how sad it was that we no longer do this.

I never told Zac how I felt about this lost tradition. In some ways he truly knows me. But in others . . . well, there are others he has never come close to imagining.

I slip the bracelet on my wrist. 'I do want it.'

'The rest of her ashes are with Peggy. I thought you might want to bury them with your parents, or scatter them near there, maybe in the sea. It's for you to decide.'

'What about you?'

'I didn't just hurt the two of you, Holly. I hurt myself too.' He pushes up the sleeve of his shirt. Around his wrist is a narrow band of white metal, with a large oval capsule. 'There's a chamber in the bead like the ones in the charms. It binds me to her.' He lowers his voice. 'It also binds me to you. I hope you don't mind. If you do, you can have this one too.'

'No. You keep it, Zac.' I meet his gaze and he flushes.

'I'm so glad you came.'

'Me too.' I touch Alice's hair, and she opens her eyes. 'I don't want to say goodbye to you, little birthday girl.' I slide my booted foot from the bench.

'Big.' Alice is fully awake again. 'Big, big, big.'

I laugh. 'You're right. Big birthday girl.'

'Don't,' says Zac.

'Don't what?' I say, though I know exactly what he means.

'Don't say goodbye.'

Alice pulls herself from Zac and throws herself at me, presses her face into my chest. 'No. No go.' She dissolves into tears, clinging like a koala bear as I soothe her. At last, she relaxes across my lap, though her arms are tight round my waist.

Zac says softly, 'I'm with Alice. Don't go, Holly. You and I belong together. We can get it right this time. I'm different. I'll do anything to make it work, to make it up to you. We can get married. You can adopt Alice. You only have to say yes and I'll put the legalities in motion.' He moves closer, draping Alice's legs over his thighs, while her upper body continues to rest across my lap, her head in the crook of my arm. 'It's what I've dreamed of since you ran away. Getting you back.'

No better way to get a man to love you forever than to run away from him. That was what Eliza said. She knew the truth of that. Maxine, who is an expert at identifying human desires, and understanding precisely how to use them in order to purchase information, knows this too.

I cannot fathom how long Maxine has been planning this. When did she foresee the circumstances that would allow her to put it in play, given the innumerable contingencies? She can envisage the impossible, figuring out the solution to a complex puzzle made of constantly moving pieces. And Martin, too, letting me walk away with Alice's identity documents. And George, helping me find that medical data. At every point, they knew what to do with me. I couldn't give them Jane, but I can still give them Zac, who they always wanted just as much. Because Zac remains their best chance at getting Frederick Veliko.

I have looked at it all. I have considered everything, aided by the clear-thinking Maxine. She spent a lot of time by my hospital bed, before I was well enough to leave Yorkshire. Explaining how it can work, spelling out how she and I can each grant the other a very fond wish.

As things stand, I have no legal rights to Alice. She will be alone with Zac and I won't be able to protect her. Would Jane have wanted that, after everything she sacrificed to keep Alice safe? It is inconceivable that social services would take Alice from him. If by some miracle they did, she'd end up in foster care.

Even if I were to complain to the police about the things he did to me, there is no way I could prove them. MI5 and GCHQ would never admit the evidence I needed even existed, and his films have been consigned to Maxine's dark caverns, where they belong.

Three different women ended up without a child, yet he is the one who gets to walk away with a little girl in his arms. The intelligence agencies of two countries, bolstered by the life-destroying might of the IRS, couldn't find Jane, couldn't catch her. It was love that did that. Love that made her vulnerable. Love that killed her. That love was more powerful than any of those relentless institutions.

I can hear Maxine's voice, echoing over the glass table and across time. Asking how far I would push it. Asking where the line comes. Asking if I would sleep with someone for the role, to save my country, to save my own life, to save the lives of hundreds of others. I said then what I thought she wanted to hear.

But what I know now – and know deep in my bones – is this. Whatever anyone says to that interview question will be a lie. You have to be in the situation before you can know the true answer. And when it comes to my child, and Jane's child, the true answer is that I will push it as far as I humanly can. The true answer is that there is no line. The true answer is yes. Because I cannot abandon this child. I could never walk away. I will climb back into Zac's bed, deliberately and with full intent, in order to claim her and keep her. I will move on with Alice, move on with my life, but keep her sister with me always, inside us both, so she moves on with us. I will not leave her behind.

Zac's hand is in my hair, on my face. He murmurs my name as he presses against me, whispering, 'Is that a yes?' and I say, 'Yes.' He kisses me, a lover's kiss, and I kiss him back, with Alice warm in my lap. His eyes are half-closed, and I see a crescent of blue in the left and one of brown in the right, because mine are wide open.

Acknowledgements

I am indebted to my agent Euan Thorneycroft for his wise guidance and the many wonderful things he does. Here is one of them. When Euan and I first discussed my idea for this novel, he said, 'How about calling it *I Spy*?' I don't think novels necessarily find their true names, but this one did, thanks to Euan. My editors, Sarah Hodgson and Emily Griffin, saw from the start what *I Spy* could be, and helped me to realise that vision, never losing faith, guiding me when I was lost, and seeing much more clearly than I could exactly what needed to be done. Working with them is a great privilege and joy. Kathryn Cheshire's editorial input was also immensely valuable. This is my third novel to benefit from Anne O'Brien's elegant and meticulous copyediting. I am extremely grateful to the superb teams at HarperCollins UK and HarperCollins USA – they are the most talented and dedicated people any novelist could hope to work with. A. M. Heath Literary Agency is celebrating its 100th anniversary this year – Happy Birthday, A. M. Heath, and thank you for all that you do.

My husband Richard gives me painstaking support. His acute critical eye is a rare and precious thing, and *I Spy* gained immeasurably from his expert feedback. My parents, my sister Bella, and my brother Robert never waver in their belief and love. And now for my daughters. Imogen acted as my specialist medical reader, applying her considerable knowledge to ensure I got things right and making suggestions I would never have thought of. Her expertise and passionate encouragement made a huge difference to *I Spy*. So did the training event that we went to together at the Royal Society of Medicine, who do so much good. All mistakes and fictional liberties are my own. Lily makes me laugh harder than anyone, and lets me read my work-in-progress aloud to her. She has fantastic editorial judgement and a huge capacity to forgive me for the amount of time my writing takes. Violet spent many hours in my study, my sweet companion as I worked. When it all got too much, she would make me take a break and we would watch films and music videos and eat ice cream. As ever, my love and thanks go above all to my three magical girls, and to Richard, who is magical too.

The epigraph is from the first edition of Anne Brontë's novel, *The Tenant of Wildfell Hall*, originally published under the name Acton Bell. Printed by T. C. Newby, London, 1848, Volume I (of Three Volumes), Chapter V, 'The Studio', pages 85–86.

For those affected by the issues in this novel

Sands – Stillbirth and Neonatal Death Charity
https://www.sands.org.uk/

Tommy's
https://www.tommys.org/

International Stillbirth Alliance
http://stillbirthalliance.org/

The Lily Mae Foundation
https://www.lilymaefoundation.org/

Petals
http://petalscharity.org/

Bliss
https://www.bliss.org.uk

Women's Aid
https://www.womensaid.org.uk/

National Domestic Violence Helpline
http://www.nationaldomesticviolencehelpline.org.uk/

Refuge
https://www.refuge.org.uk/

National Centre for Domestic Violence
http://www.ncdv.org.uk/

Respect
http://respect.uk.net/

Victim Support
https://www.victimsupport.org.uk/

The
BOOK
of YOU

You left me no choice, Clarissa.

I just want to take you home, Clarissa.

I know your darkest secrets, Clarissa.

Clarissa is becoming more and more frightened of her colleague, Rafe. He won't leave her alone, and he refuses to take no for an answer. He is always there.

Being selected for jury service is a relief. The courtroom is a safe haven, a place where Rafe can't be. But as a violent tale of kidnap and abuse unfolds, Clarissa begins to see parallels between her own situation and that of the young woman on the witness stand.

Realizing that she bears the burden of proof, Clarissa unravels the twisted, macabre fairytale that Rafe has spun around them – and discovers that the ending he envisions is more terrifying than she could have imagined.

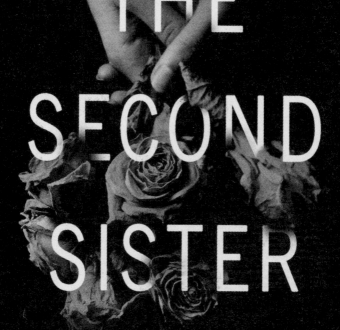

THE SECOND SISTER

**I'm the sister who got away.
The lucky one. Until now.**

It is ten years since Ella's sister Miranda disappeared without trace, leaving her young baby behind. Chilling new evidence links Miranda to the horrifying Jason Thorne, now in prison for murdering several women. Is it possible that Miranda knew him?

At thirty, Miranda's age when she vanished, Ella looks uncannily like the sister she idolized. What holds Ella together is her love for her sister's child and her work as a self-defence expert helping victims.

Haunted by the possibility that Thorne took Miranda, and driven by her nephew's longing to know about his mother, Ella will do whatever it takes to uncover the truth – no matter how dangerous...